PRAISE FOR VÍCTOR CATALÀ

"[I]n its evocation of landscape and myth, as well as its incipient feminism, *Solitude* prefigures the work of several later and better-known British women writers. Virginia Woolf, Doris Lessing, Edna O'Brien, and Jeanette Winterson all come immediately to mind."
—*The New York Times*

"While Caterina Albert i Paradis had little choice but to use a male pseudonym, she wrote *Solitude* from an intensely feminine viewpoint, delving deeply into the thoughts and emotions of a young woman caught by circumstance. It has been called 'the most important Catalan novel to appear before the Spanish Civil War,' when Franco took power and outlawed the Catalan language for more than thirty-five years. To find it translated into English and in print may be more remarkable still."
—**Erica Bauermeister, author of** *500 Great Books by Women*

"It is not surprising that [*Solitude*] has been hailed as a Catalan classic."
—**The Modern Novel**

ALSO BY VÍCTOR CATALÀ

Solitude

A Film

(3,000 meters)

Víctor Català

Translated from the Catalan by
Peter Bush

OPEN LETTER
LITERARY TRANSLATIONS FROM THE UNIVERSITY OF ROCHESTER

Library of Congress Cataloging-in-Publication Data: Available.
ISBN-13: 978-1-948830-44-7 | ISBN-10: 1-948830-44-2

This project is supported in part by an award from the New York State Council on the Arts with the support of Governor Andrew M. Cuomo and the New York State Legislature.

The translation of this work has been supported by the Institut Ramon Llull.

Printed on acid-free paper in the United States of America.

Cover design by Alban Fischer

Open Letter is the University of Rochester's nonprofit, literary translation press:
Dewey Hall 1-219, Box 278968, Rochester, NY 14627

www.openletterbooks.org

A Film

(3,000 meters)

Translator's Note

What's in a name?

From the start, Víctor Català had to confront the prejudices inspired by the machismo and clericalism rife in Catalan society. In 1898, at the age of twenty-two, she anonymously submitted a poetic monologue, *La Infanticida*, to a literary competition in the town of Olot. The work won a prize, but the story of a mother killing her baby shocked the Catholics of Olot, and they were even more appalled when the author was revealed to be a woman, Caterina Albert. As a result of the furore, Albert decided to adopt the literary pseudonym Víctor Català, which she would use throughout her life, though it was soon public knowledge that the name belonged to Caterina Albert.

Ramon Nonat Ventura, *A Film's* central character, is hugely symbolic, and the reference would have immediately been recognized by Catalan readers in 1918. Sant Ramon Nonat was a Catalan saint born between 1200 and 1204, in the village of Portell in the region of Urgell. There are differing stories about Nonat, Catholic and non-Catholic. He was born via a Caesarean section possibly carried out by the count who fathered him; his mother, the daughter of a local farmer, died as a result. He was thus called "Nonat," or "not born." His father saw to his bastard son's education, and he eventually worked for the Mercedarian Order in Barcelona helping to free Christians being held in Moorish prisons in Arab parts of Spain and North Africa. He was himself captured; his jailers made holes in his lips by using red-hot skewers and padlocked his mouth because he was always pontificating. He was eventually made a saint in 1657, and became the patron saint of orphans, midwives, victims of gossip, and silence. There are Nonnatus Houses in the UK and USA that are orphanages for children of single mothers. One such house features prominently in the popular BBC TV soap, *Call the Midwife*, now in its ninth season.

Nicknames:

Nonat earns himself the nickname of El Senyoret because he acts posh: a "senyoret" is typically the son of rich parents who doesn't have to work.

Maria la Gallinaire, Nonat's godmother: Maria the Chicken Woman.

Nas-Ratat, the street-porter: his nose looks as if it's been nibbled by a rat. Catalan has an adjective "ratat," meaning just that.

Paperines, the innkeeper: plastered, implying violence and stupidity, in Barcelonan Catalan slang.

Nadala, the apprentice seamstress: Christmassy, after Nadal, Catalan for Christmas.

Xe, the Valencian: a jokey way of referring to Valencians, similar to "che" in Argentina.

La Pelada, Xe's girlfriend: someone who is a straight talker, or flat broke.

The Catalan language is the main language as well as a feature of the narrative—Nonat feels at a disadvantage when speaking Spanish, which he sees as a "foreign" language. Upper-class characters tend to speak in Spanish, and I indicate when they do so. The working-class characters all speak Catalan though it's flecked with borrowings from Spanish, for example the use of the Spanish "duro" for a five-peseta coin. Víctor Català was opposed to the *noucentiste* purists who didn't want this hybrid Catalan to feature in literary fiction. I've tried to reflect this hybridity in the translation by retaining Catalan or Spanish lexis according to context, for example pesseta and peseta, or Les Rambles, the Catalan plural of Las Ramblas. This is still an ongoing polemic in Catalan literary circles and in the works of Víctor Català, a pioneer in giving literary space to different registers of her mother tongue, thus living up to her own pseudonym!

Peter Bush

God Be With You

GOD BE WITH YOU, MY READER! It's been years since you and
I bumped into one another in the helter-skelter of a new book.
Circumstances gagged my garrulous pen, and a long pause was
opened in our dialogue. If I'm piping up again, it's not because
I have anything very riveting to tell you. My modest heading
is proof I have not been overambitious. Besides, it's not a bad
idea to see a movie now and then, when there's nothing better
to do. In the rapid succession of scenes across the blank screen,
one relishes the contrast, the beauty of being able to relax;
the quantity and extreme nature of the violent acts on display
remind you it's only a tale, and you have no need to probe too
deep; the general rule of the scant substance and psychological
fetters at work in miming theater; the lethal leaps made beyond the realms of verisimilitude, the many twists and turns,
tell you it's neither an exquisite nor a fully fashioned fantasy,
and you're freed up, for a while, from the torture of straining
your eyes in attempt to catch all the threads . . .

That says it all, really almost all I need to say, by way of apology. I have made a film, and as an individual I like as much as I can to give everyone their due, when writing; I also like to keep to the specific rules of each genre and not confuse or mix the different terms and conditions. So, dearest reader, if you manage to get over the threshold of this book and start to follow the plot unfolding in its pages, don't say you weren't warned, don't complain about what you find, don't demand I give you more than I promised, because here and now I simply promised you a film, in all its simplicity, in all its disarray, in all its coincidences, in all its excesses . . . in a word, all the freedom the genre brings with it.

The literary value, small or great, you may have kindly granted my previous work is null and void in such an enterprise; it guarantees nothing at all. The novelist on this occasion surrenders his tools to the filmmaker, and that comes with no obligations or puritanical restrictions. Like the comb of a countryman, merely cutting a parting through a thick mop of matted hair, hoping to make a straight, continuous road of it, the novelist's pen has today tried to steer a smooth, clear path through the entangled virgin wood—woods being always virgin!—of life, of the ups and downs, thick as a head of hair, of the men and women who pullulate on this planet. On both sides, the unexplored, inexhaustible, impenetrable undergrowth endures, but a simple, straight furrow opens up and invites you to survey at leisure its gleaming, untrammeled light, its raw cruelty and elemental disposition, with no malice aforethought or hidden fancies.

Consistent with the innocence of his aims and accomplishments, the author has serviced his plot with tales stripped of

pompous rhetoric, elaborate inflections and subtle reliefs, for-
mal elegance, hidebound purity, dazzling pyrotechnics of the
pen, that would have suited him as much as Christ the pair of
pistols mentioned by that proverb . . . No, none of that: each
to his own, as we said at the beginning.

For now, just watch the film, and if you like it, dear reader,
don't give yourself or me too many headaches over whatever
you may find lacking or superfluous. For both our sakes, let
this long, inconsequential sequence of scenes without excess
dressing or substance prevail a while and relax your brain; for
both our sakes, let it simply provide a small, reinvigorating
oasis of calm amid the anxiety-ridden demands of more urgent
tasks. And another day will be another day, when, if God
grants us life and health, we will make new commitments.

Au revoir, then, loyal reader. I shake your hands, delighted
to have found you anew, after such a long absence, your friend,

THE AUTHOR
Barcelona, 2 July, 1919

Part One

Part One

Mid-afternoon a blustery north wind whipped the sea into a roiling mass of foam and furiously swept the streets, emptying them of every scrap of trash and grain of sand.

At twilight the cobblestones, stripped bare by the *tramuntana*, gleamed like whitened shells in the purple haze and a deafening whistle filled the air.

Seeing the door bang to and fro, flapping like a flag, and fearing it might shatter, Maria la Gallinaire slammed down the bar, and asked her husband anxiously: "Well, Jepet? Why don't we eat early and get to bed? There's nothing doing in this storm and we'll only waste electricity and catch our death of cold."

As usual Jepet thought what Maria said made a lot of sense, and, also as usual when home at that time of night, he went to light the fire.

Honoring their biblical names, they lived like Joseph and Mary. He worked mooring ships, and the oilskin hanging on the back of the door had been his second skin for over thirty years.

His leathery face and hands were cracked and gnarled like rocks; his rough, ruddy, stony features seemed sculpted rather than alive, and his short, stubby fingers never altered, never fully uncurled, because they'd lost the ability to make any other movement than the one required to haul mooring timbers up and down beaches.

Maria was fat, with the reassuring plump folds of a pillow. She'd never tolerated the torture of a corset, and her body's ample expanses were testament to an easygoing nature. Nonetheless, despite both her size and a flexibility of mind that seemingly kept her burgeoning flesh in check, Maria was a vigorous, organized, hard-working woman.

In the early days of her marriage to Jepet, she had found it hard to resign herself to the tame, lonely life of a sailor's spouse, and looked for work to occupy her free time and garner some helpful cash.

At the time, Jepet was working on a small merchant ship and was often away for days on end, if not weeks. Every morning, the moment the fishermen returned from the sea, Maria ferried dirty nets to the cleaning areas with the jenny and second-hand cart they'd bought, though she reckoned it was small beer and when her husband's absences lightened her housework load, she went to remote farmhouses to buy eggs or hens, which she then sold in the markets of Girona, generally making a handsome profit.

Lolling back on the cart's backrest, holding the reins—for appearance's sake, because her honest little jenny was never skittish, she sped down lanes and byways, outwardly placid, but inwardly a bundle of energy and enthusiasm.

Naturally alert and observant, she had the measure of those countrywomen whose husbands gave them little leeway, those who struggled to buy a scarf or a new apron for their marriageable daughter, those desperate for chocolate or other tidbits, and, wheeler-dealer that she was, once she knew the weaknesses of her parish, she skillfully exploited them for gain. Her bag on the cart always contained roasted almonds to tempt one customer, needles and thread needed by another who was too busy to go to town herself, curling irons for a presumptuous farmer's wife, small loans for the skint or indebted, strange herbs to cure mumps . . . and, at once up-front and discreet, she plied or encouraged deals that were, naturally, always to her advantage. Those countrywomen—who, when their husbands or neighbors weren't looking, sold their wares for rock-bottom prices—breathed a sigh of relief at the sight of Maria la Gallinaire approaching. In turn, when she espied them from afar coming out alone to the roadside to haggle, she smiled contentedly, convinced she'd not made a wasted journey. And, if that wasn't enough, she found time to do the washing in her own inimitable style for the grand houses in town.

Things being thus, it isn't surprising that in a few years wife and husband had saved a tidy sum between them. They stopped renting and bought a house, small and white like an eggshell; they stopped cultivating the vines of others only to reap a fraction of the fruit, and bought their own; the notary gave them a profit of some three thousand pessetes and they exchanged three or four thousand more for government bonds, from which, every three months, they extracted a small amount, which their legal man—their trusted aide—took to Girona and brought back converted into hard cash.

When they saw old age was in sight, and Jepet began to feel broken by life at sea, he stopped voyaging and became a man who helped moor and launch boats from beaches, and Maria, who couldn't leave her husband's side, gave up her poultry trade, and transported nets and washed more clothes than before. With such an orderly, quiet existence, you'd have thought they were completely happy if it hadn't been for the *but* that never fails to show up in the unfolding of earthly life's rich tapestry and leave its drop of bile in even the most select of hearts. The drop of bile, for our poultry pair, was the fact that there was no sign of children.

At the height of youth, both had dedicated themselves to making money and, as they had plenty of opportunities to exhaust their energy reserves, they didn't fuss over their abnormal situation. But when they realized the years had stacked up, their barrenness reared before them like a stretch of wall, destroying the impression of infinity people love to cherish, and emphasizing the way nature had sold them short.

"Good heavens!" Maria exclaimed sadly one day, when they were calculating their earnings after Jepet returned from a voyage. "Why push ourselves so hard if we don't know who all the toil is for?"

And from then on, they could only think of the child that hadn't come and never would, and miss him sorely.

That was as far as it went for Jepet; he was a man with little imagination and took things as they came without trying to seek out underlying causes, while Maria was the one to ponder—and ponder she did. Feeling she was strong, healthy, and all there, and knowing of no issues or faults in herself or on her side, she told herself she was free of guilt, and, unawares, deep down, was convinced the issue *was* with her husband. "By the Holy Virgin! Men are sealed boxes. What does a woman know when she marries, when she takes a man for life? Not a thing, and that's the truth . . . Then look how it turns out!" As she went on her rounds, she'd heard many women say: "But these are crosses nobody looks for; they fall from the skies and land where they land . . . and if it happens to land on you, all you can do is pick yours up and bear it . . . that's why you need to keep an eye out on this earth."

And Maria took her cross as a levy God imposed on her for the good health and prosperity He had granted, and she complained to nobody, though from then on, without doing so expressly, she adopted a watchful, warmly overbearing tone toward her husband, as if he were a big, irresponsible child, a dimwit son who must be protected and loved even more because he doesn't have quite as many marbles as the others. And so their intimate married life took that twist. When people noticed, they smiled and used that common expression—"Maria wore the trousers"—but they never suspected the human warmth and generous forgiveness her attitude generated.

Only, now and then, like a breath of air escaping from a vent, a thwarted mother's remorse arose from Maria's heart to her lips, bearing no relation to whatever had been said previously: "When I think about it, I should have kept the child I took to the orphanage . . ."

"You're so right! But who'd have thought . . . ?" Jepet replied, quite matter-of-fact and meek, never imagining what was going through his wife's mind.

And years and years passed like that until that night when that north wind buffeted.

They had done what they'd agreed. They prepared supper in next to no time, ate it in a good, affable mood, and, for dessert, said an Our Father for the souls of the dead, and were about to clear the table, when they suddenly heard loud coughing on the other side of the front door, followed by two loud knocks.

Husband and wife gave a start, and exchanged panic-stricken glances.

"What on earth is that?" they wondered silently, their eyes wide-open.

Then all was silent before they heard two more knocks. Maria stood up and strode toward the door.

"Who goes there?" she bawled brusquely, as if that untimely visit bordered on the insulting.

"Open your door, I beg you, my good folk . . ." replied another voice, that was young and modulated, between two further bouts of coughing.

"Who are you?" repeated Maria, frowning and firm.

"You will not know me, but I come on behalf of someone who knows you . . . If you're frightened, I'll be off, because it's grim out here . . ." the voice retorted impatiently.

Maria glanced at her husband, all nonplussed at the other end of the table.

"What shall we do?"

Jepet was in no state to say yea or nay.

"Don't know . . . You decide . . ."

Maria did just that.

"I'll open up and we'll see what . . . who by the Holy Mother of God it can be . . . "

And without finishing her sentence, Maria lifted the bar, but before she could open the door, it swung violently into her and something devilishly dark and icy flung itself over her, blinding her, making her stagger and lose her wits. The north wind had blasted its way inside, shamelessly sweeping her skirts over her face and top half. When she managed to disentangle herself, she was shocked to see a man standing in front of her, wrapped in a cloak, a beret pulled down over his ears, holding the door steady with his outstretched hand.

"Do forgive me!" muttered Maria, all flustered.

A corner of the cloak dropped, revealing a smile beneath a black mustache on a pallid face.

"I must say this is a fine old time to be up and about!" said that courteous voice. "If I'd have known, I'd have left it to another day!"

And, as Maria slotted the bar back down, the other corner of the cloak dropped, the beret was tipped back, and the man came into full view.

The meager light from the oil lamp allowed husband and wife sight of a slim young man with a friendly face and gentle demeanor, staring at them, half grinning.

Indeed, they did not recognize him.

Maria addressed him politely: "I'm sorry, senyor . . . Are you sure you're not mistaken . . . We . . . ?"

"Aren't you Maria Celles, the one they call Maria la Gallinaire?" asked the stranger.

"I am, God willing . . ."

"Then I have come to see you." And the young man smiled, flashing two rows of even, white teeth. "I've come to give you a hug . . ."

Maria stepped backward, in shock, while Jepet took a step toward the stranger. The latter laughed and coughed again.

". . . Or, rather I should say I've come to return the hug you surely gave me years ago . . ." and he removed his cloak entirely and placed it on a chair.

Husband and wife couldn't think what to make of him. When the stranger again moved toward them, they both felt their legs quiver.

He noticed.

"Don't be frightened . . . Am I not allowed to want to meet my godmother?" And to put them at ease once and for all, he added: "I am Nonat Ventura." Then the couple were more panic-stricken than ever.

"What do you mean 'godmother' . . . ?" 'Ventura' . . . What on . . . ?"

And as at ease as if it were his own home, the stranger took each of them by the hand and led them to their table.

"Be seated. I see you've forgotten me, but let me remind you and you'll soon see I'm not trying to trick you."

And he grabbed a chair and sat quietly next to them.

Maria stared at him. He had a handsome face and very pleasant demeanor, a half-smile always dancing on his full lips, though his gaze seemed rather penetrating and hard from chiaroscuro eyes that were bluish-green like the wine vessel on the table.

"Yes, you *are* my godmother. If the certificates don't lie, twenty-two years ago you took a bastard to be baptized in the church of this town and gave him the name of Ramon Nonat Ventura; later . . ."

Maria jumped to her feet, a smile spreading across her face.

"You mean, you're the child I . . ."

"The very same . . ." the stranger replied, smiling as ever.

"Ay! What a pleasant surprise . . . !" exclaimed Maria, though suddenly beset by suspicion.

"The child you took to the Orphanage with a blue cord around his neck, a Montserrat medallion on his chest, and the certificate of baptism in his sash . . ."

"Praise be to the Lord . . . ! This seems a veritable fairy tale . . . !" but, worried again by a deep-seated fear, she locked her inquisitive eyes on the newcomer, explored his serene, graceful face, his gentlemanly features, his new, elegant suit, his shiny polished shoes, gleaming brightly in that darkness . . .

The stranger read her thoughts, interpreted them and replied solemnly: "I see. You think I don't look like someone from the Orphanage? I don't live there anymore."

Maria calmed down.

"That child had a mark . . ." she whispered.

"What was it?" the stranger interjected brusquely.

"A cross . . ."

"On his chest. Take a look."

And he quickly unbuttoned his waistcoat and shirt and bared his chest.

His skin was as white and pure as a young girl's, and a blue tattoo, two thin lines stood out clearly, a finely drawn cross against that silken whiteness.

There could be no doubts now, and at that unexpected revelation, Maria's generous soul poured out all her love.

"*Fill meu!* It *is* you!" and tears filled her eyes. "Who'd have thought it? When I left you there it was around the time I stopped taking poultry to Girona; on the last two or three trips I made after that, I always went back to ask after you . . . The nuns told me they were bringing you up elsewhere and that you were well . . . That was all I ever heard about you . . . And now, good God, just look at the man you've become . . . I'd never have dreamed . . . it makes me so happy . . . !" She sat back in her chair. "Tell me everything, *criatura*, I can't wait to hear . . ." But another idea suddenly interrupted her flow. "I expect you've not supped yet?"

No, the stranger hadn't supped, but he said he wasn't hungry . . . he would do so later at his boarding-house.

"What do you mean 'boardinghouse'? You must be joking! I can't treat you like a bishop, much less stock up at this time of day with this weather. But you'll soon bear up with my poor little offering . . . We've known each other so long, no need to stand on ceremony," and Maria burst out laughing, her sides shaking, while the newcomer didn't have to be asked twice and meekly accepted her invitation.

Then, diligent Maria shelved all her other questions and cheerfully went to the fireplace, revived the smoldering ashes, and in no time had boiled up a pan of broth seasoned with thyme, and fried bacon and a couple of eggs.

Despite what he'd said, the orphan swallowed it down

hungrily, and while he ate, Maria left him with her husband and went to get the bedroom ready. She only had one, their double room, and a small spare room. She took the cot from the spare room and carried it to their barn; she changed the sheets on the double bed, put a clean towel and the new washbowl on the trestle, refilled the water-jug, but the newcomer hadn't eaten the dried pear or peeled the apple that, with a glass of mellow wine, comprised dessert by the time Maria had everything ready and was sitting down again, wanting to hear all he had to tell.

And the bastard told them his tale; a short version that went straight to the point, leaving out all rhetorical frills; a tale that we, who are less in a hurry and perhaps better informed than even the protagonist, will fill out so our readers can better understand what happened.

For sure, the nuns reared him outside the Orphanage, but then he was returned there, and lived and grew up for years between its gloomy walls amid those hapless companions crammed inside. And it was fortunate nobody had to set eyes on them! Inside, they were all one and the same and weren't ashamed to look at each other. But when they were taken out for a walk in a procession, dressed differently from other people, attracting everyone's attention, the children suffered and found themselves disgusting! It was even worse when the Orphanage had visitors and the bastards were exhibited like freak animals, like poor beggars regaled with charitable glances and words of pity that, rather than encourage them, made them feel sick, insulted, and bruised inside. As a very young child, Nonat had always rebelled against those shameful displays of the orphans' misery. He never wanted to go on walks; he hid wherever he could when the nuns called out his name because they wanted to show him off more than any of the others; he was a pretty little boy, didn't have boils or sores, and was a good advertisement for the institution. That was why he was punished when he tore his clothes to make them seem older and shabbier. He always wanted a new apron, and when someone else had one newer than his, he claimed it through guile, force, or whatever means he could find, and naturally when the nuns spotted his sly tricks and carried him off, he spat, bit, and kicked!

One day a gentleman visited the Orphanage and asked after a child who had such and such features. Nonat was playing with the others in the yard. The gentleman begged them not to summon his son, because he wanted to pick him out. He went into the yard and nervously inspected the boys. Suddenly, he stared at him, at Nonat, his eyes beaming contentedly, and he cried: "That's him, that's him! I feel it in my heart!" And before the nuns could say a word, the man grabbed his arm, pulled him in, and started to kiss and hug him . . .

Then Nonat smelled something he'd never smelled before. That gentleman gave off a lovely, subtle scent, which the child, quite unequipped to draw comparisons, thought smelled like ripened fruit, and his frock-coat brushed against the orphan's face with the gentlest touch, making the marrow in his bones tingle . . .

The nuns were rather embarrassed and patted the gentleman on the shoulder: "But that's not him, it really isn't . . . It's the one over there . . ."

The gentleman looked at them quite bewildered. The child they were pointing to had sunken cheeks, a squint, and one leg shorter than the other.

"Impossible!" exclaimed the gentleman, gripping Nonat even tighter, as if defending him, as if he wanted to stop them from taking him away, and Nonat, frightened they *would* take him away, clung to the gentleman's chest, stuck to him like a limpet. The heat passed from one to the other, and whenever he remembered that heat, Nonat got goosebumps.

But the nuns insisted, swapped details, whispered something in the man's ear, and only then did the gentleman loosen his grip, suddenly morose and limp as he let Nonat slip out of his arms, took the child with the gammy leg, and without even a glance, gave him a perfunctory kiss. Immediately, Nonat felt wretched and burst into tears.

The nuns were surprised, asked him what was wrong, but he couldn't find the words to tell them; the deflated visitor put his hand in his pocket and produced a handful of sweets; Nonat hurled them to the floor, the nuns rebuked him, saying he was a nasty piece of work; the gentleman gazed at him as if he were a long way away and muttered, "What a pity!" then walked out, giving his hand to the ugly boy, followed by the nuns. Nonat sobbed until supper time, and, not ever knowing why, from then on he couldn't stand the nun who had said: "But that's not him, it really isn't . . ."

That was the last they saw of the ugly boy, and the rumor went round the Orphanage that that gentleman was a millionaire who'd been widowed and had come to collect the bastard son he'd never mentioned to his wife.

From then on Nonat expected his own millionaire pa to come and collect him too. He always reckoned it would happen the next morning, always the next morning, but as the days, months, and years went by and such a natural deed was never done, he decided to ask a nun: "When will my pa come for me?"

"What pa?" retorted the nun, blinking.

"Mine."

"Oh dear! And who might your pa be?"

"A pa like little Jordi's . . ."

The nun gave him a motherly look: a gaze of infinite compassion.

"Ay, by the Sacred Heart of Jesus! You don't have a pa, little chap . . . You're stuck with us . . ."

Nonat flew into such a tantrum they thought he would go mad. It took hours to pacify him; then they couldn't get him to eat, he was delirious and wanted to escape from his bed.

Once that attack was over, his character changed radically: he grew taciturn, introspective, suspicious, and prickly. He hated the nuns.

They'd lied to him! He *did* have a pa; of course he did, but he didn't know where he lived, and if his pa didn't come to fetch him from the Orphanage, he'd go and look for him. And he plotted and tried to escape several times. The nuns were forced to keep a particularly watchful eye on him, and he took his revenge by being as naughty as could be. Until, one day, his childish brain spawned a grown man's way of thinking. Nobody else opened his eyes, he just realized it wasn't the way, that he could never force his escape from that place, that other ruses were needed . . . So he pretended; he acted as if he

was self-absorbed and persnickety; as if he were always rumi-
nating. Until his pondering confronted a situation, blessed by
chance, that seemed to come to his rescue.

From time to time, adult men who'd joined the orphan mi-
litias, bought themselves out and paid the Orphanage a visit,
with a sense of deep elation, as if returning to their ancestral
home. They scrutinized everything, as if it was all new to
them, spoke to the children, laughed, and never knew when
to stop . . . The nuns followed close behind, joked, asked hundreds of innocent questions, hovering over them with happy,
loving glances, preening like mother hens . . . Nonat, on the
other hand, looked at them askance, he didn't know why, as if
those men were accusing him of something, reproaching him
for his hidden sins. But, one day, a man turned up who was to
change the course of his life. His face was broad and flat; his
nose, dirty. He was a locksmith and had established his own
shop. He came to the Orphanage solely to tell the nuns that
it was opening. He was beside himself with joy, recounting all
the ups and down of his youthful odyssey. But now the bad
times were behind him and he was starting out on a beautiful, free life . . . He owned a workshop . . . He was boss! He
craved nothing else . . . Then he stopped. "But no! I do need
someone . . . an apprentice . . ." He turned around and looked
at the kids around him and blurted: "Who'd like to be one?
I'll take him today. I'll teach him my trade and he'll keep me
company . . ."

Whose voice was first to cry out: "I do!"? Nonat couldn't
have said, because he hadn't felt the words leaving his lips,
but everyone swung around to look at him, and the locksmith
glanced at him affectionately, and was happy to declare: "I like

you, my lad, you've got a smart face. It's a deal. Ask Matron
for permission, pack up your things, and home you come, I do
need someone . . . I'll make a man of you in three years . . . !"

After the paperwork was duly signed, Nonat was entrusted
to the locksmith, who lived up to his word. The new shop soon
prospered, and after three years of metal-beating, the apprentice became a full-fledged tradesman, and a first-rate one at
that. If his first earnings were only little treats his master gave
him, later, of his own accord, encouraged by nobody, happy
to see the lad applying himself and learning, the locksmith
began to pay him in the form of presents he could choose
for himself, and invariably, the boy opted for clothes, usually
the showiest and most attractive. To set them off, in his free
time, he forged rings and watch chains from knitting needles
and scraps of brass, and even though he didn't own a watch,
he hung a chain from one waistcoat pocket to another for the
pure joy of seeing it gleam brightly. When he'd finished his
apprenticeship, his master allotted him a monthly wage that
he spent entirely on fashionable ties and shoes, embroidered
handkerchiefs, all manner of shoes, hair creams, and scented
soaps . . .

When his master saw him squandering his pay, he said:
"Oh, Nonat! With those hands of yours, if you weren't such a
show-off, you'd soon save a few pessetes. But I can tell you one
thing, your liking for smart clothes will land you in the work-
house . . . unless you can find a dozy heiress . . ." whispering,
as if only for his own ears, "and anything *can* happen . . ."

Because the locksmith was an innocent abroad, unbecoming, odd, and grizzly, who wore cardboard patches on each
knee, with feet as big as a town square, and who couldn't

touch a piece of paper without leaving his grubby fingerprints, who'd never contemplated marriage or set his sights on any woman, he felt a kind of bittersweet satisfaction, mingled with blithe admiration, when he looked at his slim, smart protégé who lit up the shop's smoky shadows with his suave charm, who captivated maids in the rich households where he was sent, and who was greeted cheerfully everywhere in the neighborhood, his glinting finery, like soaring larks, attracting all the single working women and artisans who attended the soirées organized by the Locksmiths' Company to which they both belonged. And, as everyone knew the young lad's tale, his master asserted with great conviction: "When you think about it, what's so surprising? It's in his blood. . . Because he isn't from any poverty-stricken stock . . . At the very least he's the son of a marquis . . . They're quite right to nickname him El Senyoret. Nobody in the whole of Girona does that better than him!"

And, indeed, people knew him by the name of El Senyoret. It stuck from the moment he entered the trade, and summed up the general impression people formed of him.

"They've opened a locksmith's on the corner. And such an El Senyoret apprentice works there!" chorused housewives straightaway.

"El Senyoret from the locksmith's has come to fix the door handle," the lady on the second floor told her husband.

"Who's that El Senyoret coming down the stairs?" asked the farmer's wife at the seed merchant's.

Even the local kids, when they met up on a Sunday to go and play in Sant Daniel or the Devesa, would ask: "Hey, Senyoret, why don't you come too?"

And with a "Senyoret here" and a "Senyoret there" it soon became the only way to refer to him.

Likewise, El Senyoret wasn't as vain and as much of a spendthrift as people believed, since one day, when he realized he was amply furnished with everything he'd craved in terms of clothes, though still keeping himself spruced up, he began to resist temptation, restrained himself, and began to save. An idea that, like an underground stream, had been stirring for years, suddenly surfaced, its murky, tempestuous flow flooding his mind and driving out all other worries.

As soon as he saw the pile of cash his master had left in a corner of the drawer in his bedroom, he reached a decision. He'd go back to the Orphanage and talk frankly to Matron. So he went. Until then, he'd felt quietly confident, but the moment he asked for an appointment, he turned white as a sheet and a frown knitted his brow. He understood that this was a turning point in his life, a fateful knock on the door of destiny, and that whatever happened, his freedom from then on would never again be entirely his to enjoy in a leisurely, casual manner; his life would no longer be happy-go-lucky, a carefree experience from day to day, but a life shaped by hidden anguish, a life governed, enslaved by a unique, single-minded focus, secured diligently by him, like a wheel by its axle.

Once he was in Matron's presence, he explained himself. His voice trembled with emotion, but his smooth patter flowed as usual, just as an El Senyoret's speech should.

"I would like to know . . ."

"What . . . ?"

Well, just about everything. Who his parents were . . . Where they lived . . . Why they took him to the Orphanage, why, after so doing, they hadn't ever returned to reclaim their son, to restore the rights they'd taken away, if they'd been forced to go to such extremes. Once and for all, he needed to know the nature of his birth. He could stand it no longer. He had to know, he simply had to . . . he'd been living and working to that end alone, to be restored to his rightful place, and he believed such a longing was humane, just, and natural . . .

Matron was still young and romantic in a saintly fashion, with an ingenuously pure heart, despite the painful years spent confronting the depravation and misery that rivers of debauched desire landed on the Orphanage's doorstep. She was moved by Nonat's plea. Perhaps that poor boy, so keen to know his origins, *was* merely expressing a secret impulse of nature . . . She must respect that. After a moment's reflection, mentally committing the matter to the mercy of Our Lord, she ordered a search of the Orphanage's archives. She even ventured the possibility that a clue, a sign, might come to light in that first round of enquiries, but it wasn't to be, and they were both disappointed. They found only Nonat's date of entry, a mention of a bastard's baptism from the parish of Sant Pere de Ruelles, and a silver Montserrat medallion on a blue silk cord.

Cold sweat beaded Nonat's forehead; his lips quivered like a young child's about to burst into tears. Those clues were scant; he was utterly downcast. Later he poured out this bitter, rancorous bile.

It was beyond belief! Bringing children into the world only to throw them away, to cast them in the Orphanage like people ditch a new-born puppy on the dung heap to save themselves the bother of killing it . . . ! Unbelievable! He sensed his parents were well-to-do, people with clout . . . He was absolutely convinced of it because a mysterious, inner voice kept telling him . . . and he pounded his chest with a hand already callused and hardened by work, the only visible stigma of a lowly birth. "If that was the case, how could they want to close down my future and sentence me to a life of slavery and deprivation, in total silence . . . ?"

Hurt by his tone and the abrupt, demanding force of his un-Christian recriminations, Matron initially protested, but then, moved by the suffering she felt at the heart of his violent outburst, she tried to temper him with motherly advice.

"You shouldn't take things like this to heart. I'm sure it seems quite wrong at first sight that people don't confront their guilt with courage, if guilt there was, or misfortune, if misfortune there was, but you cannot make righteous accusations when you don't really know of what you are accusing someone . . . Sometimes, what one imagines isn't everything it seems! Who knows? Perhaps your parents aren't as responsible as you think. You think they were prestigious, but what if they weren't? There's no evidence to show that the opposite wasn't true . . ." and I've heard that in ninety-five percent of cases, bastards weren't any kind of perversion, but blind acts by poor, ignorant individuals who behave instinctively, quite unaware of what they were doing, like little animals, and then, afterward, must conceal the damaging consequences by finding a solution that conceals the horrors of their crime as well as their shame from the public eye, which is so unmerciful toward everything that exceeds the limits of the law . . ."

But Nonat vehemently rebelled against those humiliating

insinuations, which pierced his heart like the most treacherous thrust the dagger of fate could deliver. No, he refused to accept the obscure parentage they wanted to foist upon him with every ounce of energy he could muster, as if it were unbearably shameful.

Whenever he reflected on the enigma of his origins, a kind of magic loom surged before his eyes, as if in a hazy dream, where silvery spiderwebs crisscrossed, weaving an array of carpets that quietly undulated, like layers of gauze blown by the wind of fantasy, and he would stop and draw breath, watching the different, changing scenes come together—now picaresque, now bawdy, now romantic—but always graceful and in good taste . . . They were fragments of novels, hewn and framed by a dark strip of mystery that made them even more luminous and attractive . . . They were pristine, lordly visions, imprinted on that intangible gauze, which vibrated, shaking off a delicate dust, as from a butterfly's wing that hovered in an atmosphere shot through by the sun's rays, before slowly settling on his benignly distracted spirit, leaving a delicious sediment of poetry. Perhaps a decisive part *was* played in those scenes by betrayal, licentiousness, infringements of the law, even crime, if you like . . . but never the grossest, elemental acts of bestiality that was so repellent and disgusting, and was relegated to the terrestrial graveyard of all debasement . . .

And that arbitrarily immaterial substance nourished his own dreams of grandeur; in a sudden about-face, he, who had only just attacked his parents as unnatural, now defended them so as not to lose his grip on that resplendent, fabled world he so admired.

"No, they aren't hicks! Hicks don't go out of their way to

do things without purpose . . . It's only in other spheres, when other plans for the future exist, that people take precautions. And surely the baptism certificate, the medallion, and indelible mark were all signs that pointed to their eventual return?"

Matron turned her head, smiling sweetly but skeptically. "Many children come to the Orphanage with marks, but nobody ever returns to ask after them. They reflect scruples, fleeting remorse that life's hardships, prejudice, and the corrosive acid of new passions or preoccupations later erase, slowly or swiftly, but usually leaving no trace . . . And it is in those cases, when nature acts as a heartless stepmother, that Charity appears as a tender-hearted Mother . . . No, the Orphanage isn't a stinking dung heap for human beings, but a blessed sieve of impurities, from which cleansed souls emerge rid of the original stains that sullied them. That's why it is best to cherish hopes and jealously preserve them than to know for sure . . . So many hopes have been dashed by the rash desire to delve into depths of doubt!" And, believing such a presumptuous obsession might be bad counsel for that youngster, she tried to drive it from his mind.

"Better not to worry yourself. If your parents were as you believe, they will eventually appear and do their duty, and, if they don't, you must forgive without judging them . . . Human beings know nothing of the distant reason behind things or the designs of Our Lord . . . If He wished, for example, to finally pull the veil from the circumstances around your birth, it would be an act He'd have to consent to, so it's best to resign yourself to His divine will . . ."

She rounded off her speech with words to curb his

impulses: "We shall later see what God's designs may be . . ."

In the meanwhile, she would be so good as to give him whatever information she could find, and he could then decide what he must do.

He walked out of the Orphanage in a rage, much paler than when he'd entered. He stared deep within himself, as if expecting something to come from outside the world of the senses, and he felt he'd aged ten years.

At supper, his boss, though he had little insight into anything outside his trade, did notice that he was upset.

"What's wrong, lad? Aren't you feeling well? You don't seem yourself. You're not eating, not talking . . ."

He put the locksmith off with a few words and a grin. "I have a thick head because I've been studying a clock's complicated mechanisms . . ."

And Nonat left his master gawping at the head of the table, went to his bedroom, and climbed into bed. At least there he wouldn't be subject to inquisitive looks and an interrogation, he'd be able to ruminate at will. And for one, two, and three hours he ruminated, his mind spinning around thousands of times . . . He wasn't happy with the nun's counsel, or her parochial perspectives; they would poison his longings, rather than offer any balm . . . He had to investigate, all alone, on his own behalf. He felt with searing clarity that nobody ever showed an interest in their neighbor's plight, and that maybe nobody would ever be sufficiently engaged to sense his needs, to identify with his joys and his sorrows. Every individual's woe is theirs alone: baggage that can't be transferred. And that's why the tag "look after yourself"—encapsulated real wisdom, which he now grasped for the first time. The desire to find his parents was his, felt by him alone, and he was the only person destined to seek them out . . .

And as if the path he must follow was now lit by a clear, well-defined idea, he suddenly felt released from his obsession and truly liberated from that inner struggle, his mind calm and free. He smiled, just as he did when girls stared at him at the Locksmiths' Company, breathed deeply, turned on his side, and slept like a log.

In the morning, the moment he got up, he went to find his boss and ask for a few days leave of absence.

His boss was surprised because he had never before left the shop.

"Where do you want to go?"

"To Sant Pere de Ruelles . . ."

"And where on earth is that?"

"I'm not sure . . ."

His boss's eyelids flickered.

"It's where I was baptized . . ."

"Where you . . . ? And what are you hoping to do there?"

"Speak to my godmother . . ."

And Nonat told him some of his preoccupations. His boss listened attentively, and watched as something like thick mist gradually rose and wrapped his thoughts in a cloud. "What a lad he is! He's one clutch of great expectations!" And just like Matron, his first instinct was to warn Nonat off, to tell him to ditch his silly ideas, to forget about ready-made parents or ones selected in a lottery . . . What did it matter if you were sired by this man or that; we all come from the same root: Adam the father, and all end up in the same place: the ossuary . . . What did it matter if the steps leading from one end to the other were hewn rock or clods of soil? Things are what they are, everyone passes through the same strait and nobody can escape . . . What was important wasn't knowing who had given you life—it was living, breathing, running, working . . . feeling the blood coursing through your veins, and joy through your heart . . . All else was window dressing, stuff and nonsense . . . a vain desire to squeeze blood out of a stone . . .

But his boss didn't have the gift of gab and couldn't think of a word to say.

So his young tradesman left the following morning and reached Sant Pere de Ruelles on that windswept evening.

"And now, godmother," Nonat exclaimed, as he finished explaining himself, smiling as ever, "by now you must have understood why I'm here. I want you to tell me everything you know about me, everything I imagine only you can tell me. One makes one's bed and lies in it, and one doesn't expect others to foot the bill. And it can't be right if my parents, after bringing me into the world, aren't called to account, and enjoy a life of leisure while I break my arms beating hot metal, and sentence my children, whenever I have any, to be the lowest of the low, like me, and suffer all kinds of misery and privation, when perhaps, by rights, I could be offering them a comfortable life."

As soon as Nonat stopped talking, a deadpan Maria, who'd been listening to his tale, seemed to wake up from a dream, as did Jepet, who, elbows on table, hands gripping the bar from the door, had been all ears, in a blissful haze, like a child listening to a nursery rhyme.

A minute's silence followed. Once the spell was broken, Jepet put down the bar, stretched his arms, flexed his shoulders, which tingled as if drops of cold water were streaming down, and opened his mouth in one big yawn.

In turn, Maria quickly wiped her forehead, as if to remove something that was irritating her, and brightened her stern, blank features, as if donning a mask, preened, and tidied her skirt that didn't need tidying, a sign she was about to make a move.

"Praise the Lord! I can't see straight after listening to what you just said . . . That never happened in the stories and romances they read in the barbershop when I washed their linen . . . That old dear who never wanted to die was right . . ."

She stopped for a second, and, as nobody said a word, she asked innocently: "So what *are* you going to do?"

Nonat stared at her.

"What do you expect me to say when I'm still in the dark? First, I must get to know . . . my parents." (He hesitated, but didn't dare say "pa and ma"; despite all his swagger, he felt uneasy after what Matron had insinuated)

A harsh, obsessive idea haunted his eyes and voice, as it had when he talked to that pious nun.

"And then it depends. If they are who I suspect they are, I'll force them to do their duty . . ."

"And what if they can't, my son?"

"So what if they can't? They ought to have thought about that before . . . !" He paused, then continued: "Dear godmother, I've been neglected and forgotten for twenty-two horrible years, and that's quite long enough!" and, trying to temper the harshness of his words, he smiled again, "Please tell me *all* you know . . ."

But La Gallinaire had already made up her mind. She laughed out loud: "Good God, my lad, you go straight to the point! Like a gust of wind . . ." And she parroted: "'Tell me *all* you know!' Just like that, as if I'd thought only about you from the day I took you to the Orphanage . . . Just imagine! All those years and my poor memory . . . Everything gets so mixed up inside this head of mine!"

Jepet interrupted his yawn and stared at her. Why was she saying she had a poor memory, when she never lost track of anything that entered her head, however trivial? But, as he was used to never challenging what his wife said, he hid his surprise and completed his yawn.

Meanwhile, Nonat, distressed, gave a start in his chair.

"Are you saying you don't know . . . ?"

Maria's face was as placid and ingenuous as could be.

"I'm not saying I don't know . . . I think I must know what happened to me and that sinner . . ."

Nonat calmed down.

"But what I'm saying is that, put on the spot like this, I can't remember anything clearly . . ."

The young man shouted anxiously: "For God's sake, god-mother, make the effort . . . ! Think . . ."

But La Gallinaire stopped him mid-flow.

"You must understand, my son . . . I won't beat about the bush . . . I'm shocked by what you've said . . . Besides, it's late and we don't usually stay up . . . When I'm feeling sleepy,

I'm good for nothing . . . as if I were already in the land of Nod . . ." (That was also news to Jepet, who'd always found her awake and lively as a rooster at any time of the day). "Please believe me! Let's go to bed. Tomorrow, when I'm wide awake, when I've revived and am clear in the head again, I'll think back on everything that happened, I'll put it all together from A to Z and tell you every little detail . . ." And, seeing the orphan was about to protest, she continued, "I'm telling you, if you try to force me to talk now, I'll get it all wrong, make a mess of it, and nothing will make any sense . . . Right now, I don't know what's wrong with me! I feel all queasy!"

And there was no shifting her. She went to get the tin candleholder with the still colorful length of altar candle, and holding it in one hand and an oil lamp in the other, Maria and her husband accompanied their visitor to his bedroom, and after showing him everything he might need and wishing him good night, they retired to the barn.

Jepet looked at Maria, an alarmed expression on his rough, granite face.

"Don't you feel well?'

"Me?" his wife retorted, taken aback.

Jepet was even more confused: "You said you felt queasy!"

Maria grinned mischievously.

"You know, I didn't feel like chatting with him," then, on a more serious note, "What can I say, Jepet? I'm not too sure about that young man . . . At first, I liked him, but then . . . I mean, I found him rather odd . . . And it didn't seem right to tell him things straight out that might bring a lot of distress to the families . . . Don't you agree? It's better to think things through before putting your foot in it . . ."

And while Nonat, gripped by more devastating soul-searching, leapt acrobatically over his hosts' imposing bed and crashed down on the squeaking, protesting mattress—which was unused to such athletic agility—Maria was in the barn clutching the bed rail to avoid falling on Jepet, who'd comfortably placed his whalelike bulk of becalmed flesh in the dip of the sheet. She herself spent a sleepless night reviewing the ins and outs of that distant episode when fate had forced her to intervene a lot or a little.

What she knew of those events: just over twenty-two years ago, a stranger by the name of Donya Tulita had come to spend the winter months in Ruelles—for health reasons, they said at the time. She lived on the outskirts of town, past the main gate, in the only large house to rent in the village. Donya Tulita had a six-year-old daughter. The young child's wet nurse, the sister-in-law of the Ruelles midwife, stayed on in the house after the child had been weaned to take care of her, so her mother, a delicate, simpering lass, didn't need to worry about a thing.

However, one day, the wet nurse caught typhus and her relative, the midwife, was summoned. The latter traveled to the city to make the acquaintance of her sister-in-law's master and mistress. The sister-in-law was recovering, chatted to all and sundry, and had started to eat, when she overtaxed herself and had a relapse that would be the death of her. Subsequently, the midwife returned to the village, bringing a secret with her; a secret known only to the ailing woman who had confided in her. Her mistress had a lover, a military man.

As a very young girl, the Senyora had worked as a maid in a magistrate's house. Back then, her name was Tuietes, and she liked a spot of fun. One of the sons of the family, a student, fell in love with her, she returned his love, and the moment the magistrate found out, he sacked the maid.

Tuietes moved on to the household of a childless, well-to-do couple from South America. The wife was consumptive; she struggled for months, then died. Tuietes never left her side, and her master was very grateful, became infatuated, and married her. The gentleman was twice her age and had big business concerns in South America. He took her there on their honeymoon and she became terribly homesick and after their daughter was born, it was even rumored she'd been affected mentally. They returned to Europe. Soon afterward, chance brought Tuietes's—now Donya Tulita's—old flame to her side—the student, now a first lieutenant in the army—and they resumed their relationship, and it was much less innocent than before. When the husband next spoke of returning to South America, where his enterprises were in urgent need of his presence, his wife resisted the idea of accompanying him, and in a veiled, though tenacious manner, alleged that her state of health didn't allow her, cleverly drawing on medical opinion. In the end, her husband was obliged to leave by himself, and when he returned, after a long absence, the same issue arose, in the same terms, and he was forced to agree to a compromise and resign himself to spending one year in South America and the next in Spain, subsequently alternating on an almost regular basis.

During one of her husband's absences, the wife was caught in a sticky situation and had to flee the city and hide from her acquaintances . . . She remembered the midwife and wrote to her, asking her to find her a house. After renting it, she planned her move, fired the old servants, contracted new ones, and traveled to the village. The midwife immediately understood what was happening and that she must be careful to employ only folk she could trust. She called on her friend Maria la Gallinaire to wash clothes and do other jobs, and, as she didn't feel able to bottle up the secret, she told Maria everything.

When difficult times were nigh, Maria was available to do the necessary and was instructed to quietly take the newborn baby boy to the Orphanage. Before the child was born, Donya Tulita had insisted he or she should be indelibly marked; the midwife took a sewing needle, scored two deep lines in the loose, wrinkled skin around the baby's left nipple, dipped a piece of cotton in an inkwell, soaked the wounds, and kneaded the tender skin so the liquid penetrated the fleshy folds.

But his mother became very distressed, got into a big tizzy, afraid that the mark might be erased too easily, and insisted he should be given something else so he would stand out from all the orphans for a longer time—"Two years, at least two years!" she moaned feverishly—the midwife removed a Monserrat medallion from the mother's neck and placed it around the baby's, complete with blue silk cord.

Once that was done, the sobbing mother gave him a slavering kiss, and the babe was quickly handed to Maria, who was charged to arrange for him to be baptized, before she took him to Girona, by the name of Ramon Nonat, to which, half an hour later, the priest added Ventura and Miquel.

As the mansion was outside the town gate, that scene took

place in the middle of the night; the maids were lodged in an annex to the main building, attached at the end opposite to the one occupied by the midwife's bedchamber—in any case, they slept the deep, bombproof sleep of the young. As her mistress had been ill for two days, the midwife stayed at her side on the excuse of her sickly state and allowed nobody to come near her. As her isolation continued a few days more, when the mistress got up, she pretended she was still fat, and nobody suspected what had really happened.

The housekeeper spoke of a mysterious baptism and spread a romantic tale whose lead role was played by a poor girl who'd been abandoned by her fiancé and suddenly had to leave the village, disgraced and shamed, in order to go and help an old aunt.

Soon after the said lady left, Maria shut down her chicken business and the midwife died. Before the midwife's passing, Maria had asked her what she knew about those people, and the midwife told her Donya Tulita had written to say they were well, that she often remembered the village, the midwife, and her, and that for her part, she could never be happy or peaceful as long as she was separated from her absent loved one. When she said that, she seemed to refer to her husband, but the midwife knew it wasn't him, but the boy.

Not long after the midwife's death, another letter came from the lady. The midwife's nephews and nieces read it. It told the recipient to go to the city immediately: something very unfortunate had happened and they must talk. The nephews and nieces sent news of the loss of their aunt and never heard anything more from that lady.

As Maria was aware that Donya Tulita's husband suffered

from a very poor stomach and that the doctors didn't give him long to live, when she heard of the letter, she concluded that the misfortune must be the death of the lady's husband, and prayed an uplifting *Pater noster.*

When dawn broke, Jepet was awoken by the cold, empty space Maria left when she abandoned their uncomfortable shared cot in the barn; he felt disorientated by the new arrangements, and he had to think hard. The previous night's scenes and Maria's last comments came back to him, making him feel jittery, which wasn't like him at all.

He was the mildest of men, not because it was in his nature or he willed it to be so, but because he tended not to react. His awareness of things lasted like rain on thin topsoil: it immediately filtered through, sucked downward, leaving not a drop on the surface, scattered, silted, and hidden from sight in the dark, mysterious depths of his being. And he never spoke spontaneously, nor had a word to say about whatever he might have seen or heard; though if asked, he was one to tell the whole truth, not out of natural honesty, but because he lacked the wit and guile to fabricate a lie. His Maria, the Chicken Woman, had had to wage war on the poor man's natural tongue-tied state, though he had no padlocks or bars to defend himself against inquisitive neighbors, who, whenever he returned from a voyage or after the sale of a catch, sank their claws into him, on the cart or in the tavern, and dragged out of him everything they were after, simply by forcing him to let slip a "yes," or untoward information.

Thanks to repeated warnings from his wife, he'd learned to curb this weakness of his, but he was always terrified by questions to which the two of them hadn't jointly prepared a reply.

"I mean, when Jan Fuma from across the road comes and asks how much cash you got as your share from the catch, tell him only the half of it, say prices were down . . ."

"But . . ." Jepet was about to protest feebly, given the huge difference between the price suggested and the real one, when she deftly demolished his scruples.

"No ifs or buts . . . First, there's no earthly reason why he should know how much we make, and second, he's council secretary this year, and will pile on the taxes if we give him half a chance."

Delighted by a wife who'd think and sort everything out on his behalf, with a clear conscience Jepet repeated the lesson he'd learned whenever he had to, making her entirely responsible, and then avoided further conversation for fear he might stumble. Which was usually the case. However, that day was quite unlike any other. It wasn't merely the quantity of grapes or profit from a fishing trip that were at stake—that was his business when all was said and done—but something much more serious and unusual, because Maria had stated it might cause more than one family upset: he didn't have a clue what he should say. There were lots of gray areas in Jepet's memory, which was never too secure or well-nourished, though he did know something about the matters the young visitor was so desperate to hear about. Because La Gallinaire loved him, led him wherever she wanted, and because her expansive nature required it, she confided everything to her husband, convinced, as we have said, it was tantamount to consigning it to a tomb. However, the sudden appearance of the inquisitive locksmith and his hunger for facts threatened Jepet's unguarded reserve, and as Maria had said she didn't want him to speak before thinking it through, yet she'd fled their bed without telling him what she'd decided, or telling him what he could and could not say, Jepet was as terrified as if there was already a noose around his neck. If he could be sure all the questions would be fired at his wife, no worries; she was well spoken, had a silver tongue, and could deal with anything. But if he was unlucky and they were misfired in his direction, he might make an awful mess of it. He might say the exact opposite of what Maria had said . . . Because he imagined she'd been speaking to the young man for a while . . . It was broad daylight, the young man was in a hurry, and their house was so silent; he could already imagine them by the fireside . . . However, that wasn't the case. Jepet had got it wrong: as he was pulling on his clothes, he went over to the barn window overlooking the yard, and saw Maria alone on the bench, next to the laundry basket, opposite the bushel of grain, stock still. Poor Jepet had another nervous turn. Oh dear! His blessed wife wasn't well . . . Or else, at that time of day, when she'd usually be going through household chores like wildfire, why would she sit ramrod on the bench? Even the hens, fearfully, then shamelessly, twisted their heads to look at her, with one eye on heaven, and one on earth, pecking at the grain, yet she said and did nothing to shoo them away . . .

Suddenly, as if sensing she was being watched, she looked up, and, as on the previous evening, seemed to wake up from a dream. She lifted a finger to her lips, signaling her husband to keep quiet, and then motioned for him to come down.

Barefoot, tiptoeing as much as possible so the floorboards didn't creak, Jepet hastened to obey.

Maria told him to pull up a rock and sit next to her. Then she whispered falteringly, as if in the confessional: "You know, Jepet, I've been chewing all night over what came through our door . . . and I can't think what to do and keep a clear conscience . . ."

Jepet felt even more anxious. It was the first time he'd seen Maria fret and struggle to reach a decision. She was always one to make her mind up instantly, without a moment's hesitation.

"What do you mean, Maria?"

"What do I mean? That I wish this lad had never come . . . It might have spared me a lot of agony in my old age."

More upset than ever by such a statement, Jepet ventured to offer some advice: "If it's going to make you suffer so, you'd better tell him everything . . ."

Maria gestured to him to shut up.

"I'd suffer even more . . . I promised the midwife I wouldn't say a word, and her mistress had her make me swear an oath . . . You see, the lady was married, had a daughter, her honor was compromised, and she was terrified somebody might get an inkling . . ."

Jepet felt confused and stared blankly at the bushel of grain, where not just one or two hens were pecking away: making the most of their mistress's inattention, the whole flock had gathered around.

"Don't say anything then . . ."

Maria reacted impatiently.

"That's easily said! Anything goes if you couldn't care less . . . But I'm not like that . . . That lad speaks good sense, depending on how you look at it . . . He has wealthy parents but he's beating metal, like one of God's forgotten . . . If I speak up, I'll make him a rich man; if I don't, he will never learn the truth . . . I mean, it really is as I said: a case for the conscience . . ."

It was all too complicated for Jepet to risk voicing an opinion. He let it go and yielded to his sluggish stream of thought, while instinctively following the movement of the hens. A red one, with oil-colored eyes, a small, cropped crest, and folds of fat hanging like a turkey's glanced between Maria and the basket for some time before finally jumping into it. Unsure whether to follow her or afraid of being attacked, the other hens circled around, twittering as if they were squabbling. Finally, one of them, black as a crow, its huge comb tilted to one side like a Carlist leader's beret, daringly stretched her neck and stuck her head into the bushel. No sooner had she done so than she was quickly repelled and a drop of blood even redder than her crest appeared.

Christ, that red one's a tough nut! thought Jepet, vaguely amused. And whenever the other hens tried to share in the booty, the sharp beak in the bushel defended her prize, keeping them at bay.

"Tougher than La Ferriola!" thought the master of the house to himself.

La Ferriola was a fishwife neighbor, with a temper like

tinder, ready to take on anyone, if only over the miserable scale of an anchovy.

In the meantime, Maria wracked her lonely brain, between Jepet's mental void and the chickens' hue and cry.

"Besides, when they handed me the baby, the mistress told Magdalena (the midwife) that she wasn't putting him in the Orphanage because she hated him, but because she had no choice. As she was pledged and couldn't show her face, his father, the soldier, would take care of him . . . But as the military man was a professional, and those people are always on the move . . . And as he himself probably married . . . The truth is he must have forgotten the boy . . . Men will be men! Good at doing things on the side, and then . . ." The hidden pain in her life was spilling out again, though her spirit of fairness didn't allow her to put all the blame on the soldier, however much a man—and a fly-by-night—he had been. "You'll say if he hadn't done his duty, she could have done *hers*, after being widowed . . . After all, it was her son!" But when she was on the point of assigning blame, doubts took her along a different path and a thousand and one times she encountered the same hurdles that had prevented her for hours from moving forward. "Praised be the Lord! I can't think of what could have stopped her . . . Perhaps it was her reputation . . . perhaps she didn't want to harm her daughter, perhaps it was her husband's legacy . . . perhaps, if you press me, she was sick, or even died. I'd put it down to that rather than anything unbecoming . . . Because Donya Tulita was extremely generous and thoughtful in everything she did . . . She couldn't bear to see anyone suffer . . . You saw how she wept when she left the baby . . . She couldn't sleep, and within two days sent me back to Girona to find out whether he was all right . . . And she missed him every minute! And even said it would be the death of her if God didn't find a quick solution . . . And look at the solution! Now, if I believed she'd pushed him to the back of her mind, as if she never had a son, if I believed that was the case, I'd encourage Nonat to fight for his legal rights . . . But, now, like this, in cold blood, not knowing what actually happened, I wouldn't want to put her on the spot, and betray her to her son . . . I couldn't, I couldn't possibly, even if I hadn't given my word . . . If she's alive, her daughter must be married or about to be, and if the truth were trumpeted around, that might end their peace of mind, and all their fates . . . And if she's dead, what would be the point of speaking up and sullying her memory? Do you see? If she were alive and I knew where she was, we could—for example—secretly go and see her, inform her of the situation, and ask her to look after her son without going public." But then she started to falter and hesitate. "Except *he* wouldn't accept that . . . Once it began, he'd want to take things to a conclusion, then it would be a disaster . . . Because there's the catch! He's set on doing this without heeding anyone, and it's clear he'll not stop short of causing havoc . . . I told you as much yesterday, Jepet: I don't like this young man . . . he's too full of himself . . . If he wants to find his parents, it's not because they're his parents, but because he thinks they're rich and will give him a life of luxury. And if he finds them, he'll be pitiless; he'll drive them into a corner, you mark my words; he'll drive them into a corner, and all hell will break loose. He'd only leave them in peace if he discovered they were poor, without a cent to their name . . ." She stopped. A clever idea had just flashed across her brain: an idea she'd been chasing all night. Her anxious face brightened into a sly grin. "And if so . . . let's give it a try, I'll bet you I'm right."

But Jepet couldn't bet anything because, though he seemed attentive, he hadn't been following Maria's thread of thought. The hens had seized all his energy. None outside the basket had been able to get a single grain. The one that had established herself like a sovereign queen was in complete control. Clucking contentedly, she scratched with her yellow legs, claws full of dirt, in that God-blessed granary, discovering endless treasures: a black bean gleaming like jet, the small whitish-gray cadaver of a desiccated insect, a broken ear of corn, a shiny pebble, a vetch the size of a chickpea . . . Her sieving revealed surprising riches. Her coop-mates, the other hens, bristled with envy, and seeing they weren't strong enough to force her off her throne, were taking it out on each other, skirmishing furiously, beaks pulling out feathers . . .

Until a bitter, frantic sound suddenly issued from the warm depths of the coop, and all at once, as if shot out from a blowgun, another hen emerged, disheveled and flustered. The soldier of the yard, who'd been amorously accompanying his favorite while she laid an egg, then appeared, solemn and erect, imposing respect. And at the sight of their magnificent lord and master, the hysterical hens around the basket lifted their siege, fluttered off forlornly, and, alerted by the turmoil, Maria, with an angry swipe of her apron, frightened away the delinquent, greedy red hen.

Jepet now heard the buzz that till then had barely reached

his ears turn into something intelligible, and he grasped what Maria was saying: "People are so quick to say that you think you've got it right when you've got it all wrong! I so regretted not holding onto him at the time . . . If I'd been tempted to do so before I took him to the Orphanage, we wouldn't be so happy today. Because it's obvious he would never have accepted our poverty-stricken lives! I mean, he gives himself such airs!"

And, as if she'd finished wracking her brain, she stood up, affectionately telling her husband to go and get the egg from the coop, while she went to see if Nonat was awake.

"And don't get it wrong: the best layer is the one with the black squiggle."

But Jepet stopped her, panic-stricken: "But what if he asks me something?"

Her response came loud and clear.

"If he asks you? Say you haven't a clue . . . It's all a mystery to you . . . Better do that, so you don't muddy the waters . . ."

Jepet was fully on board, and, peace of mind restored, went to look for that egg.

The conversation between godmother and godson was a curious tug-of-war: a subtle game of defensive diplomacy on her part; on his, a spirited, impetuous dive into the deep end, its sole outcome a leap into the void.

She rehearsed the story that had been agreed upon years ago: "One night someone knocked loudly on the door, as you did yesterday . . . Jepet was out to sea"—she hastened to add in order to spare her husband an interrogation. She had been terrified, had leapt out of bed, and peered out of the window . . . She asked what they wanted and nobody answered, but she saw a woman, her face hidden behind a headscarf, depositing a whitish bundle on the doorstep, then running off down the street . . . Curious, she went down to see what was in the bundle and found the baby . . . ("You were red, red as if you'd had chicken pox, and sucking your little fists rather than the sweet wrapped in cloth they'd put in your mouth.") She was taken aback. She couldn't think what to do with that little hunk of flesh smelling of the cradle and clean linen . . . If Jepet had been there, he'd have calmed me down . . . ("If he'd said, 'Let's keep him,' I'd have done just that . . ."). She stared at Nonat with a concerned, motherly smile ("You see, then you'd have been heir to this household!"). Nonat smiled too, but said nothing. She closed her eyes, swallowed, and continued: But Jepet wasn't there, and she had to decide . . . The next morning she had to go to Girona to sell hens and thought she'd take him to the Orphanage . . . That must have been why the baby was left in her doorway . . . But, before doing that, naturally she decided to make a Christian of him, as she imagined nobody else would have thought of that . . .

She stopped. Nonat rasped: "And what else?"

"What else? End of story!" She laughed pleasantly. "Would you like there to be something else? You're not like me. I think that was enough, more than enough! If you'd have been in my place . . . !"

El Senyoret was stung by his obsession.

"For Christ's sake, godmother! You seem to take it all so lightheartedly, you're not thinking that I . . . You've said next to nothing. Even less than the Orphanage . . . And that can't possibly be right . . . That cannot possibly be. Try to remember. Think hard. You must know, you do know something that can give me a clue . . ." And when Maria flinched imperceptibly, he redoubled his efforts: "What about the woman? What were her features like? Who was she? Everybody knows everybody in this village, and you must at least suspect . . ."

But she hadn't recognized her, she had no suspicions . . .

"I'm telling you the truth, my son! She was so wrapped up and I was so bleary-eyed because I'd just jumped out of bed . . . Besides, she didn't dally or let me get a look at her; she seemed to fly off, and was out of my sight in an Amen, Jesus . . . That's why I couldn't tell you anything else for certain . . . Now if you want to hear the gossip, what the gossip-mongers said . . . Who can stop those tongues when they get a whiff of something racy?"

You can imagine how frantically Nonat rushed through that breach opened before his demented brain. Which was when the Chicken Woman quietly and warily began to tell the story that had to come to her in the yard minutes ago. Recalling the kerfuffle caused by the bastard's birth, she recounted the rumors sparked by the disappearance of that girl who'd been abandoned by her fiancé, and while caviling and protesting she knew nothing, she suggested there might in fact be some truth in all that chatter . . .

"Might be, or might not . . . What do we know? And God forbid I should bear false witness . . . What I'm telling you . . . was just a rumor making the rounds."

As Maria spoke, El Senyoret felt constricted by the metal hoops tightening around his ribs, and sweated blood and tears. Once again they were claiming he had poverty-stricken parents he should be ashamed of, and were trying to block his path and persuade him to desist from his search. It was horrendous! The opaque malevolence of chance . . . the cruel mockery of malign powers! However, his violent reaction soon made him see things in a fresh light. No, it was anything but random and innocent, it was a premeditated, deceitful act . . . And vaguely—because he couldn't grasp a motive—he felt, he *intuited* an unknown factor, that wasn't insoluble in itself, that nobody wanted to shed light on; he guessed strange elements were conspiring to mislead him, to put him off track, to keep him away from the truth, basically ravaging and destroying what he firmly believed within himself; his hunch that he came from illustrious stock . . . And his rebel nature surged; once again he found cold, razor-sharp words.

"Let's forget all the gossip, godmother . . . I want to know what you know and what you saw and nothing else!"

And, angry and angst-ridden, he tried to prompt new leads that would enable him to tie up loose ends, and find the flimsiest thread to lead him back to his origins. To no avail. Quite naturally, she piled on the futile detail, repeated what she'd already said in different guises, wandered unnerved this way and that, but never once contradicted herself or added anything crucial. Until, tired of flailing and tripping in that relentless murk, Nonat felt his spirit ebbing, as it had hours earlier, and curtailed his frenzied interrogation. And that was the moment the Chicken Woman calmly chose to introduce her next cunning ploy.

"That woman . . . Your . . . the one they said was your mother was very pretty . . . She looked like the Virgin

Mary . . . She was a good lass, like her family, and nobody ever had a bad word to say . . . Apart from that business . . . which if it were true, was certainly a blemish . . . But she was blinded by one of those loves that stops us from seeing what we are doing . . . But she wasn't ashamed . . . The best proof of that was how the poor girl fled, and how nobody has ever seen her in these parts again . . . First they said she went to Vilafranca or Granollers, or somewhere up there. She met a baker, they liked each other, married and left for Algiers . . . I bet they're still there, trying to make a bit of money . . . Though they were both sensible and hardworking, my feeling is their business can hardly have prospered . . ."

She paused, and then as Nonat said nothing, she added affectionately: "I can see you're upset, my son . . . You don't believe it . . . The idea you might find parents that you've never known, is like being born anew . . . It's true what they say: blood runs thicker than water. But don't be taken in by my words. All that could be wind in the trees, senyor, as they say . . . You know there's no stopping gossips, that they make a snowball out of the smallest flake . . . Before you go any further, you need to investigate properly . . ." She felt a sudden twinge: "If you like, I could make the first contact . . ."

Nonat had drifted off, but he came around and scowled aggressively at his godmother.

"What do you mean?"

"I'm a friend of that lass's mother and of the whole village, though, naturally, we've never talked about any of all that . . . You can imagine what a blow it was, and it didn't really affect me, you know? But it's different now . . . I've met you and feel sorry for you . . . I've given it some thought and I'd like to help you as much as I can. As for your father, if it really was him, forget it. He worked as a farmhand near here, and after the scandal, as people gave him the eye, he took off, and God knows where he is . . . But as far as she goes, we could find out more than the gospel truth. If you agree, I'll try my luck with her grandmother and use my cunning, my soft, soft touch, and see if I get anything out of her, confirming it or not . . . And once you're sure you've got the facts, nothing can stop you from hopping on a boat to Algiers and meeting the woman who brought you into the world . . . Your *mother*! Lucky the man who has one! And even the worst are saints in the eyes of their children . . . And that lass was as good as gold, she really was . . . I tell you! She might be on the poor side—but what's wealth by the side of love?—her heart was so big . . . After what she must have suffered, you turning up will remove that thorn. As well as knowing she'll have your support in her old age . . ."

Nonat was seething with rage; white heat frying his guts. She was lying! He didn't know why, he couldn't imagine what hidden intent led her to playact, but he was sure he was right, he'd have wagered his life on it. He'd seen her the night before when she recognized him, and was effusive, welcoming and cheerful, opening her heart and mind . . . and then, when he'd explained himself, she suddenly clammed up, entrenched herself behind evasions and enigmatic silences, and that had been a warning. And now her glances, her words, her gestures, the thoughts lurking behind her temples, were slippery like an eel; she sidestepped all his questions, zigzagged from one lie to another; she was all deceit and imagination, the sand-like figments she tried to fling into his eyes to make him lose his impetus, to blur everything. That bundle on the doorstep was fake, fake too the woman running away, fake the farmhand, fake the bakery . . . His godmother knew much more than she was letting on, probably the whole truth, but what she *was* trying to do with her foolish tales, he suspected, was to shut him off from the truth and plunge him irrevocably into the black pit of ignorance. But why would she do that, for God's sake? There lay the key: in the reason for all her maneuvering. It must be something big and powerful for her to adopt such a cautious front. He was convinced his suspicions weren't betraying him . . . His parents *were* classy people . . . Only high status and largesse could muzzle anybody like that, could guarantee such keen loyalties . . .

And that was why Nonat was more sure than ever that he was right, and why, against La Gallinaire's hopes, the precautions she'd taken to put him off track only reinforced and consolidated the deluded bastard's hopes. Momentarily, he felt murderous impulses. If he'd followed his heart, he'd have grabbed her by the throat and choked her to death. But from very early in life, he was used to swimming against the tide, to pitting his chest against the waves, to being plunged into deep water just when he thought he'd reached a safe harbor, and he'd learned the art of self-control, of recovering his sangfroid quickly, and hiding his impulses. In that dark hour, in the midst of the storm whirling around him, he was calm enough to grasp that nothing would be gained by wreaking havoc. The woman standing before him was an honorable soul—he recognized—and wasn't lying for the pleasure of lying, but had been obliged to do so by a power that controlled her, and, enslaved to that power, she'd die rather than speak out and yield the solution to the enigma. If he destroyed her, he might destroy his last hope of ever finding the truth . . . He must respect her, at least until he had lost all hope of ever extracting anything from her.

The truth existed, and, however remote it was, however much they wanted to keep it from him, he was sure he'd discover it someday, and who knew if that woman might not prove useful . . .

He ran his hand nervously through his hair, his fingers tapping his skull, like the fingers of a reed player . . . Then he stood up, straightened his jacket, tidied his shirt cuffs . . . He picked up the chair he'd been sitting on and placed it back against the wall. He looked around at the Chicken Woman . . . As in the Orphanage, his gaze and his voice receded into the distance, assuming the somber shadows of a chasm.

"Godmother, you're lying, telling me the opposite of the truth. I don't know why . . . But it's evident you're being forced to . . . For the moment I intend to respect your scruples . . . But tomorrow will be another day . . ."

Maria was dumbstruck.

"But, my son . . . I'm . . . I'm saying that if you want . . ."

Nonat laughed half-contemptuously.

"No, though thank you very much. We should leave the farmhand and baker in Algiers in peace . . . They're doing no harm . . . And now, godmother, please do excuse me . . . Who knows if we'll meet again in the future, when perhaps your memory will be working better . . ."

And after a few bland, colorless words rejecting other invitations and affectionate pleas for him to stay on at least another day, he bid farewell and left, as if he felt a desperate need to abandon that house and those folk who'd only made him taste more rancor and bitter defeat.

His cape over his arm, with a lordly, leisurely gait, he walked down the dark side of the street, women neighbors peering inquisitively from their doorways. From hers, Maria watched him go and when he turned the corner, she went back inside and looked at her husband.

His snarling grin had naturally faded as it was now quite pointless.

"What did I tell you, Jepet?" she muttered gloomily. "Such a fuss about knowing who his parents were, and look how he reacted when I said they were poor . . . Just like when I suggested he should stay on with us . . . He couldn't care less about honest people, honest souls, the salt of the earth . . . What he's after is money . . . getting more sun than shade . . . He thought ill of me . . . He said I lied to him . . . So what! If he'd not fallen into the trap, if he'd not shown his intentions so clearly, perhaps I'd have taken pity on him and said something I'd regret . . . But, with him being like that, I was never going to do anything stupid . . . I did well to seal my lips . . . I pity poor Donya Tulita if she ever falls into his hands! There's a glint of evil in that young man's eyes!"

"So, how did it go?" asked Nonat's boss when he saw him walk into the shop.

Nonat tried to act as naturally as possible.

"Waste of time! The poor woman knew nothing . . ." and he went to his bedroom to cut the conversation short and change his clothes.

His boss was overjoyed. She knew nothing? Thank God! I hope he'll forget all that nonsense now . . . However, he soon saw Nonat's obsession hadn't gone away. The whole day his apprentice worked silently, anxiously, distractedly, as if he was planning a new tack, and that night he complained of a thick head, said he wanted to try to relax and walked out.

His boss shrugged his shoulders and shook his head in disappointment.

That lad was on the wrong road, as plain as God was in heaven! But he didn't know what he could do to change that . . .

Nonat wandered around Girona until late into the night. At first full of activity and noise, the city gradually quieted down until the sounds seemed to subside altogether. The only signs of life were the glare of artificial light, the thunderous revving of a saloon car, and people going in and out of a downtown café.

Air didn't seem to circulate down the narrow streets of tall, brown houses; enchanted layers of cold, as in a cave, hung between heaven and earth and thick, sticky patches of damp stained the walls' invisible flagstones and cobbles, as if sweating in a protracted death throe. Now and then the monotonous black countryside was broken by a bend in the road that opened up a large, gleaming sapphire eye; a moonless tract of sky dotted with tremulous stars . . . Or else, the walls' precipitous sides were jarred by an unknown cataclysm and seemed to crash down on El Senyoret, that bird in the night, and imprison him in a long, low ravine where he struggled to breathe and his footsteps echoed, treacherously betraying him . . . The arches of an arcade bore the bulky weight of the buildings in a square, resisting gravity like the shoulders of Atlas . . . Further on, a random noise or the sharp edge of a street corner made his heart thud with instinctive panic, as if a hand wielding a cruel weapon was about to emerge from the murky depths and a gruff voice, buzzing like a crazed hornet, would bawl the terrifying classic: Your money or your life! Then came the graceful, sturdy silhouette of the belfry of Sant Feliu looming out of the gloom and laying a finger of dense shadow across the sky's translucent darkness . . . And later, the arch of a bridge, swelling up from ground level, bestrode the river, peering at the muddy water trickling turbidly beneath, sullen and silent like a shabby tramp, boxed in between cheap and nasty buildings that systematically turned their backs on the water, displaying all the ugliness that stifled the poetry rather than illuminating and ennobling their façades, as opulent Venice would do with its fairy-like touch. . .

Staggering from one side to the other, like the arcades in the square, like a miniature Atlas, carrying the weight of a world on his shoulders, Nonat had walked almost the whole of Girona, and, feeling tense after expending so much energy, calm on the outside, raging like one of the shop's furnaces on the inside, he returned home in the early hours, when Girona's roosters cock-a-doodled to each other from one end of the city to the other, from one gallery to another, and carts began to stir, their wheels and axles squeaking lethargically . . .

His boss, an upright fellow, heard him come in, thought

the worst, and, regretting another uneasy moment his protégé had made him suffer, muttered between sheet and pillow: "God forbid, God forbid, he's not satisfied with wasting his money, now he's damaging his health . . . He must have found a den of nymphs, or the Four Horsemen are after him . . ."

However, as we have seen, neither youthful distractions, knuckles or fake cards had consumed the young lad's time. In that closed city, walled in its pious solemnity, he had merely been trying to discover the seed of the secret folly, misfortune, or sin to which he owed his life. From one street to another, like someone turning the pages of a memoir, he'd been rifling the memories dormant in the tales he'd heard over the last few days, rumors of sins, big and small, sullying the names of distinguished families, of all the impurities, that in life's seething ferment surface daily in a big city and are swept benignly or malevolently away by that great colander of dross. As a little boy, tortured by the enigma of his origins, his ears had eagerly seized on the stories, slander, or nonsense that reached them, and had zealously hoarded them like a collection of precious stones, and on that nervy, restless night, he had stood in front of every suspect house, scouring his mind for every detail, marrying dates and eras, weighing up possibilities . . . But, after long, exhausting hours, as he retired to his home like the cold light of a firefly meandering between tombstones, he had felt a fresh sense of disappointment, but then new hope lit up . . . He would *never* find anything there. The novelettish episodes he'd cherished were too thin or rehearsed for him to be in doubt, some far too old, others far too obvious, their provenance only too visible, to be at all connected to himself.

No need to underline that he wasn't abandoning the higher echelons, rather he would consider only a very select band of suspects; he was jettisoning everything else, scorned with Olympian disdain.

Part Two

It had been painful to tell the boss he was leaving, and the unpleasant aftertaste lingered. Anticipating the inevitable, Nonat made his preparations on the quiet and out of sight. A colleague of his in the Locksmiths' Company, Peroi, had quarreled with his foreman and decided to leave for Barcelona. The colleague had never been before, but an aunt of his lived there and he'd stay with her while looking for work. If Peroi liked the city, he'd stay, if not, he'd find somewhere else.

All of a sudden the sky cleared over Nonat. Girona oppressed him; he hated the place. From the moment he sensed he was going nowhere, he'd broken all emotional ties to the city. He reckoned that the city and its inhabitants owed him something; they'd made him victim of a swindle, of an immoral con; all things considered, he was being held there against the law and his rights, like in the Orphanage, and he wanted out, though he couldn't decide how and when. He'd started hatching a thousand plans and spawning countless escape routes that all fell short or were silly in one way or another. And though leaving was constantly on his mind, he stopped worrying and, like in the Orphanage, he trusted that his freedom would come by chance. An obscure instinct—the instinct of the born adventurer—told him chance was the great provider, that where human guile and foresight failed, chance would resolve his dilemmas. It had opened the doors of the Home for Bastards, now it would bring the walls of Girona crashing down, lead him to his parents, and put him on the road to fame and fortune. When? When God willed! His goal could remain more or less distant—though not by much, the mysterious voice whispered deep inside him—but he *would* get his own way, and find the source of his fate—of that there was no doubt—however much they hid it from him, whatever hurdles they placed in his way . . .

Such stubborn self-belief curbed his impatience, ensuring he did nothing stupid, or acted inopportunely . . . That confidence again produced a small miracle and gave him the opportunity he was seeking: the aforementioned colleague's departure to Barcelona. Nonat had been attracted to the idea of Barcelona for some time. He always thought of his *parents* and *Barcelona* together. The two ideas were always entwined, inseparable. After the disappointments dispensed by Matron and his godmother, after his retrospective scrutiny of scandal-mongering in the old city of Sant Narcís, he had unconsciously focused everything driving his filial inquiries on Barcelona. That city had to be the ark where his secret was hidden; he *would* find the answer to his enigma there; wandering its streets, one day or another, out of the blue, a hunch would suggest: "That's your father!" And he was certain his hunch wouldn't disappoint him, as that gentleman's had in the Orphanage, the millionaire who mistook him for his son . . .

And so, Nonat asked to join the departing Peroi.

"It's all I needed to make my mind up to go . . . A colleague: to have an acquaintance there . . . So I wouldn't be a total stranger . . ."

Peroi was delighted, because Nonat was highly regarded in the trade. His haughty, supercilious manner belonged to his innermost life and character, and wasn't part of his daily attitude at work. He was perhaps the best tradesman on the block, since his wonderful manual dexterity went with a fertile brain and consummate patience when it came to analyzing problems and the mechanics of his art, and he never flaunted that superiority in an offensive or demeaning way to others, and was always ready with a perceptive word of advice or a helpful hand to get them out of a fix.

They agreed the colleague would look around once in Barcelona, and if Peroi found anything suitable for them, he would send Nonat a couple of lines.

That letter took a week to come, meanwhile Nonat suffered the feverish anxiety he'd felt in the past, that struck at times of great mental tension, when he was perpetually on edge and a victim of high hopes. A strange luminosity created a blinding veil that blurred everything in his sight. It was as if he'd been looking at the sun too long, and his eyes saw only a glittering, phosphorescent dance, a shimmering shower of golden dots in an electric atmosphere that was uniformly red, blue, or green; his blood hammered his temples, rushed to and from his face so fast that one minute it flared up like a turkey's wattle, but the next it blanched as if he were about to faint . . . And an ominous black cloud overshadowed that tempestuous turmoil. What would he tell the boss? How could he sugar the pill of his escape? They'd never signed a contract, they'd never talked about it, but quite naturally, by force of circumstance, they'd forged an understanding that they would be together for life. The boss had rescued him from the Orphanage, the boss had generously taught him everything he knew, the boss had treated him and loved him like a father; he never scolded him, left the management of the workshop entirely in his hands, often alluding to what Nonat could do when he, the boss, was no longer of this world. Reckoning his youthful fantasies and hopes of finding his unknown progenitors were unlikely to be fulfilled, that upstanding man considered Nonat to be his one and only heir . . . How would his boss now react to his planned desertion? What pleas, what imploring would he face as the locksmith tried to dissuade him from leaving? When he thought about it, Nonat felt a painful twinge in his heart; something deep inside sternly reproaching him, disapproving of his behavior, telling him, whether he listened or not, that he was acting disloyally and wasn't repaying his debt as a grateful human should . . . However, as usual, Nonat angrily rejected a sentiment he found disconcerting and tried to quash it with a derisory shrug of the shoulders.

"Hey! Let's not jump to conclusions before the evil deed is done . . . Who knows if Peroi will ever find us work!"

But Peroi did. Here's the letter he wrote to El Senyoret:

Dere frend: cum wen you like. Heer you got job and home I think we'll be all rite.

Then he'd scrawled his address and signature; the latter an uncouth scribble, like the battered rings of a broken chain, set out in a wobbly line that feigned an impression of insouciant savoir-faire, pretentiously surrounded by a huge labyrinth that had it all: curly spirals, arcs, circles, straight, curved,

crisscrossed, broken, or freely added, as if it were an embryonic locksmith's project created by a mad artisan.

Poor Peroi had been born in a mountain farmhouse a good
four hours from the *la incompleta* . . . But Nonat—when Nonat
had been apprenticed to a blacksmith in the biggest clump (a
dozen) of scattered houses in the parish, he had also started
school, and the priest taught him for an hour every Saturday, imparting basic knowledge later supplemented with the
radical newspapers Nonat devoured and the trade unions he
began to join, which injected into his bloodstream the idea
of his own distinct social and individual merit as a member
of that vague, mysterious thing that was, nevertheless, refer-
enced continuously in those printed pages and endowed with
formidable unknown power via a hugely evocative phrase: *the
working class.*

So there was no way Nonat could delay the day. The time
had come to pluck up courage and deliver the mortal blow to
the boss. And El Senyoret did so with determination, jettisoning any scruples.

It was indeed a mortal blow. The wretched bachelor was
all but floored. That lad was his family, his pride and joy, his
only love, his only hope . . . He had ingenuously nourished the
illusion that, apart from bringing him into the world, everything about that young man was the work of his own hands,
of his own skill and endeavor. He even contemplated Nonat's
physical beauty with a father's modest appreciation And that
sense of paternity wasn't any less intense for being secondhand; it constituted for that hapless fellow the axis, pinnacle,
culmination, and crowning—indeed, the alpha and omega of
his life. He'd also cherished another illusion: that the bastard

loved him. And, despite the youthful follies now obsessing him and monopolizing his brain, follies that were sure to melt away as he matured, he was convinced Nonat loved him with all his heart, the heart of a true son. He would never have dreamt that Nonat would forsake him on the threshold of old age, when he was almost good for nothing, when, thinking he'd found a proper heir, he'd already begun to cut free from his business as the boss and obeyed the young man's orders without ever arguing, as if Nonat, and only Nonat, was the journeyman, when, say, only a couple of days ago, he'd let him dismiss a good, intelligent young worker, who could have been a good companion, helping to extend their trade and giving it real drive. The boss was so ingenuous he'd never have suspected a thing, hadn't even had an inkling.

When El Senyoret told him to take it in his stride, that he needed to go to Barcelona, the boss replied simply: "*Bueno*, that's up to you . . . but try not dilly-dally there too long . . . I don't understand how the new factory operates, because you did the deals and signed the contracts, and you know they are a scheming bunch and you can't negotiate with your eyes shut."

But, as he began to get a clear grasp of what the lad's words meant, the boss was so stricken his mind went blank. None of the pleas or sermons Nonat had feared issued from the boss's lips. He tilted his head to one side, started trembling as if he suddenly had a fever, and tears streamed silently down his cheeks; despite his best efforts, he wasn't brave enough to hold them back, and . . . that was all. No complaints, no criticism, no comments followed Nonat's terrible declaration. It was precisely that silence, that blankness in the face of the enormity of the disaster that changed Nonat's attitude. He wanted to do

what he wanted, always what *he* wanted, but to do it as someone exercising his rights, serenely, not as someone committing
a violent act or crime, the unfair imposition of the strong on
the weak that always leaves in its wake an unpleasant, trou-
bling aftertaste. If the boss had resisted, protested, even come
out with a hostile tirade, Nonat could have defended himself,
spelled out his reasons, argued for them, passed them off as
the real deal . . . But rather than that, the boss was crying,
and Nonat couldn't fight those tears prompted by pure emotion that exposed, without camouflage or fig leaf, the naked
selfishness of his act.

Nonat frowned.

"Come on now, it's not so bad. Don't take it like that . . . I
was bound to leave one day or another . . . You'll find another
tradesman like me soon, we're hardly needles in a haystack . . .
The business has a good reputation, and when people know
I'm leaving, they'll come in swarms, like flies to a pot of
honey . . . I might even come back . . . depending on how
things turn out . . . And supposing you still need me . . ."

But the boss, who'd slumped on a chair, sprawling face
down over its back, slowly raised his head between his arms,
and feebly waved a hand: "You'll never come back . . . I'll
never see you again . . . You'll never give this workshop or this
wretched old man another thought . . ."

And a sob he'd been choking down erupted from his gullet. His words of misery and his tears showed how futile it was
to attempt to offer hypocritical excuses and vapid consolation,
and Nonat didn't dare respond.

In the three or four days that remained to collect his things,
put some order into the jobs going through the workshop and

inform his friend that he'd arrive in Barcelona the following Saturday, his departure was not mentioned again, yet even so the bastard's final days with that silent, depressed man were long and drawn out. His boss was at all over the place. He'd start a job, leave it, walk up and down, move things for the sake of it, and didn't know what he'd done. He couldn't eat and every now and then went to the café on the sidewalk and sipped a coffee, he, a man who never drank or snacked between meals.

Whenever Nonat made an effort to gather his tools and picked one up, his boss placed three or four more in front of him.

"Hey, take these. Whatever you end up doing, they'll come in useful . . ."

Nonat protested. "They belong to this workshop and you'll need them for some job or other . . ." The boss shook his head.

"No, I won't . . . I can't use those things . . . I no longer have the eyes or a steady hand . . ."

The young man talked about buying a big trunk, and his boss responded immediately: "If you want, you can have the one I had when I was a lad . . . As you're emptying the drawers, I'll have more than enough space for my clothes . . . It's not exactly the latest fashion, but it's strong and could hold a cathedral . . ."

So Nonat took the boss's old trunk, and as the boss was taking his things out, he found a set of new vests he'd never worn, and said: "I'll leave these. It's very drafty in Barcelona, and you youngsters are always short on money, you think of everything except keeping warm . . ."

Finally, on the day of Nonat's departure, the boss went to

the young man's room where he was tidying up, and wordlessly handed him a cardboard box. El Senyoret opened it and saw a doubloon bearing the king's head. That minted gold coin stood out regally and sumptuously against a sky-blue cotton cloth. The young locksmith's eyes glowed; he was surprised and entranced.

"What is it?"

"The first wage I ever earned, that my boss wanted me to preserve like that, in a single coin, to bring me prosperity . . . and, thanks be to God, as far as my luck goes, I've had no complaints until now . . ."

"So?" asked Nonat, moved, albeit reluctantly.

"It's yours now . . . It can be your memento from this place . . . Don't sell or lose it . . . do what I did . . . Who knows what power such things possess? My boss was well-read, and when he said something, it was for good reason. You're one for showy baubles, hang it from your watch chain; I knew a notary who did that . . . Well, maybe not; it's not for a worker . . . Who knows what people might think . . . ? Better keep it in the box, as I did . . ."

That was the present that most touched Nonat; like everything that glittered, like everything that suggested wealth, it gave him a deep sense of wonder, and owning it, and knowing that it was *his*, without any doubts or cavils, suddenly infused him with an extraordinary sense of well-being and confidence. The robust optimism emerging from the dark depths of his subconscious was bolstered by that beautiful object which, according to his boss, brought good luck . . . He'd always been subject to small superstitious manias, to surges of fatalism that directly related any trifle to unknown causes and effects. On

Sunday, for example, it was always a good idea to go to festivities near a fountain. He would tiptoe slyly along the edge of the pavement, telling himself: "If I don't slip up, Sunday will be my lucky day . . ." Or else: "If the first person I meet is a woman, the cobbler will soon be making me some new shoes . . ." And he'd say that time and again. We hardly need to say that the gold doubloon soon became his lucky charm: hadn't he said it was *right* to go to Barcelona? That he'd find what he was searching for in Barcelona? And lo and behold, that coin now linked his good fortune to that new enterprise just as he was setting out, proof that it would turn out as he wished . . . And, cheered by the prospect, he checked all the packets and lists he'd prepared to make sure he wasn't missing anything. As someone unaccustomed to traveling, he'd been thorough in his preparations; he was afraid he'd get everything wrong; he packed every little item, didn't forget a thing, and had a mountain of luggage: a box here, a bundle there, a knotted scarf . . .

His boss appeared with one last gift: two bread rolls, an omelet, a slice of cold sausage, and a bottle of wine he'd had filled at the café next door, and had clumsily wrapped in newspaper tied up with black, fraying string.

"Here you are, a bite to eat . . . If you get off at a station, you might miss the train . . ."

His boss walked around for a moment, as if he wanted to say something but didn't dare. Then he made up his mind: "Got everything ready?"

"Yes, nearly . . ." Nonat glanced at his watch. "Almost an hour until the train, but I don't want any last-minute . . . It's a good stretch from here to the station."

His boss closed his eyes, and, as if his head was in a spin, he leaned on the dresser full of rubbish, its drawers hanging out: "I've a little job to do . . . I have an errand . . . you might not be here when I get back . . . So it would be best . . . to say goodbye now and . . ." He rubbed his big black paw on the leg of his pants, looked around, his eyes full of tears, and the floor creaked as he held out his hand casually, matter-of-factly . . .

Nonat was shocked. He was still stunned by the gift of the doubloon and the speed of his pending departure, and he too felt his heart breaking for a second. He took that rustic hand between his own and squeezed it. He tried to say something, but the words caught in his throat; he struggled to free them; he blinked . . . and suddenly felt a huge void in his palms . . . His boss's hand had vanished, as had the boss from his bedroom.

After donning his jacket and carrying his numerous parcels to the workshop, Nonat searched the building for the old man and said a final goodbye to his neighbors, asking them if they'd seen the boss . . . Nobody could say . . . That was the last time Nonat was ever to see his boss . . .

As a final farewell to his life in Girona and callow youth, he heard news of his boss some twenty months later, from an old work-mate, Granaire, whom he bumped into one Sunday in Plaça de Catalunya. When he enquired about his boss and the workshop, Granaire clamored: "You know, you'd barely recognize the place. Big cobwebs hang like aprons in every corner, and we often don't have metal to make so much as a key . . . People are never where they should be; no job is ever finished on time; every week, there's a new tradesman; each steals what he can and runs off. It was once so prosperous and now it's going downhill! You were the drive behind everything, and with you gone, the workshop is dead in the water . . . It'll shut down any day now . . . That's obvious enough! The old man has lost his way . . . When he drops by, he turns everything upside down . . . He's taken to drinking, would you believe? And it goes to his head rather than his feet . . . He never moves from the tavern . . . Who'd have thought it? He always seemed so sensible . . . He must have kept that vice well hidden, and now he's alone he lets it rip . . . Ever since you left, he's gone to pot . . . He looks a hundred years old . . . His legs shake so much it's a wonder he can stand straight; his hair is snow-white and his eyes are bloodshot, as if someone had thrown quicklime at them; he only goes for a shave every two or three months, and when you speak to him, he never answers . . ." Granaire gave a little smile. "I think that those tufts of singed hair sprouting out of his nose and ears are stifling all his energy . . ." Then he went all solemn again. "Believe me, lad, wine and rotgut make animals of men . . . God save them! Otherwise, I've advised him to go to the Sisters . . . if only to be rid of the sickness that's eating him alive . . ."

After telling Nonat a string of other things about his old neighborhood, Granaire walked off and El Senyoret, prey to an emotion he couldn't explain, stood alone for a minute, sticking out like a sore thumb in the middle of the square.

He looked at his waistcoat. The gold coin gave it a regal, seigneurial touch. The young locksmith hadn't been able to resist his boss's initial suggestion, and had hung the doubloon from his watch chain . . .

So: it was true the coin was the key to his boss's good

fortune? Getting rid of it and going downhill was one and the same . . .

He gripped the coin tightly, as if it were a bird trying to escape . . . And half-bared by a grin, his teeth gleamed under his dark, silken mustache like the whitest shards of porcelain.

Life in Girona! Ever since Nonat had come to live in Barcelona, that city had sunk deep into the recesses of his mind. So much so that he now thought that resigning himself to so many years there had been a dream, in which he always saw the same people and things, always did the same jobs, always languidly engaged in the same diversions, which, even when they were a tad out of the ordinary, felt strangely nostalgic, a throwback to some family gathering, some homespun debauchery . . .

When Nonat arrived in Barcelona, he had experienced a clear sense of freedom and transfiguration, like a prisoner seeing the prison gates suddenly open wide before him.

Peroi had come to welcome him. His glee at seeing his old friend and being able to give him good news restored his previous rural simplicity, and made him forget his social martyrdom and rancorous rebel airs, as well as the affected, sententious patter his laughably sectarian views had led him to adopt.

The second Peroi glimpsed Nonat from afar, he shouted: "Didn't you know? We're staying at my aunt's. It was her idea . . ." He gave Nonat a big hug. "It's a bit off the beaten path and dingy, but who cares? It will do us for supper and bed . . . As long as it's clean and the food's hot . . . And that's guaranteed . . . They both gleam like a church plate and Carlota's a good cook."

"Carlota?"

Peroi looked at Nonat, put out.

"I mean, my cousin. Didn't I tell you? She's a good lass and worth her weight in gold! She gets the grub ready, tidies the house, sews and mends clothes, and is at it all day clickety-clack, clickety-clack on the sewing machine . . . She takes my aunt her lunch . . ."

"Is your aunt ill?"

"No, she's very well. She looks after the public toilet in the square, and earns a pesseta *a day* and is away from the house from 8 A.M. to 9 P.M. . . . You'll soon see, they're a lovely twosome, they always help each other . . . Carlota sews shoe uppers . . . Till now she earned enough for her board and Auntie for the flat . . . They prefer to be in their own place rather than renting. They made that decision when Auntie was widowed and robbed of everything . . . After having the fright of their lives, they now want to keep to themselves even if it means working double overtime . . . And our income will help them out . . . You just see how at home we'll be . . . Carlota is such a laugh!"

They divided up the baggage and, weighed down like ants, jumped on board a tram. That was Nonat's first big revelation. His expert eye immediately saw how smoothly it sped along, how precisely the artifact responded to its driver, and he thought: "That's what you call a proper engine!"

One idea led to another.

"Hey, where are we going to work?"

"Christ, that's the bad news . . . The workshop is past Travessera . . . We'll have to walk a few kilometers there and back every day if we don't want to waste all our money on trams."

"Why didn't you look for something nearer?"

"I did, real hard . . . It was hopeless! Bombs were still being thrown so nobody wanted to give us work. I looked everywhere but found nothing decent . . . Luckily, Auntie . . . Auntie remembered a woman from her village who had married a tradesman in Gràcia, and she got Carlota to go with me and vouch for me . . . And, you know, whether it was because they were acquainted or they liked me, we hit it off straight away . . . And even if there'd been two more . . . and we *are* two with you . . . The firm's very busy . . . You'll like it . . . There's not much manual work, it's all machines . . . And it's a hoot! When we finish, we walk the local streets, and you just wait until you see the maids in those mansion gardens! We crack all kinds of jokes and they laugh like mad, and they're always hanging over the rails or standing behind the wrought-iron bars waiting for us . . . I like it best when they come out on the excuse that they're fetching milk, and we trip them so they break the jug . . . I've done that to three . . . They feel so flustered and mad, but make nothing of it so as not to get anyone into trouble . . ."

While he absentmindedly listened to his friend, Nonat gawped out of the window . . .

If it hadn't been for the greater hustle and bustle and the wide street, he'd have thought he was still in Girona . . . The severe, windblown façades from the days of Señor Don Carlos

IV seemed very familiar, a similarity that depressed him.

But he soon reacted differently. The splendid sight of Plaça del Palau, glimpses of the sea, the double row of palm trees mounting guard on Passeig de Colom, were things he'd never seen before, that spoke of a life quite different to the limitations of life in Girona. Finally, the dark mountain looming ahead against the bright sky, the gray mass of Montjuïc, was Nonat's second revelation. He'd seen the monument to the great man from Genoa on postcards, and thought of it as a small clay figure, and now he had to strain his neck to inspect him high on his pedestal. Noting the wonder in Nonat's dazzled eyes and chuffed with his role as guide, Peroi immediately declared: "Right, you know, what you see now, people say is a column made of concrete blocks and with an inside hollow like a tube. You can go up in an elevator, and they say you can see half of Spain from the top. We'll do that one Sunday with Carlota; we've already planned that . . . You know, mate, we have to make the rounds to get the sheep's wool off our back . . . Carlota says the fact I'm a hick sticks out a . . ."

Peroi spoke at the top of his voice, gesticulating and laughing as if they were alone, and everyone in the tram stared and grinned. Nonat was annoyed by this and tried to distract his friend and deter his patter.

The tram turned onto Les Rambles and Nonat surveyed that large space, which seemed to suck him into a kind of whirlpool. He was forced to close his eyes, and when he opened them again, he couldn't stop himself asking his friend: "Hey, what's all that? Has there been an accident?"

He was referring to Carrer d'Escudellers, which at that

time of day was teeming with people.

Peroi laughed loudly and told him that lots of streets were always packed like that: so many people lived in Barcelona . . .

"You can't believe your eyes, can you? I mean, it's just like the day we went to that Republican rally and there were so many folks in the square like so much rice in a pan"

The other passengers in the tram were now openly laughing and staring, and Nonat blushed bright red, ashamed he too was playing the part of the hick for which his future landlady had reproached his friend. Nevertheless, the sight of the throng on the city's streets was to astonish him for some time yet.

The swarming anthill of Plaça de Catalunya on a Sunday, the thick carpet of apparently motionless heads filling Les Rambles whatever the time of day, struck him as a curious spectacle especially when traveling down from Gràcia by tram, and he would struggle to get used to it, as he would to not saying "good day" or "good evening" to passersby on the sidewalk or to shop assistants hovering in doorways.

The two friends got off near Carrer de l'Hospital and walked to their lodgings. When they reached Plaça de Sant Agustí, Peroi said: "Come on, we'll stop by the public toilet so you can meet Auntie."

Peroi's auntie, who'd just set aside her knitting because of the waning light, was standing in front of her shabby kiosk and cheerfully welcomed the two lads.

She looked like a small, plaster-colored mummy, all skin and bone. Originally from Sant Llorenç dels Cerdans, she'd lost everything in "this blessed Barcelona," as she liked to call it, apart from her headscarf. A piece of spotless linen—almost a wimple—that made her look like an elderly nun in an old folk's home, the headscarf that now covered the wisps on her seventy-year-old head was the very same one that had once covered the thick, shiny tresses of her youth. Auntie and the newcomer got on well, and when they said their goodbyes—since it was still too early to shut the public lavatories—Peroi happily remarked: "I told you you'd like her . . . You'll like Carlota too . . ."

But Carlota was another kettle of fish.

Carrer de l'Hospital was buzzing with people, and now and then the two friends had to push and elbow their way through. Nonat was afraid to open his mouth but Peroi never stopped.

"Hey, you! Keep an eye on your parcels . . . This isn't Girona! It's so crowded! And there are quick-fingered pickpockets everywhere . . ."

Nonat was amazed nobody took offense or challenged the insults so glibly aimed at the throng.

A few steps later, Peroi asked: "What do you think of these shop windows? You didn't see displays like them in Girona, did you? I'm telling you, there's no place like Barcelona . . . !"

All of a sudden, Peroi stopped in front of a window full of small earthenware pots of cream cheese with honey on the side and dishes of cream as pale as an anemic adolescent girl's skin: his eyes lit up.

"Take a look at that cream, it's the most delicious in the world . . . The other day I ate two dishfuls . . . What madness! I tell you, if it weren't for the cost, I'd eat one tasty plateful after another!"

Nonat smiled as he remembered Peroi's sweet tooth. When they drank coffee at the Locksmiths' Company dances, he'd pocket all the sugar left behind by his friends, and suck one cube after another the whole evening, or drink three or four cordials in a row and kick up a fuss because they were too watery. Sugar was his vice.

As they walked on, they bumped into a woman heading in the opposite direction. She was ambling along, baggy clothes billowing, features flat as if they had been hit by a mallet. Nonat thought her face powder and smoking rings around her eyes made her look like a death's head, but Peroi nudged him with his elbow and exclaimed gleefully: "Look at that, you horny sod! Pure cinnamon! Want a mouthful?"

Although people on the streets didn't seem to take any notice of them as they had in the tram, Nonat's fear of looking ridiculous sealed his lips, and he was appalled by his garrulous friend, who wouldn't shut up even when they were mounting the long staircase to his auntie's apartment.

As they panted breathlessly and bright gaslight spread their shadows luridly over the flaking walls, Peroi kept up his running commentary and warnings, which hurt Nonat, who felt he was being treated like a donkey or a fool . . .

"Take care you don't trip, if you fall, it'll be like dropping from a belfry . . . It's high up, ain't it? Imagine we're walking up a mountain. Mountains are high up too, but the rich go there for pleasure and we go because we have no choice . . . That's how things are . . . !"

At last they reached the door to the apartment. They were

still knocking when the door opened wide and the cousins greeted each other with an effusive "God be with you!" Then the cousin addressed Nonat, sounding very surprised, "Senyor, is this your friend?"

"At your service . . ." replied Nonat politely.

They gazed intently at each other but reacted quite differently.

At fifteen, Carlota had been a tall, graceful girl, and was celebrated in the neighborhood for her cheerful gait, incredibly small feet, and pretty, velvety face. Then one day, she caught St. Anthony's fire, and from one day to the next, in very few years, she was unrecognizable; unsightly patches and bright red blotches surfaced and ate away her beauty. What's more, the long hours she spent seated and sewing rearranged her flesh into huge mounds that distorted her silhouette and completed the destructive process. When she turned twenty-five, her facial features became horribly puffy and further blotched, her bright eyes almost disappearing between bloated eyelids, and, like a Normandy mare's, her haunches seemed even heftier next to her still slim, svelte waist: the sum total was conspicuous in its ugliness.

Ill-prepared by Peroi's constant praise for her and his incessant, "You'll like her, you'll like her . . ." Nonat found her quite repugnant and had to make an effort to hide his feelings.

They showed him around the apartment: a dining room the size of the palm of a hand, a clammy kitchen, a largish bedroom with a double bed where mother and daughter slept and the latter worked, and finally, the small sitting room now transformed into the guest bedroom. It contained an old cot for Peroi and an iron bed with a mattress for Nonat they'd just bought in instalments. Nonat's trunk, sent in advance because it weighed too much, was already waiting at the foot of the bed.

Peroi spoke as naively as ever: "Would you believe it? Carlota wanted me to have that bed. I said no, because I could sleep at the top of a post, but you, you're more delicate . . . If things aren't *just so*, you can't cope . . ."

Carlota's blush deepened and she responded quickly: "I didn't know this young man, so it's hardly surprising if I thought you were made of the same cloth . . . Don't worry, I won't make that mistake again . . . I now know what suits the pair of you . . ."

She said that evidently wanting to please Nonat, but he couldn't find it in him to acknowledge her compliment. He saw everything as gloomy and small, and incredibly threadbare. He'd have felt deeply depressed were it not for his pleasant memories of what he'd seen on the journey from the station to their lodgings and, above all, for the invigorating idea that he was finally in Barcelona, the promised land . . .

They opened their parcels and put away their things, and as soon as Auntie returned, they ate supper. Carlota suggested going for a walk to show the newcomer around the neighborhood, but the men preferred to go straight to bed: they had to be up early in the morning.

As he undressed, the exhausted Nonat had to listen to his friend burble on; he just wouldn't stop.

In the two weeks they'd not seen each other, the once ardent rebel had become totally infatuated with his cousin and couldn't decide whether or not he dared ask her to start courting.

"You'll soon see. I know she's five years older than I am, that she's hardly a pretty face, but her hands are worth an empire and her feet, her lovely feet! Did you see them? Her shoes look like pine shells . . . I don't know how she manages to walk . . . And there's really something about her eyes! Her stare makes you tingle all over, and if she wanted, I'd follow her like a sleepwalker. What I most like is her mouth . . . It's as cute as a Baby Jesus's in a shop window. If I didn't put the brake on, I'd be all over her. . . I mean, the other day, in the tram, when we were going to Gràcia, an old fellow couldn't keep his eyes off her . . . as if he'd been bewitched . . . And the haberdasher on the corner likes to joke with her . . . That's what scares me . . . But I have to bite my lip and keep quiet, because I have no right to interfere . . . if we were betrothed, it would be different . . . Oh! If I could only give her some hope . . . but how can I say anything to a woman I don't have the money to support . . . !"

"And what does *she* think?" muttered Nonat, for want of anything better to say.

"She hasn't said a word . . . I mean, she really hasn't! She knows I like her, but she acts as if she didn't . . . Women will be women, right? And even though they're throwing themselves on you, they have to act that way, just as a precaution . . . Auntie is the one who gives me most hope . . . When she sees me looking at Carlota, she laughs, and when I praise Carlota, Auntie weeps . . . The other day she told me she won't rest in peace until she's married Carlota to somebody upstanding. You see! Our poverty always gets thrown in our faces! We won't leave that behind until we've turned everything upside down . . . That newspaper hit the nail on the head, only 'the era of the working-man is the epoch of equality' . . ."

At that very same moment mother and daughter were also swapping impressions.

"Ma, what do you think of the new fellow?"

Her mother was delighted.

"My love, he seems a proper gentleman! He's so nice, and did you notice the way he eats? Tomorrow we'll give him a knife . . . I thought he was looking for one . . . He acts like your pa, may God forgive him . . . as if they'd been to the same school . . ."

Carlota looked unusually serious.

"Yes, he's not as sappy as my cousin . . . We must make sure we treat him well . . ."

"As long as he's not as full of nonsense as your pa . . . He dresses very smart . . . Not very sensible for a working man!"

Carlota didn't reply; she preferred to cut short their conversation so she could indulge in vague thoughts that lurched strangely this way and that.

Her mother, Janeta, didn't say another word either, and sat deep in thought, but unlike her daughter, she wasn't swayed favorably by anything going through her mind. Rather, she felt a thorn prick her, a sharp, invisible thorn, that had lain buried in the folds of her heart for years, and that still stung at the slightest stirring of her memories.

She'd been orphaned as a young girl, and her uncle, her

father's brother and practically her only remaining relative, took her in. He'd left Sant Llorenç years ago. He lived in Barcelona, on Carrer Robador, where he'd established a dairy. His niece owned some property and livestock in the village, and before taking her to Barcelona, he did a deal with different locals who agreed to manage everything, and after that he only went back to Cerdans once a year to collect the income from the land, none too carefully, as he knew his niece didn't have to rely on those pittances to live because he and his wife had no children of their own and their business was prospering.

From then on, the young girl from the mountains lived quietly in the dairy and was spoiled by her aunt and uncle, and although there was no shortage of hideous corruption and promiscuity, she was spiritually isolated, pure as a single flower in a vase.

But one day, she fell in love. Because of what she was worth, what with the dairy and everything else, she'd been pursued by suitors and would-be fiancés, and she, the commonsense sort, who seemed to ignore their blandishments and handsome offers, suddenly opted for the worst: a no-good, apprentice tailor, a lazy braggart, who moved house every day, whose hair was always bunched high like a pile of wood chips. Her uncle and aunt were devastated and formally opposed such a lunatic match. The young tailor's apprentice, who simply saw the girl as a way to support his life of leisure, suggested they elope, to guarantee she remained his. She resisted for a while, struggled with all her might against the current sweeping her away, but in the end, early one morning, she vanished from the house.

The moment he found out, her uncle, sturdy and robust

as Saint Paul, with a bull's neck and tinder-dry temper, was felled by a stroke, and after weeks of ebbing and flowing between life and death, he was declared cured, though the battle he'd won left him with a drooping eyelid, a twisted mouth, and a gammy leg he had to drag along.

Meanwhile, poor Janeta, his niece, saw through her strange infatuation, and drank the first cup of bitterness from her ill-omened marriage. In dispute with a succession of bosses, her husband would bring home either a meager sum, or, instead of money, a bad headache because he'd not earned a cent. To boot, he was obsessed with the theater and every night went off to a local amateur dramatics group where four bums like himself spent hours rehearsing roles, and, naturally, the morning after his wife couldn't drag him out of bed, even though she employed all her muscle.

Prompted by the tailor's apprentice, they'd tried to build bridges with her uncle and aunt, who refused to hear a word of it. Frail and frightened by her husband's seizure, the aunt might have yielded, but the moment her apoplectic husband found out, his one good eye glowered and scared everyone so they would flee and stop mentioning Janeta in his presence.

Six months after marrying, Janeta suffered a miscarriage that left her at the cemetery gates. The tailor, who couldn't find succor anywhere, went personally to the dairy to seek forgiveness and help, but Janeta's uncle sent him packing, and then, with no fire in the hearth, no bread on the table, and not knowing which saint to pray to, he signed up to the Odeon Theater company. However, though God had given the young tailor an excessive love of the stage, he hadn't made him a skilled performer, and his disastrous acting was soon a black mark for a splendid group of young actors who otherwise displayed exceptional talent and character. They gave him secondary roles, relegated him to bit parts, and, finally, occasional walk-on characters who said nothing and, of course, that couldn't provide even potato stew for the table. Janeta was desperate and begged the sidelined thespian to change course, to go out and find real work, but he was so besotted by the stage that he wanted to be an actor and nothing else. But then a day came when the couple's penury was so pitiful that, for the first time ever, Janeta removed the white headscarf that singled her out and stood on a shadowy street corner holding a hand out to passersby . . . Chance had it that her uncle, on his way to a rendezvous in a café that evening to discuss the sale of a cow with a livestock dealer, limped around that corner past the poor woman, and as she recognized him and he didn't go to put his hand in his pocket, a screech pierced the gloom. Her uncle stopped in his tracks and, as he scrutinized the scene with his one trembling eye, a word, as straight as a bullet, suddenly penetrated his heart.

"Uncle!"

She caught him just as he was about to collapse, and that single word and the shameful sight of that unhappy wretch did more than any number of self-interested pleas and theatrical monologues . . .

The young couple returned to the dairy like prodigal sons, but Janeta's uncle's tardy generosity couldn't counter the effects of the last few months.

Janeta was again carrying death within her, and her second child came still-born, just like the first. Her maternal organs seemed to have espoused a tragic bent, repeatedly leading her to the graveyard like the driven snow. Her uncle and aunt despaired, all the more so because they couldn't change their nephew-in-law, the scourge of the parish, whom there was no way to get to bed at night or out of it in the morning, who had no nose for business, and who was totally useless, except when it came to wearing fancy clothes, getting a haircut, and glowing on a Sunday like a good Jesus.

Luckily, Janeta recovered from her anemia and was more like her former self, namely the willing, helpful hand that showed more than a daughter's care for the old couple. And that lasted until they were gone—first her aunt, then her uncle—at which time the sun set yet again on the well-being of the unhappy Janeta, because as soon as her head-in-the clouds devotee of the stage inherited everything, he huffed and puffed and, like a hen, started scattering first the seed-corn of their money, second of the family business, and finally of the small family farm in Sant Llorenç dels Cerdans.

When he'd scraped the bottom of the barrel, as if gripped by a sacrosanct mission, he suddenly seemed to sort out the screws in his head. An old colleague from the Odeon, now working in the new Romea Theater, found him a job. Not as an actor—because his pitiful state and aging body, together with past upsets, had left him battered and useless even for a small role—but as an usher, a well-defined job to which he gradually added a thousand others that were much vaguer: stagehand, errand boy, mender of costumes, etc., etc.

He'd finally found his natural habitat and was happy. He came home with the stars, slept all morning, lunched on the road, and, with his mouth full, rushed to the theater, which he only left for a quarter of an hour to eat supper, also on the road. The theater was his home; much more so than his real home, as he adored the place more than words could say. Apart from satisfying his love for glittering lights, it enabled him to let himself go, dancing with St. Vitus, as he couldn't sit or stand still. He changed jobs every minute; he was upstairs, then downstairs, everyone wanted him for this or that—since the Tailor, as they called him, was an irreplaceable jack-of-all-trades. He'd notice a stall that was loose or a squeaky hinge that needed oiling; he saw to jobs for actresses, and always found a pesseta in his or someone else's pocket for a brother—which is how he addressed all the actors—down on his luck; he poked his nose in other theaters or among out-of-work actors, looking for a new idea or something his theater company was missing; he always carried a little bag of needles and thread of every color for every eventuality, and often got the temporary wardrobe assistant out of a jam; he was alert to all necessary details when a new show was being rehearsed or when an old one was being brought back into the repertory; he advised—like a tailor who knows his cloth—the scissor cuts needed to shorten an over-lengthy scene or the most suitable characterization for this or that individual, just as he knew better than anyone where to find cheap, secondhand clothes . . .

And naturally, although his basic wage was quite modest, he managed to supplement it with the proceeds from his many extra activities, which varied but were never to be sniffed at, and allowed him to provide for the upkeep of himself and his wife, who could finally live without constant torment now that he had a stable, busy life and spent his rare moments at home telling her about the world of theater, exclusively about his beloved theater. He only kept silent about one aspect: his romancing. Because nobody could deny that he was perpetually enamoured. He became infatuated in turn with all the famous, fashionable, or merely attractive artists who graced the stage. His loves were platonic, intensely romantic surges within his little tailor's heart, which he only expressed externally in histrionic praise for the latest candidate's acting or good looks, in his greater interest in serving her, in spontaneous, ridiculous outbursts, and, above all, in keeping at bay any other man's attempt to flirt, any third-party interference on his terrain.

One day, shortly after the performance had begun, the Tailor was summoned away from the theater because Janeta had had an accident.

He delegated his duties to someone else and ran to see what was the matter. At suppertime, the Tailor had told his wife to get something from Les Rambles that he needed; after supper she went to do just that, and as she was turning a corner, she had been hit by a car and knocked to the ground. She'd been carried off unconscious and bloodied to a pharmacist's, and once treated, she was driven home in the very same car that had done the damage, whose owner proved to be an honest soul who stayed to take responsibility for what he'd done. Janeta had nothing worse than a cut on her forehead and slight bruising on one arm and leg, but she'd been given a real fright and was a bag of nerves, which made the Tailor decide not to abandon her, but spend the whole night by her side.

Exactly nine months after that fright, with Janeta past forty, a baby girl came happily into the world. At the time the Tailor's ardors were being stoked by the renowned actress Carlota de Mena, and the love-struck fellow, who performed daily in the dazzling purgatory of his dreams as the first love of his blessed first lady, implored her to grant him the honor of being his daughter's godmother and bestowing her beautiful name upon her. The actress was delighted by the prospect—and this is how Peroi's humble cousin came to bear the grand-sounding moniker of Carlota.

When the usher died, the young lass was of an age to work and help her mother pay their way. She had inherited at least a quarter of her father's dreaminess, but life's hard knocks kept it embryonic, never allowing it to surge. Even so, in an ironic or acerbic way—depending on whether she was in a state of war or peace—she harbored a hidden inclination for novel-ettish swoons and onslaughts of passion. And when her St. Anthony's fire faded, as her eyes lost their cobwebs and any prospect of love requited grew unlikely, these dreams retreated only to intensify beneath endless layers of rejection that were as aggressive as they were fictitious. Finally, Peroi, the tardy, innocent paladin, rode up to the gates of that turreted castle built on the absurd.

Nonat and Peroi had fallen asleep like little angels, Nonat so deeply that God knows when he'd have woken up the next morning without a nudge from his friend.

A good douse of freezing water from the faucet, four gulps of coffee that Auntie had boiled up for them, and Peroi asked: "Are we off, lad?"

"We're off!"

They each took their little pack of food, Nonat took both

their tools, and they left the house.

Once on the street, Peroi, who was heading to cross Carrer Hospital, thought better of it.

"You know, today is a day to celebrate . . . We should celebrate your arrival like proper gents . . . We'll take the tram."

They caught the first one going up Les Rambles. On board were only two countrywomen with bags and baskets, a fair-haired young girl with a shawl, and a middle-aged man who looked like an office worker. One or two other trams went up and down, still entirely empty, but signs of life and renewed activity were beginning to spread like oil stains along city streets just awakening from their nighttime slumber. And Les Rambles *was* where life was mainly happening.

Lukewarm rays of sun were dispersing the misty haze over the horizon, and birds chirruped cheerfully before flocking toward the distant plain.

Busy workers rushed to and fro like pistons, gripping blue or yellow kerchiefs full of provisions, alongside shop assistants and pen-pushers, many also carrying their lunches wrapped in newsprint; florists quickly emptied their cellars to fill dew-damp tables, and bunches of flowers scented the air; cheery, brawny ragamuffins in the street-cleaning brigade began to flourish their brooms and spout nonsense to female passersby; long poles over their shoulders, house painters nonchalantly took up their positions in the entrance to Boqueria, shooting the breeze with broad-backed, slow-moving porters; cooks descended, white aprons gleaming like walking clotheslines, then huddled, clotting the entrance to the market; and seamstresses, delicate and stylized like living figurines, promenaded light and graceful like swallows in flight.

Newspaper boys shouted morning headlines that echoed down the street; horses pulling vegetable carts neighed as they lined up from Carrer Hospital to Betlem, and all you could see in the workshops, whose doors opened like eyes on the blink, were apprentices diligently engaged in their daily tasks, and window cleaners demisting glass, caged in shop windows . . . And over and above everything else, like a shower of holy water, chiming church bells sonorously summoned the faithful to Mass, while the loud hoot of a distant steamer pierced the air . . .

Nonat looked on in astonishment, and felt the delightful sensations of the previous day spill from his heart and rush to his head, spinning in a drunken delirium, and when the sweep of a bend confronted him with the glorious Plaça de Catalunya, then Passeig de Gràcia, the sense of wonderment he'd bottled inside lit up his face, turning it pale with excitement.

For the first time he had a clear idea of what a big city was like and of boundless horizons that could satisfy any whim. Peroi kept naming the important buildings he knew, piling on trivial details, but Nonat wasn't listening; he only had ears for the vibrant rhythm of the city's serial enchantments and the magical word he kept repeating to himself: *Barcelona . . . Barcelona . . . Barcelona . . .*

They zigzagged rapidly down Travessera to make up time, and soon reached the workshop. An expansive Peroi introduced his friend to all his workmates and showed him around the building. Nonat felt the turmoil in his head subside, and, with renewed sangfroid and peace of mind, quickly absorbed all around him. The owner, a man in poor health, even more delicate at that time, had yet to put in an appearance.

"You'll meet him at the mid-morning break," the foreman told El Senyoret.

The foreman was a character like Peroi, with a kindly face, but thicker-set, and whose biceps rippled like a fairground strongman's. He was very proud of his hammer strikes and the flourish with which he delivered them.

The owner was a different matter. Tall and thin as a bean-pole, he kept his head down, slightly twisting it like a clerk; he was a deeply jaundiced color, with sunken cheeks, jutting cheekbones, and a squint; he wore white, metal-rimmed spectacles and his hair and mustache were completely gray, and trimmed like a brush. He suffered from a nervous tic that often made him stretch one side of his mouth, and, gripped by a vice he couldn't control, he chewed one end of his mustache. As a result, that end was always shorter than the other, which was unsightly, and though he kept it trimmed, driven by habit his fingers kept nervously mashing his lips until the mustache, however short it was, reached his teeth.

The bastard didn't think he looked like a tradesman. He later discovered the owner had inherited the firm from his father, a very handy man, and followed in his father's footsteps, but, as his poor health prevented him from physical work, he'd had to keep tight control over every little detail and devote his spare time to scrap metal—a business, people said, that had brought in lots of money. He espoused reactionary ideas and was a fierce defender of the principle of authority; he said little, but was succinct, and only smiled at the annual fiestas. He had been a district mayor and the president of a Catholic

Center.

Scattered across the yard in front of the works, the tradesmen had just finished their mid-morning snack, when the owner arrived.

"Hello . . ." was all the boss could manage.

"Good morning, Senyor Ramoneda," they chorused, as they filed inside, and the foreman pleasantly asked: "Feeling better today, senyor?"

But the director had spotted El Senyoret and didn't answer, rather asked in turn, more with a wave of his hand than his voice: "Is he the new man?"

When he received a positive reply, he bid him to come over. The foreman summoned Nonat, who approached them with his trademark poise and half-smile. For a minute he was the object of a silent, relentless scrutiny that he found disturbing. Finally the director spoke up: "How old are you?"

"Twenty-two."

"Where are you from?"

"Girona."

"How many firms have you worked for?"

"Just the place where I did my apprenticeship."

"Why did you leave?"

"Because I wanted to come to Barcelona."

"Was that the only reason?"

Nonat frowned imperceptibly and answered aloofly: "Yes, senyor. To see the world . . . and learn."

The director, who till then had failed to snare his mustache, cruelly nibbled a couple of hairs and seemed content.

"Well, let's see whether you can last a few years here, too; all good, hardworking men do . . ." He turned to the foreman:

"Rovira, accompany him to the rotating table, show him how it works, and how to finish what's started. We can't wait for Guillemet to come back from the cemetery to do it."

He acted as if he was going to smile, but it never materialized, and with a curt goodbye nod the owner entered the factory, reviewed everything, and slunk behind a glass-paned partition that hid a desk. That corner, away from the workers but with a view of the entire floor, was Senyor Ramoneda's office.

Nonat's gaze followed him for a while, then he shrugged his shoulders. He wouldn't have been able to say what that shrug meant, but all day the memory of the workshop owner was vaguely worrying. Apart from that, he felt perfectly at ease. The factory felt familiar to him after only an hour; he felt safe and in good spirits, as if he'd spent his whole life there. He'd realized that without overexerting himself, he could be as good or better than its most skilled worker. It was only a matter of adapting to the machines, and not being too clever; machines had always been his easy-going, generous friends, who committed to him at the first approach without demur.

When they finished for the day, Peroi and his new workmates showed Nonat the streets around the factory, and they went up Gràcia's Carrer Major and down Muntaner at an hour when there was a dizzy flow of cars and carriages, in which the newcomer saw lightning flashes of mouths, bosoms, hats, or whole profiles: fleeting fragments that stood out strongly against a blurred backdrop of expensive cloth or extraordinary faces. They were snapshots of sophisticated, urban luxury: flying along, languidly posing on soft cushions, enjoying the voluptuous pleasures of twilight, speed, and the covetous eyes of the poor . . .

Nonat looked up at the sky, a huge concave of burnished topaz, and at each sidewalk dotted with magnificent mansions between lush but sternly regulated green gardens of bygone days or the showy, polychrome patchwork of more youthful parks; he looked ahead and behind at the evanescent vistas descending on both sides of the mountain and joining on the skyline. He remembered the stunning morning emptiness of Passeig de Gràcia . . . This was real life . . . This was *life* . . . ! And, gradually, a frenzied, almost aphrodisiacal desire possessed him . . .

Nonat's spirit was totally in awe of those two parallel streets that had framed his first day in Barcelona—Passeig de Gràcia and Carrer de Muntaner.

The following day the owner didn't turn up at all; someone said he was taking a rest: El Senyoret felt relieved, as if after a sedative or cold drink, and worked in a light-hearted, lively way all day. However, the day after, the moment he saw his new boss walk in on the other side of the yard, with a sallower face and more prominent cheekbones than two days before, his heart thudded and the plane he was holding juddered and made an incision on the piece he was making. Hey! the bastard reproached himself, What's wrong with you? But later the same day, a memory suddenly shone through his anxiety like a ray of light, and he saw things as clearly as could be. When the owner gestured, turning around to reply to Rovira, the sad, sickly image of Jordiet, Nonat's former companion in the Orphanage, came to mind. The squint eye and sallow hue made that child and man seem very similar, and this similarity, striking his heart rather than his memory, was what made such an impression on Nonat the infant that had sprung back from his earlier life.

That was when the bastard realized, much to his surprise, that his deep, inner obsession hadn't surfaced since the day he'd arrived in Barcelona. As he became aware that three days had passed without him remembering his dispute with destiny, he felt happy. When he fell back on the treadmill of that *idée fixe*, he also fell back into the isolation of his feudal castle, now raising the drawbridge that had once descended over the surrounding moat to connect him to the world of ordinary mortals.

From that day on, the owner, the innocent cause of Nonat's renewed inner turmoil, inspired a secret rancor, like Maria la Gallinaire and the nun in the Orphanage before her.

However, Nonat's entry into that new world wasn't what you'd call difficult or unpleasant. Like a fountain in full flood, good feelings flowed spontaneously around him, flattered him, and he didn't have to make the slightest effort to provoke them or keep them in check. After a few days, everybody doted on him: Auntie, not for nothing once seduced by her presumptuous little tailor, was thrilled by Nonat's suave refinement, nothing like the coarse manner of her nephew or so many other journeymen; Carlota's lively, sparky spirit glittered like a firework display, galvanized by the presence of such a handsome young man; as for Peroi, his friend was an oracle he listened to in a state of intense reverence; in the factory, Nonat soon overtook his workmates in status; the latter asked for his opinion, the foreman gave him the most challenging tasks, and the owner, despite being the serious, meticulous sort, soon deigned to accept the practical solutions Nonat found for all kinds of problems.

He was also admired and respected far from his usual habitats. When he walked from Carrer de l'Hospital to Carrer del Carme, he often crossed the Boqueria market and the greengrocers, fishwives, chicken women, and butchers stared at him, and dubbed him "the luvverly handyman." When he walked between stalls, knives hovered in the air, sentences were left half-finished, one fish after another dropped on the scales, and the price of lettuce suddenly tripled, as if he'd just come from Peking; conversations stuttered or were interrupted as every female eye was hooked on his figure.

And it was no different in La Maravilla, a bar on Carrer Arribau, a working-class haunt where on an evening before a holiday workers played dominoes, argued, and read the newspapers, or in the cafés on Carrer Major, where they also gathered in numbers to sip cold drinks at terrace tables and watch girls go by. After a very little while, and without him having to say or do anything unusual, he naturally became the focus of attention; it was so obvious that Peroi noticed and commented in his warm-hearted way: "Christ, I don't know how you do it! Everyone's hanging on you . . . You've got that special thing, like Carlota . . . You seem to be alone in this world, or smelling of catnip . . ."

Nonat smiled, but didn't reply or acknowledge tacit or

explicit homages; he welcomed them as the most natural occurrence in the world; he was neither petulant nor contemptuous; he acted with aristocratic insouciance and polite indifference, as a mythical hero or blue-blooded prince would have done, accustomed to ruling over the masses as a matter of right.

And thanks to the waves of innate attractiveness he radiated, the air with which he dismissed the presence of his neighbor was effortlessly forgiven or went almost unnoticed; that cold selfishness with which he pursued his objectives, never thinking or feeling the hurt he could inflict on those who crossed his path, that electric circuit encircling his mind and enclosing him within himself, which constituted a threat of mortal danger to anyone who dared enter. Because while he exerted his influence on all around him, he never suffered any in return; nothing that tempted other lads of his age and estate tempted him. He was measured and sober in what he said, only gambled to please friends who invited him to play; he hated fights and squabbles, was repelled by all political ideas, wasn't drawn to young men's sporting activities, didn't like reading; even women, who might have lured him out of instinct, struggled to make an impact. To interest him, it wasn't enough to be young and physically beautiful: something extra was needed.

He much preferred mature women, even if they were ugly and in decline, to the fresh, piquant, spontaneous grace of a young seamstress. His fondness for the Eden Concert and other such dance halls, much criticized by his acquaintances, came purely on account of his desire to feast his eyes on the racy exuberance and licentious appeal brought to dance floors or stages by a constellation of French women who, in those early days, represented the sum total of elegance in the neophyte's eyes.

That was his weak spot, the vulnerable heel of the young Achilles. Just like in the Orphanage, his outward appearance continued to be his central obsession, and, second to the enigma of his origins, the vital key to his happiness or disillusion.

He never found it in himself to walk the streets like an anonymous blob, and brought to the factory a worn outfit and espadrilles that he donned on arrival, and also a towel, tooth brush, and hair brush to spruce himself up before changing back when he finished work. What's more, to ensure he didn't dirty or scuff his shoes, he spent half his savings on the purchase of an old bicycle soon after coming to Barcelona and, as Peroi was upset at having to walk by himself, Nonat lent him the other half—to be paid back in weekly installments—to buy one as well.

It was around that time that Nonat felt an impulse to do wrong.

He saw a tie he judged to be the latest fashion in a lit shop window. He went into the shop and asked after its price; six pessetes. He didn't have six and they were only mid-week. He was downhearted. From then to pay day he was sure someone else would buy that tie.

He worked bad-temperedly throughout the day and passed by the shop in the evening. The tie was there in all its solitary uniqueness, a true pearl among a mass of vulgar tawdriness.

The temptation wasn't simply strong, it was violent. He thought of asking for a loan from a workmate, or Rovira, but was stopped by a kind of inner restraint. Those in his trade already felt Nonat was too much of a beau and he was repelled by the idea of laying bare his inner desires and being in debt to anyone. A work errand the next morning meant he would head in to the factory later and cycle by himself: the tie was still in the shop window as he rode past, entrancing and luring him in. He stopped, one foot on a pedal and the other on the ground. A young man had just walked into the shop and was asking for something. An assistant went to retrieve something from the window display, and as he returned, his hands full, he left the window slightly ajar. It was at that moment the lethal impulse surfaced in Nonat, as if springing from the murky depths of instinct: to stick his hand in the window, grab the tie, and pedal off at top speed . . . However, before impulse could lead to action, the shop assistant returned to fetch one last item and closed the window.

For hours Nonat experienced a bitter aftertaste of regret, but not remorse, and it was even worse when he cycled back past the shop and saw the tie was gone.

Days went by, and he let life drift and develop as it suited him. At the end of the work day, he found no pleasure in roaming the streets and chasing maids, nor was he entertained by gambling and arguing in bars. He preferred to spend his time differently. As a result, he asked the foreman, who in turn asked the owner, to be allowed to stay on at the end of the day and work on small commissions and new-fangled things he liked to make, quietly and unobtrusively. The owner willingly agreed, as Nonat wasn't asking for a raise and they'd noticed that his little extras always benefited business. Once Nonat could excuse himself like that, he felt relief: his emancipation had started. Of course, some workmates initially offered to join him and Peroi decided to stay on as well, but by the end of the week, outside attractions and the desire to escape the walls that caged them in for so many hours won out and drew everyone away except for Rovira, the foreman, who, more for the pleasure of seeing him work than the fact the factory was open, stayed until Nonat finished. Though one day Rovira had to leave midafternoon for a funeral and, rather fearfully, asked Nonat to take charge of everything, to see to this and that, leave this like that, and that like this, and finally to shut up shop and take the key home with him.

The next day, Rovira found everything so much to his liking he no longer worried about leaving Nonat by himself—first, when it suited him, and then every evening. And that wasn't all: he soon gratefully started to share all his responsibilities with Nonat, making him his substitute, a sort of deputy fore-man. From that moment on, Nonat was free. He didn't stop being friends with the lads; occasionally he still went out with his mates and meandered, and, with single and married, went to La Maravilla, but he preferred to stay on at work, and once everybody had left and he'd done what he wanted, he washed and spruced up before leaving. Despite being such a beau, he loved his trade and the blue overalls that went with it.

Never patched or darned, made-to-measure, and carefully adapted to his specifications, that outfit bore the distinguished lines of a military uniform. Now that he wasn't being watched or hustled, Nonat could spend all the time he wanted on his appearance and emerge on the street as a *dandy*. His naturally attractive features were better set off by his modest attire, and you'd have said he wasn't a real worker but a famous actor *disguised* as a worker. Then, by tram or on foot, depending on his pocket (he only took his bicycle when he was going shopping or on errands, because he wouldn't have known where to leave it), he went downtown and strolled along Carrer Fernando or sat on a chair in Passeig de Gràcia. El Senyoret felt blissfully on top of the world, eying elegant goods in shop windows or mingling with the bourgeois languidly enjoying the shade from the plane-trees.

Nonat's gleaming shoes, bright white collar, and cuffs enhanced the somber simplicity of his overall, and combined with his tastefully slanted tie-pin and sleek hair, his appearance didn't jar in such surroundings.

Something about him did stand out, however: on workdays he never wore anything on his head, though he owned caps of all kinds. He considered a cap to be an unsightly item that didn't go with his ensemble. If it was English, he found it made him look common, even thuggish, and if it was leather-peaked, it didn't go with his blue dungarees; the latter cried out for white piqué or raw silk that he was too embarrassed to sport for fear of being ridiculed. As for the ugly little outfits worn by Peroi, Nonat would rather have been dead than seen wearing them. So, unable to find anything suitable and after lengthy soul-searching, he decided against them, suppressed the problem by suppressing the cause, and initiated, perhaps even pioneered, the hygienic, fetching fashion of going bareheaded at all times.

Comfortably ensconced in a wrought-iron chair on the corner of the central sidewalk, his pant legs hiked up to avoid baggy knees, and one leg across the other, Nonat whiled away his time, listening to the gossipy chatter of nearby groups of girls, pursuing with an attentive eye the carriages going up and down; especially the latter, given that those vehicles carried the cream of Barcelona's high society, and he silently enjoyed the glorious spectacle provided by the grand boulevard and its parade of the latest touches of high fashion.

One day, though, he was no longer content simply to look . . . On the excuse that he had a prior commitment, he took the afternoon off, dressed up to the nines and went from street corner to street corner looking for an elegant horse-drawn carriage with a coachman whose jacket wasn't threadbare or coming apart at the seams. When he found one, he jumped in, and, breathless and inhibited, gave the order to be taken to the city outskirts and then along Passeig de Gràcia.

It was a fine day, beyond words. Under the canopy of the hood he'd left raised out of a sense of fear and timidity, Nonat's heart galloped and his blood throbbed at his temples like a hammer striking an anvil. He'd settled himself well, in a premeditated pose that wasn't too stiff, as if he'd never traveled in a carriage before, or too casual, which might seem affected and in bad taste. He crossed his feet; a slim calf, visible above the lower Russian leather shoe, was finely shaped by a dark-green silk stocking. His face remained stubbornly hidden by the hood, but an off-white cotton glove played with its partner on his knee. If a fellow tradesman had happened to pass by, nothing about that foot, ankle, or hand would have made them suspect they belonged to a workmate; nor did Nonat feel like an intruder or an oddity among the grandees rushing up and down the boulevard at that hour.

When darkness fell, he ordered the coachman to drop him off far from his neighborhood, to avoid any unpleasant surprises, and walked home. He felt a fire burning in his chest, its devilish flames rising to his bluish-green eyes, and then he told himself, with utmost conviction, that if he didn't find his parents very soon, he'd kill himself: "Either the life that is my right, or none at all!"

Carlota opened the door to him. She was alone. Peroi had come home, but when he'd seen Nonat wasn't about, he'd gone down to the barbershop.

Nonat made to hurry to his bedroom so nobody would see him dressed in his finery, but, noticing that Carlota's bewitched, carnal gaze was following him, in a moment of unconscious indecision, unsure why, perhaps driven by the emotions he'd just experienced, he swiveled around and smiled warmly. Carlota blanched like a slab of wax, shut her eyes, and staggered against the wall. The journeyman had registered her interest some time ago, and would have clipped her wings right away and acted standoffishly if that hadn't threatened his own interests. Carlota's energy was consumed by her love, and by her endless efforts to add more meat to the pot, to provide Nonat with special treats on Sundays, or a nosegay of flowers in his bedroom every day; she went to bed late and got up in the middle of the night to wash and iron the white underwear he frequently changed, and always wore under his more colorful outer attire; she ironed his stockings and polished his shoes, starched his collars, purchased and embroidered handkerchiefs she then secretly mixed in with his others so he couldn't protest at her gifts. And all that made Nonat's life more comfortable and saved him money he could then devote to other expenditures, so he let her get on with it as if he hadn't noticed, never showing a moment of sympathy or gratitude toward the hapless girl, who always melted away like a candle, but instead looking with sullen irritation at the ugly eyes that always stared at him as if bewitched.

Peroi never suspected a thing. As his cousin was always more affectionate and talked more to him than with El Senyoret, as he never found rips in his clothes and ate the very same special dishes, as the flowers were for their shared bedroom and he never saw the young woman starching Nonat's collars or embroidering his handkerchiefs, nothing seemed different. However, her mother did notice, and once again, after years of relative peace, she began to watch the oppressive haze of acute anxiety mist the shadowy valleys of her heart and rise slowly to cloud her horizons.

Not only was their double income not benefitting them as it had initially, but now Carlota was working harder than ever and still not punctually paying the installments owed on the bed; she was damaging her already poor health with excessive physical effort and a burden of simmering sentiment, and was in danger of throwing her future out the window. Experience meant her mother's clear-sighted eyes saw what the martyr's dimmed vision didn't; Nonat never showed the slightest interest in her daughter, and he would destroy her only possible betrothal: to Peroi. Her maternal heart rebelled against that terrifying possibility and prepared to fight back. When veiled criticism and lists of cavils began to supplant Janeta's hitherto gushing praise of the young man, Carlota immediately suspected she'd been found out and put herself on the alert; from the moment her mother decided to open her eyes, a confrontation was inevitable. For the first time, Carlota disrespected the woman who'd brought her into the world, telling her she was a scandal-monger, that she cared no more for her cousin and Nonat than she did for some lad she'd met yesterday; that everyone should mind his own business, for Carlota herself had enough work as it was and wanted to be left alone; she was adult enough to look after herself.

That clearing of the air led to tears, and from then on Carlota avoided her mother's gaze and company as much as she could. In the morning she arrived from the market when her mother was leaving for work, and at night she quickly slipped between the sheets, turned her back on her mother, pretended to sleep, and drifted, and drifted, and drifted . . .

The glum Janeta saw the miserable story of her own youth being repeated: the same blindness, the same stubborn silence day after day, the same kind of torture; another tailor on the horizon, a worse one, no doubt, because this fellow was a tailor who knew how to make the most of his hands and wouldn't let himself be duped by the offer of a dairy. And the haze clouding her heart gradually turned to tears, tears that streamed nonstop by day over that black stocking that never grew, and by night drenched the meager pillow where she rested her head, tears that brought no relief because they were simply the product of hapless impotence. It was only too obvious: Carlota would treat her as she had treated her own uncle and aunt; nobody would ever deflect her will or change her path and, come what may, she would head straight over the edge of the precipice. Only God's will could save her.

And indeed, God's will did finally come to help poor Janeta, and His chosen instrument was Peroi's jealousy.

One day he appeared at the public lavatories, face distraught and lips trembling. His aunt thought nothing of it at the time because her nephew had been tossing and turning the previous night and before going out she'd prepared him a cup of chamomile tea and left him resting comfortably, advising him to stay in bed . . . But no sooner did Peroi enter the public toilet than he gripped her arm tight and started crying like a baby.

"Ay, Auntie! Ay, Auntie!" he repeated.

Auntie was alarmed.

"What's wrong, my love? Do you feel poorly?"

Peroi looked around.

"No . . . no . . . It's Carlota . . . Carlota is . . ."

His aunt was horrified, she thought something dreadful must have happened to her daughter, but her nephew calmed her with a wave of a hand.

Let's ignore his rambling explanations and get straight to the point.

As Carlota had taken longer than usual to surface that morning, his aunt had left to preside over her public lavatory before she could see her and warn her of Peroi's indisposition, and, as her daughter didn't have a key, she'd left the men's bedroom door ajar. Exhausted after a sleepless night, Peroi was dozing and daydreaming in his cot. He didn't hear Carlota come in, but suddenly opened his eyes and saw her walk across the room carrying a nosegay. He wanted to call out to her, but he was still half asleep and didn't manage to rouse himself. He watched Carlota approach the table with the small vase, take out the previous day's nosegay, and kiss it three or four times, staring into the air as women do in vaudeville, then she extracted a flower from the bunch, unbuttoned her blouse, tucked a little purse inside the opening, placed the flower in the purse after kissing it yet again, and pressed the purse back down her cleavage. She threw the water in the vase from the balcony that looked over the inside yard, refilled it from the bottle on the table, and arranged the fresh nosegay. Once she'd done that, she walked over to Nonat's bed. At the foot of it, on the ground, was a small pile of handkerchiefs, dirty collars, and cuffs. Then, motionless in his cot, Peroi watched his cousin do something so strange it shocked and paralyzed him.

She picked up the dirty items, looked at them rapturously, as if they were things of wonder, and lifted them to her face, rubbing them, pressed them hard against it for a good five minutes, whimpering as she did so . . . And that wasn't all . . . She suddenly threw herself on Nonat's cot and wallowed like a madwoman, crying, moaning, kissing, and biting the pillows.

Horrified, Peroi sat up in bed, thinking his cousin must be having a fit, and with the noise he made, she too sat up, writhing like a snake, hair standing on end as if scared to death, looking around . . . She saw her cousin, howled like a scalded cat, jumped off the bed, and dashed into the dining room as if she'd gone crazy.

Peroi understood at once.

"She loves him, Auntie! She loves him! If you'd seen her kissing everything! It was horrible . . . That's why she's been ignoring me, because whenever I spoke to her, she'd put me off, or make it a joking matter . . . And yet when it came to him . . . who isn't even our blood . . ."

The poor boy was too overwrought to continue, but his aunt saw a vestige of hope in that saddest of situations.

She grasped Peroi's hand affectionately.

"My dear . . . Let's rejoice now the abscess has burst; perhaps we can cure it . . . Don't lose hope, my son . . . That young man is not for her, and when she realizes that, her lunacy will go . . . because that's what it is, a kind of lunacy . . .

But Peroi's head was in a spin.

"No, Auntie, she loves him, she loves him . . . She's infatuated! It's clear as day!"

His aunt soothed him as best she could and kept repeating: "Don't give up hope . . . don't give up hope . . ." until she saw he'd calmed down.

That same morning—a black mark in Peroi's simple life— would also be exceptionally important for his friend.

It was Friday. On Thursday evening Nonat had gone for a stroll with his mates and to the cinema at night, and had had to walk back home. He took the route through the market and up Xuclà. When he was halfway up Balmes, a cyclist who'd not rung his bell pedaled by frantically and almost clipped Nonat, who, if he hadn't jumped out of the way, would have been knocked to the ground.

Nonat yelled out, angrily shaking his fists at the cyclist. Two young lasses walking on the sidewalk opposite, carrying baskets, snorted and disappeared down the street, splitting their sides with laughter at the way he'd leapt in the air like a hare and followed up with a furious tantrum. Nothing pained El Senyoret more than feeling he'd been made to look a fool. His rancorous gaze pursued the cyclist like a silent curse. The cyclist had crossed the next street and stopped at the beginning of the next block. He took a scrap of blue paper out of his pocket, looked at it, and then at the house opposite. He was obviously checking an address, since he immediately entered that building. Nonat was in front of it in seconds. It was a large store; two men walked across at the back and vanished from sight; he easily recognized that accursed cyclist. The bicycle was parked by the doorstep. It was a magnificent, brand-new specimen that must have been worth a fortune . . .

On this occasion, impulse and deed coincided, and before realizing what he'd done, Nonat was flying down Balmes like an evil genie astride the stolen bike. He turned the first corner and raced on as if someone was in hot pursuit.

He took a long, roundabout route in order not to reach the factory too soon, so his workmates would be inside and hard at it. There was a door by the yard entrance that couldn't be seen from inside the factory: it was the scrap metal store, which was only visited twice a week and was shut with a bolt. Nonat hid the bike behind a large, busted boiler.

When he walked into the factory, he was pale and kept swallowing as if his throat was dry. Nobody suspected a thing, but, even so, from midafternoon onward he kept glancing at the clock. He was desperate for work to end.

No sooner had everyone gone than he shut up shop and went to salvage his theft. His first glance hadn't deceived him: it was a perfect specimen that had only recently left the factory; that web of silver had been wonderfully well-made. He wheeled in his old, battered bike: from one mudguard to the other, it was as different as a bullring nag set next to the finest steed in the royal stables. He was so proud to be its rightful owner. Then he started the conversion. He took bits from both and interchanged them, put parts from the old one on the new and vice versa; tapped here and there with his hammer, making small, repairable dents; tarnished shiny bits, removing the gleam; added fake scratches and soldering, and when his deft handiwork had disguised the bicycle, aging it by two years, he gave a sigh of satisfaction. Nobody, not even its owner, could ever discern his morning trophy under that disguise. Then he cheerfully cycled home.

The only one who might have asked bothersome questions was Peroi, but he didn't appear until suppertime and barely managed a few words. In turn, embarrassed by the morning's scene, Carlota had stayed in bed and her mother had to take supper to her . . . So, for the moment, everything went smoothly.

The next morning, the first thing Nonat did was buy the previous evening's and that morning's newspapers. He peered anxiously at the crime reports . . . Only two or three mentioned his deed, and one jokingly referred in Spanish to "a theft on wasteland." All stated there wasn't the slightest clue to the identity of the thief.

As a precaution, Nonat didn't ride to work for several days, then sold his old bicycle and explained he'd picked the new one up on the cheap. He had no regrets. Whoever had the money to purchase that splendid bicycle was sure to have plenty of spare cash to buy another.

In that respect, one might have said it was smooth sailing; in the apartment, on the other hand, the weathervane seemed to have turned dramatically.

After the welcoming smile Nonat had given Carlota the day he rode in the carriage, she no longer held back and openly besieged him, even making it unpleasant for him to be in the apartment; Peroi, on the other hand, once so candid and friendly, had suddenly become sullen and sour, and only ever contradicted and mortified his friend.

If Nonat said he would walk, Peroi wanted to take a tram, if Nonat carried an umbrella saying it was about to rain, Peroi retorted he must have no eyes in his head to say such a thing . . . And if out of the house Peroi tried to be with Nonat as little as possible, inside he never left him for a moment, afraid he'd talk to his beloved. Until Nonat, who was impatient by nature, got the bit between his teeth and bawled: "Hey, you mangy cur, what's making you so edgy?"

Peroi refused to say, but Nonat had cornered him, and finally Peroi said he wouldn't allow him to pursue his cousin.

"Who, me? Well, that's one for the books! What a joke . . . !"

Nonat laughed sarcastically, then gazed at Peroi pitifully.

"May God rush her back to your bosom, you fool! Make sure you butter up your lovely cousin . . . and lie beside her . . . Tomorrow I'll have someone fetch my trunk . . . It was only gathering moss in this hole . . ."

No sooner said than it was done. Nonat left the lodging house the very next morning. Auntie was overjoyed, but Carlota despaired and they thought she would go mad; she wouldn't eat or see anyone, and developed a nervous sobbing habit that resonated throughout the house. Peroi watched over her for several days, then returned to work looking haunted, his beard as prickly as a hedgehog's spines, his face anxious, exhausted, and sallow.

Peroi summoned Rovira and told him he wanted to speak

to the owner. Once in his office, he began to tell him that Nonat was an evil man who'd ridiculed his family, finally declaring that the owner should choose: it was him or that other fellow, because both couldn't work for the same firm. Then what was bound to happen, happened. The owner fixed his squint-eye on Peroi, first in shock, then sternly; he brusquely enquired how much Peroi was owed, opened his desk drawer, took out some bills, and handed them over without another word. Peroi was fired. When he walked past the foreman, he asked him to listen to what he had to say: "Rovira, tell my workmates I'm leaving, and that I'm sorry for all your sakes. . . If you ever need a pair of hands, you know where to find me. I say that sincerely . . . because I'm not like that other fellow . . ."

He handed Rovira the money he'd just been paid: "Here, please give this to Nonat; I don't want to see him. It's seventeen pessetes short of what I owe him; tell him I'll get them to him as soon as I can, and, if he can't wait, he can sell my bicycle . . . He has my permission to do that . . ."

And Peroi left.

That was the end of all contact between Peroi and El Senyoret.

Part Three

Part Three

Rovira, the workshop's foreman, was married and had a six-year-old son and a forty-two-year old sister.

Rovira's wife, Pepita, was a shortish, thinnish woman, and almost an albino straw-blonde. Her mouth was small and puckered—fish-like; her big teeth protruded, her skin was milky-white, and she had bulging eyes with pink eyelids, bloodshot pupils, and long white lashes that completely obscured her stare. As she also lacked breasts and hips, she and her family liked to imagine she possessed the profile of a fine gentleman.

She was the daughter of Sant Gervasi haberdashers. As a girl, she only ever sold from behind the counter, and learned to read music and play the piano.

She was the youngest in the family and her mother doted on her; she curled her hair, perfumed her, dressed her as if she were a doll, and never allowed her, as they say, to wash the dishes; her father and siblings, only a little less doting than her mother, brought her sweets and the scores for waltzes and polkas that were in vogue. Her most remarkable, idiosyncratic habit was to add ruffs and frilly cuffs to her dark dresses, because a commercial rep who'd been to Madrid once told her she looked like a portrait by Velázquez, and her mother also thought the style favored her. What's more, she wore extremely high-heeled, cut-back leather shoes, and at home, a variety of small, showy pinafores her big sister made for her.

The whole neighborhood believed the haberdashers were rich and wouldn't give Pepita's hand to anyone who couldn't keep her in fashionable millinery. However, the workings of fate are as surprising as they are mysterious.

From 12 to 1 P.M. every day Pepita, went to her music and piano lesson at Senyor Bonafont's Academy. She'd leave home, hair just so, sweetly scented, shoes tap-tapping, clutching her case of scores. The young blacksmith from the street that crossed hers had just left work and was running to eat his lunch. They turned the corner at the same time and collided so violently her case flew into the middle of the street, and the young girl would have too if the tradesman hadn't reached out and grabbed her when he saw her stagger. That collision and involuntary embrace decided both their futures.

Rovira—the tradesman—apologized thirty thousand times and asked thirty thousand times whether he'd hurt her.

"Ay, senyoreta, how clumsy . . . ! Please forgive me . . . I am so sorry . . . believe me, I really am."

"Don't worry . . . It was an *ayccident* . . ." Pepita replied in an affected accent, touching her curls and bun in case they'd been disheveled.

"No, no, no, it was my fault, completely my fault . . . I was steaming along like a train . . . I always do, and it's a bad habit . . . Please forgive me . . ."

Calmer, after checking her turret of hair, she now looked vaguely around.

"What are you looking for, senyoreta, if I might be so bold?"

"My music . . ."

Rovira kindly went to retrieve her case.

"You mean this?"

Pepita held out a hand to take it.

"No, senyoreta . . . You are still in a dither . . . I'll take you home, if you'd like."

Pepita told him she wasn't going home, but to the Academy around the corner. Rovira begged her to let him accompany her there, and Pepita could not refuse, thanking him mellifluously so as not to cause offense. That flurry of "please, senyoreta," and "thank you, senyoreta," had appealed to her innate vanity.

The following day, at the same time, they met on the same street corner, but this time didn't collide. The tradesman burst out laughing and his face puffed out.

"God keep you, senyoreta . . . We did better today . . . Hope you're not still feeling the effects of yesterday?"

Pepita was equally thrilled by this second encounter.

They stopped for a minute to chat about the previous day, and as Rovira was saying goodbye, Pepita asked quite ingenuously: "Aren't you going my way? Why don't we walk together as far as the Academy . . ."

Rovira should really have gone the other direction, but he didn't say that, so proud was he to get that invitation, and, courteous by nature, he wanted to carry her case as he had the day before. The following midday, a fresh encounter and rehearsal of the scene, with small variations. And the next few days too. The tradesman couldn't believe his luck and his mornings rushed by as he waited for the moment to go and meet his blonde little lady.

He hadn't been working at that blacksmith's for long and didn't know who she was, but felt she was so high-class he could never imagine she might one day be his wife. While the whole neighborhood was commenting on that unequal relationship, Rovira had yet to make a single move; he was just happy to see her and be granted his wish to carry her case. After their second encounter, Pepita insinuated something, but he remained tongue-tied, shocked and wary of reading too much into her hints, until she added "she wasn't wrong," she "too" was in love with him.

That unadorned, almost pastorally idyllic exchange decided the matter.

The neighbors, who'd thought Pepita would have set her sights higher, wondered what she'd found so special about her betrothed to make her decide to seek his hand in marriage, as they say. The chiropodist opposite the haberdashery came up with one solution to that enigma: "Why does she like him? Quite simply, he's the only man she's ever come across, thanks to that first collision . . . Till now she's been chasing Chinese shadows."

Indeed, quite literally, Pepita saw nothing beyond the end of her nose.

When, even more amazed than the neighbors, her girlfriends asked her how "all that" had come to pass, she puckered her mouth in a familiar mawkish grimace, and always produced the same enlightening explanation: "Good heavens . . . An *ayccident!*"

Rovira was in seventh heaven and spent the rest of his life equally amazed by such "*ayccidents.*"

The news hit the haberdashers like a bucket of cold water: they'd dreamt of somebody quite different for their daughter, who was so pale, fair, and refined, but, as they only ever did what she wanted, in a resigned rather than joyful mood they agreed to let her marry the young man of her choosing.

Pepita wanted to marry immediately; the reason for her haste was threefold, each being equally transcendental.

Firstly, she was looking forward to a white wedding with a grand train. Secondly, she wanted a Napoleonic portrait, wherein she was photographed at the top of a long stairway, her train gathered at her feet and cascading down the steps like a waterfall, with the bridegroom standing by her side, gazing into her eyes. And thirdly, because she could fulfill her lifelong dream the moment she married: visiting cards that announced, in the most flowery script: *Pepita Tomaset de Rovira*, and, in one corner: *At home on Wednesdays . . .*

And she executed her plan step by step. The wedding was quite an event for those parts. Nobody could wait to see the cortège—stuffed into six or seven carriages—or, above all, the bride, who, as everyone said who knew about such things, was "a sight for sore eyes."

Once the blessing was bestowed and the traditional rides down Les Rambles and Passeig de Gràcia accomplished, they all went off to a packed hostelry.

Innuendo and chatter abounded. Midway through the meal, Pepita's haberdasher father, Senyor Tomaset, who until then had seemed the one least happy with that union, felt an evolution taking place within himself—though it wasn't an evolution, rather a manifest revolution—and suddenly leapt to his feet, glass in hand, to launch into a speech that, while not entirely lucid or fluent, was most eloquent. Among other infinitely interesting things, he said it was the happiest day in his life, that now he could see his posterity in the wake of the marriage, which is what every paterfamilias wants, and what he most deplored was that his ancestors, *vulgo* grandparents, were not there to partake in the joy and preside over the wedding banquet, because years ago he'd had to take them to their final resting place . . . Senyor Tomaset's occasional *faux pas* didn't matter because it was drowned by a salvo of enthusiastic applause. The loudest applause came from Pepita's haberdasher mother, whose eyes shone brightly from so much laughter as if all the condiments she'd ingested had blended to inspire hallucinations.

At the end of lunch, the bride whispered something in her husband's ear, and they both rose to their feet and disappeared to cries and hurrahs from the guests. At that moment, Rovira believed, at the very least, that he was leading away the Princess of Asturias and, from then on, he only ever saw life through his wife's practically blind eyes.

As the bridegroom's only patrimony were the fingers of both hands and a sister he had to maintain, the haberdashers furnished a flat, looked over their finances, and took out a loan for the items the couple needed. Pepita would have liked a maid, but as her parental budget didn't stretch that far and they'd already used most of it, Rovira's sister served as both maid and butler. We hardly need note that Pepita was good for nothing: as a result of her natural inclinations and lack of training, she was utterly useless. It was just as well she was resigned to being like that, for when she felt the occasional, belligerent urge to be the mistress of the house and tell people what was what, her sister-in-law was truly horrified. Since she couldn't see and had never done a stroke of housework, if Pepita wanted to dust, whatever she touched fell to the floor and smashed to smithereens; if she tried to cook, she burnt the sauce or knocked bottles over without noticing; if she put washing out to dry, she dropped it on the flat underneath, and apart from needing to be salvaged, it all had to washed again . . . Everything followed a similar pattern. Carmeta, Rovira's sister, sorted those calamities and was only happy when she saw Pepita focus on her own world, because at least, if she didn't help, she wasn't getting in her way and Carmeta didn't have to witness more slaughters of the innocents. Pepita's world was: waking, getting up, washing, eating breakfast, getting dressed, and going to the haberdashery so her mother or sister could curl or comb her hair, since being her own hairdresser didn't appeal to her and, in any case, as she'd never practiced, she had no idea where to begin.

Pepita came home for lunch; she and her husband enjoyed a leisurely meal, and Carmeta left the table now and then to serve them. When Rovira departed to the workshop, Pepita retired to their *salon*. Their salon was furnished with a settee, half a dozen chairs, and the piano and music cabinet her parents had given her as a wedding present. The traditional portrait of the bride and bridegroom sat on the piano in a red, plush velvet lyre-frame with leather flowers—a gift from Senyoreta Bonafont. The couple was conventionally posed, him standing, her sitting at the top of the stairway, her long train gathered by her feet and cascading down like a waterfall.

When Pepita's mother gave her that piano, her father had said: "Whatever you do, my love, don't give up the piano after all the sacrifices we've made to give you lessons . . . Although you're married now, practice a little every day, and remember that a piano is the finest adornment a lady can ever have."

And Pepita heeded her mother and practiced a little every day after lunch. Behind a bolted door, nose to the score, she tinkled away on the ivories while Carmeta washed dishes and tidied up to the rhythm of a Boston two-step or mazurka, and when Carmeta was ironing or darning stockings, Pepita emerged from the salon, powdered anew, clasping her crochet bag and invariably declaring: "If you don't need me, I'll go and keep Mama company for a while."

Of course, Carmeta never needed her and Pepita went off to keep her mama company, spending the whole afternoon with her until her husband came to collect her after work, and in the summer, after chatting to his in-laws a while, he took her for a stroll before supper; in winter, they went straight home in order to be in bed nice and early.

That complex existence suffered slight variations: Sundays were more for husband and wife, and on Wednesdays Pepita was "at home." That day, she'd dress more fetchingly than usual and stayed in her *salon* the whole afternoon receiving visits from her lady friends: the daughters of Senyor Eusebio, the chiropodist, the daughter of Senyor Bonafont, her music teacher, the herbalist's granddaughter, and, from time to time, Senyora Anneta from the shoe shop, as well as her mother, who would take time off that day even if the haberdashery was bustling.

Her mother was the star attraction in Pepita's salon and the one who ran the "at home" show. She knew perfectly well that to attract and retain each customer—in this case, visitor— one had to talk to each guest about her special interests; thus, she talked to Senyora Anneta about how expensive life was compared to when they became established. "Back then we could do more with a two-cent coin and a copper from Morocco than with today's pesseta. Fish cost this, meat that, and sugar slightly more . . . And as for our goods . . . I mean, elastic cost us . . . etc., etc." And she'd practically insert her lips into the ears of Senyora Xirau, who was on the deaf side, or so she claimed in order to be the center of attention all afternoon, for in fact she heard as well as the walls of Montjuïc Castle, so Pepita's mother spoke slowly: "So how are the public lectures going?" to catch her attention. "It's scandalous, truly scandalous, Senyora Tomaset; I don't know where the sick come from . . . It's unbelievable . . ." And she gossiped to the chiropodist about pharmacists. The pharmacists' wives— apothecaries, as the women at the "at home" scornfully labelled them—were their *bêtes noires*, because they eschewed contact with the neighbors and socialized only with *la crème de la crème* downtown. Pepita's mother talked to Senyor Bonafont's daughter about her sewing and knitting. Senyor Bonafont's daughter was a forty-year old who ought to have been awarded the great cross of some order if there were any justice in this world. If it is true, as someone once said, that the most beautiful sacrifices are the most pointless, Senyora Bonafont's life was an example of articulated beauty, an interminable gold chain, a kind of cord running from the void to the infinite. As it was only her and her father, and they had both income and the Academy, plus an old servant who saw to everything, Senyoreta Bonafont could do whatever she pleased with her life, and dedicated her entire existence to her sewing and knitting with a martyr's frenzy and the strenuous efforts of a rubble-carrying mule (if you'll pardon my poetry). She knew all the stitches for hemming, embroidery, stockings, crochet, and needle work; she owned all kinds of samples of all kinds of things, in the dozens, the hundreds, the thousands; she knew what was going out of fashion and what was coming in; she was a living manual of everything that had been in vogue and when, from wax fruit to beaded flowers, from rugs made from remnants and curly sheeps' wool to gold filigree slippers and Bristol-board watch pouches, from triangular shawls to dainty baskets and paper candleholders, etc. etc., and possessed exclusive patents to achievements that would make Hercules a laughingstock, like, for example, two particular paintings—one of which was five feet by two, and showed a train going at top speed, spewing out smoke, thick and dark like something evil.

A green meadow dotted with white daisies stretched out in front of the train; behind it a range of mountains; one covered in snow, another blue as the Virgin's mantle, yet another with a scattering of pine trees, and finally the fourth, magnificently crowned with red, volcanic flames: behind the mountains, a paler blue sky streaked with shimmering-gold sunlight. That tableau was embroidered in silks—which had cost over seven hundred pessetes—and she'd worked on it, off and on, for nigh on twenty years. The other tableau wasn't a tableau, but a varnished wooden box with a glass lid and a hook to hang it from the wall. She'd embroidered the inside of the box, in the highest relief on a background of crimson damascene. Employing every kind of stitch, material, and imitative procedure, a life-size parrot in equally life-like colors sat perched on a contorted tree branch, carrying in its beak a white card, where one could read, in thin, straggly script the classic line: "To my dear father on his saint's day."

Years ago, the train that flew and the parrot that didn't had been the pride and joy—before such taste went out of fashion—of Senyoreta Bonafont, and had been continually admired by the old servant and the young pupils who passed in waves through the Academy. The maid, who had bad lungs, always declared; "Ay, Lord! That wisp of smoke looks like it's about to escape the frame, and dampens my spirits as much as the fumes in the kitchen . . ." And the tiny tots were overjoyed; boys imitated train noises and girls stood in front of the varnished box and shouted: "Lovely, lovely parrot, give me a leg and I'll give you my love!" Additionally, Senyoreta Bonafont made mats, eiderdowns, pillowcases, lace curtains, lace bows, and all kinds of godly wonders for saint's days, birthdays, weddings, and christenings throughout the neighborhood, and she took her exemplary generosity to such lengths that she'd even go to the homes of lady friends and acquaintances to teach them stitches they didn't know or combinations they couldn't get right . . .

And with the herbalist's granddaughter, the haberdasher found plenty of material to chew over in the contrary behavior she was forced to endure, and that shop assistant her daughter wanted but her grandad didn't, and the cousin her grandad wanted and her daughter didn't!

When she'd talked a bit to everyone about their problems, the cutter of cloth and seller of pins and needles decided to talk about her own, which came closer to her heart, to the extent that she couldn't put them out of her mind for a second.

"Now we've had our say about our work . . . or the weather, our groceries, or our gout—all roads lead to Rome—my love, tell us what you're studying . . ." and when Pepita had done that: "Come on now, don't be such a shrinking violet, play us a tune and we'll see how pretty it is . . . Us ignoramuses like music too, don't we, ladies?"

And Pepita played until everyone had left.

It was all Pepita ever did, apart from listen, on her days "at home."

Those days brought hustle and bustle to the house and extra work for Carmeta, even if it was only cleaning and coming and going to the front door, and that along with her sister-in-law's calamitous management of the household annoyed her no end. Every Wednesday she'd tell the neighbor. . . "You see, Angeleta? More of the same . . . I'm telling you loud and clear: this simpering soul my brother has landed will be the death of me . . . And the saddest part is that the day I depart, they'll have to go begging . . . Because nobody will be able to salvage her from her fatuous limbo . . . Her mother spoils her, and that will be the ruination of us all."

Carmeta Rovira was a wholly unhappy woman. She'd longed for one thing in life—to be a midwife—but had never managed it. When, as a young girl, she had asked her parents, they said: "That's not work for a decent girl. When you marry, you can learn how to do it, if your husband lets you . . ." And Carmeta would have willingly married in order to become a midwife, but the years passed, and, as no suitor presented himself, Carmeta couldn't marry or learn her preferred *métier* and that profoundly embittered her; she saw the whole world as a sad, dreary place, as if through tinted glass. A tiny light only entered her life when her nephew was born.

Pepita spent her whole pregnancy being sick and watching the calendar. She couldn't think what name to choose from the ones she read there. She wanted one that sounded distinguished and gentlemanly . . . Finally, after lots of arguing, doubting, and consultation, she reached a decision. The "offspring," as Senyor Tomaset called him, would be Margarita if a girl, and Octavio if a boy—or "Uuctavio," as Pepita always pronounced it.

It was a boy. White and fair like his mother, with a head almost as big as his father's. As he grew, that lack of proportion only augmented.

Octavio had small, insipid features and a blank, soporific expression, but his high, broad forehead protruded from beneath his lank, stringy hair, as if it were hydrocephalous: a forehead so vast it seemed a well of wisdom, though it was hard to say whether the well was full or empty. The baby had only two redeeming features that delighted the whole family. One consisted, from a very, very early age, in bellowing like a carter, and the other in calling his parents and relatives by their Christian names in his half-lisping way: Dovira, Pepitta, Cammetta . . .

After the huge binges of wedding, apartment, christening,

wet nurse, and almost completely meeting the expenses of both households for three or four years, the haberdashers were finally cleaned out and were obliged to tell the couple it had to stop, and that Rovira couldn't stick to his day wage but must procure a higher income. However, as he was hard-working and knew his trade, he soon found a position in Senyor Ramoneda's firm, on a decent fixed wage and a little bonus for additional jobs. That was when they went to live on Carrer de las Ximeneies to be closer to work.

The day when Nonat had that argument with Peroi, he had as usual taken the firm's key to the foreman's house after work. The latter wasn't in, and as Nonat needed to see him he sat and waited on the doorstep on the street where Octavi was playing.

The boy ran in and out of the house opposite, which was a greengrocer's; one time he came out with a calabaza squash that he went to show Senyor Nonat. Nonat asked: "Do you want me to make you a horsey?"

Since the boy was keen, Nonat looked for a few branches that he cut to size. As he was attaching the legs to the horsey, Rovira arrived and they all went inside.

"Hey, ask Auntie to give you a piece of string or cord and we'll give him a bridle . . ."

While the boy went to get it, El Senyoret told his friend what had happened. When the boy returned, he continued to talk while he tied the cord to one of the horsey's legs: "So you see, I'm out in the street and have to find new lodgings. As I have no choice, I'd rather it was nearer to work than my last place . . . Do you know anywhere around here that would do?"

Octavi made the horsey gallop across the table, and seemed unusually elated. He appeared to be absorbed in his new game, not seeing or hearing anything else, but out of the blue, he interrupted the list of houses Rovira was enumerating, bellowed, and cheerfully kicked his feet: "I don't want Thenyor Nonat to go . . . I want Thenyor Nonat to thtay here . . ."

"Where do you want him to stay?" asked his father, taken aback.

"With uth, with uth . . . I want Thenyor Nonat to thtay with uth . . ."

The child was showing how pleased he was by the horsey the locksmith had made for him.

Everybody was amused by his outcry, but if at first they thought he was joking, they very soon had to take it seriously when the little chap was so insistent he grabbed Nonat's leg and threatened a huge tantrum if they refused him . . . And as the child was the apple of everyone's eye and nobody had ever refused him anything, they were helpless. The game was soon up. When they saw the boy didn't want to give in, digging his heels in the more his father tried to dissuade him, the adults yielded, particularly when Pepita and then Rovira decided that there was no reason why Nonat shouldn't stay with them. In fact, they did have an empty bedroom he could have without displacing anyone.

Nonat initially didn't accept out of politeness in that affable, courteous way of his, until the foreman insisted forcefully that he should accept their offer, invoking imaginary advantages to living together. And Nonat accepted, to everyone's delight, except the only person who would have to deal with the extra work the guest would bring and the only one not consulted: Carmeta. Naturally, when she heard the news she went through the roof, and, if till then she'd had only two loves in her life—her brother and her nephew—and one pet peeve, from then on she refocused her feelings and divided the latter between her sister-in-law and the intruder.

And once again what tended to happen, happened. In a flash, the bastard became lord and master of the wills of Rovira and the child. Without intending to and never unfairly, he gave the orders in their home as he did at work, since the only opposition he might have met was amply countered by Pepita's apathy and the warm reception afforded by everyone else, including all those who worked in the haberdashery. He'd made their acquaintance when accompanying Rovira, who went there after work to collect his wife and son. At first they had reacted poorly to the idea of their daughter starting a lodging house because they thought it demeaned her socially, but when they met Nonat they were so pleased that, from then on, they welcomed him like one of the family, whenever he went to visit with them, even though he went bare-headed.

One evening when he was there, they all sat outside as usual to enjoy the fresh air and watch people go by.

The bastard was sullen and bad-tempered. He was obsessed with buying a gold watch, but however much he tried to save, small temptations triumphed and consumed all the money he earned. It was precisely that day the screw had turned again and made him angry with himself. The other men were talking politics because a government crisis had just erupted. Senyor Tomaset, so fond of holding forth, was in full flow, attacking the sacked ministers with thumping diatribes and luminous phrasing. Suddenly, his wife's hoarse voice rudely interrupted his bluster mid-crescendo.

"Look, look how beautiful the consul's wife is today! What a *bird* she's wearing! I'm sure it's the first time she's worn it. I can't remember seeing it before!"

All eyes turned toward the road. A luxurious Victoria carriage was riding by, where a lady was lolling, dressed equally luxuriously. She was very fat and the magnificent bird on her hat was indeed flapping gracefully in the breeze stirred by the carriage.

Nonat enquired quietly: "Who is she?"

"A consul's wife . . . They've lived in a mansion up the hill for years. You can't imagine how rich they are and they have just one sad son . . . She was gorgeous before she got so fat, but she always dresses very smartly . . ."

Nonat followed the path of the carriage as it disappeared, and his bluish-green eyes retained a vague impression of the soft, soft plumage flapping over the palest, freshest complexion.

That and his stress over the watch combined to ratchet up his bilious depression.

To think there are so many people who don't know what to do with their money apart from spending it on whatever they feel like, whereas others . . .

And he again recalled his parents. His ingenuous desire to find them on a Barcelona street corner one day was set to make him lose his marbles.

He himself had recognized the foolishness of those wayward hopes. Barcelona was a vast expanse, and the moment of revelation he so longed for, with so much space to cover and no clear path, seemed remote, and he'd lost his impetus. When he strolled along Passeig de Gràcia and saw the people and items parading past, he always wondered: "Who knows if that's . . . ? Who knows if here . . . ?" But as he wondered, he felt suspended in a void, with no firm ground to hold on to, as evanescent as a coil of smoke wafting upward, destined to fade and melt into the infinite, because he, Nonat, couldn't stand in front of every door like in Girona and interrogate the innumerable secrets lurking behind it. He could never penetrate that glittering, gloomy world, to which he belonged by right, if he wasn't granted the lucky break of a precise clue or an audacious, unfettered lockpick. However, it was his resolute wish to penetrate it, however and whenever, and the unremitting faith nestling in his heart told him, today like yesterday, that he *would* make it in the end. And whenever he was feeling that way, like in Girona, he sensed that Lady Luck would be the anchor to save him. Whether guardian angel or lowly bawd, she was bound to help him when the moment came.

In the meantime, he carried on at the small factory as if that was his lot in life. His situation improved daily. Rovira had taken his deputy entirely into his confidence and trusted him implicitly. In turn, the eagle-eyed director had grasped the journeyman's unrivalled talents, and consulted him daily and considered his advice and initiatives with the utmost seriousness. Under El Senyoret's supervision, new areas of work had been opened and new departments and services established. Another team of workers now supplemented the one based at the workshop, one operating externally, its members scattered here and there according to the urgency of a demand that grew daily.

"As there's work that doesn't come straight to our door, we must go looking for it, otherwise it will go elsewhere," the bastard declared.

And it had also been his idea that, given they couldn't rely exclusively on wholesale offers or sales of scrap iron or other metals, which always brought in more revenue, they should hire a few rag and bone men to work full-time for the firm to ride around Barcelona and the surrounding area, foraging everywhere, visiting every backyard and buying item after item, at prices high and low; then they would divide up the purchases; on one side, scrap metal, and on the other, all that could be sold as antiques and all that could still be used after proper restoration.

Of course, this led to huge changes in how the firm organized itself. As the outside work could lead to disputes and losses if they weren't properly managed and as, moreover, the scrap-metal department required special attention and aptitudes, a new kind of deputy management or inspectorate had to be created, and, predictably, it was entrusted to Nonat, the initiator of that new departure.

By the day, he gained more freedom of movement and prestige. He was no longer obliged to spend hours and hours shut inside that small factory, hammering metal or operating machines like an ordinary worker. No, now he'd had made at his own expense an oak box with filets, embossed initials, and a fine nickel handle and catch, and, carrying that box—more a surgeon's case than anything else—he visited the places where the firm's workers had been and inspected what they'd done with a fine-tooth comb, or else, cloistered in the small office he'd arranged for himself at the far end of the scrap metal warehouse, he imposed order on the chaotic avalanche of objects arriving as a result of the excursions of their rag and bone men.

However, that greater freedom of action and professional status wasn't accompanied in ratio by other advantages, whereas Nonat's needs didn't diminish; on the contrary, they increased by virtue of his circumstances, so the ex-orphan began to suffer frequent bouts of Tantalus-like torture. If at first he'd simply been satisfied by all that glittered, he'd long since lost his liking for *plaqué* and fake stones, realized how naïve and pretentious it was to be laden with flashy baubles, and, consequently, increasingly coveted genuine gems and quality metals—the good things in life—and a thousand and one expensive bagatelles dotted around the city, but beyond—so very beyond—his modest worker's wage. Senyor Ramoneda was ruthless, with a sly, hypocritical meanness he camouflaged behind a studied air of absentmindedness and a no-less-studied air of austerity. At all times, if he could get by with giving three, he never spontaneously offered four, and he accepted and was grateful for any out-of-the-ordinary service or contribution, as if they were the most normal, natural acts, not requiring any out-of-the-ordinary reward. Hence, one of the things that immediately attracted his attention, and had been instrumental in his embrace of Nonat, was the latter's lack of a tendency to ask for more. You would have said he was a new potentate, a new Louis XVI who worked for the love of art, never attempting or needing to profit from the fruit of his labors, or shamelessly thinking about asking for a bonus. Just in case things changed and demands did ever surface, the director held back, and meanwhile discreetly enjoyed the real savings and considerable profits his new supervisor brought.

Nonat was perfectly aware of all of this, but disdained raising a finger. He wasn't a pathetic beggar scrabbling after a cent somebody dropped on the sidewalk, but rather the proudly Olympian, insouciant fraudster who holds on to the only bill in his pocket or takes what he wants wherever he finds it. He prodigally expended his energy and ingenuity, without deigning to haggle, to the benefit of that sickly, unlikeable fellow he hated and scorned with equal gusto.

Since El Senyoret hadn't come as punctually as usual and Rovira knew he'd gone into Barcelona to look into some special protective metal boards they were considering, which might detain him for a good while, he had lunch served, and the moment they'd finished eating, Rovira returned to work and Pepita, with her unerring sense of routine, returned to her piano. Carmeta was clearing the kitchen, as usual, and Octavi was playing on the front doorstep, also as usual. It was a sweltering day with the sun blistering down on the urban bustle, where soil and cobbles stung when touched, like blister beetles. It must have been almost 3 P.M. when Nonat strode around the corner. The moment Octavi saw him, he ran to welcome him with open arms. Nonat responded with a broad smile from far away, and two yards from him he held his hand out instinctively, though when the boy grasped it, he noticed something strange and unusual, and his large, dim eyes stared in a state of shock. Nonat's hand hadn't come toward him palm open, as normal, but with its fist closed around the top of a walking stick. Children are extremely observant and miss nothing: Nonat had never carried a walking stick, and the boy was stunned by the sheer novelty of it all.

"Good heaventh! Thatth's a lovely th'tick, Theenyor Nonat!"

Nonat frowned.

"When did you buy it?"

"This morning," came the locksmith's curt response.

"I knew I'd never theen it before. Can I hold it?"

Nonat let him have it without protest, albeit reluctantly. It was a walking stick with a blunt tip and a silver knob with a patina of dark, gilded blotches, or shiny patches, polished by the rub of hands. The handle consisted of two naked entwined figures fiercely wrestling with each other. The goldsmith who'd conceived and carved that couple had created a wonderous thing. The woman—a nymph—caught with her head arching backward, her tresses disheveled, was furiously trying to extract herself from the coarse caresses of a fawn who, glued to her breast and clutching her, was avidly seeking her lips. The design and detail of that daring miniature were remarkably apt and precise, but the most perfect features were the finely hewn expressions on each face. The woman revealed her angry, hostile anguish at that unpleasant assault, and, between his incipient ram's horns and beard, the fawn projected on his prey a mocking, throbbing, surging Dionysian lust.

Nonat had seen that walking stick for the first time when going down to Barcelona on a tram, in the late morning. A tall, well-built gentleman in a long gray jacket and trousers, white spats, and spectacles—a foreigner no doubt—had lodged it between his legs. That foreigner was attentively reading an equally foreign newspaper. Halfway down Passeig de Gràcia, another gentleman climbed aboard, exclaimed loudly when he saw the reader, and patted him on the shoulder. They exchanged greetings and sat next to each other. They occupied the bench nearest the rear platform, on the right; Nonat occupied the one opposite, by himself. The bespectacled foreigner showed the other man something in the newspaper he was reading, then decided to show him something on another page. As he opened it, the newspaper hit the top of the stick, knocking it onto the corner of the bench opposite. In turn, the second foreigner extracted a different newspaper from his pocket and the two men began to compare passages, striking up a lively debate that neither the people getting on and off, nor the passing conductor succeeded in interrupting. Alone on his bench, Nonat stared at the two foreigners quizzically. They alighted in Plaça de Catalunya, still arguing, and still deep in debate they made for one of those cafés garlanded with tables packed at that time of day with a huge variety of men. Nonat then crossed to the other side of the tram and simply grabbed the walking stick, which had been forgotten. A minute later, he alighted and quickly crossed back over Les Rambles, and as he had to walk toward Passeig de Colom, he caught the tram on Carrer de les Corts that was going uptown so he could make the reverse journey . . .

While Nonat ate lunch, Octavi kept him company, chattering all the time. He was very alert, noticed everything, and spoke like an adult.

"I like your thtick a lot, Thenyor Nonat . . . When I'm a grown up, Papa will buy me one . . ."

The whole time Nonat ate, the lad burbled on about the stick.

Nonat was furious. It was so unpleasant to be with acquaintances, with people one had no alternative but to tolerate. He got up impatiently and walked out into the street with the lad hanging onto his hand.

The fruit-seller opposite was also on her doorstep, holding a golden melon.

"What a lovely melon, Senyora Quima!" exclaimed Nonat.

"As fresh and crisp as an apple it is . . . Look, I just took it from the ice box and I'm going to snack on it. I've got at least six in the box . . ."

"Will you sell me one?"

"Of course, Senyor Nonat! Come in and choose one for yourself . . ."

And Nonat went in, followed by the boy. He selected his melon. His neighbor gave him a knife and a chair, and on that same side of the street, which the sun was then leaving, man and boy ate the whole melon slice after slice, the boy almost consuming as much as the man.

Five minutes later, when Nonat was on his way to work, Carmeta peered out and saw the boy sitting in the blistering sun, still chewing. When she realized what he was eating, and discovered who'd given it to him, her face reddened.

"How could he give him melon only two hours after lunch! He doesn't think, he doesn't think for one second . . . !" she spat in the direction of the factory. "That blasted show-off will bring us no good!"

She tried to drag the boy out of the sunlight, but Octavi was annoyed by his auntie's attitude and refused to budge; his auntie insisted, and he threw a tantrum as he was being dragged tearfully along the ground, until she too lost her temper and left him to it.

"All right, you damn little fool . . . If it makes you sick, so be it . . . Don't come asking me for help . . ."

And she walked in, muttering to herself.

As if Carmeta had been a prophet, that very same night the boy was limp and languid, but, even so, when he saw his father come in, he announced: "Thenyor Nonat has bought a thtick! Papa, Papa, Thenyor Nonat has bought a . . ."

Rovira, who was talking to Nonat, didn't hear him or heed what he was saying, but the latter glanced angrily around and told himself: "Never again with people I know!"

Octavi was asleep in his little high-sided cot in his parents' bedroom. Pepita spent the whole night fast asleep, all her worries under her pillow, but her husband noticed the boy looked off-color and whimpered now and then.

Next morning, when he woke up, he told Carmeta: "Dear, you must change the boy's sheets. He was tossing and turning all night and was all hot and sweaty . . ."

And he left.

Carmeta's heart skipped a beat, but as Pepita was still asleep, she didn't dare enter her bedroom. By eight o'clock, however, she could bear it no longer.

The boy's head and whole body were on fire. When her

brother came back home, she told him, though she was afraid of alarming him. They went for a doctor, who took over two hours to come. Octavi was feverish and had a temperature of 40°C.

Carmeta was in the depths of despair but didn't dare say what had happened the previous day, because as she'd caused the child to cry she was afraid she would be the one blamed.

And the fever and queasy stomach followed their course, more worryingly by the minute; finally, a strange, shrill howl and a rolling of the whites of his eyes indicated the dreadful presence of meningitis. It was a drama with few twists and turns.

Rovira only half-realized what had happened when he saw poor, motionless Octavi stretched out on his little white bed, in a small shift, completely covered by a white veil, white as marble, his little face wan. Rovira prowled listlessly around the house, struck dumb by the grief he was suppressing. Finally, he burst into tears; no words could comfort him.

For Pepita it was like an anxiety-ridden dream. She couldn't see the terror on the shadowy faces encircling her; conversely, her own lack of gumption and natural frivolity didn't allow her to accept the possibility of catastrophe. "Mama was there, seeing to everything, without fussing, so what could go wrong? If the boy had been really sick, Mama would have told me, and when Mama said nothing, I was sure he would pull through."

And she walked this way and that, and back again, like someone intending to do something, but all she ever did was get in the way and spill the medicines from the glass or spoon, tugging at her pinafore, clean and spotless as ever, and powdering her nose after every little tear shed. The only real change one saw during Octavi's illness was that she stopped practicing the piano and perming her hair. So when somebody suddenly stated in an emotional, solemn tone: "The poor boy has died! Praised be the Lord! His suffering has ended!" it took her completely by surprise and she refused to believe it. She'd always been so ingenuously happy, had always gotten what she wanted and willed, that she found it hard to grasp that something so devastating could happen without her consent; until her sobbing mama hugged her and confirmed that it was so. She collapsed in a fainting fit.

Like a wounded animal, Carmeta had slipped away into the junk room, where, all alone, forgotten by everyone, she bit her nails and pulled out her hair. Rancor and remorse slid and slithered in her soul like a couple of poisonous snakes. "And to think that I, yes, I made him cry! Only a few days before the poor little thing died . . . !"

Angeleta, the neighbor on the landing who'd been looking for her, finally tracked her down.

"What on earth are you doing here, my blessed child?"

"Ay, Angeleta! They've killed him, they've killed off 'my heart's delight!'"

And as Angeleta looked at her askance, as if she thought she was going mad, she could restrain herself no longer and blurted out: "That nasty, stuck-up piece of work is the cause of all this misery! I never could stand the sight of him . . . Never . . . ever . . . I was always wary of him, as if he were an evil genie . . ."

Angeleta's eyes opened wide.

"Come, dear! You don't know what you are saying. He may have made him sick by giving him that melon . . . (men never think of these things), but he is a very sensible, well-spoken young gentleman; he doesn't sing, make a big fuss, knock you over if he bumps into you, and never swears . . ."

When she heard that sharp rebuff, Carmeta felt a twinge of pain in her heart and her eyelids closed over glinting tears, like the wings of an injured bird . . .

The boy's burial caused a big commotion in the neighborhood, just as his parents' wedding had done in its day. It took place in the morning and the onlookers—neighbors, market stall holders, maids, and artisans going to and from the square—lined the route of the cortège, as if it were a celebrity's funeral, dispensing comments and condolences in everyday tones.

"God's little angel!" muttered a young girl, peering at the small white coffin.

"Be that as it may, better now when there was help at hand!" exclaimed an elderly lady, dressed in black, by way of response.

"It makes no difference for parents. You love and mourn your children no matter their age . . ." a third woman added in turn, a true stalwart, tears streaming from her eyes.

The elderly woman dressed in black spun around and retorted sourly, sizing up the sobbing stalwart with a venomous glance.

"Listen to her! As if we don't all know that. But it makes a big difference if you can have more children, or if you can't and instead see them die in bed, one after the other, and lose all your anchors in life, as I did!"

"If yours died on you when they were young, mine died on me as little children, so I know that loss," added the other, wiping her eyes.

A quarrel was about to break out between those two mothers, their past sorrows revived by the spectacle of the present mourning, when a young apprentice girl, leaning on one hip to balance the weight of a huge box she was carrying on her other arm, yelped: "Ay! Look at that old fellow! He looks like a fat hen!"

All the young people burst out laughing, but the lady in black berated her scornfully: "So that's funny, is it, ducky? If I'm not wrong, that fat hen is the boy's granddad."

"Yes, senyora, that's who he is!" a neighbor added.

"A real good reason to split your sides laughing, if I ever heard one!"

At that the apprentice girl turned red as a robin's breast, and had to stuff her headscarf between her teeth and bite it hard to keep a straight face. The tufts of short hair sticking out of her pigtail shook like little flames stirred by inner tremors.

Senyor Tomaset did in fact inspire comic pity; his get-up and grief had a regrettably cartoonish air.

He'd put on the morning coat he wore to his daughter's wedding, now short in the sleeves and tight in the girth because its owner had put on considerable weight since he'd had it tailored; the front of his bowler hat was pulled down over his eyebrows and the back perched on his skull, revealing a slice of bald pate under the rear brim. His beard was stuck far into the hollow of his neck as if his head had been dislocated by a sudden clout and his arms dangled in the breeze as if hanging by a thread from his shoulders; his right hand gripped a big white handkerchief into which he blew his nose and which he used to wipe away the occasional tear, and his uneven, Roman-style hair hung down over his ironed collar. While the boy's illness had lasted, the poor man hadn't thought to go to the barber's, as he was always rushing from the shop to Carrer de les Xemeneies and then back to the shop, and after Octavi had died, his wife, who amid the direst upsets never lost her *savoir-faire*, had refrained from mentioning it to him because she felt it would make him even more grief-stricken.

Senyor Tomaset, who was stooping very low, suddenly stumbled, and if he hadn't held on to his bowler with both hands, it would have flown down the street. When she saw that, the girl apprentice could restrain herself no longer: she erupted into a non-stop titter that almost choked her, and she fled that spot at top speed before the crowd turned on her.

Someone further up, in another knot of gawping bystanders, exclaimed: "Look at those wreaths, my dear! That carriage looks like a proper window display . . ."

"I know, there's four! One on each side . . . You'd've thought the kid was a member of parliament!"

"And what does it say on the broad ribbon?"

"*To . . . o-wer . . . most be-lov-ed grand-son.* The grand-pappies have really gone to town, eh? Those big white velvet pansies are what the stinkin' rich like!"

"They'll make the kid sweat in this weather," quipped a local jester.

And a defiant response came once again: "Don't joke about the dead! It's not nice and will bring woe!"

"The elephant in the Park . . . is even nastier! You're the one who'll bring woe, you fool, with that face creased like an accordion," and the jester snorted and gleefully slapped the back of the plump artisan at his side.

As it had lower down the street, the crowd here too started laughing, ignoring the grumbling lady's grouses, while the apprentice girl reappeared and fired more spicy barbs from beneath her sleek, tidy hair.

The hearse passed by, followed by all the workers from Senyor Ramoneda's firm, and, finally, the neighbors and acquaintances of both families.

"Christ, they've even got a priest! What a luxury!"

That priest was a distant cousin of Senyora Tomaset, a clergyman from a small Penedès village, whom Pepita had insisted they summon to give a refined touch to the funeral ceremonies.

"And what about that elegant gentleman? He must be the boss of the factory where Senyor Rovira works?"

"No," said the shopkeeper from the corner store, "that's the young man who lives with them . . . I think he's a tradesman . . ."

"You know, he looks like the company president . . ."

It was indeed Nonat whose elegant clothes and naturally distinguished airs attracted attention as usual. As on that day when he'd ridden in the carriage, he wore Russian leather shoes and off-white gloves. Buttoned up from top to bottom, his jacket gave him a military allure, and the walking stick he'd "acquired" in the tram was tucked in his grasp with the utmost calm and tranquility.

Senyora Tomaset, who'd arranged the ceremonial program down to the tiniest detail, appreciated Nonat's decorative, eye-catching appearance and placed him next to Rovira, so that, together with the priest, he could enhance the funeral. And a recondite maternal regret made her think to herself, as she compared that outsider to her son-in-law: Ay, Lord! If Pepita had to go and marry a worker, she might have chosen that fellow, who's more her style and ours . . . !

And when everybody had left and the funeral party moved off, Senyora Tomaset slipped furtively out of the sitting room, where neighbors and acquaintances were keeping Pepita company, spoiling her like a child, and went to peek out of a crack in the closed side-window.

Her homespun vanity was satisfied: one could not ask for more, one really could not! It was a good, grand crowd. As she surveyed the scene, she saw all the neighbors of the haberdashery, the undertaker's staff, relatives, a scattering of acquaintances, the child's father's work colleagues etc., in what was like a kind of lunatic serpent that at each step lightly contracted the colorful scales on its back. The rear of the serpent's neck was formed by the clergy's liturgical garments and a gaggle of children with lighted candles, and the head by the white and gold hearse—which seemed more like a beautiful toy than anything funereal—the case of the small casket was surrounded by wreaths: theirs and the grandparents', which were the most expensive and showiest, in the top spot, at the head, ribbons spreading in every direction; the parents' wreath at the bottom, and on each side, wreaths of real flowers; from brothers and sisters, from Pepita, and one from Ramoneda's workers, out of respect for their good-hearted foreman.

However, what most overjoyed the haberdasher were the lines of onlookers simmering on the sidewalks. Of course, she'd lost her baby grandson, but everybody could see that, in death as in life, he'd never gone wanting, and see the high esteem in which the Rovires and Tomasets were held everywhere.

When the men returned from the cemetery, one serious issue was raised. Pepita's mother said to her daughter and son-in-law: "Collect your things and come to our house for a while. What will you poor things ever do between walls so full of memories?" As the haberdasher made no reference to Carmeta, who understood she was being discarded, a flash of genius made Carmeta respond immediately to the inconsiderate way she was being treated.

"Senyora Tomaset is right; that's the most sensible thing to do. You go with her and I'll go to El Clot with cousin Pepa until you return here. I couldn't stand living between these four walls either."

The haberdasher moistened her lips because she saw a hailstorm in the making. It was what Rovira ingenuously suggested by looking at Nonat: "That's all very well, but . . ."

Nonat's reply came just as swiftly: "Don't you worry about me. Like you, I'd feel very sad to be here without the little lad. I'd rather fly to a different nest . . ."

They all protested sharply, except for Carmeta. "Meals would be no problem . . . he could go to the haberdasher's, but he couldn't sleep there because they don't have room . . .

If he's fine staying in the apartment . . . Clearly a man doesn't feel loss like a woman . . ."

However, Nonat saw in this unexpected situation a way to regain his freedom, and resolved the issue at a stroke: "No, no need for that, don't worry on my behalf. I have an idea. I'll look for a small room around here, and eat at a restaurant . . ."

There was no way to budge him. Then Angeleta, the neighbor on the landing, mentioned an acquaintance of hers who'd been widowed and had more than enough space for herself.

"She might rent you a room. She lives by herself, and is very tidy and very nice . . ."

They agreed that, after lunch, she'd accompany him to see whether or not he could stay there.

And they all stood up to leave. Wanting to make up for her involuntary slip, Senyora Tomaset begged Carmeta to come with them, but Carmeta stood her ground: "No, no, don't worry, thanks all the same . . . I have to tidy up and get my things together . . ." Then Angeleta caught on and interjected: "Leave it to me. You can go, without a worry in the world. I'll help Carmeta clear up and then we'll have lunch together . . ."

As soon as the others had left, a tearful Carmeta gripped Angeleta's hands tightly: "Ay, Angeleta, you did me a real favor! I'm fed-up living with those people! Pepita is a fool, her mother's all façade, and the men . . . all hen-pecked! I don't miss the others, except for my brother, but they've turned him inside out like a glove . . ."

Carmeta hid the main reason for her rebellion: her repugnance toward Nonat, her desire never to see him again. They were in the sitting room, which was a mess, and she glowered at the photo of the gentleman-tradesman that was hanging on the wall; a photo he'd given them a while ago that Rovira had taken the trouble to frame and place among the family photos.

All was sorted by late afternoon: the house tidied, and Nonat's belongings sent to his new staging-post—which turned out to be an average-size bedroom, freshly wallpapered, with almost new furniture too, which the landlady, a widow of four months, had bought when she got married a little over seven years ago. Angeleta, charged with keeping the key to the apartment, had no sooner said goodbye to Carmeta, who'd left in tears, than she locked the door and rushed into the street in the grips of a terrible depression, as if she'd been left imprisoned, alone with the wretched child's ill-omened spirit.

That night, as always when he severed a link tying him down, driven by a pleasant, invigorating sense of excitement, Nonat ate double portions and found his supper doubly tasty. He had made a deal, on a monthly basis, with a cheap restaurant on Carrer Major frequented by people short on money; apprentices and tradesmen from local factories, shop assistants, tram workers, clerks, office workers, and fly-by-nights. That restaurant comprised a long, narrow room with two rows of tables along either wall (tables, set from early morning, with napkins, plates, and glasses—upside down for reasons of hygiene—but with no cutlery, because occasionally it had "grown legs and walked away"), and chairs, a bar counter, shelves of bottles behind it, an ancient pendulum clock with a cuckoo that came out to sing on the hour; a large, murky, cracked mirror where they wrote up the days' specials, and a host of adverts for this, that, and the other dotted over the walls, the top half of which were covered by discolored, fly-blown paper, while the bottom half had been rubbed, cracked, and dirtied by customers' shoulders. The clock's cuckoo had given the establishment its name, fancifully translated by a delirious ornithologist. Above the broad, low exterior and the double doors (painted an apple-green and edged with a large strip of bright red) that extended against the wall on the street side, were white letters which read: *The Grand Quail Dining Room*, and inside the tiny window display a desiccated hoopoe had once stood, perched lightly on a branch of natural cork, which had for years presided over little pots of fresh cheese, dusty custard in twisted cups, and plates of beef stew, because the establishment had long since lost any claim to good taste. However, the sun, weather, and above all, moths had seen off the hoopoe, and the owner didn't think twice about replacing it with a handsome, glass-eyed, bushy-tailed black squirrel. But, as in times of yore, the inscription *The Grand Quail Dining Room* still graced the cheap restaurant, though the customers, a more easy-going, take-it-or-leave-it crowd, referred to it in plain, homely fashion, as The Father-in-Law's.

From then on, Nonat went there every day for breakfast, lunch, and supper at the most isolated table, tucked away in a corner, feeling no need or desire to strike up friendships or conversations. That abrupt change marked another new departure in his life.

After his son's death, Rovira acted as if his brain was shot; he stood rooted to the spot for ages, stared aimlessly, and never replied, as if he didn't hear when people spoke to him, his mind wandered when his hands were busy on a job, he muddled the director's orders, walked from one machine to another . . . and would have wrought real damage if Nonat hadn't almost always followed him out of the corner of his eye and rushed to right his mistakes.

At the onset, nobody took any notice.

"He's upset, he'll soon get over it . . ." reckoned his workmates, reckoned the director, reckoned his in-laws, the haberdashers. But far from getting over it, Rovira's daydreaming and semi-apathy gradually worsened. If at first only close acquaintances noticed, day by day, it became increasingly obvious to everybody. You'd have said Rovira's brain was porous, more lethargic than other men's, and his pain had made greater inroads there than was usual, leaving it deeply scarred.

That was why his deputy had to do all his work and entirely assume his responsibilities for real, not for show. Anticipating as a matter of course what Rovira did and said, Nonat stepped in and took direct charge of everything, everywhere, with director and workers, negotiating all deals and signing external contracts; he met whomever, went wherever he was needed, and executed jobs much more expertly and swiftly than his friend. Under his say-so, time, the workers, and the enterprise seemed to give more of themselves, as if by magic, and, in view of the outcomes, the boss seriously began to contemplate a change of management.

Rovira was always withdrawn and non-responsive and didn't register what was happening around him, that he was being replaced, that his deputy was adopting a naturally authoritarian attitude toward him and everyone else.

"Rovira, do this or that . . . Rovira, tell Senyor Ramoneda . . . Rovira, put away those wrenches, watch where you leave them, don't misplace any . . ."

"*Bueno*," was all Rovira would ever say, before obeying mechanically.

One morning, on his way to work, a voice from behind startled him, exclaiming: "Francisqueta!"

Rovira turned around and was surprised to not see a living soul in the street.

"Hey, who said that?"

And he gawked this way and that . . .

He didn't catch a trace of anyone. Tears came to his eyes.

"They saw me dawdling along in a dream and made fun of me . . ." he thought.

That same day the director summoned Nonat to his desk.

"I say, Nonat, what do you make of Rovira?"

Nonat said nothing and stared quizzically at his boss.

"I'd say he's useless . . ." the boss continued. "Did you see the mess he made of the job you delegated to him at the Garriga company?"

"Of course."

"You must see we can't carry on like this . . . It was a disaster . . . Rovira isn't himself . . . He must be replaced . . ."

Nonat said nothing. The director, rather hesitant initially, decided to blurt out . . .

"Tell me, Nonat, how about you take his place? You've got everything at your fingertips . . ."

"If you say so . . ." the ex-orphan responded matter-of-factly.

And as he didn't add anything, as if proposal and acceptance were a formality and foregone conclusion, the director, rubbing his hands, quickly dismissed Nonat with these equally matter-of-fact words: "Good, then that's settled . . ."

But when Nonat had walked a few strides, the boss shouted: "Nonat . . . !"

Nonat turned around.

"Don't say anything to Rovira for the moment."

"If you say so."

Seeing that the director had nothing to add, Nonat returned to his work,

At the end of the day, Nonat accompanied Rovira back to the haberdashery, where he'd not set foot for a few days. Just before they arrived, they watched an open carriage occupied by a lady slowly come up the street. Nonat recognized her at once: it was the consul's wife. A twenty-something young man was riding the most elegant thoroughbred steed by the side of the carriage.

The consul's wife was whiter and fatter than the first time Nonat had seen her, and she wore an exquisite pendant on her bosom; the young man accompanying her had handsome features and looked distinguished in every way. Nonat thought he looked familiar, one of those folk you see in sketches of horse races published in illustrated supplements or foreign magazines. Nonat stopped in his tracks, turning pale and wan. He was paralyzed by a feeling of infinite envy that had never before stung so sharply.

"Just look at him, now there's someone I'd have liked to be!"

Rovira, who'd carried on walking without noticing a

thing, suddenly discovered Nonat wasn't with him and turned around; the bastard was still gazing at the horseman and carriage receding into the distance, as if awestruck.

"What's the matter, Nonat?"

Nonat slowly caught up.

"The fellow riding with the carriage is the son of the consul's wife, right?"

Rovira glanced at him, surprised.

"I don't know . . . Maybe . . . I don't know them personally . . ."

Rovira's brother-in-law was standing in the haberdashery doorway. Nonat repeated his question.

"Yes, it's her son . . . He accompanies his mother home most evenings . . . I don't know where they're coming from. Though not in the morning, which is when he rides out alone or with friends. They'd kept him in England until last year; the housemaid here told us . . . he does look a bit foreign, doesn't he?"

It was exactly five days after they buried Octavi when Angeleta, the Roviras' neighbor, heard a knock at the door. When she opened up, she was astounded to see Carmeta standing there.

"What are you doing here? Didn't you say you'd stay in El Clot until they came back?"

"Yes, I did, but I missed . . . My cousin Pepa really wanted me to stay, but I . . . You see . . . there's no place like home . . . I have all the mementos of the little lad here . . ."

"But, my poor dear, what *will* you do here all alone?"

The spinster didn't reply.

"Well, I'll come and keep you company . . ."

"Do you know how they all are?"

"Good, for now. Senyora Tomaset came yesterday to get some of Pepita's clothes."

"And . . . and . . ." she hesitated for a second, then added: "What about . . . *him*?"

"Who do you mean?"

"Him . . . the *quiet* man . . ."

Angeleta laughed.

"Well I'll be, my love, I hadn't realized! I thought you couldn't stand him . . . !"

Carmeta's face darkened and she muttered: "Believe me, I can't get him out of my head . . . He's inside here night and day . . ." She jabbed her forehead with her finger. "When I think how he's to blame for everything . . ."

"Now, now, leave well alone! What's past is past. Better not to brood on things you can't alter . . . He also came on Sunday, for garters he'd left on his bedside table. He looked gorgeous! You don't know this, but he now wears a gold watch, slim as a sliver of cardboard . . . I don't get it, he must earn a mint . . ."

"You think?"

"Yes, my girl! You only have to see the pretty things he. . . Everything he wears is always brand-new . . ."

"That nasty piece of . . ."

"You know," Angeleta suddenly exclaimed, a glint in her eye and a smile on her lips. "Perhaps he's some old lady's boy toy!"

As she put the key in the hole, she didn't see the glazed, sorrowful expression that momentarily disfigured Carmeta's face.

They walked into the apartment and the young Rovira lass surveyed the scene. A light layer of dust covered the varnish on the furniture; the light slanting in from the small window over the inside yard was grayer than ever; it was starting to smell dankly of a house that had been shut up, of a mixture of ether, sewers, and eau-de-cologne . . . There was a prescription on the sideboard . . . When Carmeta moved the basket of clothes she hadn't ironed the previous week, something dark rolled out from behind . . . The women screamed, panic-stricken; then looked . . . It was the boy's ball . . .

Carmeta could stand it no longer; she slumped into a chair, rested her head on the table, and sobbed mournfully.

She'd returned from El Clot in worse shape: thin as a rake, a dun brown color, black rings under her eyes . . . limp, languid, and worn out. Like the whole of that small apartment, she too had a damp and dismal air, and a layer of dust all over . . .

"Come now!" shouted Angeleta. "What's the point? You'll be the one falling ill if you carry on . . . Enough is enough! You know, I'll bring the lark that's your brother back, who's been acting just like you; I've treated him royally, but he's moping . . . he's not happy away from home. In the meantime, clean yourself up and we'll go buy some fish. Today you'll have supper at home . . ."

When Rovira discovered that Carmeta had returned, he went to see her, then dropped by for a while every day. Those little chats revived brother and sister. They opened their hearts to each other, talked about Octavi, gave full vent to their sorrow, held nothing back.

Carmeta also found her brother was down, like someone convalescing after a long illness, and watching him over a number of days deteriorating rather than improving, she decided to have a serious heart-to-heart.

"Joanet, don't deny it! You aren't well; something's giving you grief, and I can't watch you suffer without doing something. We'll go to the doctor's tomorrow. If it upsets you to think the family will find out, we'll keep it to ourselves, but I want someone to take a look at you."

Rovira burst into tears. Carmeta took fright at a reaction she wasn't expecting.

"Dear brother, what *is* the matter?" she asked, giving him a hug.

"Ay, lass! I'm going mad, I'm going mad . . ." and, convulsing and sobbing, he placed his huge head on her old-maid's chest, flat and smooth as a plank of wood.

For a moment she went blank, as if thunderstruck, but as she recovered, she succeeded in coaxing it out of him by dint of her maternal caresses and warmth.

When Octavi had died, Rovira had felt his memory going fuzzy in his head. Sometimes he was sitting down and felt like he was walking; sometimes he was walking and felt he was flying . . . But one day . . . one day he was strolling down the street and heard somebody shout out a name behind him, he turned around and nobody was there . . . Right then he hadn't worried . . . Some idiot was having a laugh . . . But another day at work he suddenly heard a whisper in his ear: "Four keys!" He turned around with a start, and again nobody was there. He asked all the workers, who were busy far from him: "Who asked me for keys?" The workers looked at each other, then it was knowing glances, and in the end they all smiled, not wanting to make anything out of it . . . "Keys? you must have been daydreaming, Rovira." But he wasn't. And that's happened a lot since . . . There's definitely a voice telling him things . . . A clear, sharp, yet softly spoken voice; a voice speaking as if in a normal conversation . . . Except the voice isn't coming from outside . . . it's in his head . . . The more distracted, the more unwary he is, that voice utters a word precisely, and though it doesn't sound unpleasant, he feels panicky . . . Because he alone hears those words . . . And it happens daily, whether he's by himself or surrounded by people . . .

Carmeta turned pale. She sensed her brother's condition was no laughing matter, but something extremely alarming. She soothed him as much as she could, but never mentioned a visit to the doctor's again. The following day, she went to see the doctor on her own. When she explained the situation, that doctor referred her to a renowned psychiatrist, who said he could make no exact diagnosis without seeing the sick man, but, in any case, he asked if there were precedents; what was the rest of the family like, what illnesses had they had, what had they died from . . . Carmeta was alarmed, and quickly and confidently answered that they'd all been as strong as oaks, died of old age, and never suffered from malingering diseases. But the doctor interrupted her with a measured wave of his hand, a gesture that seemed to raise silent objections and stir unsuspected doubts . . . Later, cornered by his apparently innocuous questions that led, as they say, quite unawares, to the conclusion he was after, Carmeta began to recall . . .

"Odd things? Well, no . . . I mean, it depends how you look at it . . . If you delve into your family, who won't find someone on the eccentric side?" For example, their great-grandfather married twice. Their grandfather, along with other children, belonged to the first marriage, but he and his siblings had been well respected in the village: Carmeta had never heard of the family doing strange things, except for one man with a mania for chasing cats; the second he caught one, he'd quickly hang it by its tail over a bucket full of water and leave it there for days on end as it meowed furiously and swung around like a thing possessed. The family was appalled by the spectacle, the neighbors complained about the frightful caterwauling, but he smiled, shrugged his shoulders, and muttered: "Let them try and scratch me again . . . !" He'd once explained that a cat had scratched him when he was a kid, and from then on he'd had it in for them, and if people said the cats he strung up were not to blame for the scratches he'd received, he'd add: "It's a cat, so as good-for-nothing as its mate . . . They've all got claws, and if one doesn't scratch, it's because it can't." There was no shifting him. Those tragedies sometimes lasted weeks, because cats can be tough, but that uncle never softened and woe to whomever dared touch a cat before it starved to death or went mad . . . Apart from that, nobody had a bad word to say about that uncle . . . His brother, Rovira's grandfather, also had four or five children; they were all good, intelligent, and hard-working; one of them, *L'Oncle Xocolater*, as they dubbed him, had even gone to South America and made lots of money . . . That money brought misery to his family, however, because worried by his fear of being impoverished again, he made them go to bed by the light of day to save on electricity, and put the bread in the sun so it went dry so they'd eat less . . . Even so, he was such a live wire that the friars asked him for advice, and so handy that, though no cobbler, he made his own shoes. He never had more than one pair, but, as the soles were an inch and a half thick, they lasted for years. And something very amusing happened when he died. Following village traditions, they didn't bury him in his shoes, but gave them away to a poor man, who one day noticed that with every step he took a gold coin dropped out. He examined the shoes and found they were stuffed with half doubloons . . .

Great-grandfather, as already mentioned, married twice; the second time to a young woman, at which time his heir was already an established man and had a son of his own, who would one day be Rovira's father. In turn, the son was at that time a bit older than his father's stepsister—his great-grandfather's only daughter from his second marriage. Carmeta had distinct memories of that great-aunt, by the name of Aunt Manela, the only dim or simple member of the family. When she was growing up, and as an old woman, she always carried a rag flower in her bosom and constantly cradled a dirty, shabby doll in her arms (nobody knew where she'd found it) that she said was her baby. As a child, Carmeta would infuriate her great-aunt and split her sides stealing that mangy doll, and dim Auntie would get into a temper and chase her with a broom, shouting: "I'll flay you alive! I'll flay you alive!"

The doctor listened to Carmeta very attentively, maintaining an enigmatic silence and merely said: "Bring your brother to see me. . ."

His silence, his failure to offer her comfort or give her the slightest hope, appalled the poor woman.

The doctor obviously thought Rovira was losing his mind because it was in his blood; his family had peculiar features going back and his father's half-aunt—a half-aunt, for Christ's sake—from the dregs of the family, as they say, who'd been a simpleton: whereas she, his sister, knew for certain that Rovira had as a young boy been as sharp-eyed as a magpie and as an adult always an honest, reliable individual, a reasonable, intelligent man, a front-ranker, until he was hit with the dreadful blow of his little boy's death. And she tried to protest, to make the doctor see reason, to erase the dismal impression given by her own thoughtless, plain-speaking . . .

"When you hear it like that, all at once, you might think . . . but don't jump to conclusions, doctor; they were people . . . We don't come from . . . we really don't . . . And as for my brother, my brother . . ."

Her sobs choked her, stopped her flow . . . The doctor took pity on her, and as he led her gently to the door, he patted her affectionately on the back.

"For heaven's sake, don't take it like that, senyora . . . I've said nothing to upset you so . . . One can never say without examining the patient . . . Who can tell, who can tell? Bring him to see me, and then . . ."

Carmeta walked out of the office, where she'd been dealt the cruelest blow, dismayed and devastated. A few steps from the green door that was closing behind her, a thunderbolt had suddenly felled her brother, and the spinster's hair bristled with horror as she moved away from a door as ominous as the door of destiny. No, she didn't have it in her to bring her poor brother to hear his sentence confirmed . . . She preferred to continue as before, even if it meant being tormented by the most terrifying fears . . .

She reached home feeling that she had lost *her* mind; she didn't know where she'd been or the route she'd taken: all she remembered was a nasty youngster with a new spinning-top who'd cracked the cord like a whip near her eyes, stuck his tongue out, and spat at her.

She put her black, knitted shawl on a chair and walked into the living room. Her eyes flew to the photo of her enemy like two red-hot coals; it was a dark blotch on the wall. She ripped it down, nail and all, and threw it to the ground. The sound of breaking glass seemed to calm her slightly, as if her rancor had been dissipated by the damage done to the picture, as if she'd injured the hated figure in the flesh.

"You're an evil creature, murdering us all. First the little lad, now his father! Poor us! My wretched brother! If you'd not brought that man into our home, we'd all still be happy. And now you've gone mad. And I'm not far behind!" She smiled a tragic, sarcastic smile. "It's in my blood, as the doctor would say. What a fine inheritance! Such awful, god-sent woes!"

Feeling more reasonable after that violent outburst, she went to get a dustpan and brush to clear away the broken glass; then she wanted to put the battered frame back in its place, but couldn't find the nail. She shrugged and tossed it onto the table.

Rovira became increasingly intent on spying secretly, furtively, on the intruder who'd lodged in his brain, who continued to become a greater presence, who lorded it over him a bit more by the day; he began to forget everything that wasn't his infernal obsession. At work he took no initiative and managed nothing . . . He moved instinctively, with the skill and deftness of an experienced tradesman, but that was all . . . At home he sat in a corner where he'd have spent every self-absorbed minute if the others hadn't dragged him into the to-and-fro of family life. His mother-in-law, the haberdasher, the first to notice the disaster threatening them, had also been the first to take precautions. Without her caring hand, if he'd been left to his own devices, Rovira would have walked around like a dirty, ragged, pitiful beggar, because apart from work he'd let himself go and had ceased any form of cleaning, change of clothes, or orderly activity. But she used her gentle, motherly ways to keep him in hand.

"Joan, my son, did you forget to change your socks and shirt? Didn't you see them on the chair? Off you go, you're free now . . ." she'd tell him on a Sunday morning, before instructing her son to take him to the barber's.

When it was mealtime, she summoned Rovira to the fountain to wash his hands, served him at the table, kept him conversing so he didn't relapse into morose self-absorption, and made him drink "revivifying" herbal wines specifically to fight anemia. She tried to hide her son-in-law's growing delusion and apathy from the eyes of family and strangers alike, as if by not drawing attention to it and refusing to recognize that deadly, frightening *thing*, it was sure to beat a retreat and melt away. She'd only been sorely tempted to mention it to Nonat. That young man was so pleasant and understanding!

But Nonat was Rovira's workmate and Rovira was still bringing home a wage, a wage the household really needed, as they were behind with their own work and had been so badly hit by poor Octavi's death, which had been so costly in every way! If she spoke out and admitted that Rovira was good for nothing, what might happen?

The haberdasher, like Carmeta, preferred to put her head down and plow on, silently waiting for whatever might ensue.

When Senyor Ramoneda paid Nonat his weekly wage, Nonat held the bills in his hand and stared him in the eye, but Senyor Ramoneda quickly looked down, intent on counting out the other workers' money. Nonat frowned, shrugged brusquely, said nothing, and stuffed the bills in his pocket. Although he'd gone up yet another rung, Senyor Ramoneda was still paying him the same basic worker's wage.

Nonat went for an early bite at *The Father-in-Law's*, hurried home, and shut himself in his bedroom. When he emerged after a good long time, the mistress of the house took a step backward as if she were witnessing a wondrous apparition.

Nonat wore a black dinner jacket and trousers, white tie, embroidered silk waistcoat, and leather boots. The fingers of the white gloves hanging from his pants' pocket had a braided trim.

As he put on his overcoat and wrapped a fine, knitted scarf around its white collar, he told the widow: "Senyora Maria, don't be alarmed if you hear noises in the early hours. I'll be back late."

"You getting married, Senyor Nonat?" she asked, half-joking and extremely curious.

"Not for now, thanks be to God! I'm going to the theater . . ." the bastard said with a smile.

He tapped his pockets to make sure he had a handkerchief, wallet . . . and took his hat.

"Good night, Senyora Maria."

"Enjoy yourself, Senyor Nonat."

The widow stood gawping behind the door as it shut until the sound of Senyor Nonat's footsteps faded on the stairs.

It was the first time he would be entering the Liceu through the front door. Till then, his place had been among the onlookers waiting for people to exit, or perched up high in the cheap seats with music lovers and other workers like himself.

From those other vantage points, with desperate longing and titivating envy, he'd spied on the dazzling world of the wealthy, studied their airs, manners, fashions, and customs . . . but incompletely, in fragments, as the remote perspective distorted the whole . . . No, he hadn't *seen* the Liceu, he'd never been inside; if he'd been inside and seen it, it was from outside the zones where the *grandees* were permitted.

He realized all that, to his sudden astonishment, when he was about to alight from the tram, and, for a minute, sensing he was a complete outsider, his quiet daring vanished and he didn't want to go in by himself.

He dusted his pants, straightened his waistcoat, patted his pockets again as if looking for something, and pulled on his gloves . . . in a word, he dallied. Another tram emptied out a group of men, and two ladies alighted from a carriage . . .

Nonat went in with them, as if they formed a single contingent. The men preceding him went to the right, and, feeling at a loss, Nonat followed. As he climbed the stairs, he saw those figures reflected in the large mirror dressed *comme il faut*, in attire that seemed to be receiving its first outing, and in the middle of the throng, a jarring note, a loose-fitting English overcoat in last season's style. He turned around to look. The people he'd come in with had already started up the second flight of stairs and he was alone on the last step of the first. Behind him, the heads of the two ladies from the carriage stuck up in the far mirror like heads at a hair stylist's. Nonat suddenly went red as a cherry; he'd just recognized himself as the man in the secondhand coat. He was dreadfully upset by that mortifying illumination and his neophyte gawking.

He blushed many a time on that memorable, testing night, constantly scrutinizing what others were doing and afraid he'd look foolish, but he was almost at the end of his initiation and apprenticeship. The young man, who'd seemed hesitant and inhibited like a foreign student on his first foray, was soon no stranger to the dress circle. He was simply an unknown quantity, undetected by gossipers, and his natural refinement exhibited all the self-confidence and savvy of a regular at the Opera House.

Senyor Ramoneda always spent every evening at his political party's Circle playing billiards with the same few colleagues. One afternoon, one of his closest, an old, wealthy contractor, appeared later than usual.

"Where've you been?"

"Don't ask, my friend! All hell's been let loose at home! Do you remember that cigarette holder with the diamond and ruby clasp my children gave me as a housewarming present? Well, it's been stolen! You know, life in Barcelona will soon be quite impossible. You're not even safe in your own home!"

"How did it happen?"

"Your guess is as good as mine! We thought it was the maid, though she swears she is innocent and went berserk when we confronted her with the law. We obliged her to open her trunk, but we found nothing, though we threw her out on the street anyway. It could only have been her. And you know I hadn't touched that holder since it was given to me! I don't like using expensive things like that every day . . . But last Thursday I brought it along when I was attending the lecture here, and when I returned home, I hung up my overcoat, forgetting it was still in the pocket. My wife keeps telling me I'm a careless soul. She has a spring-action box where she puts her rings and valuables and wanted me to put mine there too, but I never remember. *Bueno*, the next day I had to go to Badalona, as I said. I told the maid to give my coat a brush while I ate breakfast. She found the case, showed it to me and asked: 'Shall I leave it in your pocket?' 'No, give it to the Senyora . . .' 'The Senyora's gone out.' 'Well, put it in our bedroom, and tell her to put it away later.' She went to our bedroom and came back empty-handed. I left for Badalona. My wife got back late, almost at suppertime, and the maid says she told her: 'Senyora, the master said to put away what's on your bed.' She was tired and decided to do so later. Then when she went to bed, she picked up the case, opened it, and . . . it was empty!

She says she thought it was strange I should take the holder without its case, but reasoned: 'He's one who doesn't like to fuss!' and didn't give it another thought and put the case away. I was in Badalona three days. I came back today, and, while I was having a wash, my wife said: 'It's not very sensible to take the holder without its case! Someone will steal the jewels!' 'What holder?' Then it all became clear. Imagine how annoyed I was! The only people who enter our bedroom are my wife, myself, and the maid . . . Naturally, my wife didn't take it, and I was away . . . So, do the math . . . I don't think it could be clearer . . . I reckon the maid gave it to the trashman; she's a good friend of his and she always spends ages chatting to him . . . My wife tells her not to, because he stinks up the place . . . and the trashman is not somebody to trust, according to a neighbor on the stairs . . . I wanted her arrested, to tell you the truth, but the municipal police say we should forget it, because we have no leads, and it would only mean expense and headaches, they say any day now they'll summon us to make a statement . . ."

They played their usual game of billiards, and in the late afternoon when it was time to leave, the contractor told Senyor Ramoneda: "Oh, by the way, I almost forgot! My wife says the bathroom tap is still dripping and it keeps her awake at night."

"You told me last week, and I gave instructions for someone to be sent."

"No, that was the pipes, and that was fixed. It's the tap now."

"I'll tell Nonat to drop by again."

And they bid each other farewell.

Carmeta was skin and bones; her face was earthen, and her eyes gleamed mysteriously, like a cat's. By day she ate nothing and by night she hardly shut her eyes, and even when she did sleep, the torture intensified: she always dreamed the same dream. Her enemy was the stuff of all her slumbering and waking hours. When she was awake, he pursued her pitilessly, nonstop; no thought was left unsullied by his image or memory, so much so that he finally swept away her whole horizon—sad, gloomy, full of dark storm clouds, but a horizon all the same—and not only that, it was darkened and befogged by other memories and images she adored; of her little nephew and her brother, too . . . Her nostalgia for what she'd lost, initially so vivid and poignant, was now turning rancid and dank like something buried in the remote past; the vision of the sick, hapless man, with his long hair and nails, his flapping pants sagging on a body that was slipping away, only brought tears at odd moments, while his immediate presence sapped her . . . *He*, and *he* alone, reigned within her, controlled all her energy. Because, in the middle of the night . . .

Carmeta, when she was a scrap of a girl, had heard her grandmother and other old dears speak of people possessed by spirits or demons. The malign spirit often appeared to those unfortunate souls in human form . . . if they were men, as a woman, if they were women, as a man . . . It caught them at will, and like it or not, provoked and mocked them; it made them laugh or dance, made them spew fire or mouth obscenities, act foolishly or shamefully . . . She must be in the grips of such a demon, an evil spirit had gotten his claws into her . . . or . . . or what that doctor suspected was true: they were descended from a line of lunatics, and she and her brother were equally crazy . . . And she felt powerless to fight that madness, that terrible avalanche crashing on top of her, sweeping her into the abyss . . . What was the point of refusing to think about Nonat, of refusing even to look at his photo, however much that was the order of the day, if that person, like the voice her brother heard, stayed inside her head, not outside? What was the point of her, a woman who'd previously been only half-heartedly devout, praying fervently the whole day, fasting to the point of screaming from hunger, if still she didn't fall exhausted on her pillow, and heard footsteps around her bed, and suddenly felt herself in his horrible embrace which wouldn't let her go, however furiously she struggled, scratched, or bit? She was crazy, quite crazy, or possessed by a demon; that was all there was to it! How horrific was that?

The following Saturday, when Senyor Ramoneda summoned Nonat to settle their accounts, he said he couldn't leave what he was doing for the moment; Senyor Ramoneda had to pay the other men their wages. The latter were leaving the works when Nonat went over to his boss's desk. Senyor Ramoneda was still busy tidying the paperwork. There was a small heap of coins on the table.

"There you are, Nonat, help yourself . . . I'm too busy adding up . . ."

But Nonat had measured that pile with a swift, hawkish glance, and the idea he'd been incubating for days erupted, leaving his lips wan and pale: "Senyor Ramoneda!" he shouted, his voice choking violently.

The director half-raised his head, alarm lights flashing in his squinting eyes.

"Is that all you will give me?"

"Oh! As . . . that . . ."

He too had blanched, and his words trembled, hung on his lips.

There was something sinister about Nonat's stare and his determination.

"Is that what Rovira earned? I mean, *is it*?"

The director cowered, shrunk back, like the communion wafer when it feels the cutting edge of the knife.

"No . . . obviously . . . but . . ."

"Well, then?"

"As Rovira is still here . . ."

"And what the hell do I care about Rovira?"

"Very well, very well . . . Don't you worry . . . As you didn't complain . . . I imagined, I believed, you were interested in . . . No matter, I'll arrange that now."

He didn't know what to say. Nonat stood at the foot of the desk and waited. An ominous frown knitted his thick, manicured eyebrows. Senyor Ramoneda understood there was no point arguing; he pulled out the drawer, counted out a sum of money, and added it to the pile. It was exactly, to the last cent, what Nonat should earn. Then the wily director looked up at him.

"Count, count and see . . ."

"That won't be necessary." Nonat pocketed the money in one handful and, before turning around to leave, he sternly eyed the man opposite and declared drily. "I warn you, Senyor Ramoneda, don't ever try to pull a fast one on me . . . It will turn out badly. Good day!"

And he left the workshop.

Senyor Ramoneda, who, without warning, had already reduced Rovira's wage, didn't even intend to continue paying him.

Midday on Monday, he summoned his old foreman.

Rovira dragged his feet to his boss's desk. He was a pitiful sight.

He was half his normal weight, his face was drawn, and his flaccid cheeks and chin hung limply like an old hag's. His gaze was blurred, lifeless, and anxious, his lower lip kept turning down as if carrying an unbearable weight; his hands were trembling . . .

The director avoided looking him in the face and took a step forward so as not to have to enter into explanations; he was struck by the level of deterioration when he saw him close up . . . Even so . . .

"Rovira, you say you're not feeling well? You must be tired . . . You need to take time off to rest . . . Then you'll get better . . . I'll allow you to take some early vacation days . . . I'd advise you to stop working . . . But if you can't sit still and do nothing, and want to try your hand . . . you know only too well . . . the workshop will always be open to you . . ."

Rovira knew Senyor Ramoneda and, despite being so dejected, he knew what his boss was getting at.

"He's seen the state I'm in and is getting rid of me . . ." Rovira thought.

He held his head in his hands and squeezed it as if he wanted to make it explode . . . When he got home, he didn't dare tell anyone what had happened. He was aware the haberdashery was spending more than they should on him and needed his wage . . . After lunch, he paid his sister a visit.

"What are you doing here at this time of day? Aren't you at work today?"

"Yes, of course . . . But you know . . . I went to see a client . . . and as I was passing by, I thought I'd drop in."

"How are you feeling?"

"Better . . . I think I'm better."

Carmeta looked up at the sky.

"They'll certify him, they'll certify him one of these days!" she thought, exclaiming with all her soul, "My Lord Jesus Christ! Spare me that heavy cross!!!"

As Rovira went off, he kept turning around and shouting: "Goodbye, my love! Goodbye, my love! Do you hear me, my love? Goodbye!"

"Goodbye, goodbye, my love! But don't keep turning around! You'll trip . . ."

Later, as night was falling, Carmeta, who was going to dinner, heard two quick knocks on the door. It was Angeleta, who walked in, panting breathlessly, deathly pale, eyes fearful, expression distraught . . .

"For heaven's sake, what's wrong, Angeleta?"

"Nothing at all really . . . I mean something . . . but don't you take fright!"

Carmeta howled: "Joanet!" and made to rush downstairs. Angeleta held her by the skirt, ripping her belt.

"Where you going, my dear? Wait here and I'll tell you everything!"

Two other neighbors walked in: Angeleta beckoned to them. Between them they managed to drag her into her bedroom, and as Carmeta had suffered a big attack of nerves, they didn't know where to put her and tried to lay her on her bed. Angeleta hurriedly pulled up the sheets and as she straightened the pillow, a dark, heavy object fell from under it onto the floor. She picked it up and was flabbergasted. It was the photo of Nonat.

Rovira had returned to the works late, at an inconvenient time, yet even so, and although the workers knew he now represented nothing there and had been fired, they welcomed him naturally and let him work at whatever he wanted.

"It's quite obvious," thought Rovira, "they know I'm crazy, and are letting me do whatever I want . . ."

"Strike a light! Easy as pie!" the voice suddenly said inside his head, down low, by his shoulder.

"That's right," thought Rovira, remembering the matches they sold in his village when he went to school. "Strike a light!"

The whole afternoon that voice kept telling him one thing and another, sounding clear and precise, but uttering

incoherent, odd words or half-sentences, as it always did . . .
That voice no longer scared him; rather it had become almost
a familiar friend he found amusing and vaguely soothing.

At the end of the day, he asked the bastard: "You coming,
Nonat?"

"No, Rovira, I've still got work to finish."

"Really?" he answered, as if he couldn't decide what to do.

"Yes, lots."

"Well, good night to you then."

"Good night."

"Good night, good night, good night," the sick man repeated as he walked off.

Two other workers behind him couldn't stop laughing.

"When he gets going, the poor man . . ."

"Yes, what an unlucky fellow," said another wistfully.

"So right! He used to be the salt of the earth!"

Rovira walked out of the factory and away from his workmates. Slowly, dragging his feet, he kept crossing the street
though it wasn't his usual way home. Suddenly he felt someone yank him so sharply, he almost fell backward. And as the
tram hurtled past his nose, blasting his face with a shower
of cold air mixed with snatches of obscenities, an angry gentleman, eyes bulging from their sockets, gesticulated and
screamed at him: "You idiot! You fool! Is that any way to walk
down the street? If you want to jaywalk, join a procession!"
and turning to the bystanders gathering around, he added, by
way of explaining his outburst: "Look, I'm still shaking! If I
hadn't grabbed him, he'd have been on the rails, even though
the poor driver was honking frantically . . . And if there's a

disaster, the trams get all the blame. These people should be garroted. He gave me a real fright!"

Rovira looked down and silently moved away from the bystanders, who kept exchanging opinions, and, as if he was half-blind, he continued down the street by the rails . . . A quarter of an hour later, he looked up, glanced all around, then back . . . Another iron beast was galloping toward him . . . He waited, and when it was so close the driver would be unable to brake, he stood astride the rails and faced it. A scream arose from heaven knows where, drowning out all other sounds in the city twilight, and there was a somber judder in an earth-quake of metal as the tram carriages shot past like an arrow.

There was a horrendous uproar. Angry bystanders stoned the tram, smashed all the windows, overturned the carriages, attacked those in charge, who were forced to flee as fast as they could; in other words, there was one hell of a riot. In vain, the gentleman who'd first recognized the suicide and now understood the motive behind Rovira's previous deaf-ness and self-absorption, tried to remove any blame from the fleeing tram employees and explain what had happened. But the people in the street were beside themselves, refused to listen, and talked of lynching those individuals, of setting fire to the innocent instrument of homicide and everything con-nected . . . Until a contingent of police arrived and cordoned off the accident site.

Poor Rovira had died in the act, even though his flesh went on shaking and quivering for several minutes. The tre-mendous crash had spun him around, turned him over like an omelet . . . The entire convoy had run over his body . . . His legs had been broken, one shoulder ripped from his torso, and his head lay open like a pomegranate, part of his brain spilling over a strut of track.

Someone brought brown paper from a nearby bakery and used it to cover the steaming, bleeding heap of flesh and hide it from the sight of the wild, fearful, nosey crowd until the duty magistrate arrived . . .

In local pharmacies they continued to revive a number of women who had fainted.

Part Four

El Senyoret had gone upstairs to doll up before going for dinner—not to The Father-in-Law's, but to the Mallorquina, where he often dined before going to the opera. One of the senses he'd taken time to refine was taste. The lure of all other forms of sophistication had preceded a gourmet palate, but, once he'd tested it and grasped the difference between cuisine that was ordinary and cuisine that wasn't, between young or blended wine and vintage, his demanding new aptitude became his new must-have, and from then on, however impoverished his purse, he fled slices of smelly cod or stringy hake with peas—and, most of all, the loud guffaws, vociferous squabbles, rough earthenware dishes, stench of cheap oil, tobacco, and rabble, the waiter's rudeness and the filthy rag used to clean tables and glasses, the periodic, philharmonic appearances of the cuckoo above the clock, and everything else that characterized the humble, easy-going place that was The Father-in-Law's.

He'd just placed his overcoat over his arm—no longer that baggy, unfashionable English cut, but a somber item in the latest style with a lush, shiny, black satin lining—when his landlady's knuckles quietly rapped on his door and she informed him that a gentleman was asking for him.

"For me?" And mildly surprised because he never had visitors, Nonat went into the passageway. He recognized Rovira's little eighteen-year-old brother-in-law, standing there cap in hand, and pale as a wax figure in the dim glow from the gas light.

"Senyor Nonat!" the youth exclaimed the second he saw him, holding out his arms as if seeking help.

Nonat was taken aback.

"Hullo, Ricardet! What brings you here?"

"But . . . haven't you heard? You haven't?"

His voice strained and faltered; he couldn't get a word out.

"Not a word! Do tell me what . . ."

"I've come straight from the restaurant . . . Mama . . . come with me now, I beg you."

"But tell me . . ."

The youth told Nonat in bursts as best he could, in the end begging him to accompany him home, where everyone was at their wit's end and couldn't think what to do.

"All right!" Nonat replied brusquely. He took the key to the apartment and they left. On the way his companion gave him the terrible news in more snatches.

Rovira hadn't come back and it was late; first they thought he must be at work, then they thought he'd had a bad turn. When night fell and he still hadn't returned, they were sure something awful had happened. Even so, his mother-in-law had given them hope. They hadn't been able to convince Rovira to go to the barber for a shave for two weeks, and when his mother-in-law had insisted the previous day, he'd answered her rudely: "I'll go tomorrow . . . tomorrow." So, no doubt, he must have remembered and gone for a haircut by himself? They'd rushed to the barber's, but with no luck, then to the workshop, and found none there either; everything was closed and shuttered, and a local they'd anxiously questioned clearly remembered that Rovira had left with all the other workers . . . They were about to go to the Town Hall when they heard people say there'd been a riot on Carrer Balmes . . .

The older lad had rushed there, his heart racing . . .

At the moment he arrived the police were turning the body over . . .

"What? Was he dead? Not a breath of life?" Nonat asked.

"I'm afraid so, the poor fellow! I didn't see him, but my brother said it was horrible . . ."

"Let's go and see," the bastard responded.

"But . . . Mama asked me to . . ."

"Later. Let's go there first."

And Nonat strode off.

They had to elbow their way through the heaving crowds that packed most of the street, and zigzag to dodge carriages that had been turned upside down. In a new wave of vengeful fury, the crowd had wrought real damage; a gang of students had appeared on their way to night classes; there was a smell of oil, a dozen matches were lit, they set light to several newspapers, and soon tongues of flames were licking the derailed tram. More police, municipal constabulary, and soldiers arrived and extinguished the fire. The forces of order were stoned and hissed; they issued warnings and threatened to charge, it looked as if it might become a full-scale battle, but finally the duty magistrate arrived.

"Where's the body?" Nonat asked a bunch of dispersing onlookers.

"Look there, they're carrying it away."

A hundred yards up the street, a lugubrious contingent of half a dozen shadows was walking on both sides of a stretcher, preceded and followed by the flickering light of torches. In that glimmering light, despite the huddles of people and dull, intermittent buzz of fresh chitchat, the whole street seemed dark, deserted, and mysterious as a graveyard.

Nonat saw to everything and spared the haberdashery folk the worst worries.

The body had been identified thanks to Pepita's brother, but it was Nonat who spontaneously appeared before the magistrate to clarify the circumstances leading to the disaster. He explained he was the director of Casa Ramoneda, in the metal trade, and that Rovira was one of the workers under his orders; that Rovira had lost his mind, was a vacant presence, though the firm had kept in consideration the good work he'd done on its behalf; for days everyone had noted a marked deterioration in his health, work rate, and appearance; that very afternoon Rovira had drifted in very late, hadn't lifted a finger, and when he left, he'd kept repeating his goodbyes in an unusually insistent way, as if wanting to draw their attention to them, although Nonat and the others hadn't taken any notice, as they knew what his mental state was; it was only now, when he thought about it . . .

When the judge asked, Nonat declared the dead man was a fine, upstanding character, esteemed by the owner, his workmates, family, and all acquaintances . . . That, to the best of his knowledge, Rovira had never experienced any problems before the death of his son—the sole factor to which everyone attributed his loss of reason—that he was an entirely placid madman and Nonat had never suspected any suicidal tendencies, for if he had, he'd have accompanied Rovira home that night, as he'd done so often before . . .

When he'd finished with the magistrate, the bastard went to the haberdashery. Shop, rear-of-shop, and upstairs were as crammed with people as Carrer Balmes because all their acquaintances had rushed there the moment the sad news leaked out.

When they saw the well-dressed, sophisticated Nonat, those who didn't know him respectfully parted to let him pass, thinking he must be an official functionary, and those who did know him led him straight into the dining room, where most of the family had gathered. As soon as he appeared, numerous arms stretched out toward him, and the haberdasher, coming out of a bedroom, hugged him effusively, as she would a son . . .

"Ay, Nonat! Look at the misery inflicted on us! And saddest of all now, our daughter . . . she has gone mad too . . . Come in and see for yourself."

And, whether he liked it or not, she made him go into what used to be poor Rovira's bedroom, where the widow, after suffering various attacks, was reclined on a rocking chair, sobbing and convulsing. Her skin, the color of flour, her eyes, bulging and red as rosebuds, and her hair, a flaxen mess, made her look extremely peculiar, as if it was merely a disguise, a cardboard mask and wig made of bits of cane. In contrast, by her side, her sister-in-law, horribly silent, hermetically sealed in her profoundly tragic grief, seemed like a Fate. As Nonat approached her, despite his usual cold reaction, he felt the sight of her send an icy shiver of terror down his spine. She was awful to behold, dreadfully, indescribably ugly, and her stare was deep, dark, and glowering, as if coming from far away, from mysterious barren wastes, from macabre dreams, it looked inhuman, the cowardly, fleeting glower of a dangerous beast that scents distant peril. By her side, Angeleta, her neighbor, seemed to lend a mantel of ingenuous compassion amid the vacuum created by the general indifference of Tomaset's friends, who were exclusively intent on soothing Pepita.

Nonat said a few polite words to both women in that measured, self-possessed tone he maintained in all situations, and his words, though they expressed nothing special, brought great relief to all and sundry because *he* said them, a luminous element to brighten the anxiety-ridden gloom. Then they talked to the family about what must be readied for the following day. Suddenly, Nonat glanced at his watch: *I could still catch the last act*, he thought, adding out loud: "Now, all of you, get some rest. You're all exhausted, and if you spend the night like this, you won't be able to cope tomorrow . . ."

As if he'd issued an order that brooked no appeal, everybody stood up and, without protest, started to say goodbye. Only two of Pepita's friends insisted on staying, all the same, to keep her company.

Carmeta had also stood up; she was going to sleep at Angeleta's.

"You're walking alone at this time of night?" someone asked.

"I'll accompany you . . ." answered Nonat quietly.

The glower of the dangerous beast sunk even deeper into her bowed head.

As they walked, Angeleta chattered away, nervously and emotionally, about how one had to accept the happy and sorrowful moments in life, because everything is "take it or leave it," like on a stage set . . .

Nonat listened to her absentmindedly, not hearing a word, nodding now and then as if agreeing to wisdom as commonplace and ancient as walking.

Carmeta kept her lips sealed the whole time, and only said a curt goodnight to Nonat when he left them by the door to their house.

A new nail had been hammered deep into her heart and mind.

You asked God to spare you the cross of seeing your brother locked up, and you *have* been spared that blow! Truly, you have!

Arriving late to the opera gave Nonat a pleasant thrill. When he was less *au fait* with those things, he had been irritated by banging doors or stumbling people blatantly faking apologies, but of late he'd enjoyed that blasé attitude, that scorn for an only too familiar spectacle, that lordly lack of a need to scour the princely barrel . . . He didn't go to the opera late of his own accord because, like it or not, he felt very impatient, and besides, he thought doing so without good reason was the height of affectation, but considering the events of the day, he could give himself those airs without making a ridiculous fuss, and was delighted.

He walked in casually past the flunkey who had run to open the door for him, and contentedly surveyed his elegant profile—now so familiar—as he walked past the mirror.

When he appeared in the dress-circle, his leather shoes squeaked slightly, pleasantly, like everyone's in the house, and lots of ladies in private boxes turned their heads to look at him. It wasn't the first time they'd done that; he often felt he was being spied on by eyes lurking behind opera glasses, as if he were just one more lady, and moreover, like one more lady feeling herself *under observation*, he gorged on that delicious homage—accompanied by various flights of fancy—of which he was the object. As he saw his seat was occupied, he sat in the first empty one he could find. He suddenly heard people conversing about him; seemingly above his head, perfectly audible whispers a few yards away—also the established custom of the house—voicing these words in Spanish:

"But do tell me, Pepe, who *is* that fellow who just arrived?"

"I have no idea . . ."

"Good God! It's as if he were an elf! I ask everyone and nobody can tell me . . . He landed here as if he'd rained down from heaven, and no one has ever seen him talking to a soul . . ."

"He looks like a parakeet . . ."

"What do you mean a 'parakeet'?"

"Sorry. I meant a South American. I always call people from there parakeets . . ."

The inquisitive lady chuckled throatily, and went on: "Yes, he could very well be foreign . . . He looks to be . . . Though I'd say Portuguese rather than South American . . ."

"They're all the same . . ."

"I see somewhat of a resemblance to Delmiro . . ."

"To Febrer? So there you are, I was right! He's Chilean, or Peruvian, or God knows what from across the pond . . ."

A loud, defiant hiss halted their exchange, and Nonat waited a while before discreetly inspecting the whisperers. Four people were sitting in a box right behind him: on one side a young courting couple, with eyes and feelings only for themselves, and on the other, an elderly man and an astounding mound of flesh who'd attracted Nonat's gaze more than once. She was a lady one imagined must be a widow, a great beauty now flaking and disintegrating from age, but with a dewlap that was still relatively fetching, monkey-eyes a cunning blue, and neck, shoulders, and back worthy of Rubens's brush, splendidly exposed by the swooping décolleté of an olive-green velvet bodice to hearten jaded, ogling males. That old couple were undoubtedly the garrulous pair who'd spoken about him, and immediately Nonatus felt a current of sympathy flow from his heart toward the faded beauty who'd found him foreign, and contemptuous repugnance toward the old skunk who'd labeled him a parakeet . . .

Movement started in the boxes where there tended to be early leavers, noise in passageways to distract the already lax attention of those who'd stayed on.

The young man in Nonat's seat got up, and walked silently toward the exit.

The lady's voice from behind Nonat asked hurriedly in Spanish: "Look at him, Pepe . . . What a straight back . . . ! Compare him to the other fellow when he leaves . . ."

The young man walked past, greeting the occupants of the box with a smile and a wave, and Nonat stared hard at him, intensely fascinated.

Had she been referring to *him*? Was Nonat like that other young man? He was devastated.

His tailored evening costume sheathed a statuesque body that was well-proportioned and well-hewn, full of feline energy and agility, but also molded by natural grace, nourished by distinction he'd learned in social circles.

Suddenly Nonat felt a stabbing pain in his heart. He'd now drawn comparisons with beady, cobweb-free eyes. That man was younger than he, more elegant, more gentlemanly, wore nothing fake, as if everything you saw was real and quite natural. He sunk the nails of one hand into the back of the other.

Things never changed! Never! Everyone was legal, of sound stock, except for himself! He always bore the stain of a mongrel, his name, blood, soul, and social situation all blighted! Whether he liked it or not, he was always the child of a fraud, perhaps of a servant girl, perhaps of a . . . when someone asked, like that lady: Who was *he*? They could say "who" of everybody but himself, Nonat . . . Everybody, except himself, had a father behind him, with proven origins and status . . . It would be extraordinary if someone came out with the truth: "He's a blacksmith! A damned bastard to boot!"

What would the women with the opera glasses think of him then? What shock, horror, and jeering there would be! No, he would always be the intruder, wherever and whatever the occasion. "I curse you, my father, a father still shrouded in mystery. The day I find you, I will repay humiliation with humiliation, shame with shame, cruelty with cruelty."

Feeling venomous, rent by hatred, and wanting all that, he stayed in his seat and didn't move until the lady in the box had left to deprive her and her laughing cavalier of a comparison he intuited would not be to his advantage.

Clenching his jaws and brooding under his dark brow, he walked into the Mallorquina and ordered supper. He'd not eaten since midday, but the hunger that had been teasing and turning his innards for an hour in a normal, youthful way seemed trapped under an avalanche of stones that had killed it dead. The dishes he'd so pleasurably savored on previous nights now tasted bitter, of bile, the salt of tears and pale gray ash . . .

Before getting into bed, he wrenched his shirt open in front of the mirror. The slender blue cross rested on the silky skin of his chest like a protective shield; the Montserrat medallion hung alongside on the blue cord, like a seal on noble parchment. Why had they branded him if they intended to throw him out? Why perpetuate the stigma alongside dashed expectations?

He grabbed the medallion and pulled hard; the cord scored his flesh, like the blade of a dagger, but didn't yield. Doubly driven by grief and blind rage, he pulled furiously again— the cord snapped and the medallion clattered to the floor; he stamped on it. He'd started wearing that medallion a long time ago in a moment of superstition, as if appealing to fate to magically attract the millionaire who'd given him life and insist he recognize his offspring.

The magistrate had summoned relatives, Senyor Ramoneda, colleagues . . . Everyone agreed on the main points: that the deceased was mad, but honorable and much liked; his sister described his last visit, which supported the notion of suicide; a tavern barman related how the previous evening he'd seen a stranger pull him off the track and what that gentleman had said. Senyor Ramoneda said nothing about sacking the poor lunatic, and as he'd not mentioned it to anyone, his extreme measure remained occluded.

The outcome was as clear as running water, and it seemed a waste of time to look for needles in a haystack. Nevertheless, before declaring the end of his enquiry, the magistrate called Nonat back.

When Nonat was opposite him, he stared at him hard and continued his interrogation in Spanish:

"Yesterday you said the deceased was a worker under your orders."

"Yes, señor."

"But the other workers said quite the opposite . . . They stated you were a mere journeyman like them, and the suicide, on the contrary, was the foreman in the shop, and, consequently, your boss . . ."

Nonat felt his face go as red as a rose.

The magistrate's observation was doubly wounding: because it hurt his vanity—which was beginning to expand at speed—and because he'd been caught in the act of mystifying the truth, if not exactly lying. After a moment of confusion and a penetrating stare that—even through spectacle lenses—prompted his rebel instinct and his impulse to protest, he explained in his inept, derisory Spanish—suited to the illiterate character he really was—what had happened: his entry into the shop as an ordinary worker; the leadership status he'd immediately attained; his friendship with Rovira; the latter's illness that made him make one big error after another; the way Nonat had taken care of the poor, sick man because of their friendship, which had led him imperceptibly to assume his role, responsibilities, and duties . . . And he'd been confirmed to the post of foreman he was already carrying out *de facto* only a few days ago . . .

The magistrate interjected: "How do you explain the fact that the other workers said quite the opposite?"

Nonat was again stung by the magistrate's insistence and replied curtly that the change hadn't been officially notified to them, and he wasn't sure why. That was down to the owner . . . He'd been advised to say nothing to Rovira, and, as he obeyed orders, he'd said nothing.

"And why do you think the owner acted in such a way?"

Nonat hesitated . . . "He perhaps wished to avoid upsetting the madman by making his dismissal public knowledge . . . And perhaps to avoid provoking the other workers' envy . . . He knew for a fact what he'd said and that sufficed."

He adopted a prickly tone, slightly tempered by the great difficulty he encountered when speaking a foreign language, and now looked the magistrate in the eye, quietly defiant, as if to say: *That's how it was if you want to believe me, and if not, too bad* . . .

He was so used to being treated effusively and openly that the judge's impenetrable reserve and suspicious, blank face angered him like an affront he didn't deserve. If he'd had to spend any time in the judge's presence, he probably wouldn't have tolerated it and would have expressed his outrage. Luckily, the judge seemed satisfied by his explanation and waved to him to leave, though his confident, unflinching stare stayed with Nonat until he left his office, and even hovered there for a lengthy minute in the open doorway. Then the magistrate slowly picked up a sheet of paper, thought for a moment, and, with the end of his pen between his teeth, scribbled three or four words.

When Nonat returned to his bedroom, he saw that his landlady had retrieved the medallion from the floor and placed it on his bedside table; he grabbed it, tied a knot in the broken cord, and humbly hung it around his neck.

If I'd have worn it, he thought, the magistrate wouldn't have given me such a hard time.

He thought the medallion, like the coin from his boss in Girona, was an amulet protecting him against all harm.

Rovira's death left disaster in its wake: economic collapse for the haberdashery; red-faced exasperation and spasms for Pepita; total despair for Carmeta.

"What do you intend to do now?" her neighbor had asked.

"What do you expect me, a poor wretch, to do if I have neither trade nor income? I can never forgive my parents for what they've done to me . . ." Tears streamed down the face of the wretched spinster, who'd been left flat broke with no help. "They are the ones to blame if my only solution is to go into service night and day, or leave the apartment, rent it out, and go selling wares from door to door . . . But, before I decide anything, I must go and see my cousin Pepa."

Cousin Pepa had been the housekeeper of one Mossèn Vicenç Canalies, a stipendiary of Santa Maria del Mar, and had lived with him in the vicinity of the parish for many years. The stipendiary had saved a lot of money; they were both economical people and survived on the bare minimum, so they were soon able to buy government bonds. When they accumulated a good number, they felt it wasn't a good idea to put all their capital into paper. "God save us from a fire, a burglar, an earthquake, a *revolation* . . . You never know!" and they bought property: a house in El Clot, land in Montjuïc . . . And to ensure that in the future relatives or third parties couldn't make claims, they bought those properties in Pepa's name; later, a busy bee by nature and with little to fill her time, Pepa established a small shop in an entranceway in partnership with a bankrupt silversmith, as well as, on a daily percentage, a booth for bootblacks run by a bright choirboy who helped Mossèn Vicenç every day at mass. When the latter, who was much older, surrendered his soul to God, the Vicar's Pepa—as she was dubbed by those who'd known her when she entered his service—or Senyora Pepa Canalies—as she was addressed more respectfully and obsequiously by those who'd only dealt with her after she became established—could have the last laugh at those who had laughed at her. She only had one source of sorrow: being lonely as an owl night and day, since fear of being robbed wouldn't allow her to let anyone stay in her house. That was why she was always asking Carmeta Rovira to come and see her, and when Carmeta spent five days with her after little Octavi's death, she would have been in wonderland if Carmeta had been a little more communicative. When the second misfortune led Carmeta back to her house as a safe harbor, Pepa was almost happy and repeated Angeleta's question: "So what will you do now?"

When she heard what her cousin was planning, she exploded indignantly: "You must be joking! You should forget all that! Do you know what would be best for you? Come and live with me, and we'll share the little I have and the housework like good sisters . . ."

Her generous proposal was prompted by the most selfish calculations that had ever visited the brain of Mossèn Vicenç's former housekeeper.

Carmeta was past the marrying age, so Pepa could count on her forever; they were more or less the same age, and she wouldn't hope Pepa died first so she could inherit; she was a first-class toiler and would serve as her maid at a cost of little more than upkeep; since she had no other relative or heir, she would treat Pepa well so as not to lose her, and she wouldn't take things from the house to give to people who came and went . . .

Carmeta burst into tears at that providential offer of help and was so grateful she was reduced to silence.

She needed to go to San Gervasi to sort out the apartment with the haberdashers. The two cousins paid them a visit the following day. The haberdasher, who could be a cold fish, had anticipated trouble from Carmeta, and was immediately soothed when she heard of the ex-housekeeper's solution, and, putting on her usual "friendly local shopkeeper" front, she kindly accompanied them upstairs where Pepita was still corralled with her girlfriends. Pepita hadn't recognized the visitors, but the moment her mother introduced them, she quickly stood up and, as if prey to a new surge of sorrow, hugged her sister-in-law and sobbed her heart out.

"Ay, Carmeta! Ay, Carmeta!"

Her sobs choked her, her legs wobbled, she put her head on Carmeta's shoulder . . .

Carmeta was astounded because Pepita wasn't usually very emotional, least of all with her.

They soothed her as much as they could, and Carmeta told her what had brought them there. However, as they began, the widow realized what it was all about and interjected: "The apartment? Don't worry, you can have it all! The whole lot! We *are* sisters, when all is said and done . . . !"

The haberdasher rolled her eyes. Carmeta objected meekly: "No, I can manage on very little . . ."

"No, lock, stock, and barrel, it's yours . . . You need it more than I do . . . I've got Mama and Papa . . ."

And driven by a sudden rush of generosity, like a simpleton, she refused to hear another word.

In a sweat, the haberdasher finally suggested that Carmeta would have no need of certain things like, for example, the armoire with a mirror and the piano, whereas . . . (her voice faded and melted away, though her thoughts were clear enough inside her brain, which oozed logic and good sense) . . . "when Pepita remarries they'll do her nicely, particularly since we won't be in a position to buy new ones . . ."

Carmeta seemed to understand and exchanged knowing glances with the haberdasher, and muttered: "Yes, senyora, quite right . . . Don't worry, I'll leave them and anything else you can think of . . ."

She knew only too well that almost everything in her brother's apartment had been paid for by the haberdashery, and would have thought it wrong to lay claim to it.

They agreed to stop renting the apartment immediately and that Carmeta would take to El Clot any furniture they gave her, and when the two cousins stood up to leave, Pepita made them promise on the spot to visit her and keep her company often, more than often.

"Because I'll only leave home to go to the cemetery, you see? Everything else would be too depressing . . ."

And she burst into floods of tears again.

Someone said, "It all had to pass, life is life, and it is good to remember those departing, but we must also think of those who are still with us," etc., but when Pepita insisted on something, it was futile to try to budge her. And as from the very first she'd decided to be an inconsolable widow, she performed her role to the full, much to the disgust of her anxious mother, who had other ideas.

At the time of the misfortune, the moment they notified her of her son-in-law's death, a name and an image had appeared, almost automatically, before her eyes, embodying long, recondite plotting on her part. Nonat! That handsome, courteous young man, at once a gentleman *and* a hard worker, had always stolen her heart. True enough, he was currently spending more than he ought on pretty baubles, but that would change when he had other obligations . . . He was always so sensible and considerate, and always did what he said he would do! And the entranced mother mentally imagined the fine couple her pretty, refined daughter and the equally refined, accomplished Nonat would make, while calculating the support that a second son-in-law would give to all of them . . .

In keeping with these ideas, she did whatever she could to keep the bastard nearby despite the severance of their original bond, and to diplomatically point her daughter's mind in his direction. But Pepita understood nothing about diplomacy and was in turn hatching her own plans, little by little.

"I want a plain, tight-fitting dress with a smooth finish and no other feature apart from a row of buttons and lower hem of mourning crepe . . . So all can clearly see it's a widow's dress . . ." she'd told the dressmaker. Tucked into that garment and wrapped in a fetching, capacious black mantilla that enhanced the whiteness of her face and her flaxen hair and endowed her, thanks to the material's silken rustle and subtle transparencies, with the graceful allure of a black Tanagra figurine, Pepita would only leave home on the occasional morning to go to Mass, where she received compliments from the neighbors, and on the occasional afternoon to go the cemetery.

She simply took what she wanted from the till, went to the nearest florist's and bought a bunch of flowers, and, embracing her sheaf of colors, walked off to pay her respects to her late husband.

That new expenditure worried the haberdashers, but they dared not say a word. Their lass was so pretty in her widow's weeds, and it was all so natural and respectable. Besides, as she said: "The least a woman who has lost her husband can do is take flowers to his grave!"

Only once was her mother proud of Pepita's attitude. It was a mid-week holiday and she had invited Nonat for coffee. El Senyoret arrived, smart and suave as usual. They drank their coffees, and, as they were finishing, Pepita announced that she was going to get dressed without offering a word of explanation.

As soon as she left the dining room, the haberdasher exclaimed mournfully: "Ay, Lord! This child of mine will die on me after poor Joan, may he rest in heaven! Her heart is so very loving!"

The whole family chimed in to praise Pepita's qualities, and their guest had no choice but to nod politely, when he was suddenly surprised by the haberdasher's request: for him to accompany her daughter to the cemetery.

"It greatly distresses me when she goes by herself on days like this, when the streets are so packed . . . It's not for me to say, but she looks so attractive, and there are so many rascals around with no respect for what's sacrosanct!"

Nonat was seething, but was obliged to accompany Pepita: first to the florist's—and to pay for the flowers, naturally—and then to the cemetery.

The excited haberdasher ran to spy on them from behind the shutters, and the passersby they met along the street kept looking back and admiring the well-matched couple; nevertheless, that whole afternoon was one of the most boring the tradesman had ever experienced, and, as a result, he conceived a new mania: a mania against Pepita and her simpering ways, a mania against the folk at the haberdashers for being so pathetic, and a mania, most of all, against the haberdasher herself for her hypocritical wheedling and shameless, obvious attempts to pair him off with her daughter. To round off his disgust, a last-minute insult put the seal on an afternoon of almost total mortification: the sudden, brief, luminous sighting of the young man from the Liceu who, according to that loquacious lady, was similar to himself. He came riding along Passeig de Gràcia with a few other youngbloods, and was distinguished by his understated swagger.

The Ramoneda engineering enterprise had experienced swift expansion under the new manager's leadership. Even so, the owner didn't seem happy or satisfied. He had been very ill, and his doctor had forbidden any involvement with the business for a time. He couldn't even go down to the workshop, and when he was at last allowed to do so, everybody found him to be sallower and more sunken-cheeked than before— which beggared belief—and his gaze was so somber it seemed a wick must be smoldering deep in his eye sockets. His attitude appeared to have changed, too. The sullen, taciturn fellow, always crouched behind his glass-paned partition, had become prickly and fretful, walking nonstop from this side to that, rummaging around, making notes in his pocketbook, asking his workers pointed questions, but he did so particularly when Nonat was out or enclosed in his own office in the scrap iron warehouse, because, in Nonat's company, he mostly held his peace and kept his jumpiness in check, as if embarrassed to seem interfering or afraid of upsetting him. In contrast, Nonat grew more assertive by the day, with the aplomb and confidence that come with knowledge and the trust of others; he gave out orders and organized the workshop with almost total independence, increasingly so after the boss's illness had transformed him into the visible head of the firm and placed all the levers of the business in Nonat's hands.

Apart from the boss's bureau, there were two sets of keys for every section in the workshop; Senyor Ramoneda kept one and Nonat the other so they could go freely in and out and without the bother of having to inform each other all the time.

As El Senyoret's workload had recently been considerable on weekdays, he devoted Sunday mornings to putting things into order and distributing the tasks for the coming week.

One Sunday, he entered his office looking particularly anxious.

The previous day, when the boss had paid him, he'd told Nonat on the sly, without looking him in the eye, as usual: "Now I feel a bit better . . . when you are ready, we should review the accounts . . ."

"Whenever you want," replied Nonat, after a slight hesitation. That whole night he seemed to be itching between the sheets.

Senyor Ramoneda was methodical and extremely devout. On holidays he always accompanied his wife and daughters to Mass: Nonat, like all his workforce, was familiar with his routines and had even seen them in church more than once.

Nonat was sure he was safe and was so feverishly absorbed in tidying calculations, invoices, and letters of exchange at the back of the store that he didn't hear the outside door open, nor the one where he was working eased slightly ajar. He'd picked up a smoking habit some time ago, and at that point a blue haze of tobacco smoke was shaping a kind of halo around his head. Suddenly, a dry, searing rasp like the grating of a saw hissed next to him: "You thief!!! I've caught you!!!"

As if a clockwork spring had violently propelled him from his chair, Nonat was on his feet and face-to-face with his boss. His face was contorted, his eyes panic-stricken, his lips pale and his mustache stiff and erect like a brush.

Senyor Ramoneda, leaning forward and clenching his fists like a boxer, seemed about to attack him; he was laughing sinisterly.

"Where did you get that cigarette holder, you hoodlum? Where?"

The amber holder slipped from Nonat's rigid, gaping mouth, as if by magic. The boss picked it up; his voice lashed like the crack of a whip: "It's Pagès's holder . . . and he was in such a rush to get rid of his maid!"

Nonat felt that everything was spinning, as if he were drunk: he steadied himself instinctively on the table, blinked, swallowed . . . Senyor Ramoneda's sarcasm was stinging him, somewhere, in a mysterious spot in his guts, like a bunch of simultaneous needle pricks.

"So that's how you paid for your silks and finery, your binges and opera-going!"

The holder with its diamond and ruby clasp shook nonstop in the boss's trembling fingers, like a drop of quicksilver. That restless item was the first thing Nonat saw when he recovered from that thunderbolt. He wiped his icy hand over his brow, now white as snow; the stiff hairs of his mustache began to droop and soften, but his heart raced like a galloping horse and his flexed facial muscles maintained the terrifying rictus of a hanged man.

Senyor Ramoneda was still laughing, his squint-eye stirring in its dark hollow, venomous as a viper.

"Why shouldn't we spend and cavort! While others are paying, why not? Collecting debts and staying in debt! Selling and embezzling hand over fist!"

Nonat's face soon regained its serenity, his mustache became silken and flexible again, though his features communicated a singular iciness, a superhuman stillness, as if sculpted in marble.

"What a thief! Worse than a thief! Let's see the accounts! You'll go to prison! To pris . . ."

He couldn't finish his sentence. He was flung on the ground, his back impaled on a pile of iron hoops, a heavy weight on his chest, fingers tightening around his throat . . .

Gritting his teeth, Nonat was spitting words into his face: "Oh, really? Are you going to turn me in? Prove it! Prove it and you are dead! Deader than the dead!"

The shock and attack had left Senyor Ramoneda defenseless. He squirmed, almost suffocated by the knee of oak pinning him down . . . He sunk his nails into his executioner's hands, trying in vain to pull them from his neck. He was an old dodderer; the journeyman's lithe body was equipped with the drive and energy of youth and robust health from a life of hard graft. The struggle was so unequal that the boss sensibly saw he had no choice but to capitulate, and meekly surrendered. When he saw this, El Senyoret relaxed his grip, but still sat astride his accuser, transfixing him with a piercing stare, exclaiming with that haughty contempt he affected when angry as he returned to the matter in hand: "Really! What on earth were you thinking? That I'm the kind of man to allow you to get your way?"

He smiled scornfully; then stood up, straightened his clothes, tidied the strands of hair flopping over his face, now almost completely calm and in control, as if he were by himself and nothing had happened.

Bruised and battered, Senyor Ramoneda also got to his feet: mouth bleeding, lips swollen, the side of his face cut, his sleeve ripped. Cowardly fear lurked deep within his quivering eyes.

And the bastard dictated his conditions: "I will leave . . . as soon as I have somewhere else to go . . . At the end of the day, there is no shortage of bosses . . . If only! But now you know: keep your trap shut, because if you don't, I swear, I'll . . ." and his determined tone left no doubt his threats weren't to be taken lightly.

Senyor Ramoneda felt totally defeated, but even so, he tried to pretend and make his silence count.

"All right . . . I don't want to lose you . . . You're younger . . . Give me back my money and . . ."

Nonat, who was knotting his tie, stopped and looked at his boss askance.

"What's that . . . ?" and sneering, he retorted: "You must be joking . . ."

There was no room to haggle or exact the slightest benefit

from that situation. When he realized this, Senyor Ramoneda suddenly began to shake so violently he couldn't even bring his handkerchief to his face to wipe the blood from the gash caused by the rim of the hoop.

Nonat collected the paperwork, tucked his gold-initialed wallet in his inside pocket, grabbed his walking stick and hat, and, as he was about to leave, issued one last warning: "You know what's what . . . Don't you dare forget it . . . !"

His boss barely registered that threat. He was staggering, feeling queasier than when he'd taken a boat trip around the harbor. After agonizing for five minutes in that unnervingly solitary warehouse, a furious spasm released waves of bile that flooded his stomach.

As a consequence, he had to keep to his bed a further two weeks.

The contractor's cigarette holder, in turn, had rolled across Nonat's office floor and under a pile of scrap metal.

At a crossing of paths in a Pyrenean valley close to the French border, at the beginning of the last century, there was once a dingy tavern much favored by smugglers, passing thieves, spies, conspirators, and armed brigands. That tavern was known as the Four Ways Inn or the Rat Hole—the first, as the name indicated, because of its location, and the second because the place had lots of entrances and exits that suited the shifty, motley crew lodging there, who attacked as much as they were besieged.

Those filthy, flaking walls had witnessed many curious events, but we will only make mention of one that has a direct, if distant, connection to our story.

Just before the Napoleonic epic began, when French society was still in the grips of the revolution's final convulsions, on a cold, raw, midwinter night, the illustrious tavernkeeper heard a quiet tap on the bottom window in the kitchen, where three or four guests had gathered to drink, converse, and warm up by the side of the open hearth wherein the whole trunk of an olive tree spat and crackled.

Assuming it must be discreet news of some deal, to which he was well accustomed, and seeing there was no musket of the law to inspire fear, he lifted the metal catch and opened the window. A whitish gleam in the darkness disappeared. The innkeeper was intrigued, lit a lamp, and, sticking a dagger in his belt and putting a cape over his shoulders, he went out into the night. A man was lying on the ground by the window. The inkeeper stooped down, shone the lamp over the body, and saw a face that was deathly pale, seemingly already dead. Perhaps he was, because the man showed no signs of movement. The innkeeper called to the people inside, and between them they carried the stranger in, but, as they picked him up by his armpits and legs, to their surprise they found a child in diapers in the folds of his overcoat. When they saw him, one of those present, who had just come out of the tavern, Ossuary Flix—a gravedigger from a village in the valley and sometime muleteer, smuggler, or whatever came his way—abruptly stepped back into the shadows.

"He's dead," someone said.

"No, he's been wounded," affirmed the innkeeper, who'd just put his hand on the man's heart, but when he pulled his overcoat aside, he saw bloodstains all over his ridged collar.

They carried the man into the kitchen. He was an adult, age indefinable, well dressed, unshaven, and a city-dweller. He had been stabbed twice, and the gashes flowered like two dark roses of clotted blood in the middle of his chest. As he warmed up, he regained consciousness, looked hazily around, and uttered a few words . . . Nobody understood him, and they realized he was from foreign parts. The innkeeper put a glass of wine to his lips, which the man swallowed with difficulty. Then he started speaking again, patted his coat, and looked at their faces in terror . . . They gathered he was asking to see the child, and the innkeeper's wife, who was holding him by the fireside, showed him the babe. The wounded man calmed down and, seeing nobody understood him, reinforced his words with gestures, until he made them vaguely understand he'd come from afar, fleeing through the mountains on horseback . . . He pointed to the child, indicating with his open hand that of the five members of his family, five, had been beheaded and only that hapless baby had survived; that the baby was high up, very high up, and he himself, low, very low—a servant? a butler? they weren't certain—that he had been carrying a lot of money in his belt, his pockets, and his steed's saddle-bags . . . He had met a man on the track, they had been riding together when, suddenly, slash, slash, that fellow had stabbed him twice, and he'd collapsed to the ground and lost consciousness . . . When he came around, his horse was gone, his belt was gone, and his pockets were empty, though the child was still alive at his side, and he'd taken the babe in his arms and dragged himself slowly across the mountain, he didn't know for how long . . . Finally, when he had hardly any strength left, he'd seen the light of the tavern, and he wanted something now, before he died . . .

"*Prêtre . . . prêtre . . .*" he mouthed painfully, joining his hands in prayer, repeating three or four more words that were always the same and that none of them understood . . .

"He's asking to confess," said the innkeeper.

The foreigner felt instinctively that he'd been understood and nodded vigorously.

The innkeeper scratched an ear.

"Ah! The Rectory is a long way, and at this time of night . . ."

The wounded man's eyes looked into his, imploring yet again.

Ossuary Flix, who was standing behind everyone, tapped the innkeeper on the back and gestured to him. The innkeeper came over.

"I'm going home . . . Do you want me to call in at the Rectory?"

That was agreed. Flix went out to the stable and saddled his horse—a young, powerful thoroughbred, exhausted and covered in flakey scabs like dried foam—and rode off immediately, without returning to the kitchen or saying a word to anyone.

Hours went by and, as the priest didn't appear and the wounded man's strength was slipping away, as he suffered one relapse after another, they sent word again to the Rectory when day broke and learned that nobody had seen Flix or received any instruction from him; Flix's family knew nothing of his whereabouts, and his face was never seen again in the vicinity.

By the time the Rector arrived at the Rat House, carrying Our Lord, the foreigner had already surrendered his soul to God, minutes before. Feeling death was nigh, that he was in his last throes, and not finding a living soul to tell of the enigmatic world he was carrying within, he made a supreme effort and scrawled a few strange words with a burnt branch from the fire on the sooty wall of the kitchen, and, as he wrote those words, he repeatedly pointed to the child, as if wanting to indicate they were closely related, then flipped over and died.

They worked out that those scribbled, distorted, almost unintelligible letters read: *Laurent Philippe de Grisau . . .*

The priest assumed it was the child's name, and christened him there and then. The innkeeper would have willingly adopted him, but as his own wife was about to give birth, he didn't want to deprive his yet-to-be-born baby of any rights by keeping the bereft stray in his home. His wife gave birth to a girl, time passed, and that lass married Felipó Grisau— as written in Catalan—and she and her husband became the owners of the establishment that, from then on, was not only the Four Ways Inn or the Rat House, but also Frenchy's, which was what Felipó, the French lad, was called.

In turn, Frenchy now had two sons of his own, one of whom was working in a Barcelona tavern the family had owned ever since the priest who had rebaptized Frenchy gave him a relatively large amount of money and a miniature framed by a line of pearls. The priest had received these things, so he told Frenchy, in the secrecy of the confessional, from a dying man who declared he had been the author of the two stabs that took the life of the unknown foreigner. and described in gory detail how he had committed the deed. He had met the foreigner by chance in the mountains, offered to act as his guide and porter, and, the moment the opportunity presented itself, his fingers acted, intending to rob him. Which is what he did: when he saw the foreigner lying at his feet, thinking he was dead, he carefully removed everything the man was carrying, and, riding his victim's white steed, fled the scene of the crime. He inspected his booty in a remote spot in the mountains. There was a large number of jewels, lots of silver and gold coins, and a bundle of papers. Thanks to a good fire, those were soon hot ash: he then sold the horse and went to Algiers. He had only returned to his land to deposit his bones and reclaim what was left of the stolen fortune: a handful of coins and that miniature, which a strange scruple of conscience had led him to keep "in case it was the portrait of Frenchy's mother." In the small, shiny oval, a delicately feminine brush had painted the lovely head of a young lady, with a haughty hairdo and powdered white . . . A beautiful head that had every similarity and feature of a Marie Antoinette, as drawn by a Vigée Le Brun . . .

With the money that had rained down from the heavens, Felipó Grisau, alias Frenchy, had refurbished the crumbling tavern he was to bequeath to his heir, and purchased a tavern in Barcelona where the second was to serve, thus putting both sons on the right road.

From this second son, Grisau the innkeeper, came another Grisau, a silversmith, who one day caught the eye of Mossèn Vicenç's old biddy, Pepa.

When we made his acquaintance, Senyor Benet Grisau, the foreigner's grandson, must have been in his sixties, and was tall and stout, though worn down by a long, poverty-stricken and disorderly life. He was round-shouldered, bleary-eyed, and his heavy legs were pitted with sores. He had been a redhead in his youth, but now the meager St Anthony's crown encircling his head was completely white; white too were the four, spikey tufts crossing his rubbery cheeks, which were flaccid and puffy, a peculiar, sickly fat, enameled with red, herpetic stains and constellations of dark lumps scattered around like chaff. His red nose was bulbous, striated with purple veins full of chilblains or blackheads in winter and transparent, crystalline dew in summer. He always wore thick woolen shoes and a yellow weave jacket with baggy pockets, and when nobody was looking he'd stick the stub of the extinguished cigar that he always carried between his teeth up his right nostril in order to smell the strong tobacco more intensely, which gave him huge pleasure . . . Short-sighted and uptight by nature, his hearing was poor and he didn't liven up unless a woman walked by.

His fondness for a bit of skirt had been his ruination. The principal craftsman in a renowned jeweler's shop, his future would have been guaranteed if his liaisons with women of every stripe hadn't led him to commit his first crime: siphoning off precious stones that, however stealthily done, had finally been discovered because he tried his luck too often—not in any way that could land him in court, but flagrantly enough for him to be fired ignominiously and prevented from joining any other high-class establishment.

From then on he lived as best he could, with ups and

downs, until he became embroiled with others in a trial over counterfeit money, and though he was absolved, it dealt a lasting blow to his reputation. He had played a barrel organ in the street, trapped dogs, and openly begged by the entrance to Santa Maria when Senyora Pepa offered him her aid. With her unexpected help, he could have survived with relative ease into his old age—helped less by income from the kiosk than the fact that his years and battered physique turned off most of the women he chased—if now and then he hadn't degenerated into the lowest, errant ways that threatened to throw everything to the wind.

The noble, poetic enigmas in his blood coursed through the hardened arteries of an old lecher's and degenerated into in the lowest, most obnoxious bestiality.

As the mountain didn't come to her, she went to the mountain.

They hadn't seen Nonat since the day he accompanied Pepita to the cemetery—which was long ago—and the haberdasher, who had at first been thrilled by her cunning brainwave, fretted more and more. Had she been wrong to precipitate matters?

She had no doubt that Nonat was quite unlike other young men in his trade and one must tread softly when dealing with him.

She decided prudently to make it up as if she had offended him in some way, or to remind him of their presence, no less prudently, in case it was true that he had put them far from his mind after the death of his friend; so Pepita's mother invented an excuse to turn up at the works and ask for Nonat.

"Nonat, Senyora? He isn't here now," said the worker who came to the door.

"Is that so? Well, when he comes back, please ask him after work to . . ."

"No, Senyora. I meant he doesn't work for this firm anymore . . . He runs his own concern . . ."

The haberdasher was shocked and a film of ice seemed to harden around her heart. Her worst fears had been confirmed: if he had made such a change and hadn't told them, it meant something highly disagreeable. However, she put on a brave front as was her wont, smiled, and asked if they knew his address, since she needed to see Nonat urgently. The worker told her, she noted it down carefully in the diary she always carried in her pocket, then said goodbye. She wasn't yet prepared to give up her scheming, but there was no doubt her motherly hopes had been severely dashed. What with the cold response her hints always got from the ingenuous Pepita, ever more locked in her widow's grief, and the bastard's rude desertion, the poor woman sensed that the foundations of that beautiful castle of cards she had erected in her imagination were falling apart.

It cost El Senyoret greatly to clamber out of the swamp into which Senyor Ramoneda's discovery had sunk him. For the next few days, it was as if nothing had happened. Sickness and depression had sealed the boss's lips, and Nonat carried on handling the firm's business and activities with nobody there to control or check him. But that was short-lived. Like Rovira, Nonat knew the district's former mayor very well and realized that if fear for his own skin resigned him to accepting what was lost as lost for the time being, his rabid character and self-interest would ensure he made no more concessions, whether or not his life was at stake. So Nonat felt exposed, he could be imprisoned any minute, and understood it was vital to find a way out, to flee, to vanish, so his presence didn't make the wound fester and keep the temptation to seek revenge or take him to court alive. But what could he do? What path should he take? His inflexible, rebel temperament meant that surrender was odious, and any will that tried to influence or *might* influence, rightly or wrongly, his own drove him crazy to the point that he lost his appetite, his sleep, and even the desire to live . . . He had shown that clearly after being caught: "No more masters ever!" And every step he took was to that end. He needed to feel free, to fly with wings fully extended, not ricochet off the bars of that blasted cage. His struggle for total emancipation was driven by bilious anger. Finally, he had no cache of money because the arrears in the accounts and recent embezzling had devoured his legitimate earnings and the extras he brought to the table; conversely, he couldn't knock on doors that were too well-known or provide references, so as not to tempt the devil, but he wasn't perturbed.

Once more, he entrusted his fate to his guardian angel, Lady Luck, though he never let it out of his own hands and was always on the lookout. He scoured the streets in search of an indication, any sign that might put him on the right track;

he read adverts and more adverts in the press, spoke about his plans to friends and acquaintances, tried every port of call for a slice of good fortune . . . But days went by, and good fortune never came his way. Lady Luck seemed to be asleep on his case . . . The few things that cropped up had little to attract a man of his standing.

Conversely, one worker said the boss was up and about, that he'd seen him standing behind his balcony windows. He would soon be back rummaging around at work and Nonat's situation would become increasingly tenuous. Nonat began to doubt himself, to anticipate the unpleasant possibility he would have to compromise and go into hiding. Then, out of the blue, when he was least expecting it, a rabbit jumped out of the hat.

One evening he went to La Maravilla, the bar on Aribau, and the barman serving him asked: "Say, Senyor Ventura, didn't you say that if you found the right place, you'd like to set up your own shop?"

"Indeed I did . . ."

"Well, I might have just the thing . . ."

Nonat's heart leapt.

"Tell me more . . ."

"Just listen to this. I live next to a very old smithy all the locals call the Forge. The owner had two sons, one's been in South America for some time, and the other is a friend of mine. We always went out on the town together and people thought we were brothers . . . Well, last year this lad caught typhus and died, and soon after his mother did too. The blacksmith was left in a pitiful state; lonely as a scarecrow and in bad shape . . . He wrote to his son in South America, but the son replied saying he had too many commitments to bring his father over straightaway, though to be patient, because he would soon have better news. And, you know, three or four days ago he received another letter saying it's all arranged, he should try to sell the shop and be ready to leave at a moment's notice. I was at his place when he read the letter and he asked me: 'You meet lots of people in your bar, don't you know anyone who'd want to buy it? I'll sell it cheap.' And I immediately thought of you."

Nonat didn't wait around. The next morning, he went to the Forge and negotiated a deal with the owner. It was hardly his ideal solution. The shop was a long way from the city center, almost on wasteland on the city outskirts, the work it did was backbreaking and poorly paid; the place was set up like at the start of the nineteenth century, but circumstances meant it was available for next to nothing and it was the only solution Nonat had.

The owner was desperate to sell and had been modest in his demands.

"We can put a price on what's in the shop and you can pay me when you take over, or, if you'd rather, in two installments, one now, and the other when I leave. And you'll see our customers are a decent lot, so we won't fight over them: you just keep me on for the two or three months until word comes from my boy and it's a deal. You see how reasonable I'm being."

So that was what they agreed.

The Forge had a middle-aged worker, who was an earnest, capable journeyman with no ambitions, and a son who was finishing his apprenticeship. Nonat calculated that he could manage with that minimal workforce and cope for the moment without forfeiting his lodgings at Senyora Maria's or his restaurant meals. He would have struggled to pay the first installment if he hadn't decided that Senyor Ramoneda wouldn't notice a little bit less or a little bit more, especially as he wouldn't be able to check the figures in some transactions.

Senyora Pepa Canalies was happy ever since she'd gotten the only thing she was missing: company. In the first place, as she'd anticipated, she felt much more relaxed; secondly, she had somebody to talk to, which was of prime importance for her; thirdly, she could go for a walk whenever she felt like it; fourthly, the apartment was in good hands.

This was because Carmeta was homely by nature, and even more so in her present state of mind.

"Go on, go out for a bit while I do this or that . . ." she would tell her cousin, aware of Pepa's inclinations and wanting to satisfy them.

"No, you'll be all on your own."

"As if I wasn't used to that, my dear! And I find working distracts me . . . And you need to look after . . ."

"You're so right. If one doesn't keep on top of one's business . . ."

"Too true . . . So off you go."

"I might go as far as Montjuïc, if you don't mind."

"On the contrary! I'd be only too pleased . . ."

And Senyora Pepa would go out three or four times a week, always after pleading with Carmeta, as if she felt she owed her that. On occasion she would go up the mountain, but generally she stayed in Barcelona: she spent time with Senyor Grisau in their kiosk—and kept an eye on how it was going—she would go and see Biel the bootblack, pray for a while in Santa Maria, and visit some old acquaintances in the neighborhood . . . She was happy.

If Carmeta wasn't happy, she was at least more at peace than before. Pepa wasn't simpering like Pepita, nor was she opinionated and snobbish like the haberdasher, and she let Carmeta get on quietly with her life, except for the slight inconvenience of having to chat nonstop when she was at home, but as she spent lots of time out of the house, the Rovira girl, used to suffering much worse straits, pretended to be enjoying herself. Nevertheless, she had been so demoralized by her misfortunes that any improvements from the change didn't reinvigorate her: her thin face didn't fatten, her sallow hue, rather than lightening and returning to normal, darkened into a dry timber hue, and her body was always aching somewhere. But she said nothing and put on a front so as not to seem wearisome or a burden to the companion fate had so kindly granted her.

Nonat's departure from Senyor Ramoneda's enterprise triggered a period of headaches and severe deprivation for him. With only the cash he had in hand to deal with the immediate situation and finding it hard to start out and establish his credit worthiness, he might have been sunk completely were it not for his stunning presence, which opened many doors and turned out to be a great help in overcoming obstacles. Thanks to that and the innate good impression and trust he always inspired, he secured extraordinarily generous deadlines and good prices without having to haggle; a month after the deal was done, the old man left for South America and, as well being spared his upkeep, the latter had recognized he had gotten his sums wrong and agreed to being wired the second tranche later, as Nonat didn't have the wherewithal at the moment . . . Nevertheless, Nonat was forced to give up his theatergoing, the Mallorquina, and the carriage rides that he had grown too fond of recently. These privations were deeply felt, and would have sickened him greatly if the feeling that he now depended on nobody, that he was the absolute arbiter of what he did, hadn't galvanized his energy and powers and to an extent compensated for his losses. And as he couldn't spend, he found outlets in his work and organizing the new business to his liking. Self-motivated—the impetus that came when he surrendered heart and soul to any challenge—with a kind of divine fury that drove him on and made inanimate objects and workers go hell for leather, he reversed the slack tempo reigning in the Forge, spurred on the tradesman and apprentice who, much to their own surprise and delight, arranged the stock like well-oiled pistons and finished jobs that seemed to multiply mysteriously as Nonat did the accounts, and put discipline and method into the chaotic mess that had been the order of the day.

He spent four or five long months concentrating on those constructive endeavors, quite oblivious, but one day, when the shop almost seemed to work on its own, even though it still tottered amid the challenges and perils from sudden changes that might bring it crashing down, Nonat was brought to a standstill in the middle of the street, as if someone had banged him on the head and violently woken him from a dream. He closed his eyes, opened them, and observed: shocked, breathless, rooted to the spot . . . Three horsemen had just trotted by, gracefully bouncing on their saddles . . . One of the riders was that young man from the Liceu, his likeness . . . That same afternoon, Nonat went to a riding school, and after leaving there, he went to the tailor's to order a riding outfit.

Something else strange happened that week. When he went to bed, he found a small cambric handkerchief with a beautifully embroidered edge and an initial he didn't recognize on one corner. He looked at it, entranced, not knowing how it had ended up in his pocket. Then he gradually remembered . . . Remembered how that morning he had been riding on the tram platform because it was full inside, and a lady by his side had taken that tiny handkerchief from her sleeve, wiped her lips, and tucked it back in her sleeve, and he had thought vaguely that when the lady lowered her arm, his fingers had felt some kind of contact. He focused on that idea. It wasn't in doubt: he had taken the lady's handkerchief instinctively, *without realizing*. His forehead broke into a cold sweat. If the lady had noticed, if someone had been alerted by the strong scent from the handkerchief, he might have been in dire straits over a trifle that was at once worthless and useless in his eyes! And he told himself to be more careful when out and about.

Senyora Quimeta, the salted-cod seller, was a widow with six daughters and a son. All set to be a salted-cod seller, the son helped his mother with all shop tasks. Her daughters came in every kind and for every taste. The eldest was married to a civil guard; the second was courting a lad from a grocery store; the third had taken to the church and spent her days daydreaming and pondering whether she would be more amenable to God if she became a Sister caring for the poor, or a nun in an enclosed order. The fourth was studying to be a piano teacher; she wore her hair gathered with a big bow and spent the whole day practicing scales and other exercises that hugely endeared her to the ears of neighbors. The fifth was a manic housekeeper, and, finally, the youngest . . . "What shall we do with the young'un?" Senyora Quimet had wondered the moment that little clod of earth popped out. After serious reflection, she had decided to place her as an apprentice with a dressmaker at the top of the street. The dressmaker went to twelve o'clock Mass on Sundays dressed up to the nines. One Sunday, Senyora Quimeta stopped her on the sidewalk and told her about her ambition. The dressmaker already had an apprentice, but she was overworked, so she snapped up the salted-cod seller's offer.

"Send her tomorrow morning and we'll see how she fares . . ."

They took her to the workshop. The girl was doe-eyed with a heart of gold. She didn't displease Donya Eulàlia, as her staff emphatically called her.

"What's your name, love?" she asked.

And the girl answered affably: "Jesusa, if I can be of service,

238

because I was born on Christmas Day like dear little Jesus."

The girls in the shop burst out laughing, and from then on called the young'un Nadala, and since the other apprentice was a Rosa and the two girls were always together, keeping themselves a little apart from the band of fully fledged seamstresses, the latter called the pair the Nosegay.

Every day as they came and went, the Nosegay had to walk past the den of Senyor Grisau, the silversmith, and every day that passed they invariably stopped to gawp at the display on his shelves.

Also every day, seeing them rooted there, the silversmith's temperature rocketed as they steamed up his windowpanes, and he blasted them with a few choice words or threatening gestures. He was rougher than a prickly mat and had never been able to stand young people. They, it must be said, repaid him in kind.

"Hey," said Rosa, lively and bright-eyed as a sparrow, to Nadala, when they were finishing work, "let's wait here a while, until this lot goes, then tease that dirty old man."

Nadala wasn't the naughty sort, but she laughed and went along with her friend. And they stopped in front of the shop window until their shadows made the silversmith look up and start bawling. They stuck their tongues out, licked his window, and ran off. The fun lasted for months until Rosa's family moved to a different neighborhood and she left Donya Eulàlia's workshop. Nadala was now orphaned there, but she kept up the tempo her little friend had accustomed her to. She stayed after work tidying up, while the older women, each driven by her own hobbyhorse, were quick to leave, and when she was alone, she made the usual stop. Except that, being the peaceful sort, Nadala didn't grimace or lick his window: she simply stuck the end of her nose against it and looked in awe at the little chains, medallions, pendants, and earrings that were so bewitching . . . And when bald-pated Jupiter raised his head, she ran off, as usual.

A few drops, a heavy shower, finally a violent downpour, splattered angrily on the cobbles, water rushing in muddy rivulets down the sides of the street.

Senyora Pepa, umbrellaless, was caught in the entrance to the booth where her bootblack worked, and with no idea how to kill time, she impatiently told him: "Right, Bieló, let's while away the time, as we've nothing else to do. Polish my shoes, but not too much, right! I don't want people laughing at me . . ."

And she sat down on one of the three red velvet chairs that were lined up along the wall, scabby and threadbare like old cats. Lolling backward, legs sprawling, one foot on each iron sole of the stand, her skirt halfway up her leg, Senyora Pepa steadied herself and surrendered her antediluvian footwear to her business partner's uncouth hands, when suddenly the entrance went dark, as if fresh, dense clouds were scudding by.

A gentleman had just walked in to shelter against the rain, and, looking out to the street, he was kicking his feet, shaking the rain off his pants, and, folding his umbrella, left it to drip, handle down.

Sitting on the stool, opposite Senyora Pepa, Biel had only

turned his head, while he took a smear of polish from the tin with his cloth and rubbed it quickly over heel and toes, whereas his boss sat still, watching the gentleman maneuvering by the door.

He was visibly irritated by the rain, clicked his tongue in disgust, and, inspecting his suit, he saw a drop here and there; leaning his umbrella against the mignonette, and, taking his handkerchief from his pocket, he wiped them carefully one by one. Then he looked sorrowfully at his shoes.

"What a fine gentleman!" Senyora Pepa was thinking, when, suddenly, she let out a full-throated scream and a foot flew off the stand, startling Bielet who jumped backward.

"Agh! You clumsy lout! That hurt! You might as well have stuck a sword from Maria's Heart into my little toe!"

Bielet laughed, and the gentleman by the door turned around.

"Senyora Pepa, why didn't you tell me you had a corn?"

"What do you mean 'one'? More than what grows in a cornfield! And in this weather they give me stick I can't stand . . . !"

The gentleman smiled, picked up his umbrella, and walked over.

"Good afternoon," he said, touching the brim of his hat.

"God be with you," answered Senyora Pepa warmly. "What a downpour!"

"You don't have to tell me . . . Not even an umbrella . . . One can get drenched in a second . . ." And he glanced mournfully at his shoes.

"Perhaps you'd like to have them polished?"

"When you're done . . . As it is, one can't venture out . . ."

"Bielet, hurry! Attend to this gentleman," the former housekeeper bid him loudly, withdrawing her semi-polished shoe.

The gentleman protested: "I beg you, senyora! You are too kind . . . But I can wait . . . I'm not exactly in a hurry . . ."

"Don't worry . . . I work here . . . And I was just giving my shoes a bit of polish to kill time."

They bantered briefly, because the gentleman wouldn't allow Bielet to abandon Senyora Pepa on his behalf. In the end, when she saw she wasn't getting anywhere, she relented.

"All right, *vamos*, if you insist . . . But get a move on, my lad; four wipes of the brush, so my skirt isn't soiled, and that will do. In the meantime, do take a seat, senyor. Relax, at least . . ."

The gentleman settled into one of the two empty seats, and, encouraged by Senyora Pepa, he had no choice but to converse with her about the weather, the filthy streets, the terrible state of the world, etc., etc. After five minutes, Carmeta Rovira's cousin felt she'd known that gentleman all her life.

After the deluge, the storm quickly cleared, and before Bielet had given the gentleman's shoes a last wipe, leaving them as resplendent as a sun beam, the actual sun, from high in the sky, seemed to look tenderly down on the rain-swept city.

"Thank God, it's stopped! As long as it lets me get home!"

And Senyora Pepa also peeped out of the door to have a look.

The gentleman took out a silver purse and paid the shoe-shine, adding a big tip, but, as he went to put his purse back in his pocket, his shirt cuff snagged on his umbrella handle and something fell and bounced on the ground. It was the button that had been severed from the link.

"Blast!" the gentleman muttered bad-temperedly. "What am I going to do with a loose cuff?"

"Don't you worry, senyor," said Senyora Pepa affably. "I'll accompany you to the house of a friend who's very good with his hands and will sort it for you in a jiffy. You'll see; come, if you're ready . . ."

They left together, and a bit farther down the street they entered Frenchy's grandson's den.

"Look, Senyor Benet," Senyora announced, feeling very pleased with herself, "I've brought you a good customer . . ." and immediately added the following nonsense . . . "And be sure to make him happy, or we shall have words . . ."

And that's how Senyor Grisau became acquainted with Nonat.

Miquel Vedià, the tradesman at the Forge, had just had breakfast and was smoking a cigarette in the doorway with his son, when he saw a handsome horseman galloping up the slope toward them. Half dreamy-eyed, half intrigued, Miquel Vedià stared at the steed rather than its rider, noticing it was slender as a reed and steady, its legs moving gracefully. Miquel thought: "Heavens! First-class fetlocks!"

His son, Badoret, had raised his eyes further, and was so impressed he gave a start, his eye lashes flickered, and a cry from deep down stuck in his gullet.

The rider was approaching at pace and when he was in front of the blacksmith's, rather than riding past, he stopped without saying a word.

Mechanically, as if pulled by a piece of string, Miquel straightened his back and lifted his hand to his hat. He thought they were going to be asked for their good services . . . He looked up and straight away, like his son, was thunderstruck.

Nonat was all smiles, amused by the impact he'd made.

"Good morning, Miquel . . . Hullo, lad . . ."

And he dismounted nimbly, handing the reins to Badoret.

"Hell, Senyor Ventura! I would never have guessed it was you . . . I'm sorry! Who would have thought you would know how to ride a horse?"

El Senyoret frowned and responded rather brusquely: "One needs to know a little bit of everything in this world, Miquel . . ."

He was mortified by the idea that all they saw in him was a worker acting above his station. And he walked into the Forge. His worker followed on his heels, gawping, excited, humbled, as if he'd just discovered he was in the presence of a prodigy . . . Badoret was no less in awe.

Nonat's gleaming spurs and the whip with its exquisite top had taken Badoret's breath away. The horse was restless, clattering its hoofs impatiently, and Badoret scratched its forehead with his black, clipped nails, his eyes still staring at the miracle worker who seemed to have sprung out of a hat.

Nonat asked a few questions, issued orders, and walked back outside.

He put his foot in the stirrup and quickly and airily jumped into the saddle, trying to control the horse as it kept prancing fantastically around.

Miquel muttered very timidly: "You will remember, won't you, Senyor Ventura? We're running out of heavy iron . . ."

"They'll bring some this afternoon . . ." answered Nonat, frowning again, and with a frosty "good day," he loosened the reins and shot down the street like an arrow.

Miquel and his son stood by the entrance to the Forge looking after him.

"Father!" was all Badoret could manage, looking at his progenitor's face with strange, entranced eyes.

"What a man, my boy! One hell of a man!" Miquel answered, perplexed, as he walked slowly inside, scratching his ear.

El Senyoret had made remarkably rapid progress at riding school.

His bodily reflexes showed admirable resistance, elasticity, and precision. He personally sensed they worked like the finest steel springs. He was incredibly light, held himself perfectly in the saddle, handled the reins with the right combination of gentleness and strength, and showed no fear at all. His teacher congratulated him, encouraged him enthusiastically with each new little victory, and soon after beginning his classes, he declared him ready to go into the street, but the bastard refused until his tailor had delivered his bespoke attire. He had found something within himself to make him advance so quickly, apart from his innate aptitude for many things, namely the stimulus of an inspiring model: the memory of the *parakeet* from across the seas whom he imitated. And not altogether consciously, Nonat started to ape him in everything: his manner, his style, specific movements, even his early morning rides ... And when, at the top of Muntaner, he fully embraced the pleasant challenge of the invigorating mountain air that clung to his face like a refreshing mask, and which slipped through his open collar and broad sleeves and explored his hidden flesh, bringing a voluptuous shudder, he experienced a feeling of utmost happiness that turned everything upside down. His audaciously erect head, his eyes captivated by the far bluish or golden haze, the feeling of his steed vibrating and swaying nervously between his legs, as if it were the animated pedestal of a monument that held him there, his flaming chest lit by the torch of a will that unfurled and flapped like a victory standard, Nonat felt he was bolder and more invincible than any conquistador, than any hero predestined to reign over other worlds or men ...

And powerfully satanic lightning-glints infused the bluish-green enigma of his diminished pupils with a superhuman intensity.

It had become second nature. In all human bustle, wherever there were packed crowds to distract eyes or drop guards, wherever the opportunity presented itself, almost automatically, almost mechanically, the deft, delicate, wingèd tools that were Nonat's fingers were attracted, like a magnet, to items that had been forgotten. Once, by a bookshop window, it was the ink pen a young man had tucked into his front pocket; another time, in the chocolate parlor, the purse a young girl had carelessly laid on the chair next to her; on yet another occasion, when he'd gone into a shop to buy something, a magnificent umbrella a lady had leaned against the counter . . . Without premeditation driving his acts, without anticipating favorable opportunities, the second they presented themselves, his fingers acted spontaneously, with sudden inspiration, on a most normal, instinctive impulse, and completed with perfect calm what seemed a legitimate and quotidian act. Unflinching, measured, serenity itself, without doubt in mind or heart, he thieved at the opportune moment, at the necessary moment, with spare, gentle movements that seemed the consequence of long study and iron discipline, and then, with similar simplicity and opportunism, he vanished and placed himself out of harm's way. As if he wasn't really conscious of what his undue acts meant, he felt no anguish, fear, or unease; on the contrary, they seemed ordinary, and afforded him the fleeting pleasure of a conversationalist who smartly rounds off a sentence, or a servant who's produced a shine on the tin she is rubbing; namely, the modest satisfaction brought by the successful completion of a routine task, not a point of honor, but if the theft was of something beautiful or useful, his pleasure was palpable, bringing the headiness of fruity wine, a savory sense of excitement that illuminated his whole day, like a glorious glow on the horizon . . .

Gorged on impunity, he started frequenting locations crammed with people, famous shops, exhibitions, cinemas, and above all, the busiest trams, each of which could be dubbed shrines in motion consecrated to the patron goddess of the distracted, always holding treasures galore for a sharp-eyed man like himself.

One day he jumped onto a tram that had seats on both sides, and sat next to a fat man who kept yawning, coughing, then wiping his nose while putting his hat on and off. A woman at the other end of the tram kept glancing at that comically fidgety gentleman, an amused sparkle between her fleshy eyelids. She was plumpish, and her face was a blotchy red; she was modestly dressed with a Swiss wool shawl around her neck and a baby around a year old on her lap. When Nonat sat down, he sat between her line of vision and the fat man, and her eyes fell on him: immediately she turned bright red, then extremely pale. She quickly turned toward the door and started playing with the child, carefully hiding her face, but keeping a wary eye on the bastard.

The reader will have guessed without too much effort that she was Carlota. Motherhood had plumped her out, making her figure more normal and, despite her stoutness, had restored a touch of her former grace. Under that bulk, her small foot seemed tiny, like a Chinese woman's foot.

The fat gentleman suddenly stood up, buttoned up his overcoat, and alighted from the tram. Carlota again felt a hot flush displace blood from her heart to her face, and back. She'd noticed that a long, narrow packet that had been in the fat gentleman's overcoat pocket now lay in El Senyoret's hands. The latter jumped off the moving tram and vanished into the crowd. He hadn't noticed Peroi's cousin.

Yet again Senyora Maria, his landlady, told him: "Oh dear, Senyor Nonat! You must forgive me . . . When I took your jacket out of the wardrobe when I was cleaning, those lovely spectacles fell out . . . I hope I didn't damage them."

The tradesman moistened his lips.

Senyora Maria wasn't what you'd call a *magpie*, but he thought she had seen too many female items around, and he decided to get rid of them. He was sometimes careless, as others are, and that was obvious enough. Senyor Grisau came to mind. His was a hidden den and humble enough not to arouse suspicion. He would go to see him that same afternoon.

Senyora Pepa also went on her usual itinerary, and when she said goodbye, her partner accompanied her to the door and stood on the doorstep, surveying all around. The dressmaker's women walked by, and behind them the apprentice, Nadala, all alone . . .

"Aren't you going to stop today, you little sewer rat?" spat the silversmith sourly.

The young woman hurried along, ignoring him. The old man's spiteful, slate-black eyes pursued her, and suddenly a strange perception brought color to Senyor Grisau's pallid forehead and bacon chops. Her small, still childishly flat torso was now supported by two sturdy, plump, womanly legs that heralded the change. The sight of those legs left Frenchy's grandson paralytic and dreamy, so Nonat had to tap him on the shoulder to bring him around. He didn't recognize him immediately . . .

"Take a look at this," Nonat began as casually as ever, at once affable and serious, as he placed the girl's purse he'd purloined in the chocolate shop on the kiosk counter: "My niece has been given another purse and she wants to change this one for a doll . . . Isn't this the kind of thing you could . . . ?"

The moment he eyed it, the silversmith felt a flash of intuition . . . Common ground had just revealed a partner in crime . . . His steely gaze fixed on his visitor like two gimlets. The latter felt he'd been found out, but he blankly returned Senyor Grisau's stare; the old hypocrite lowered his greasy eyelids, and after turning the purse over and over, made an offer . . . He paid a price, as if it were new, a generous offer to test the waters, because he anticipated his customer would soon be back. And he wasn't wrong.

What a fright Senyora Pepa had that afternoon when she returned home! After she had been knocking a while, Carmeta had come to open the door, but what a state she was in! White as a sheet, blue-lipped, blurry-eyed, staggering blindly . . . She grabbed Pepa around the waist and pulled her into her bedroom where she was confronted by further horrible sights: the bed, the patchwork rug, the towel hanging over the chair, all soaked in blood.

"My darling, what's wrong? What happened?"

Carmeta smiled sweetly, as if her whole life melted in that smile, and moved her skirt imperceptibly. Senyora Pepa saw that her undergarments were also drenched with blood. Panicking, she made to call for help, but an almost energetic, heroic gesture from a barely conscious Carmeta stopped her.

"No . . . Nobody . . . nobody . . ."

"But, by the holy saints . . . !"

"It's nothing, it really isn't . . . Give me a sip of wine . . ." mumbled Carmeta, slumping onto her bloodstained bed.

Senyora Pepa rushed to get a bottle of syrupy liquor and poured her half a glass . . . Carmeta perked up and began to explain. She had been having heavy flows of blood for some time, but had said nothing so as not to alarm Pepa, but today they had been so excessive that Carmeta had realized she'd been close to . . .

"It's all over now . . . It won't . . . But, you know . . . I can't move . . . It feels like my breath is being sucked from near my chest . . . down here . . . and my eyeballs feel like they're about to drop out . . . I'm really sorry, but I don't think I'm up to cooking supper . . ."

"Praised be the Lord! Or that I should expect you would, my blessed dear . . . That would be the last straw!"

Pepa helped her with sisterly loving care. She ignored the sick woman's protests, and diligently and briskly, as if she'd become twenty years younger, she changed the sheets, undressed Carmeta, lay her down again, washed the rug, wiped the floor, removed the sinister, blood-soaked clothes . . . and when everything was neat and tidy, she sprayed a red sugary scent that made the bedroom smell sweet. Carmeta felt she was coming back from death to life, and gradually dozed off, drifting into a warm, comforting slumber.

From then on, though she felt those flows were a chance phenomenon, Senyora Pepa never again wanted to leave Carmeta alone, and she ignored the other's worries and insisted.

"Come on now! You won't fool me! If you come with me, I know you'll be all right, I've been leaving you far too much at home. They say these things come from being thin-blooded, and thin blood comes from never seeing the sun or moon . . . We will go for a walk every day, and you see if I do or don't get rid of this *nemia* of yours . . ."

And, whether she liked it or not, whenever Pepa went out,

she forced Carmeta to accompany her and take a stroll. She didn't like to leave the house empty, but she encouraged herself thinking how it was a matter of conscience to make the sick woman's cure a priority. And when all was said and done, it was more fun to stroll accompanied, and on their return to her apartment she didn't have to worry about entering in the dark, because Carmeta always went in first!

She even took her charitable impulses to the extreme of adding more meat to the stew so the young woman got stronger quickly, and even helped her with the cleaning. She also talked of going to see a doctor, but the interested party became embarrassed and protested the idea so strongly it was never mentioned again . . .

One by one, mansions in the neighborhood began to commission the Forge to take on more sophisticated jobs than had been the custom in the past, and to ensure they were done to standard, Nonat had no choice but to do them himself, and that tied him down and stymied his plans more than once. He decided to recruit a new worker. Miquel's elder son was an electrician and worked for a Barcelona firm. Nonat told his father: "Miquel, get Salvi to come. I'll train him and he can see to these jobs."

Miquel thought he'd won the lottery. Seeing both sons at his side was the best possible news for him. And he added warm gratitude to the admiration he always felt for his boss.

Salvi was nineteen and quite different from his father. From childhood he'd grown up lean, willowy, a mass of curls, sky-blue eyes, and simpering gestures, like a girl.

His mother thought he was delicate, though he was never ill, and indulged and spoiled him outrageously: he was given milky puddings, chocolate, and sweetmeats; he ate whenever he felt like it, helping himself in the pantry if they refused to give him anything; his sweet tooth put him off their usual meals, when he would be reluctant to eat and upset the family's peace and quiet. In turn, influenced by his wife and by the boy's pretty looks, which blossomed arbitrarily, at odds with his own rough and ready nature, rather than taking Salvi to the Forge from an early age, as he would the younger boy, Miquel enrolled him in a state school so he could gain general knowledge, and on alternate evenings took him to Academies to perfect his drawing skills and learn a smattering of French. His mother's ultimate dream was for him to become an artist, but as he neither applied himself nor showed any aptitude, she had to face her husband's implacable stubbornness.

"I don't want any more playacting or tomfoolery. I've already spent too much money to let him be a lifelong layabout . . . Executioner father, executioner son . . . If I've been a worker, he can work for his living too . . . I won't say he has to be a tradesman, if he doesn't like the idea . . . Let him choose the line of work he wants, but he has to have one."

Salvi chose to be an electrician, and his father placed him in a good firm, but he soon found friends who led him away from the straight and narrow, and premature debauchery meant the neurotic, leery lad lost what little he ever had of his father's vital sap: a childlike innocence, down-to-earth goodness, innate honesty, a healthy soul, flesh or heart untouched by maggots. He was skinny and stunted; his skin was brittle, his manner soft, and his color a wan shade of tea rose cropped before its time; his chin jutted out, and his small mouth and wet lips, puckering like those of the Infantas of the House of Austria in portraits, suggested a weak will and avid propensity for every kind of pleasure, and beneath diurnally blue eyes, a hazy, twilight shadow lent his stare and every feature a listless, apathetic hue. That same tone permeated his whole frame, although it was sometimes countered and tempered by fits of youthful vigor. He was intelligent enough to understand any order he was given and skilled enough to carry it out.

Nonat had observed him, when he was more personally involved at the Forge, on the days when the boy had been locked out and dropped in for hours on end to lend a hand and kill time.

Salvi had soon established a bond with his father's new boss, and when Nonat told him of his plans, he gratefully welcomed what was on offer, and as terms were good because El Senyoret tended not to haggle when he wanted something, Salvi joined the Forge and applied what he had been taught.

"Don't stick to one line of work," Nonat advised him, in the firm but friendly tone he always employed with those around him, one that always got them to work miracles, "anyone who plays only one tune will never get this world to dance: he's like a cog in an engine that, once detached from the others, ceases to function. Better to become the whole engine. Those of us who've been schooled far from here aren't specialized, and prefer not to be. As you couldn't make a living as a specialist in the outside world, they taught us a bit of everything, and one thing helped another . . ."

Salvi understood all that and Nonat could soon rely on

him, particularly because he knew his father would keep an eye on the boy and ward off the bouts of nighttime marauding his son often succumbed to.

It was 10 A.M. and Nonat was coming from Carrer dels Àngels, where he had an appointment to see the manager of a metal firm.

The manager wasn't in and Nonat was told he'd be back by eleven. Nonat thought he'd have time to collect a tin item being finished for him on Les Rambles, one Salvi had told him the day before they needed urgently.

As he was on Carrer del Bon Succés, he stopped in front of a jewelry shop. Various jewels were displayed under little white labels that said: *Bargain*. A man's ring stood out with a big, bright diamond like a big, bright drop of water. On the corresponding label, under a Spanish word, was the figure of hundreds of pessetes. Nonat was crazy about that kind of ring, which he had always found attractive, he fell head over heels in love with them, though they were always beyond his means. What might he decide to do now that this ring had glinted like a rainbow and made him feel he'd been bewitched by a genie? Nonat stared, as if he'd been imprisoned inside the jewel, and made no attempt to give a hypothetical answer; every day he was less keen on his daydreaming and futile wandering through limbo. After a few seconds of intense contemplation, he closed his eyes, as if trying to retain that wondrous mirage, and, swallowing quickly, he stepped forward . . . and almost collided with a street porter coming from the opposite direction along the same sidewalk, his ropes over his brawny biceps . . . They faced up to each other for a moment, swayed back and forth, but didn't come to blows . . . Finally, the street porter didn't touch him, stepped off the sidewalk, smiled, and walked past, keeping his distance. The ugly, hateful image of his pockmarked face and a nose eaten away down one side lingered in Nonat's mind, after that brief flurry, against the background of rainbow glitter.

The piece of tin—a yard-long tube topped by a lion's head supporting a ring—was ready. They wrapped it up and he tucked it under his arm and walked back toward Carrer del Bon Succés. Before he got there, he heard shouting and saw people racing in that direction from Les Rambles. He joined the flood.

"What's going on?" he asked those running around him.

"Fire!" answered three or four voices excitedly.

"Where?"

"On Carrer de Ponent . . ." said some.

"By Peu de la Creu . . ." said others.

Even if they didn't know where exactly, there was no doubt there *was* a fire, because a fire engine was approaching, making the air thunder and the ground tremble, roaring like a monster unleashed. When the contraption entered the street, most people emptied out into the square, leaving Nonat among the last bystanders leaping onto the sidewalks.

The bastard's inspiration came instantaneously, as ever. He didn't even look around. As the fire engine rumbled furiously past the jewelers, making a deafening racket, he smashed the widow with a vigorous swipe of the tube, thrusting his arm inside fast as lightning . . .

There was an extraordinary outcry. Among the gaggle of onlookers suddenly clogging the shop entrance, the shop assistant, a bright poppy red, gripped Nonat's arm tight and bawled: "Yes, gents! I reckon he was after the ring! His fingers were around it when I parted them! Look where the back of my hand sent it! To the other side of the window! He thought nobody would notice with all the ruckus . . . Luckily I noticed him eying it up not half an hour ago . . ." and he turned this way and that as he repeated: "Aren't there any civil guards or municipal police around? Where on earth do they all hide?"

Pale as a corpse, shaking from head to toe, whether from shame or whim nobody could tell, Nonat shouted out, gently trying to free himself.

"Idiot! What do you think . . . That I . . . ?"

His voice had left him; his eyes bulged like a lunatic's.

Suddenly, something strange happened. Two huge hands parted the mass of people and cleared a way through for their owner's head, shoulders, and torso, and now a quiet voice calmly uttered these words: "Come on, what are you saying? That this gentleman wanted to . . . ? That's a funny old idea . . . ! If you can't see, you should put your spectacles on before accusing someone for no reason . . ."

The crowd stirred, and the shop assistant was so taken aback he even loosened his grip on Nonat's sleeve. Nonat quickly withdrew his arm and took a step backward.

The intruder, now at the center of the mêlée, turned around to look at the bystanders.

"Didn't you see how it happened, gentlemen? This fine

fellow was walking idly down the sidewalk, looking at the to-do and minding his own business; I was behind him . . . and then that man—pointing to one in the group—hears the cart coming, takes fright, jumps over here and into the gentleman, hurling him at the window . . . And as the gentleman was carrying that tube, it struck . . . And I really don't know how he didn't hurt himself . . . !"

The stranger referred to said it was true, that he had jumped on the sidewalk, like everyone else, to avoid the fire engine, but he wasn't aware he'd knocked into anyone, though he couldn't deny he hadn't . . . The heaving throng began to lose interest.

At first the shop assistant was shocked, protested, and rejected that gratuitous interpretation of what had happened. But that unexpected helping hand had partly restored the bastard Nonat's sangfroid. He gawped at his defender, and immediately recognized the face that was more perforated than a colander and the battered nose, bereft of its left nostril; it was the street porter from a few minutes ago. He held out his hand with lordly condescendence.

"Many, many thanks, my good man!" He turned to the audience: "You see, gentlemen . . . This young man has been seeing things. It was an error that could have put me in a dire predicament, if it weren't for this witness," he stared scornfully at the shop assistant, "just bear it in mind if there's a next time. But I have no wish to harm anyone, even though it was unintentional . . ." He took an exquisite, lithographed card from his gold-initialed wallet and handed it to him . . . "Send me the bill for the window at your convenience . . ."

The card fell to the ground, though nobody noticed, and the spectators greeted those dry, measured words with a murmur of approval.

More indignant than ever at that mischievous tactic, the shop assistant tried to attack the trickster again, but the crowd's murmur turned to a growl, and shut him up.

Yet again the boy from the orphanage had come out on top. Even so, he had no desire to rest on his laurels; his legs were imperiously telling him to flee. He restrained himself, looked for the street porter to invite him to a drink, but could see him nowhere. The stranger had modestly vanished into thin air after his handsome, generous deed for the day. Then Nonat raised a hand to his hat in a civil farewell that was affably returned by the crowd, and strode down Bon Succès, while the shop assistant, feeling duped, wept tears of rage and clenched his fists in front of everyone.

Once out of sight of that audience, El Senyoret suddenly lost his lofty restraint, as if his nerves had relaxed all at once. His reaction had been a thing of the moment, and the thought of the danger he had risked was still making his sense of power ebb . . . It was bad luck! Bad luck! The day before, he had taken his other wallet, and when he locked it in the drawer he hadn't taken the doubloon out . . . His memory failing him again . . . !

Sweat streamed down his body, chilling him, giving him the shivers, as if he had just gotten out of an over-long bath, and he broke out in a sudden rash of goosebumps; conversely, he was incapable, totally incapable, even if he made a real effort of will, of controlling his fearful mind, which was now in full retreat . . .

He didn't feel in a fit state to go to his appointment with the metal firm, and, instinctively staring at the solitary stone lion benignly guarding the entrance, he walked into the Chapel of the Angels to gather himself and recover his nerve in that silent, cavernous penumbra.

He came out past twelve o'clock, and as it was too late to go back to the scrap metal firm, he walked on to Plaça de la Universitat. He was still so hesitant and withdrawn that he didn't notice a man following him at a slow pace. Suddenly, a gruff, opaque voice, making hardly a sound, like a voice in a dream, muttered in his ear: "You know, slickster, it's obvious you're only a little pidgey learning to fly . . . You've got spunk, but you lack experience and knowhow."

He swiveled around as if wounded by a sword . By his side, grinning peculiarly, his ropes astride his biceps, was the man with the pockmarked face and chewed nose. He went by the nickname Nas-Ratat, and had five or six abodes in Barcelona, but not one person could direct you to any of them.

Part Five

WHAT HORIZONS UNFOLDED BEFORE NONAT'S EYES! What potential energy simmered, that he had felt vaguely within himself, never suspecting it might surface one day, the moment chance released it from an amorphous chrysalis state, gave it tangible form and substance and supplied the magic wings that would allow him to fly boldly off!

It had been a moment, next to nothing . . . A kind of miraculous, dazzling revelation of a state of grace . . .

"Shall we go inside and chat for a while?" Nas-Ratat suggested. And after Nonat's noncommittal reaction, which could have been interpreted as acquiescence, they slipped down the four or five steps to Paperines's tavern.

A bluish haze and a smell of wine and brandy were everywhere. Drunks stirred uneasily in the pestilent murk, like a nest of maggots in a cheese. Two here, five there, three or four farther away, a large number of men were gathered in small huddles, eating, playing cards or dominoes, mostly drinking and talking in hushed tones, the gentle hum of an active hive.

"Sit down, young man," said the street porter. "Have you eaten? No? Hey you!" he shouted at a passing waiter. "Got any tripe?" and after an affirmative response: "Bring us two platefuls . . . right? And to help them down . . . a bottle of red wine."

They sat down in a shadowy, out-of-the-way area behind the door. Nonat wasn't haughty or subdued, fearful or contemptuous; he said nothing; the expression on his enigmatic, sphinx-like face was untranslatable. The quiet, jovial familiarity of the man he'd met only two hours earlier made him feel strangely nervous, as if he was instinctively wary of being surprised, like a hunter approaching a wild boar's lair and catching sight of the gaping chasm . . .

A cartoonish caricature emerged from the back of the room and walked slowly over, swaying from side to side like a boat: a short, enormously fat man with a distended face and pendular paunch, like the ones clowns fake with pillows. His dark mustache was absurdly small for the size of his face and looked like two leeches stuck on either side of his lip.

"Hey, Nas-Ratat, you've finally dropped by? Not seen you for days . . ."

"Oh, I've been avoiding this district . . . You can't settle anywhere right now . . ."

"I thought you'd gone to the Estrella . . ."

"And why would I do that?"

"Because he's taken on some serving wenches, a real gaggle." He disdainfully surveyed an imaginary scenario. "But they're in for a shock! I'll be getting mine early next month, then we'll see!"

Nas-Ratat looked around.

"What can I say, Paperines? Dunno if it's a bright move . . . Where there's women, there's strife, and it'll be a hassle for you and your customers . . ."

"Not if you've got a decent whip! Treat them like dogs and you can't go wrong . . . I've got some fine specimens! One's like a finch and the other's more of a character than me. The thin'un is young and looks handy, the old'un, madder than an ass . . . she's so ticklish she splits her sides before a fingertip has touched her . . . And she dances the can-can, a frightful sight when she gets going . . ." He smirked modestly. "See . . . There'll be something to suit every taste . . . You will come and take a look, won't you?"

Nonat listened to that quaint exchange with the impassive aplomb of a lord traveling incognito. Apparently the boss of the place, used to all kinds of sleight of hand, hadn't noticed Nonat, and when the waiter brought them their tripe and wine, the boss politely withdrew. He had evidently only come over to announce his dive's latest innovation, the acquisition of waitresses "to suit every taste" . . .

Nas-Ratat now felt relaxed and spoke up, while gorging like an animal on the plate in front of him.

"Well, right, slickster, like the boy in the shop, I too figured you fancied something in the window . . . Bulging eyes don't lie . . . That's why I wanted a closer look at you, and tailed you . . . Making new acquaintances is never a waste of time . . . And look how useful it turned out to be! If I'd not popped by, that upstart would have nabbed you . . . And instead of being smart or fleeing to save your hide, you just stood there giving yourself away . . ." He smiled quietly under his horrifically butchered, stitched-up nose. "Anyone can see you haven't been working the street very long!"

Nonat said nothing, but was starting to wonder why he didn't respond by simply walking out on that repulsive fellow's shameless patter. He assumed the street porter was a professional criminal, but, being a proud, prickly man, Nonat showed no offense, big or small; no muscle on his face betrayed the slightest emotion at that denigrating putdown . . . He simply listened and listened . . . while the other man talked and talked: "But you'll soon get the hang of it, and we'll do some lovely jobs . . ." The street porter glanced at Nonat enviously. "Because you look smart, and when you look smart, the sky's the limit . . . Eh, if I didn't have this mess of a nose, I'd do over the king himself . . . Because it's not for lack of opportunities . . . More than you could hope for . . . But where can a man go quietly, if one sighting is enough, and more than enough?" He glanced back at his taciturn companion, this time warily, lowering his voice. "If I could count on somebody else . . . money would pour from my pockets like water from a sieve . . . from his, too."

He fell silent. He had laid his cards on the table and was waiting for an answer. But none came. Nonat had quickly swallowed two or three forkfuls of smoked tripe that was only fit for a man on death row. The other man filled his glass to the brim and sipped his wine slowly, as if relishing every mouthful, though it was really only to better weigh the impact of his words. His lips pursed in that peculiar grin again, that vanished straight away, like a will o' the wisp. "So, playing games, are we . . . ? You think you're a smart-ass!" And he resumed his spiel.

"With these ropes over my shoulder and this safe pass," he touched his official badge, "by day I get into lots of houses, but they always keep an eye on me because of this schnozzle and I can't try anything till it's dark. But, you know, if I had a partner, the machines in the Mint would be working night and day, if you get me? The moment I saw you, I thought . . . It's not that I haven't had good mates in the past, but what can I say? I didn't feel like getting stuck with them; they were a bit like me, their gizzards betrayed them . . . Besides, they made a racket, were rowdy, created a shindig out of nothing . . . and I'm not that type; my crimes crave peace and quiet . . . I like to do things proper, and that's why I work alone . . . But, if *you* wanted, hell! I could set you up, and, believe me, you'd only have to hold out your hand . . . And I tell you there is loot to be found in Barcelona; lots of dough going to waste that's only looking for a home . . ."

Nonat looked up. He had hid his outraged dignity behind a mask of austere distinction . . . Now he uttered a single word: "Correct . . ."

The schemer's face lit up. He half stood up from his chair.

"You mean you accept . . . ? Shake on it . . . !" and curbing his elation he extended a huge, open hand over the table; but a gesture from Nonat halted him.

"On one condition . . ."

"Out with it!"

"That you work on my orders . . . You'll give me everything I need, but will only do what I say."

Nas-Ratat gave a start in his seat.

"Christ!"

That outcome had never entered his head; he was in a state of shock.

"We'll go nowhere fast with any other kind of deal," the bastard affirmed.

"Wait a minute, what the hell kind of orders are you going to give when you're still green, still sucking milk from the tit?"

"You'll find out soon enough if I'm green or not. But right now, you just need to accept that my offer suits you best."

What did that sly old-timer see in that handsome, persuasive, youthful face to feel suddenly gripped tight in a vice? Feelings enter souls along strange paths, or spurt unexpectedly from mysterious fountains that remain closed or unnoticed till the right moment presents itself. Nas-Ratat, whose pants' seat was shiny from sitting in so many low dives, felt a flow of meek trust permeate everything, and, unsure why or how, he quietly yielded.

"I saw straightaway you were carrying a good head of steam . . . Agreed, let's give it a try . . . Take a risk, strike it lucky . . ."

"Now is that so . . . ?" asked Nonat, stiffening, as if impertinently demanding a more abject surrender.

The other man stood to attention, military-style.

"I salute you, captain! I expect that's what you wanted me to say?"

And they shook hands, both now smiling broadly.

While Carmeta was at the market, Senyora Pepa needed the scissors, and remembering that the night before, Carmeta had taken them to her bedroom, she went to look for them.

"Lord!" she exclaimed, wrinkling her face. "What a stink! You'd think somebody had left a corpse in here. God protect us!" She threw open the window. "It's odd she hasn't aired the place, she's usually so keen to do that! Ay, lord, we're starting the hot flashes again . . . When our bodies start giving off a stench . . . !"

But Senyora Pepa was wrong: as usual, her cousin *had* flung all the doors and windows open wide when she did her morning clean in order to let the dust out and the fresh air in. But the rank smell lingered on.

When Carmeta came back, Senyora Pepa told her: "*Bueno,* my girl, now you're here, I'll get ready to go into Barcelona. I'm taking some cash to Senyor Benet . . . Do you remember what he said yesterday afternoon? That he needed funds for some bargains that were coming up . . . If I go now, we can rinse the washing later . . ."

Senyora Pepa took the silversmith his cash, and since Carmeta was going to buy lunch, Pepa stayed in the shop for a while. The clock struck.

"Eleven?" she asked quietly.

"Twelve," replied Grisau.

"By the Holy Virgin! We agreed we'd have lunch early today!"

And she was about to disappear like a gust of wind when a horseman entered the kiosk. It was Nonat. They immediately recognized each other, and greeted each other affably. The most blissful smile spread sweetly over Senyora Pepa's face

(*My, my, so he's a customer of ours already? I knew I'd a good eye for these things!*).

And a dreamy-eyed Senyora Pepa told him she was so happy to see him again . . .

"Didn't it pour that day? The heavens seemed to have it in for us. And you were so worried about your shoes, do you remember? I told myself at the time: what a polite, refined gentleman! Happy the lady who hooks him! Because the fact is, if you'll excuse me for saying so . . . men can be so vile, they do you down, however gentlemanly you think they are . . . (She was recalling her Mossèn Vicenç, who was a right rascal.) Because I'm assuming you're single . . . ? Or have I got it all wrong?"

Once he'd gotten over his initial distaste at the encounter, Nonat was all smiles at Senyora Pepa's innocent chatter.

"No, senyora, you've a good eye. I am indeed a bachelor . . ."

She also laughed, frankly and freely.

"Because that's what you want! Sir, with your looks and manners, they'd be lining up!"

Nonat felt in a good temper and indulged her wit, and as she left, Senyora Pepa, who was completely won over, invited him to her home, telling him to call on her if he happened to be passing by.

Nonat promised he would, purely out of politeness.

No sooner had Senyora Pepa walked out of the door than Grisau shook a threatening fist at her back, his gesture and eyes full of repressed rancor.

"What a sacristy gold digger!" He turned to Nonat, who was looking at him, slightly taken aback. "She's loaded!"

"Really?" asked Nonat, by way of reply.

"Take a seat."

And after pushing a chair in his direction, Senyor Grisau recounted in a few venomous words the story of his boss, sticking the knife in with this pious final comment: "Whoever makes her kick the bucket will be spared a stay in purgatory . . . It would be the greatest charitable work anyone could do."

As you can see, Senyor Grisau didn't mince his words.

Then they spoke about their concerns and haggled over a range of watches of different value.

Like the first time, Nonat gave no explanations. He simply presented the items, and the other man gave him a price. Though they had never openly admitted it, they understood each other perfectly and always played things straight. Except Senyor Grisau was beginning to see the light, and, as soon as Nonat left his kiosk, the old man stuck the stub of his extinguished cigar up his nose, like someone screwing a bottle cap tight, and one side of his mouth curled upward in a hypocritical, self-satisfied grimace.

"You know this can't go on! Every day the poor girl comes back later and later . . . It's hard to believe Donya Eulàlia is so inconsiderate . . ." Senyora Quimeta told her fifth daughter, seeing that several seamstresses had passed by an hour ago and still there was no sign of her Jesusa.

For some days, the young girl had been later than she should have been, and when asked why, she'd been evasive and simply said they had a lot of work.

The fifth daughter advised: "Mama, if I were you, I'd ask her boss."

"Too right, I will speak to her . . . She may be an apprentice, but Donya Eulàlia has no right to keep her holed up for so many hours. I mean . . . ! And then she isn't hungry and doesn't want her supper."

The following Sunday, she tackled Donya Eulàlia when she was going to Mass.

The dressmaker was taken aback.

"Nadala? It's what we call her, you know? All the girls have one nickname or another . . . Well, she finishes when the rest do. She might wait around for five minutes, but they've all gone after fifteen . . . and that usually includes me too."

And, hurt by the mother's vehement tone, the dressmaker spoke to the apprentice the following Monday afternoon when the seamstresses were getting up to leave: "Listen, dear, you be off home fast now. I don't want your mother to think I'm sucking your blood."

And she told her staff what Senyora Quimeta had said.

The seamstresses accompanied Nadala out, joking and asking where her fiancé was waiting for her. Nadala said nothing, tears in her eyes, distraught.

They walked past the kiosk; Senyor Grisau was on the doorstep, in his thick woolen shoes and drooping, yellow jacket, its corners hanging down to his knees. Behind his spectacles and through his puffy eyelids, he glowered like a pool of water on a mudflat.

"Girls, take a look at that little egg yolk!" shouted one seamstress.

"Looks like a plastic canary!" said another.

"And what a schnozzle! Like a chunk of spicy sausage!" added a third.

"Not one I'd like a bite of!" quipped another.

The whole posse burst into laughter.

Senyor Grisau saw they were mocking him, and his pools of water muddied as if the stones they had thrown were stirring the mud at the bottom.

"Stinking sparrows!" he parried.

"*Adiós, pollo!*" retorted one of the most shameless of them, who had felt stung.

"Make sure you don't lose your ducky slippers, Cinderella . . ." muttered another.

"Too true! All the princesses will be fighting over them!" chortled the one furthest away, as she belched.

Suddenly they were shocked by a sudden sobbing in their midst.

Nadala was weeping, and wiping her eyes with a handkerchief.

The woman next to her, around thirty, stopped joking; she liked the sweet young thing and put her arm lovingly around her neck: "Hey, darling. You surely aren't crying because they're laughing at that saffron bun?"

"Not likely! Let her be, Cristina . . . She's got the waterworks because of what Donya Eulàlia just said . . ."

The salted cod shop was around the corner; the girl stopped to dry her eyes and the others continued on their way.

For a few days she arrived home on time; then, one day, a bit later, the next, later still. She never felt hungry, whimpered into her pillow at night, and woke her sisters with her nightmares. Senyora Quimeta scowled.

"We must find out what lecherous bastard is behind all this! She's starting early!"

She had one of those sudden revelations that come with maturity: "My God! It was so different in my day! Now they're no sooner off the tit than the sap rises!"

Senyora Quimeta seemed to forget that, at the time, she was barely eighteen years older than her oldest daughter.

Senyores Pepa and Carmeta were crossing the Diagonal on the way to Carrer Claris when an automobile and a horse rider coming from opposite directions almost clattered into them as they dithered in the middle of the street. The automobile flashed by like lightning two yards behind, and if the rider hadn't tugged his reins he would have squashed them. They scampered and screamed at the sight of the horse almost rearing over them. The rider cursed and raised his ox whip fast, as if about to lash the women as punishment for their almost suicidal dallying. But at a second cry from Senyora Pepa, now one of joy, he stopped the downward movement of his hand and his stern expression vanished as if by magic and gave way to a friendly, surprised smile. The horse, punished by his spur, bolted forward, and the rider barely had time to swing around on his saddle and greet them with a sweep of his hat.

Senyora Pepa, all smiles, waved at him repeatedly.

Carmeta seemed stunned and gripped her arm tight.

"Do you know him?" she asked, on tenterhooks.

"You bet!" Senyora Pepa declared rapturously. "He's a customer of ours!"

The Rovira girl's features contracted in the tragic mode of profound sorrow.

"We're done for."

"What on earth do you mean?"

"Something nasty lies in store! That man brings only grief!"

Senyora Pepa was speechless, as if Mossèn Vicenç had been resurrected.

Nonat had recognized Carmeta the moment his steed hurtled toward them. Her face wore the same horrendously ugly expression as the day her brother died. One idea quickly led to another. Senyor Grisau's partner was no doubt the cousin Pepa he'd heard so much about from the Roviras. She had never called on them, because, although Carmeta loved her dearly, Rovira himself was prejudiced against her as a result of her dalliance with a priest. He felt it was a stain on a liberal like himself to be related to clergy, as he liked to put it. However, in the bosom of the family, people had openly alluded to that relative's wealth on numerous occasions, the pile she had put together when cohabiting with the stipendiary of Santa Maria, and whenever conversations lurched that way, Rovira ended them with a comment that always riled his sister.

"You just listen to me: you won't make any profit from Masses . . . Their sole purpose is to cast someone into hell. These housekeepers are baits to temptation . . . and one fine day she'll die in a robbery."

"Whoever gets her to kick the bucket will spare their soul

from purgatory," was a phrase that buzzed in Nonat's memory, hazily echoing that wretched fellow's quip.

Paperines's tavern was the place Nas-Ratat and El Senyoret had agreed upon for their rendezvous. Whenever they needed to meet, they set a time there, because as the porter himself had spelled out, his face was a giveaway and El Senyoret didn't want to be seen with him any place where he might be compromised.

The first time Nas-Ratat showed up in the tavern, after that encounter when he joined forces with the bastard, Paperines had accosted him straight away.

"Say, Nas, who was that *com il flô* you were with the other day? A slippery eel?"

Nas-Ratat stared long, hard, and enigmatically, and made the only nostril of his rat-chewed schnozzle vibrate eerily.

"That fellow . . . ? Christ! A nugget of virgin gold, but either I don't know the first page of the catechism, or that man will be hitting the headlines before too long . . . You know, I'm expecting him this minute . . . But, *alto*, Paperines, don't put me in a fix, right . . . You act the innocent . . . Because you have to act sharp with him . . . He's on the ball and he'll stick you in your stomach, however tough you might think you are . . ."

A touring car coming from the station, packed with people and leaking luggage everywhere, gave Nonat the idea, and, lucid as ever when it came to making money, he reached an immediate decision. Why hadn't he thought of it before? Adventures came when you were on the road, rushing here and there . . . And, at the same time, wouldn't it be exhilarating to break the chain of routine, the monotony of a static life, the perpetual sight of the same people and same things? He went into a travel goods shop and bought the best suitcase and the best briefcase they had, instructing them to add his initials and provide protective covers. He purchased an overall, a rubber pillow, a blanket, hat, galoshes . . . Everything he thought might be useful for his future gallivanting. Two or three days later, when he had everything ready, he wondered, half-perplexed: "So where am I heading?" Then he realized he had woken up to that idea too late, because summer was over and people were returning to the city, and soon everything outside would be a graveyard. But suddenly a specific date flashed in his memory. Sant Narcís! Just the ticket! The Girona fiestas were approaching and he'd première there.

His heart felt pleasantly warm. He hadn't been back to the city of his childhood since leaving for Barcelona; he felt a kind of void, a desire to revisit that hated city, to roam its streets anew, now he was a different man, released from drudgery, almost as powerful in the potential scope of his activities as that millionaire's son in his dreams.

At first he thought he would go alone, but then thought it through and mentioned it to Nas-Ratat, who was delighted by the prospect.

"A first-rate idea, captain! No better place for rich pickings than a fair! You've come up with a good'un! Christ! We'll do a roaring trade! I'll be there for you!"

They discussed the how and the what.

"Obviously, you'll want to go as a gentleman . . . If you like, I'll be your valet . . ."

"No, we'll work in concert, but separately. Here you are . . ." Nonat handed him a hundred-pesseta note and a twenty-five note. "Buy a trinket box with all the necessary things."

"Will do. You're a natural, slickster! If you don't object, and, as we won't be short of cash, I'll buy a revolver too. I know a secondhand one that will do us nicely . . . it's always an asset for this kind of trip."

"No, a gun is a dog that barks at its master, when it isn't biting him. Forget the revolver; a man with a weapon who doesn't have a license is putting his head on the block. As long as they can't find a thing on you, if they catch you they'll think you're a poor man doing it because you're hungry, and you'll get off light . . ."

"You know it all! And I was thinking I'd have to teach you . . . !"

"Get everything ready for the twenty-fifth; we'll leave on the twenty-seventh . . . If we take it slowly, we'll extract much more . . . We'll be better prepared."

The old city of Girona seemed to don a disguise and be changing its perennial languor for youthful high spirits, as if it were entering spring rather than autumn, and Nonat could feel his blood stirring.

El Senyoret experienced a new sense of enjoyment wandering from one neighborhood to the next, mixing with waves of visitors and gawping at traditional processions and spectacles, feeling the ferment of that sudden, haphazard slice of life amid the throng.

He was magnificently established in one of the inn's best rooms; an austere, spacious suite with a huge alcove and long balcony whose thick jute and small, ironed, white linen curtains let in a discreet, chapel-like light. It seemed like a genuine bedroom from a grand mansion and, despite a profane electric bulb and shabby, cheap furniture, still retained a feeling of antique nobility and bygone luxury. Scattered around on settee and chairs, small center table, and sunken bed, Nonat's tools and brand-new travel items with his initials in silver seemed at once fitting and jarring, like a rooster's cry on a silent night. When Nonat withdrew to that room to rest and dress before going down to eat, he inhaled a strange, evocative scent, a degree of dankness and damp from being enclosed, that came from walls cracked under modern wallpaper, from grimy floor tiles under a worn rug, from desiccated timbers shriveled and deformed like octogenarian ladies under layers of flaky face paint . . . And as a child of deceit, an unexpected shoot, an urchin come good, a being with no sound foundation or bright horizons, he felt overwhelmed by bittersweet respect in that atmosphere saturated by past relics, where the tentacular roots of the objects they had once been seemed to survive magically, spread across that space with a spider's wary, encircling movement, that embraced, entwined, and secretly oppressed the soul.

Nonat spotted him ferreting, box on shoulder in the jostling crowd, during the city's collective stroll at twilight. He accosted him so directly, with such aplomb that Nas-Ratat blushed: "Got any keyrings?" Nonat asked so naturally, and when Nas-Ratat showed him different sizes, he pretended to look them over while whispering: "Come to the inn at twelve tomorrow and ask them to show you to my room. Bring a biggish box with you, like a shoe box, tied with string, like a parcel from a shop."

He chose a keyring, paid for it, and left. Nobody could have suspected a thing.

The following morning, in dressing gown and slippers, he was slouching on one of the bedroom chairs, legs stretched out and feet on another chair, when there was a knock on the door.

"Enter," he responded in a surly voice.

The door opened a few inches and a maid's smiling, fresh face peered through the gap. Nonat took his legs off the chair.

"I'm sorry, senyor . . ."

"Come in, come in."

"There's a man asking for you . . ."

"For me? What does he want?"

"I don't know; he just says he needs to see you, but as he looks most peculiar, we didn't want to show him up without giving you prior warning."

Nonat smiled.

"Ah, I know who it is . . . it must be that gold and silver

dealer . . . He showed me some antique goods yesterday, but was asking too high a price, and I told him to think it over and bring them here."

"So I can show him up?"

"Yes, please do."

And Nonat crossed his legs on the chair again.

Nas-Ratat came in.

"Shut it please."

"Turn the key?"

"Turn the key."

The hoodlum locked the door and walked over, a broad smile on his face.

"Good day . . . This isn't quite like my den. They've stuck me in with three dozen others and it's a breeding ground for fleas."

Now it was Nonat's turn to smile.

"But fleas cleanse your blood, mate . . . Have a seat."

Nas-Ratat sat down.

"So you're in the picture, I said you were a gold and silver dealer and had some antique items to sell . . . Have you had any pickings?"

"You bet I do. If you're curious, I can show them to you."

"No, that can wait till we're back in Barcelona . . ." Nonat handed over a key: "Open that armoire and give me the briefcase."

When he brought it, Nonat showed his colleague the contents, and Nas-Ratat's eyes opened wide.

Nas-Ratat's single nostril shivered voluptuously. The bastard's fingers had been working overtime: on the street, in gaming-rooms, at casino dances, in theater entrances and exits, even in the inn, wherever an opportunity presented itself. In a motley mix at the bottom of the case lay tie pins, wallets, chains, purses, watches, pocket watches, an earring, various medallions, coffee spoons . . .

"Some haul, captain!"

"Don't get too excited. Lots of trinkets, few real gems . . . Women seem to smell you a mile off, and only wear fakes. Put all that in your box and take them . . . We're leaving tomorrow."

"How come?"

"Better safe than sorry . . . Besides, they'll be after you . . . Because tomorrow I'm going to inform on you . . ."

"What in the hell?"

"You make me look suspicious, and that won't do . . . The maid's already mentioned your face . . ."

"My blasted face!"

"I won't be here this afternoon. Come back and prowl around for a while; then drop by the Cathedral; you'll find me there. There's a basketry shop near where I said that smithy was; find out what happened to the old blacksmith . . . I really don't want to be seen in the vicinity . . . Back to Barcelona tomorrow morning. In any case, the crowds are thinning out . . ."

"If you don't mind, I'll go via Figueres; a gang of bruisers in my lodgings are off there and we'll have a card-school while we're at it . . . Just to pass the time . . ."

"That's your choice, but keep an eye out."

"I'd feel at loose ends around here, but there it'll be . . ."

Nonat stood up.

"While you organize the box, I'll go down to the reception."

He took his wallet from his jacket and went down to the reception, dressed as he was.

"Excuse me, please. The salesman has brought items to sell me and neither he nor I have enough change. Could you change this bill for me?"

It was a five hundred peseta bill. The person on duty opened the cash drawer, counted, counted again . . .

"I'll have to get the boy down . . . It'll only take five minutes."

"Fine, please bring it up to my room . . . I've left that fellow alone and frankly I'm not enamored of that kind of beast."

The fresh-faced maid walked through and heard what Nonat said.

He returned to his room and they brought him his change in a split second. The street porter metamorphosed into a rag-and-bone man, then back into a gold and silver dealer, facing the door so the boy who came in would see his evil demeanor for himself.

El Senyoret sent him off immediately.

"See you in the cathedral this afternoon . . . No need to come back here now that they've seen us. At the very most, walk up and down a bit outside, as if you couldn't find the right door . . ."

Nonat started on his toilette as diligently as ever, then went down to the dining room. The happy din of the first days of the fiestas was no more, but the city was still packed.

From the day he returned to Girona, he'd had his place laid where he sat on the first day: it was a table at the back, in the corner opposite the entrance, and he had to cross the whole dining room to get there. However, he did so without having to push or be shoved, or losing his composure, and he liked that. While he waited for lunch to be served, he vaguely surveyed the scene, overhearing pleasantries and listening to the plain chant of humming voices, clinking glasses, and cutlery ringing against crockery. Suddenly, he gave a start; his blank face stiffened as it did when he was angry. At a table in the center of the dining room, he'd just spotted the old gentleman from the box at the Barcelona Liceu who'd called him a "parakeet."

Momentarily, Nonat thought his eyes were playing tricks or he'd been misled by a coincidental similarity, but he had a good memory for faces and was in no doubt: it was that old chatterbox in the flesh.

The waitress brought him his plate of rice.

"Tell me, who is that man down there who's putting his napkin in place?" asked Nonat.

"I don't know, he's from away . . . I think . . . from Barcelona."

"Did he arrive today?"

"Oh no! He's been around for three or four days . . . He has the table number next to yours . . . But he hardly ever eats there . . . He's always being invited elsewhere. . ."

Then another gentleman walked into the dining room, who noticed the old man as he put his hat and scarf on the hook, and stopped to greet him and exchange a few words. Nonat knew from the waitress that the newcomer was the director of an Academy that trained people for various professions. A year ago, he'd lost his only daughter, who was his only family, and he'd shuttered his apartment and come to live in the inn.

He always ate by himself at the small table next to Nonat's. But, that morning, as he walked over, he saw it was taken and complained to the waitress.

Nonat half got up from his chair, holding his napkin.

"If the gentleman is in a hurry and wants to join me . . ." and he politely indicated his table.

The teacher thanked him and accepted. He was a middle-aged man, round-shouldered, short-necked, with a gray beard and large, shiny pate where the light sketched changing, luminous lines. He wore a black frock coat and tie, a buttoned-up shirt, even a watch chain: all strictly mourning dress.

They conversed. The bereaved gentleman was polite and cultured and spoke about a range of subjects.

Nonat, who was focused on one idea, allowed him to burble on, injecting the odd word and getting him to open up a little, before putting the question that was burning his lips. Finally he could contain himself no longer.

"I noticed you greeted that gentleman down there . . . He's Don Ramon Calvet, if I'm not mistaken?"

"Ramon Calvet? No, senyor . . . That's Josep Martínez."

"Are you sure? I'd not seen him for a long time, but I'd swear . . ."

"I'm sorry, you're mistaken . . . He's an old acquaintance of mine. We've been on close terms for over twenty years . . ." The teacher smiled. "Just imagine! Pepe Martínez!"

And spontaneously, of his own volition, he told his story, as if doing it more for his benefit than his neighbor's, as if he derived inner pleasure from revisiting old memories.

"Pepe arrived years ago as the private secretary to a governor from Madrid. He too was from Madrid. He possessed no

real talent or culture, but was an incredibly handsome oppor-
tunist. He soon became the one the young girls idolized . . .
even those who weren't so young . . . They told lots of stories
about him . . . One, in particular . . . In a word, he always
landed on his feet . . . and was excellent company, despite
his loose screws . . . As indulgent toward his own faults as
toward those of others . . . The governor, a man of subter-
ranean influences—people claimed he was a blood relative, if
not by name, of a high-ranking member of the court—plied
his post like a sport, and as soon as he tired on one side, he
got a transfer somewhere else. Pepe Martínez followed him
across half of Spain . . . In the end, he met a woman from
the Philippines in Majorca and married her. She was fantastically ugly, ugly as a small Japanese idol, but good-hearted to a
fault and very wealthy. Pepe spoke of her and their marriage
with the utmost wit and cynicism . . . They came to live in
Barcelona, and Pepe went headlong into politics, managing,
with his wife's money and the protection of his old boss, to
become a deputy several times, and finally, a senator. If he'd
had a little common sense, an excellent career was opening
up before him, but his head was perfectly empty. He spent
like a prince, got embroiled in tremendous scandals, stupidly
undermined the dignity of his robes . . . As soon as his pro-
tector died and he lost the influence that prevented him from
being hurt, he was fired for being useless and dangerous, and,
conversely, his poor Japanese miniature, tired of suffering a
man who'd put her into all sorts of dodgy situations, filed for
divorce and returned to the Philippines after she found herself
on the brink of bankruptcy . . . That's how that castle of cards
collapsed when it seemed he would touch the stars . . . Now

he gets along as best he can—seedily, begging from friends, because he's as spendthrift as ever—and a none too generous allowance his wife sends him and . . . whatever bonus is added by a splendid, retired dancer who, they say, after years of putting up with him, still has a soft spot . . ." The teacher paused to smile a companionable smile. "He always did like a woman of the theater . . . I remember how, when he was here, he bankrupted an opera company after fisticuffs with the director and swanning off with the diva, who, you guessed it, was a beauty . . . and who came to a bad end, poor thing! He had set her up in an apartment, and as a few months later the governor was transferred, Pepe happily abandoned her, never to remember her again . . . But as she couldn't work, because she was pregnant and didn't realize it, she was reduced to poverty overnight, and everyone despised her . . . To avoid starvation and shame she suddenly disappeared from Girona, nobody knew where to, though she reappeared shortly after and gave birth in the Hospital, which is where she died in the end . . . on the day of the Virgin of Montserrat, to be exact. I remember it as if it was yesterday, because an aunt of mine told me, and when I was leaving the Hospital where I'd had to take a case from the Revenue—at the time I was working for the Revenue, do you see—I went to congratulate her . . ."

Nonat's fingers contracted spasmodically on his napkin.

"And what happened to the child?"

The teacher smiled sadly.

"Well, you can imagine! Off to the Orphanage . . . I mean, I suppose that's what . . . What do you expect? The Italian, I mean, the mother, had nobody here . . ." The teacher wiped his lips politely on his napkin. "Ah, the crimes of the careless . . . Because Pepe Martínez wasn't a bad sort . . . Simply what people call a flighty . . ."

A sinister bolt of light departed the bastard's blue-green eyes, crossed the dining room, and fell like a curse on the old rake's head . . .

A pause followed. The teacher was pensive, as if engulfed by his memories, instinctively tapping his bread roll with the blade of his knife. The light from the balcony traced two gleaming rectangles on his celluloid pate.

Coldly, slowly, Nonat asked: "Did he come from a good family?"

The teacher perked up.

"Who, Martínez? You must be joking. The son of a clerk . . . As a youngster he was an idler and collected cigarette butts in cafés."

Nonat's strong white teeth sank deep into his lip. They had finished lunch, and he ordered two coffees. There were a few points he needed to clear up.

When he left the inn, still obsessing over fresh doubts, he looked up and again noticed how the balcony facing-stones were embellished by beautifully sculpted reliefs. Then, walking up the cobbled street, he noticed, through a large, dilapidated porte-cochère, a majestic courtyard, lit up by the light of a day that was as gray and miserable as ash, at the back of which two flights of an ancient, noble staircase twisted upward.

Nonat stopped for a moment to scrutinize that house, the stone ashlars of which—a *weathered* color, as Josep Enric Rodó would say—seemed to want to avoid the gaze of the profane and the philistine, swaddled in a veil of distinction, a patina to dull any brightness.

He continued his walk upward, climbed the interminable steps, and entered the cathedral. He was overwhelmed by the faintest sense of anguish. Ever since the bastard had been back in Girona, he felt like someone else, not in a way he'd at all anticipated. Much to his surprise, he felt something new, a new aptitude that tinged afresh all he saw, all he liked. The hard edges of his old working-class spirit seemed to mellow into more varied, polished forms, like the facing stones of the inn's balconies, full of subtle shades, like the darkened stones of that seigneurial mansion yet to be sacrificed to passing fashion or human caprice. In a word, Nonat felt *taste* burgeoning within himself, civilization's blessed artificial illumination, the only one that lights up true grandeur and rescues it from darkness, creating different levels of sentiment among mortals. In that era of mysterious revelations, *that* had been a new, spontaneous one, like the sudden opening of a large, wondrous flower. Until recently, Nonat had walked past many things as if he were blind or unconscious. At Senyor Ramoneda's firm, in his little office in the scrap metal warehouse, he'd touched old items in that selection and reselection he'd suggested and executed, but they'd never spoken to his soul; battered, fragmented, and torn from their proper place as they were, when they reached his hands, they merely aroused distaste: for him they were objects to sell and exploit, an eccentric collection of leftovers representative of human idiocy, moneymakers one must profit from as best as one could, period. No longer: set in their proper location, embedded in a wall, immersed in propitious chiaroscuro, molded by their natural ambience, old things, often ugly and flaking in themselves, acquired a magical beauty, a fateful power to bewitch that they radiated, that penetrated and won you over . . .

A tug on his arm interrupted his reverie. A few people, gawping as if they were lost—strangers to the city, no doubt—were dawdling down the nave, swaying as they looked upward, hands dangling at their sides. Nonat's eyes glanced their way.

"Walk and tell me your news, as if you were showing me the cathedral."

Which is what Nas-Ratat did.

"I did what you told me. I went a-roaming when I left your bedroom. The room next door was open and I gave it the once over. They'd left a silk scarf and a shoehorn lying around and I snaffled them. Then I found a knife and napkin on a tray of hot chocolate served by the inn, and a new brush and bar of soap that will do me just right, because they don't give you any where I'm lodged. Not a great deal, but there you are . . . You'll see . . . If they're going to pin something on me, better if it's with good reason. I don't like unearned merit . . ."

The crook smiled. Nonat simply said: "Go on."

"Then I went to ask about the smithy. The neighbor opposite told me what happened. She says a lad left, whom he'd taken in as his own son; the smithy missed him so much he was always crying, sitting in a corner with his head between his hands. She says she came across him in that state a lot. Then, as he didn't know what to do with himself, he turned to drink; he lost his job and his sight deteriorated; he could only walk by clinging to walls and was always covered in bruises. She says she felt so sorry for him she would have taken him meals every day, if he'd wanted, but he said no; he wanted nothing from anybody, and when she did take him something—when he was out—the following day, she'd find it where she'd left it, untouched. One day the door wouldn't open and they reported it, in case he was ill, and the law went and found him dead, curled up at the foot of the forge. The doctors said he'd starved to death. The neighbor told me she could never get those blurry eyes and open mouth, exposing a gullet, out of her mind."

Nonat's face contracted in a rare foul grimace. The street porter looked at him askance and smiled again.

"That's all I managed to get out of her in over half an hour of chatter. Now, if you want more . . ."

"No. Here." Nonat surreptitiously handed him a watch pendant with a cut diamond initial. "If you have nothing more to say, clear off, and tomorrow morning, you know what to do . . . Better not be around here . . . Take care of the box, right?"

The crook gestured as if to say: "No worries! I'll see to it!"

"If you can't leave for any reason, at all, come by the front of the inn at a quarter to ten, but don't loiter . . ."

"I'll be off. Once I'm back in Barcelona, shall I phone you?"

"No, I won't be back. See you at Paperines's on Monday."

"Goodbye, captain. I hope you get . . ."

"Goodbye."

Nonat was left alone there, and in almost the entire edifice. Waning daylight in splashes of bright color from tall, stained glass windows left the church in semi-darkness, with a stagnant haze of smoke thickest around murky hollows by altars and distant corners. The smoke smelled vaguely of fresh wax, of burning, of flowers of Sant Pellegrino, of worn clothes, of dank . . . It was a smell remotely related to the one in his bedroom at the inn. And along with the smell, shadows spread over the damp, cold, muted silence of the graveyard . . . All of a sudden, the tap-tap of dragging feet and tinkling of keys broke the silence: a sacristan, jailer of that mystery, was doing his rounds. Almost from the same direction, two black phantoms, like two fragments chipped from the impenetrable gloom around the altars, crossed those enchanted shadows, making not the slightest sound a few feet from Nonat . . .

The bastard thought those two somber shapes weren't human, but two large owls, terrifying birds of the night, sinister creatures of the devil that made him shudder with fear. From his abnormal, inward-looking childhood, with none of the light-hearted fantasies, nursery rhymes, or measured contact with the world of the miraculous that all other children enjoy, his soul retained the seeds of ridiculous, childish fears, that now and then, when he least expected, surged from nowhere, turning him back into that fearful child despite his rebellious adult temperament. And there and then they were so strangely aggressive that he quickly looked for the exit.

Half-dazed by the movement from darkness to daylight, he watched burly youths chasing each other, screaming like swifts, up and down the luminous stairs; he saw two chaplains flapping the wings of their cloaks like flies about to take to the air; he watched four young women gossiping, rooted to the spot like so many other flies around a pot of sugar.

Stripped of its disguises, Girona was returning to its true self, with all the tranquility and profound charm of a historic city trapped in time . . .

Nonat felt a painfully tightened belt snap within him that, impelled by a hidden, expansive force, now shattered the layers of ice that enveloped his heart like a hard shell, letting something warm and soft seep through the cracks, soaking everything.

He felt something had burst through his chest, his old rancor, his deprivation and unhappy memories: another wondrous flower, a child's love for his old, peaceful city.

It was well past ten and Nonat had seen no sign of Nas-Ratat in the street; he must have left Girona already. Nonat quietly dressed and went for his morning coffee. He liked a big breakfast, because he felt hungry and was used to eating early, but, ever since he'd assumed gentlemanly airs, a strange sense of tact made him repress his working-class instincts and adapt to the general laxity around food he observed in his new estate. Once he'd breakfasted, he went to collect his walking stick, overcoat, and briefcase, and visited the reception.

The manager, who was busy scribbling, looked up.

"Look," said Nonat, handing over his key, "I'll be out all day, and as I'm leaving my luggage, please keep the key . . . And by the way, when the room's being cleaned, ask them to watch out for a pair of gold cufflinks. I left some on my night table for when I put on clean cuffs, but then I didn't change them and when I went to do so just now, I couldn't find the cufflinks anywhere. I expect they fell on the ground when the bed was being made."

The man at the desk blanched and hastily summoned the fresh-faced maid.

"Conxita, listen to what this gentleman has just said . . ." and he repeated Nonat's words.

Unlike the manager, the maid blushed a bright red, and stared at manager with a mixture of irritation and self-assurance.

"I cleaned his room myself and I don't remember seeing anything on the night table."

The manager was sweating, even though the wind was whistling through the open door.

"Anyway, take a good look everywhere, just in case . . ." He addressed Nonat without looking him in the eye. "I'm sorry, senyor. We'll do all we can."

Nonat said goodbye and went out.

The maid, tense and venomous, faced up to the manager.

"I can't stand anymore of this, Senyor Rius! The lady in number two says she's missing a bracelet; the gent in fifteen, his silk scarf; and now this fellow, his cufflinks . . ."

"And the people in six, a tie pin, and in eleven, a silver brush . . . and Rosa's missing some cutlery . . ." responded the manager, looking at the maid knowingly, quite delighted . . .

"What are you suggesting, Senyor Rius? I reckon that given the time I've been here . . ."

A gesture from the manager halted her in full flow.

"Shush! Don't get upset! We've had twenty-four hours of continuous complaints . . . You know what that means? There's a magpie in the house, my dear; he's here somewhere . . . But don't say a word . . . Someone's on the watch. You should all keep an eye out too; tell me once you get the first clue . . ."

When Nonat reached Sant Pere de Ruelles, it was almost 3 P.M., and although he could hear his stomach rumbling, he didn't want to dally and went straight up to Maria la Gallinaire's house. In the distance he saw a beggar sitting on the stone bench by the door, resting or keeping out of the sun. As he approached, the beggar didn't budge or seem to notice his footsteps.

"Must be blind," thought Nonat, but as he got nearer, he was shocked and stopped in his tracks. The man on the bench was Jepet, La Gallinaire's husband, but he'd altered so much Nonat barely recognized him. He seemed more a shadow of a man; an empty husk, like the ones some insects cast off periodically during the year, and what was left of the man in that cloth skin was a scrap of matter about to disintegrate for good. Inert and paralytically still, you'd have said he neither saw nor heard.

Tense and emotional, Nonat saw the image of Rovira in his final days rise before his eyes. And terror made his hair bristle.

With some effort, he took a step toward the old man and touched his back.

"Good afternoon, Jepet . . ."

That remnant of a man took ages to look around and vaguely focus his eyes, without a glimmer of consciousness, like a fish out of water.

"So, Jepet, I see you're in a poor state?" the bastard enquired.

"Ooooh . . . ! Oooh!" the poor fellow whimpered mournfully like a newborn calf.

"Where's my godmother? Inside?" asked the newcomer.

No answer, no sign of understanding.

Nonat put his lips next to Jepet's ear.

"Maria . . . Where is Maria?"

Now he understood! A strange commotion beset him; his hardened, owlish talons began to curl and shake furiously, as if he'd scented the rotting cadaver of an ass, and something stirred in the depths of his murky eyes.

"Oooh . . . ! Oooh! Oooh!"

That inhuman moan resounded, as off the inside walls of a cavern, like the lament of an injured animal in extreme pain, while threads of silver streamed down the cracks in his cheeks . . . The old man was crying.

A young brunette poked her head out of the next door along, and when she saw the visitor, she came out, drying her wet hands on her apron.

Nonat took his hat off.

"Good afternoon."

"May God keep you, senyor . . . "Did you speak to him? He won't understand; he's not all there, poor man!"

"Yes, so I saw . . . But he was quiet, and when I asked after his wife, he started crying."

"Oh, you know, he's always the same! He seems to understand nothing until he hears the name 'Maria.' He's been like this ever since she died."

Nonat turned pale.

"What did you say?"

The young woman looked at him, surprised, then seemed to understand . . .

"Oh, you must be the young man who came years ago. I think I remember you. I was in the street when you left their house . . ." and seeing that Nonat was in a state of shock and silent, she added: "Didn't you know she was dead? Well, senyor, it happened some time ago. We were friends of theirs, and as they had nobody, we began to tend their vines and do other jobs . . . and we were soon looking after them. You know, how were two old people like them ever going to manage on their own? One day I went in with a conger eel for Maria that my husband had just fished out of the sea . . . I shouted and shouted, but nobody answered. I went into the kitchen and saw her there by the ashcan. She'd had a heart attack while making supper and we were unable to bring her around . . . The poor woman gave us a lot of work! She'd been the busy kind, and I think when she saw she was good for nothing, she lost the will to live . . ." She suddenly changed her tone: "Oh, by the Holy Virgin, I wasn't thinking . . . Rabbiting on like that without asking you if you wanted to come in . . . I'm sorry."

El Senyoret tried to react.

"Thank you, my good woman . . . I'm in a hurry . . . Do you think I still have time to catch the train?"

"You'll have to get a move on, or else . . . unless you take the express pony and trap, because the mail train left a few hours ago!"

Nonat returned to the boarding house. Indeed, it was too late to catch the train, and, after having a bite to eat, to kill time until supper, Nonat had no choice but to accept the offer of his host, who said he'd accompany him on a stroll around the village outskirts.

He was frantic, out of his mind, again reflecting on the forces of evil plotting against him . . . When he suddenly stumbled on that imitation of Rovira, he'd felt everything was going haywire . . . Ah! Ill omens! Ill omens!

The next morning, he returned to Girona. As soon as he entered the inn, they summoned him and told him of all the thefts there had been, and as they'd found no trace of the hoodlums and there'd been no more thieving, they suggested it might have been that gold and silver dealer who'd paid him a visit, and asked for his details.

Nonat tapped his forehead.

"Good heavens! It must have been when I came down to change that note . . . I'd only just put the cufflinks on the night table. . . Fortunately they weren't worth much!"

Obviously, Nonat said he didn't know the man from Adam, that the gold and silver dealer had seen he was enthralled by old things at the cathedral and had offered him some ivory pieces he happened to have . . . and finally nothing had come of it because after agreeing to a deal, the fellow had come up with fresh demands . . . No doubt the sale was simply his excuse to get into the inn etc., etc.

And so he could now put the thefts behind him.

Next day, soon after lunch, they informed him the coach was ready to take him to the station. He came down the stairs with his coat over his arm and holding his walking stick. Two steps in front, the porter was carrying his two suitcases, his briefcase, and umbrellas. As he walked out the door, the porter couldn't avoid knocking into Pepe Martínez, who sidestepped him sprightly. The furious old gent stopped to tear a strip out of the young man. Two travelers were in the way, giving instructions about how to place their luggage on the top of the coach. Nonat had to squeeze between the two pairs. As he did so, he politely doffed his hat. When he put his hat back on, he'd tucked inside the ruby and emerald rhombus the governor's former secretary had been wearing on his tie.

We'll meet again, you rake! Nonat thought to himself, and gave the man a withering glance.

Then he climbed into the coach.

The train rushed at full tilt toward the blurred horizon, dividing the first fields into sunny, chameleon halves. Not yet satiated or bored by too much travel, El Senyoret allowed his wandering gaze to rest on tiny details in a landscape that whizzed past in a kaleidoscopic frenzy: a hummock topped by a farmhouse, a twisted trunk of a holm oak, a sienna field where a couple of mules plowed broad, purple-brown edging, a flock of sheep dotting a rocky precipice, a row of three kids rudely sticking a finger up at the train . . .

He looked out until numbness from a leg that had gone to sleep, which felt like a block of wood when he moved, made him change position. He was alone in his first class compartment. His eyes also smarted from the bright light and his wrinkled eyelids felt a peppery itch after being open too long, so he turned to look inside the carriage and relax against the cushions, stretching out his legs with his back against the side of the window. His last meal sat like a deadweight in his stomach and the insistent trickety-track of the train lulled him. In the midst of that uneasy lethargy, all his doubts from the last few days flew around his head like banks of cloud across the sky.

What he was experiencing was so absurd, it defied belief! So many years torturing himself trying to find his mysterious father, and when he'd given up on finding him, you could say, *when he no longer needed him,* lo and behold, as if by magic, the man had appeared before him . . . There were too many coincidences for it to be doubted or put down to chance. And he quickly reviewed the facts: They added up, generally speaking: the diva's presence in Girona, her temporary disappearance (the stay in Sant Pere de Ruelles. The owner of the boarding house had clearly remembered that years ago, a very beautiful lady in the final months of pregnancy, who'd met nobody "apart from the midwife and Maria la Gallinaire," had spent weeks in a mansion on the outskirts of the town): her return to the city, to die giving birth in the Hospital "precisely on the day of the Virgin of Monserrat . . ." Then, the strange airs and graces people found in him . . . his love of luxury, maybe a blood inheritance from the old Madrid roué . . . and, above all, the vicious rancor the old rake had inspired in him from the very first moment he'd seen him . . . (perversely, Nonat felt that rancor was the best proof of their direct connection,

the current linking his soul and that of his presumed father!)
His father! The father who'd popped up like a mushroom out
of the bracken, the surprise father who'd dropped from the
sky . . . And what a father, for Christ's sake! None of those
millions he'd fantasized about, nothing that might even be a
substitute: whether a name, august social status, a coat of arms,
a safe haven, a good port of call in the higher echelons . . . No,
rather an inept, corrupt fraudster . . . That is, a burden rather
than someone he could manipulate, a nuisance rather than a
helping hand . . . And behind his father, his mother: a vulgar
music hall singer, the smallest star in the firmament . . . All in
all, not much better than the baker in Algiers his godmother,
Maria la Gallinaire, had no doubt assigned to him to douse
his delirium . . . What an awful joke fate had played! Because,
although Nonat wasn't the innocent, hopeful youth of old,
he felt that new thorn keenly and rebelled against his dashed
expectations as if it was an affront he didn't deserve, and felt
deep regret at a potential future that had vanished, as if it
were a right that was genuinely his, one that had been illegally
taken away, a resurgence of the shameful stigma of his bastard
self . . . Then, when he'd pondered long and hard, how could
he ever recognize a father like that? No chance! Much better
to go it alone in life. He would always keep a tag on Pepe
Martínez, he would never let him out of his sight so he could
swoop one day if he needed to, but he would never be allied to
his fate, never! No links, no boundaries, no obligations limit-
ing his freedom and that peace and calm he'd finally attained.

That feeling of tranquil freedom El Senyoret mentally
alluded to had been born in his heart the day of the fracas on Carrer de Bon Succés, or rather, the moment he'd

left Paperines's tavern after reaching an agreement with Nas-Ratat.

He'd spent that whole evening in a state of bliss, like a child lost in an enchanted, fairy-tale wood; he hadn't had anything in particular in mind, but, as that protracted hallucination developed, his conscience, bright and piercing like a clarion call, told him he'd just enacted a change that would be decisive: the ideal synthesis of the waves of longing that had pursued and perturbed him over the years; he'd just been given the life-changing gift that a sudden, extraordinary twist of fate can produce: the recognition a master gives his favorite pupil for the first time; the discovery of a long-sought, unknown quality; the "yes" from the lips of one's beloved opening the doors to betrothal . . . namely, a new sense of dignity that anointed and hallowed him in his own eyes, salvaging him from the dismal dust where beings with no ambitions pullulate, turning him into an singular, self-motivating force.

Quite simply, his vocation had been aroused, had been fully revealed in a clear, definitive form that left no room for doubt, and, becoming fully aware of it, seeing it expressed in that irrevocable pact, he was overwhelmed by the fact it existed so vigorously.

That was it! He understood that this was what he'd *always* been, fundamentally, by his very nature, and that henceforth he would only and consciously be *that*, with all the trappings of discernment and will . . . And the quiet satisfaction, the accompanying sense of serene, exalted well-being, a logical consequence of that eureka moment, were but aspects of an organ that freely performs the function it was created for by inscrutable fate . . . Perhaps, in his heart of hearts, an incipient, fine mist, a thin layer of rarefied atmosphere, imperceptibly dimmed the intensity of his satisfaction . . . It was anxiety vaguely tempered by instinct, perplexity he had hardly encapsulated philosophically in the face of the label of immorality the world used to condemn and persecute the free exercise of a function that was only a natural result of the fateful imperative of internal impulses. However, that mist soon lifted without a trace, like the haze covering the firmament at the break of day when the sun rises.

Back in Barcelona and not feeling the least concerned, Nonat dropped his box on Senyor Grisau's counter (the mahogany box with marquetry filigree he had once used for his tools and that looked like a surgeon's box). The lightning way Grisau opened up the booty, quick and dazzling like an electric flash, was a poem in itself.

He inspected it carefully and started pricing the items.

"So much for that; so much for this; so . . ."

The bastard grabbed Grisau's wrist with one hand while his other quietly reclaimed the jewel Grisau was holding.

"Let's leave it there for today, Senyor Grisau. You're an evil son of a bitch."

Frenchy's grandson was taken aback.

"What *do* you mean?" he muttered, quite bewildered.

"That the more we do, the *less* we're worth."

"Well, I give you all I . . ." he replied, reasserting himself.

Nonat smiled ironically

"No need to bankrupt yourself."

And he calmly started to put the jewels back in the box.

Senyor Grisau was livid: that rascal was insulting him, not realizing he was at *his* mercy, and, with characteristic sourness, openly voiced his thoughts.

"Hang on, you fool, don't you see that I can oblige you to give them to me for whatever price I name?"

Nonat looked him blankly up and down, and replied in a cold, neutral tone: "If I had thought that was the case, I'd never have come to you."

And he continued collecting up the items.

The silversmith's red face suddenly turned the color of rancid butter.

Grisau's expulsion from the jewelers and the ins and outs of his trial passed rapidly through his mind . . . *That rascal knows who I am and is on firm ground; that's why he's so calm and collected! I'll have to beat a retreat.* He gently ran his hand over what was left on the table.

"All right . . . no need to be so touchy! We can work out a way . . ."

Grisau's voice faltered; his eyes glowered.

Nonat's head, on the other hand, reared up like a viper's.

"I don't like needless playacting, Senyor Grisau!"

Senyor Grisau seemed to shrink inside his yellow jacket like a turtle into his shell.

The situation had flipped quickly and now Nonat was in control.

His colleague's sudden change of heart had revealed that, for some mysterious reason he couldn't fathom, the latter had just laid himself at his beck and call. And he reacted spontaneously to a hunch, as he liked to do.

"Tell me," Nonat asked, not at all presumptuously, but completely sure of his ground, "are you a genuine silversmith, or simply a salesman?"

"A silversmith."

"Very good, then. I need a thousand pessetes. Hand it over now and take what you want. We'll talk at length another time."

Senyor Grisau looked down.

"I haven't got a thousand," and, seeing the cloud cross the fine gent's face, he was quick to add, "but I will have by this afternoon."

"Excellent. Bring it to me when you close." And after giving him a card with Senyora Maria's address, Nonat plonked the box back on the counter: "Take your pick."

Senyor Grisau angrily raised his eyebrows and waved him away.

"I'll choose when I bring the money . . ."

"Bah! It makes no difference. Take them now." Nonat's thin lips formed a cynical grin. "I believe you won't let me down."

Those cutting words, reminding the old man of his impotence, were like a slap to the cheek.

He prudently chose three or four items from the heap. Nonat put the rest back and bid him farewell.

Senyor Grisau looked at the card: *Ramon N. Ventura.* He beamed the telepathic ray of a man persecuted toward the door after the fellow making his exit.

"You sewer scorpion! I'll crush you on the corner of a door!"

Senyora Pepa was absolutely convinced. The faint, peculiar stench that hit her when she entered her house, the one lingering on furniture, clothes, and walls—"even the kitchen range, so help me God"—came from Carmeta. Rather than going away, it had worsened over the summer, and was making everything stink. And when Carmeta was walking next to her, Senyora Pepa went into a kind of swoon and practically fainted.

I wish my sense of smell wasn't so keen! she reflected miserably, because she knew that if her cousin gave off such an unpleasant smell, it wasn't because she was slovenly: she spent the day washing in the washhouse and changed her clothes every two hours. The wretched girl could smell it herself and she's upset. She must be having hot flashes. Senyor Roure's daughter (a friend of Mossèn Vicenç's, from the Santa Maria neighborhood) had stunk like that when she caught chicken pox. And she approached Carmeta discreetly, talked about cures for all kinds of illnesses, gave her prescriptions suggested by her own experience or imagination. Carmeta behaved as if she didn't have a clue what that was all about, but she *was* deteriorating by the day; her eyes sank deeper into their sockets and the circles under her eyes darkened. From the time they had seen Nonat on the Diagonal, she'd been very edgy, and sometimes when Senyora Pepa looked at her, she felt depressed. Her cousin had told her, not very flatteringly, who that individual was and how he'd hurt everybody, but Senyora Pepa, like Angeleta before her, couldn't perceive the sense of premeditated evil Carmeta attributed to the bastard, and wondered rather anxiously whether Carmeta was suffering from delirium like her brother, especially as the first time

Carmeta came to El Clot, after Octavi's demise, she hadn't said a word about any of that . . .

Senyora Pepa had two shops on the ground floor of her house. On the right, La Caprichosa (perfumery and stationery effects) and on the left, El Bambú, a barbershop of high local repute.

One evening, Senyora Pepa was returning from Barcelona when she noticed that the owner of the perfumery was beckoning to her.

"Good evening, Filomena, what can I do for you?"

The parfumier looked enigmatic and smug.

"Good evening, Senyora Pepa. I just wanted a word. I hope you won't think I'm meddling in what's no business of mine, but as you don't seem to be aware, I thought I should alert you to something . . ."

"Ay, by the Virgin Mary, what on earth do you mean?"

"Have you noticed the state Carmeta is in? She seems entirely out of it . . . And do forgive me if I seem to do her down, but she gives off such a whiff!"

Senyora Pepa blanched.

"You've smelled it too? I thought my nose was being oversensitive!"

"No, my love! She spreads it wherever she goes. You know, only yesterday, my nephew, the one finishing his degree in medicine, was here . . . Carmeta came in for a bar of soap, and straightaway . . ." The parfumier seemed to hesitate, then finally came out with it: "Senyora Pepa, your cousin's got something nasty . . ."

Pepa gave a start.

"My God, what *are* you suggesting?"

"What I said. The other night we were talking to Elies . . ." Elies was the parfumier's husband, the master barber and owner of El Bambú, the barbershop across the way. "'You should warn Senyora Pepa,' he said . . . That young woman may be about to cause her a big upset . . . From the look of her, I'd say she's about to cock her toes up!'"

"Ave Maria Puríssima!" and the hapless woman turned so pale you'd have thought *she* was about to do so right then. Then she recovered slightly. "Thank you for the interest you're taking, Filomena, but what can I say? I don't feel it can be as bad as you say. There may be something wrong with Carmeta, but nothing so serious . . . I mean, where could she have caught it?"

Then the parfumier stiffened.

"I'll be frank, Senyora Pepa. This isn't nonsense I made up . . . My nephew told me . . . He's of the opinion that Carmeta is really ill and needs treatment without delay. And he knows what he's talking about! My nephew is very smart. He gets a *first-class* every year, and the professors say he's their star . . . If you like, he can give you the card of a good doctor and will even accompany you, if necessary, so she can have a proper examination."

Frightened to death by that sudden blow, Senyora Pepa left it to her tenant to arrange things as best she could. The latter brought Carmeta around to the idea by using all her wiles, because she resisted stubbornly, almost implacably, but the consultation would take place.

"Will you come with me, Filomena?" asked Senyora Pepa. "I can't think straight and I probably wouldn't understand what they say . . ."

"Of course, no need even to ask, Senyora Pepa. I'll help you however I can. Shouldn't be otherwise, among neighbors . . ."

And accompanied by the nephew, who, in his neophyte enthusiasm, had shown a great interest in the case, the three women went to the doctor's.

The student had been right! Carmeta was indeed a dead woman walking, and only because God wished; the deadly tumor eating her insides was in such a putrefied state it had already poisoned her bloodstream, making any kind of operation futile and too dangerous given the patient's extreme state of undernourishment.

Her organism was a lamp without oil, where the light of life would gradually be extinguished on a burned-out wick.

Poor Senyora Pepa was in despair.

"Alone in my old age . . . again! Alone again!"

And she saw the future stretching out long and dark as an endless winter's night.

Nonat was on his way back from La Maravilla, where he hadn't been for some time. Now and then he liked to drop into the places he knew well, for "the benefits it might bring." He was striding absentmindedly along when, near Carrer d'Aragó, he suddenly stopped because he thought somebody had given him the evil eye. Amid the haze where his mind was wandering, a prey to his ruminations, he had vaguely registered that a figure walking by the barrier at the edge of the curb had suddenly disappeared. All his preoccupations vanished immediately, like a flock of birds scattered by a round of grapeshot, and, instinctively on the alert, he continued walking, his eyes glued to the shadows where that figure had evaporated.

A glance up and down the street showed not a soul was about.

He smiled through gritted teeth, and, when he reached the crossroads, he too clung to the barrier. On turning the corner, bang, just what he'd expected. A man reared up before him like a jack in the box.

"Psst! Shut up and keep still!" squealed a voice, and a blade glinted in the dark.

Nonat acted the second his assailant appeared. He leapt on him like a deer, gripping the arm holding the knife and twisting it hard to wrench it away. It was a brief skirmish; a pain-stricken "Owww!" rang out, the twisted arm slackened, the fingers loosened, and Nonat snatched the knife. Then he hurled his attacker to the ground and kicked him three or four times at random. His downed foe whimpered and writhed like a wounded animal on the cobbles.

"I'll teach you a lesson! When you're after spoils, you need to watch who you pick on!" the bastard spoke matter of factly.

The figure on the ground pleaded meekly: "For God's sake, don't shout!"

Nonat frowned blankly; he stared at his victim, looked at the blade, closed it slowly, threw it at his attacker's feet . . .

"Here you are. Get up and follow me."

The contempt resonated in his voice and his order brooked no appeal.

The man on the ground got up and did as he was told.

When they reached Passeig de Gràcia, Nonat gestured to him to sit on a bench, then sat down beside him.

"In other words, if you grab a toothpick, you must have the necessary teeth to use it, and you're as soft as they come . . . What do you do, apart from this?"

"I used to work as a coachman."

"And why don't you now?"

"Because I don't have a carriage."

"Somebody took it from you?"

"No, it was mine and I sold it."

"And you make a living?"

An obscenity was the only response.

Nonat looked at him. Under an old cap, he glimpsed a sallow face, bushy eyebrows, a turned up nose, small beady eyes, a drooping Chinese mustache, and pinched, dry purple lips. His neck was skinny, his shoulders angular, his torso emaciated.

He studied Nonat's quizzical stare fearfully, not daring to say a word. In the end, El Senyoret addressed him curtly: "If you had more muscle on you, I might have given you a job."

"I've been sick and haven't eaten in a day. How do you expect me to flex any muscles? I wouldn't have left home today, if she hadn't . . ."

"Ah, so you're married?"

"Yes, as good as . . . I've got a woman."

Nonat looked serious.

"What does she do?"

A simian smile moved the purple lips.

"What do you think she does? She's good for nothing, as they all are . . . . !"

El Senyoret thought for a minute.

"All right. Come to see me tomorrow evening at seven . . ."

The other man replied morbidly.

"Who knows where I'll be tomorrow? Didn't I tell you I haven't eaten in a day? And if all my cards play out like this one . . . !"

Nonat stuck his hand in his pocket and gave him the man ten pessetes. He told him to go and eat something and drop by Paperines's place the next day. Finally, the man looked him defiantly up and down and promised he'd be there.

Let's say a few words about Nonat's new acquaintance.

The second son of a Valencian noble married a wealthy Barcelonan industrialist's daughter, and went to live in her house. He brought most of his domestic staff from Valencia: second chambermaid, coachman, servant, etc. The coachman soon married the first chambermaid, who'd been the young lady's chambermaid, and both continued with the family, he in the same post and she promoted to housekeeper. They had a child, and no sooner did that boy stand on his own two feet than his parents dressed him in blue breeches with yellow hems and made him open the door and run errands. He was as useless as an unruly ass, and always argued about what he should be doing. The other servants couldn't stand him, but said nothing because the parents carried lots of weight with the master and mistress of the house.

Even so, the former were almost thrown out of the house more than once because of the young boy.

One day, when the mistress scolded him for some outrageous antic, the little devil smeared shoe polish over the pink silk lining of her theatergoing coat; on another, when the master tweaked his ears, the boy put gunpowder in his tobacco pouch, and on yet another, when the young mistress accidentally stamped on his toes, he cut off the tail of Dandy, her favorite pooch.

"That nasty piece of work is worse than the plague; you see only evil in those little open windows . . ." was what everybody said, referring to the incredibly open cavities of his flared nostrils.

When the boy, whom they'd named Batista, was ten or twelve, he was informed that the master's brother had died without heirs, and his master had inherited his title and possessions. As a result, the family upped and moved to Valencia. As Batista's mother was from Barcelona and as his father doted on his wife, they decided not to follow their masters, but rather stay in Barcelona, where she would establish a boarding house and he would work as a coachman. The master made him a gift of a horse and carriage so he could earn his living by working for himself.

They enjoyed three or four happy years. The boarding house did well and the carriage was never still. Batista would have liked to stay in the lodging house forever, but his father, who had been forced to tolerate all his mischief, put his foot down and forced him to jump in the carriage with him and take the reins.

One night, the coachman woke up coughing, complaining of a sharp pain in his side. His wife massaged him, gave him orange liqueur and aniseed in case he was just gassy, and as nothing seemed to work, they called a doctor. The doctor decided he had raging pneumonia. He was dead within four days. His colleagues at the carriage line called him the Valencian. His son inherited the carriage and his father's job. His mother continued as a landlady: one day a lodger fell in love and married her. He was from a village in the heart of Asturias, which he would still visit in a stagecoach. The new husband wanted to go to his land for their honeymoon; the horses pulling the stagecoach took fright on a sharp bend and the carriage tumbled down the slope by the road. The newlyweds and other passengers were battered and bruised, taken to a nearby peasants' house, and given rudimentary treatment; their injuries became infected, gangrene set in, and the newlyweds died within a fortnight.

On the cusp of twenty, Batista was alone in the world.

He was the devil himself: a stirrer, a drinker, as trustworthy as Judas's conscience, and explosively tempered. A disaster.

Scraping and scheming, consuming all manner of concoctions for his illnesses, which melted the marrow in his bones, he managed to make it to the age of twenty-five. One late afternoon, he'd just driven a gentleman to the port and was now trotting up the Paral·lel, his red canopy raised, when a young girl on a café terrace made him turn his head. When she saw the carriage, she seemed inspired by an idea, because she hailed the coachman, who came over.

She was thin, floppy, and seemed somehow unhinged; her face was an oily brown, her eyes long and almond, and her hair, dark as deep sorrow, cropped short.

She wore battered, twisted, high-heeled leather shoes, a tight blue skirt, and a loose red crepe blouse with sweaty armpits and faded ruffles.

The Valencian was riveted.

"What a pretty little gypsy!" he thought.

The "gypsy" climbed into his carriage.

"Where to?" asked Batista.

The lass solemnly shrugged her shoulders and responded languidly: "Wherever you fancy . . . take me for a ride . . ."

A crack of the whip, and off they went. Turning down here, going straight up there, they were still rolling along at eight in the evening, his passenger never saying a word. Batista was surprised and looked around to the door.

"Do you want to go on . . . ?"

Silence.

He jumped off his seat and looked through the window: by the light from a lamp he saw the "gypsy" was prostrate and motionless. He opened the door thinking she'd had a fit; he shook her . . . The girl opened her bleary eyes, stretched out her arms, and yawned . . .

She'd simply spent all that time sleeping like a baby; she said as much as she jumped out of the carriage.

Annoyed, Batista declared brusquely: "That will be four and a half pessetes."

She rummaged in her pocket

"I've only got thirty cents," she replied, showing them in the palm of her hand.

Batista felt his innards react furiously.

"And you wanted a ride in a carriage for that paltry sum?"

She answered blankly.

"I was exhausted and couldn't think where else to go . . ."

The volcano blasting inside Batista subsided: he surveyed from up close the listless body before him. She was pretty, so pretty! Then he whispered a couple of words.

She shrugged her shoulders by way of response.

"Get in!"

And he pushed her back into the carriage, leapt onto the driving seat, cracked his whip, and the poor knight of spades, breathless and blissful, flew to the coach house.

From that day on, La Pelada and the Valencian lived together.

Now who was La Pelada?

The daughter of a café waiter and a woman who ironed for a living.

The waiter had died of consumption after running through their savings over his eighteen months of illness; he left his wife an assortment of small debts and two young daughters as her only inheritance. But Margarideta was a strong character, and not dismayed to see she'd been left head of her household. If necessary, she would work night and day to pay their debts and rear her children. No sooner was it said than it was done. She took no holidays, not even short breaks, and was always ironing, *hiss-hiss, hiss-hiss,* nonstop until she achieved what she had set out to do. She paid off the debts, was caught up with the rent, and her girls had grown up. Praised be the Lord, she could breathe again! There was only one thorn in her side: her youngest's lazy temperament and "give-it-to-me-all-on-a-plate" attitude. The elder girl took after her mother in everything—name, character, and looks—but the youngster was in the mold of her mother-in-law, "may the Lord preserve her in heaven!" While the Margaridetes—as neighbors and customers called mother and elder daughter—were tall, well-built, and proud, white as a lily, fair as gold, clean as silver, sweet as jujubes, and festive as the dawn, the second, Amàlia, was black as a crow, thin as a thread, dirty as a fox, brittle as a fish scale, and lazier than any ne'er-do-well. Her mother had tried everything to galvanize her, without success: lecturing her, imploring her, punishing her, shaming her for her faults, broadcasting them to the neighbors. But nothing ever changed, nothing at all, as if she were a leper: she neither resisted, nor protested, nor mended her ways. There was no way her mother could persuade her to wear a dress without stains (and the saints alone knew where she collected them, because the house was so spotless you could lick it), or bend her back over a task for more than five minutes. She didn't even play with the other children so she didn't have to make the effort. She crouched in corners of rooms or on the door-step, and, lolling lackadaisically with wisps of hair in her eyes, she would spend hours watching her mother work or people walk by while she chewed her fingernails . . .

"If that child doesn't change her attitude when she gets her monthlies, she'll be the death of me," said her mother in despair.

But her last hope was dashed, as was every other.

When Amàlia started "her monthlies," her defects only grew exponentially and created new ones; as well as being lazier, more lethargic, more couldn't-care-less, more taci-turn than ever, she developed a sweet tooth and became a fan of precious stones. She wouldn't have changed her blouse, washed her face, or even gotten up at midday if they hadn't forced her to, though she always put a ribbon in her hair and spent hours out of the house on every single errand after filching money from the drawer to buy herself tidbits. However, her beauty had prospered at the expense of her blotches. Her olive skin lightened and smoothened, and there was a warm, pink glow under that brown; black as blackberries with bluish corneas, always glistening and with long velvety lashes, her eyes were like the half-open sides of a mysterious, voluptuous fruit; her thin, bright-lipped mouth, around two rows of large teeth, even and white as alum, looked like a shell the depths of which seemed to harbor all the aphrodisiacal power of marine life.

While her resplendently clean mother and sister wore white, ironed aprons and pristine oversleeves over their smooth, woven dresses, Amàlia had a passion for bright colors and flamboyant designs.

"Lord Almighty, dressed like that, with those accoutrements, she looks like a woman on the prowl, God spare us that!" Margarida senior lamented to Margarida junior, pointing to the rebel leaning against the doorjamb, her body limp as if boneless, in instinctive, resigned, blank expectation of something that would fatefully befall her.

And indeed, that "something" did come along.

Three or four doors down from Margarida the ironing woman was a tailor who was always very busy. His male clients were always walking up and down the street. And when they strolled by, they all looked lustfully at Amàlia, the skeletal adolescent with protruding hips and backbone whose lips and eyes, on the other hand, were full of tempting promise. Amàlia received those male tributes with absolute indifference; she was neither shamefully aroused nor filled with modest repulsion. Each spark from the turbulent lightning she prompted met with mysterious, feline passivity, the hieratic, hermetic pose of an Egyptian goddess . . . Nevertheless . . .

One of those men eying her went in and out of the tailor's more often than the others: he was both a customer and textile seller.

Short, plumpish, puffy-cheeked, almost bald, the man had big eyes that glinted mischievously under his fair eyebrows . . . One day, he could stand it no more and stared hard at Amàlia. Amàlia let him, and didn't react . . . On another day, he bumped into her in the street when she was on her way to return ironed clothes and idly gawping at a confectioner's window. He went in and bought chocolates, then stopped to give them to her on his way out. He said many things: he talked of dresses, of travel, of loving her, and not allowing her to lift a finger . . . Amàlia listened quietly, but never responded. He was in a hurry and bid her farewell, saying that tomorrow and every day after, he'd walk past the ironing shop to see her, that she should stand in the doorway. The next day, Amàlia was there on the doorstep and that rotund fellow walked by, smiled, and, without stopping, placed a little parcel of sweets in her hand. Two days after, the next little parcel contained a bottle of perfume. A week later, he waited for hours when she was out on an errand, and when she appeared, he approached her. He said that the following day he was going on a long trip to some delightful cities, and if she wanted to come along—he'd buy her a hat, they would stay in inns, go to the theater, and he'd cherish her like a queen. She stayed silent, and looked in front of her . . . His eyes devoured her: that dark, languid sphinx had stolen his heart and she made him delay his journey by two weeks. He'd be so upset if he couldn't take her! But he made one final attempt.

"All right, I'll be in an automobile in the square near your house at around four. The train leaves at five . . . I'll be waiting for you, right? I'll be waiting . . . You will come, won't you?" He'd turned yellow and was shaking; he gripped a hand, a small, scrawny, monkey's hand, and pressed it to his lips. "You will, won't you? Tell me one way or the other . . ." he asked longingly, "You will, won't you?"

They went their separate ways.

She shrugged her shoulders, still staring in front of her.

It was a day when Margarida senior was in an angry mood and kept bawling. She scolded Amàlia because she came back late, because her blouse was crumpled, because she'd mended a ribbon by knotting it rather than sewing it . . . She would even have slapped Amàlia if the girl hadn't raised an arm to protect her face. For the first time, Amàlia had reacted impatiently.

Next morning the man walked by, smiled, and pointed to the square.

"Four o'clock," he whispered without stopping.

By two the automobile was waiting on the corner, by three he could stand it no longer and walked past the ironer's again. The two Margaridetes, like a couple of white nuns, were making up parcels of ironed clothes and putting them in the laundry basket. His heart leapt and he jumped quickly into the automobile. Every other moment he stuck his head out, beads of sweat streaming down his bald pate. At last! Amàlia came out lethargically, swaying listlessly and moving nearer and nearer and nearer . . .

Beside himself, he opened the car door.

"What about these clothes?" she simpered, totally at ease.

"Give them to me! We'll throw them out later . . ."

He feverishly settled the young girl in and shouted at the driver: "To the Estació de França and put your foot down!"

He was terrified they would rob him of his treasure!

After long, anxious hours looking for her everywhere, the Margaridetes managed to get a lead—much to their horror. The knifemaker in the square had seen the "lass from the ironer's" get into an automobile; the chairmaker's boy had made a mental note of the number of the car that parked in front of his house for so long; a search was made for the automobile and it was easily tracked down; the chauffeur handed over the ironed clothes the couple had left in the car and told them what had happened. No doubt about it: Amàlia had gone off with a man, "with an old gent," which revealed the nature of her flight and, consequently, the irrevocable damage it had done.

She was ruined, ruined on every front! Margarideta senior was so ashamed and despairing that she went mad. The very epitome of honor and conscience, she now had to recognize that flesh of her flesh, blood of her blood . . . She didn't dare finish that line of thought; her mind was spinning around in one great fog. She had nervous attacks and was ill for days on end. Margarideta junior couldn't lift her head from her pillow . . . In the end, the harsh need to make a living put a stop to that lunacy and gradually returned the poor mother to her normal state, harnessed to the hallowed yoke of daily toil, that great reliever of pain and plaintiveness, healer and helpmate of minds in turmoil, and the neighbors soon saw how a workplace ravaged by misfortune, like a damaged nest, regained its tranquil, homespun air, glowing with activity and tidiness under the determined aegis of the two Margaridetes.

As far as they were concerned, the runaway girl was dead. Only hidden melancholy, eternally revisited by the honorable matriarch's heart, attested to her lingering sorrow.

In posh hats and dressed like a lady, in mass-produced outfits, Amàlia traveled leagues galore by rail, ate in many inns and taverns, and strolled along the streets of many Spanish towns and cities on the arm of her seducer, the rotund, bald, commercial representative. He couldn't get over the bargain that had come his way in the shape of this random debauchery in the course of duty, and slavered over the young thing despite her bland indifference. He shod, combed, and dressed her as any maid might have done; he polished her shoes and brushed her clothes; when they brought breakfast, he served her in bed, and then, before going to "show his samples," he put her to bed like a child and closed the shutters so she could sleep until he got back. He bought her everything he felt would delight her; he cherished, never scolded her. Amàlia had never been so well fed and had no regrets whatsoever. But the commercial rep's tour was coming to an end, and, conversely, Amàlia began to feel sickly; she felt strangely anxious, as if she were missing something, the back of her head hurt, her eyes hurt when she blinked, sudden hot flashes overwhelmed her, she couldn't eat a bite, fainted on the train . . . The tissue of the commercial rep's heart froze. Was it punishment for their dalliance? He couldn't take his worried, questioning eyes away from his girlfriend's face, which daily reflected her change, an ominous pallor. He hastened their return to Barcelona, where they arrived at night. Amàlia was visibly ill; she complained—she who never said a word!—of being insatiably thirsty, and started to cry and hug him, mumbling incoherently: "Get that dog to go away; it keeps looking at me and making my teeth chatter . . . I'm scared . . . I'm scared . . ."

The commercial rep entered an out-of-the-way tavern and asked for two rooms; he put Amàlia in one and his own luggage in the other, and went to fetch an acquaintance of his who was a municipal doctor.

"This lady is suffering from an infection. It could be raging typhoid fever . . ." He examined her at length. "It's the worst, if I'm not mistaken . . . She is married, I presume?"

"Yes, indeed, she was given over to my care as such by a gentleman . . . a gentleman we met in Valladolid. When he discovered we were going to Barcelona, he begged me to look after her till we got here . . . I think she's expecting someone . . ."

He didn't know which way to turn; the doctor attributed his anxious state to the fix the woman who "was given over to my care" had placed his friend in.

The rep had used up all his funds, was in deficit with his company, and had to account for his endeavors . . . And then there was his wife, his children . . . looming commitments . . . No, he had to get out of this fix quickly, by whatever means . . . He shuddered next to the doctor, pleading humbly: he couldn't stay there or take responsibility for the expenses caused by that illness, particularly since he didn't even know her . . . Could his friend please do him a favor and get him out of that mess . . . and never mentioning his name . . . Above all, *never* mentioning his name . . . The doctor looked him up and down, shrugged his shoulders, as if to say there wasn't any reason why *he* should be burdened either . . . Thanks to his good connections, Amàlia was admitted into the hospital. While she was wholly unconscious, she lost her embryonic babe and found herself at death's door. Three months later, she left the hospital, half-recovered, thin as a rail, with huge eyes, a shaven head, and holding a purse where, to her great surprise, she found a fifty-pesseta note and two five-pesseta coins. When she had used up her capital, she was starving and standing next to an inn, when a man emerged, patted her on the shoulder and nodded . . . And after him, there was another and another and another . . . Because La Pelada, despite being so taciturn and languid, was enormously in demand and never lacked a suitor . . . She welcomed them limply, but all her feelings still favored the rotund, bald commercial rep who'd shod, dressed, and combed her.

Meanwhile elsewhere in Barcelona life had also moved on . . .

Senyor Grisau was in the doorway when Nadala walked past. When she saw him standing still, she didn't look as if she was about to stop, but when he saw her, he sweetened his vinegary expression as best he could and asked: "Do I scare you? No need to be frightened, my dear, you can look in my window as much . . . !"

Nadala blushed and hurried down the street. An enraptured Senyor Grisau watched her sashay into the salted cod shop. Then he extracted a cigar butt from his pocket, stuck it up a nostril, swore, sniffed blissfully, and slipped back into his kiosk like a wild animal into its den.

The following day, he curbed his impatience and said nothing until Nadala stopped to look at his window. Then he looked up and gave her a friendly smile. She blushed and ran off that day too, but not the day after, nor the one after that . . . Now they greeted each other with broad grins. As they were now on good terms, Senyor Grisau risked waiting on the doorstep for her again. When he saw her coming, he grabbed a medallion and waved it at her from afar. Curiosity won out over shyness and Nadala stopped.

"Do you like this medallion? I wanted to show it to you."

Nadala thought it was lovely and asked which saint's it was.

"My saint: Saint Benedict . . . Because I'm a Benedict, do you know? And what's your name?"

"Jesusa."

"That's a very pretty name. I'll tell you what! I'll make one for you with baby Jesus in the stable . . ."

The astonished young girl walked off. When she next came by, Senyor Grisau, from inside his kiosk, beckoned to her to come in. She went in and they talked about the medallion again.

"Yesterday I forgot to ask you whether you liked them big or small . . . Because I want to make it the way you'd prefer."

And he took the ones out of the window and laid them on the counter; they debated and chose the size.

Suddenly, Senyor Grisau said: "Wait a minute, the ribbon around your ponytail's coming loose . . ." and he pulled it free and retied the bow with his deft fingers, covered in red hair and brown nicks from his cutters.

They were good friends now. When the young girl came and went from the dressmaker's, during the day she'd always peer through the glass and smile, and every evening, when she finished, she'd go into the kiosk and chat about the medallion. That was when the salted cod seller started complaining about Nadala's late appearance. That medallion, which was never ready, was a good excuse for chit-chat.

Senyor Grisau always talked up how pretty it would be and told the girl never to whisper a word to anyone about their rendezvous and conversations. And, before she left the kiosk, he always smoothed her hair, tied her scarf around her neck so she wasn't cold, and patted her cheek. One evening, one blissful night, he kissed her . . . The day after, he confessed he'd almost finished the medallion, and as Nadala was desperate to know what it would be like, he started sketching it . . . Nadala was entranced and stuck her head between his face and the sheet of paper . . . Senyor Grisau said: "Wait a minute, you'll see it better like this . . ." and he sat her on his thigh.

Finally, the medallion was ready. The young girl's round face sagged disappointedly. It wasn't at all how Senyor Grisau's patter had led her dreams to believe it would be, but, even so, when she saw it on a small chain around her neck sparkling like colored chips of glass, Nadala was entranced. When he saw that, the silversmith said she must kiss him on both cheeks as payment.

The following Sunday, when her mother was changing her daughter's undershirt, she saw the present and asked, "Where did you get that?"

Nadala blushed to the whites of her eyes and replied that it was a gift from Donya Eulàlia. The salted cod seller thought: "So that's why she's coming home late again! Oh dear, I can't let her do this!"

However, a few days later, a neighbor on Senyor Grisau's staircase gave Senyora Quimeta insight into what was really happening and advised her in all seriousness: "Believe me, Senyora Quimeta, don't let her spend so long in there with that peculiar old codger . . ."

The salted cod seller was terrified. It was the time when the girls finished work. She ran to the kiosk. There was Senyor Grisau with Nadala on his lap.

A hue and cry resounded through the neighborhood. When mother and sisters started shouting, neighbors came out on doorsteps and balconies and Senyor Grisau, who was disliked by everyone, was verbally attacked and assaulted with sticks, balls of wool, and scrap metal of all kinds . . . He ran off like a lunatic in his woolen slippers and yellow jacket . . . in his shameful escape he left the shop open and money in the drawer. When he hurried past the salted cod shop, the weights from the counter rained down onto his head and neck . . . Frenchy's grandson disappeared from sight, and the uproar went on.

Not even he knew how he managed to slip away.

Bareheaded, staggering, white as a corpse, teeth chattering, and stinking of reheated tobacco, El Senyoret found Senyor

Grisau sitting in the passage by Senyora Maria's house when he was about to get spruced up for the theater.

Frenchy's grandson stuttered through what had happened as best he could, and how he was broke, for there was no way he could go back to his kiosk or underground den.

Nonat smiled.

"Don't you worry . . . We'll find you an apartment tomorrow, and from this day on, you work for me."

As we mentioned, Senyora Pepa Canalies owned two shops on the ground floor of her building: on the right, the La Caprichosa perfumery and stationery store and on the left, El Bambú, a barber's shop of repute in that neck of the woods. If one could more or less relate the first moniker to the nature of the business, the second, on the contrary, would have bemused even those most accustomed to the wild fantasies many shopkeepers indulge when baptizing their stores, because nobody could guess the possible relationship between bamboo and the master barber's razor or his customers' beards. Even so, one shouldn't make rash judgments, because everything in this world has its raison d'être, which may be obvious or obscure.

As you will conclude from the following (that is, if you're still following me):

Once upon a time, a father and mother with lots of children lived in a seaside village: five, six, seven big angels . . . a flock. As well as children, the father had a brother who had gone to South America.

When that impoverished youngster left, the village knew him as Xito; when he returned as a rich, old man, people called him Don Francisco, though at home adults still called him Xito, and the children, Uncle Xito.

Uncle Xito was idolized by his nephews and nieces; when he spoke, he spoke like an oracle; when he issued an order, they ran off to do his bidding.

Uncle Xito possessed many astonishing items, but one *really* stood out.

It was a cane from the Indies with a silver knob as big as a medium-size peach. All his nephews were infatuated with his cane and would willingly have given their souls to the Devil to have one like it.

When Uncle Xito wanted to go for a walk or a coffee, he would shout out in his sibilant Spanish to the nearest nephew: *"Mushasho, traéte el bambú."*

And the young nephew was delighted yet again to bring Uncle Xito his marvelous, silver-knobbed bamboo stick.

Years and years went by. The nephews scattered around the world as if uprooted by a gale.

One of these nephews learned the trade of barber and hairdresser and worked in Barcelona.

As an adult, he was as much in love with the heiress to the parfumier on the corner as he had been with Uncle Xito's silver-knobbed cane as a child . . .

"The day I own my own shop, I'll ask for her hand," he thought.

Uncle Xito had returned to South America years ago with his silver knob, caught dysentery, and died. In his will, he left each nephew a handful of doubloons ("coins," as he called them). The young barber bought his longed-for shop with his share, asked for the hand of the equally longed-for parfumier heiress, received it, and they married. In memory of his childhood infatuation and his uncle's gift, he gave his shop the euphonic, if surprising, name of El Bambú.

We might have spared you, good reader, this detail, that has as much to do with our story as the barber's label with his trade, if it weren't for the fact that it is frowned upon in these ungrateful, positivist times to elaborate beautiful acts, even if they are dragged in by their coattails.

Conversely, as the barber was Senyora Pepa's tenant, perhaps you won't mind my little aside on him, given what was about to happen.

Namely, the following:

Barber and parfumier, although legitimate husband and wife, only saw one another when it was time to eat and sleep. Each spent the rest of the day working in his and her little businesses . . . and accounting; there was plenty to do on both fronts. Money rained into their coffers; they had no children and were savers. One day, they learned that the plot alongside Senyora Pepa's building was for sale and purchased it. They intended to build a house to their taste, with this, that, and the other . . . While they drew up detailed plans for the house, recognizing theirs was a long-term project, they enclosed the plot within a highish wall, where the parfumier laid out a garden in the latest style for her own amusement and pleasure that she dubbed her little caprice, and the barber, keen to devote his free time to more feathery matters, erected a brick chicken coop with an uralite roof. They were so absorbed by their hobbies that time flew by and they never finished the house plans that they were eternally extending and adapting, but by the time their hair was turning gray, afraid they might die without ever enjoying that new home, they suddenly made up their minds, spoke to the architect, sold their chickens, let the flowers wither, and did nothing but transport stone, tools, materials etc., to begin construction. Then they found endless things to discuss and agree upon! Lying in their capacious double bed, sheets tucked tightly under their chins, trying not to move so the bedding didn't slip, cozy inside, fending off the icicles, husband and wife looked at each other out of the corner of their eyes in order not to disrupt the neat and tidy bedclothes, and debated and debated their future house into the early hours, despite being exhausted from the day's toil and the prospect of an inevitable early rise in the morning.

One night, they unduly prolonged the conjugal conversation, and their eyelids were drooping imperceptibly when they opened them wide and asked each other in alarm: "Did you hear *that*?"

And each chorused: "Yes!"

What had they heard? A strange noise, a sort of scraping, like sandpaper being rubbed over a polished surface, followed by two muffled bangs. But all those noises came from the vacant side of the building, from their plot of land...

"What can it be?" they wondered again, afraid they might disturb the turn of the sheet, a glimmer of terror in their eyes, they tenderly inched toward each other, as if impelled by the idea of threatening danger.

The parfumier had the most presence of mind.

"You know what? They reckon we've still got chickens and

they've come back for more." She was referring to when their poultry had been stolen.

But the barber wasn't so sure.

"Do you really think so? I don't know . . . Let's just listen."

They listened. There was no fresh noise, but they continued listening, putting all their other senses on hold. Their motionless, cadaverously stiff bodies looked shrouded.

A minute went by, then two . . . Sleep and drowsiness lurked behind their eyelids and attacked them out of the blue when they were most alert, knocking them out without a fight. They'd suddenly gone to sleep—like a door slamming shut—without putting the light out. They had no idea how much time had passed—perhaps ten minutes, perhaps sixty—when a shrill, blood-curdling scream sent them nearly flying out of bed. Husband and wife found themselves standing on the rug on their respective sides of the bed, staring at each other in bewilderment. They didn't know what was happening . . . But they could hear loud stumbling and an unusual hubbub down below, in Senyora Pepa's apartment, and immediately understood.

"Ay, poor Carmeta!" and, pulling clothes on pell-mell, they rushed downstairs.

He had studied Senyor Grisau's sketch at leisure. In the front, per usual in such layouts, the living room and the cousins' shared bedroom; in the center, a junk room, pantry, etc. on one side of the hallway, and on the other a tiny bedroom and the kitchen; at the back, with an exit to the gallery, the guest bedroom and dining room.

Senyor Grisau had said: "There's nothing worth our time in the front. They have a wardrobe with a mirror facing the door to the living room, and whenever I went for "stuff," she would open it, take out keys, and go down the hallway . . . I reckon the goods're in the back bedroom, in another old armoire at the back . . . I think it would be worth our while to scour it, it's a big'un. She sometimes asked my opinion on new bonds and showed me old coins she used for change. For a time, she asked about money for jewels that she must have hoarded like a magpie, because, as soon as I valued them, I never saw any of them again . . . She's also got a lot of cutlery from those days, and each item weighs a ton . . . and a solid silver Sant Vicenç that a brotherhood gave her master as a present, as he was its president."

However, though Senyor Grisau said he perfectly recalled the house layout, once they had looked at it, he wasn't really sure what was on the right or the left, or in the central area.

Because of all the uncertainty and because he preferred to see everything with his own eyes, Nonat decided to personally inspect the theater of operations, and to that end on the previous night he had jumped over the yard wall and walked around.

The chicken coop, now a storage space for construction tools and materials, was four or five yards from Senyora Pepa's house. There was a rickety old wall between the house and coop that was falling apart, the relic of an old partition. Along the ground, amid recently dug pools, holes, and the dusty remains of that capricious garden, were stone blocks, tiles, beams, and planks, what you'd expect on an incipient building site.

After giving it a quick once-over, Nonat worked out an unexpectedly simple plan. The old wall was too rocky to be of much use, but it could still take a man's weight, as he found when he climbed onto it.

That sufficed. All three of them would have to be ready to do everything deftly and surely. They would put a plank from the roof of the coop to the window ledge nearest the yard, which was still unfinished because of the lack of the neighboring house. Everything else would simply be a matter of luck.

He measured up, selected the plank, and carefully assessed the location of the windows. He reckoned one was only pulled closed, as the shutters seemed slightly ajar. A pity their expedition wasn't today, because they could have done with that help!

However, they would have that help the following day, because the moment they dropped inside the yard, the bastard could see the window was exactly as it had been the previous day, and that it would be as easy as pie to enter the apartment. *A good start!* he reflected, and with his outstretched hand he pressed the protective amulet against his heart: the doubloon from his old Girona boss.

Nonat didn't realize that all the apartment windows were similarly ajar, despite the wintry weather, because if they hadn't been, the rancid air would have been unbreathable for the occupants.

They began the job by carefully hoisting the plank up and resting one end on the coop and the other on the old wall. Then, on the coop, the Valencian held it steady while

Nas-Ratat, from the wall, slid it gradually toward the window ledge. Nonat anxiously kept an eye on the environs and operation, ready to lend a swift hand if need be.

It was all going as smooth as silk when too rapid a tug from Nas-Ratat wasn't stopped in time by the Valencian, who wasn't the strongest of men, and the plank banged along the uralite. That scraping noise and Nonat's leap up to stop the plank were what the barber and parfumier had heard from their bed. The bastard choked down a curse, listened attentively, and, a minute later, as he didn't detect any alarm signals, jumped on the coop and slid the plank along himself. It finally came to rest on the ledge; their bridge was all set up. Nonat tested it with a foot to make sure it was safe.

Nas-Ratat and the Valencian met down below.

"Who's going first?" wheezed Nas-Ratat.

The Valencian bent down as if he were looking for something on the ground.

This Xe is green . . . The captain's made a big mistake, thought the street porter.

But without saying a word, Nonat had already walked on the plank, and signaled to his colleagues not to budge.

He reached the window, listened by the crack, pushed it gently, and the shutters parted. After a fresh scrutiny of a welcoming darkness, nevertheless full of unknown perils, Nonat disappeared inside.

He hadn't given the others any instructions; still as statues, they stared at the gaping black hole in the half-open window.

It was the first time the bastard had engaged in such an expedition, and a rookie soldier's blank, infinite terror amid the flashes and bangs of battle stopped his breath and numbed his legs . . . Even so, he felt no impulse to retreat, to run away from the adventure; on the contrary, a secret frenzy, the frenzy of the cardplayer who's put all his chips on one card, drove him on, always onward . . .

Seconds later, El Senyoret stuck his head back out and indicated to his colleagues to follow him. First, he had wanted to find his bearings, as he wasn't convinced by the vagaries of Senyor Grisau's map, but now that he'd been in the kitchen, he knew the whole place by heart

He issued his orders with authority.

"Nas, you go down to the dining room. In the sideboards are antique sets of cutlery and a solid-silver sugar bowl . . . I'll go to the junk room, and he can stay on the watch . . ."

Nas-Ratat grasped his arm.

"Just like that, with nothing to cover your face?"

"There's no need."

"Bad move, captain. An apartment is a rat trap . . . and they only need an eyeful, and you're on their map . . ."

The bastard was the cautious kind, but at that point, the warning from his subordinate, apparently accusing him of lack of foresight, wounded his pride and led him to casually shrug his shoulders. Even so, when he saw the others tying kerchiefs around their faces, like in a movie, he trembled and his heart thudded violently against his ribs.

They separated. El Senyoret trusted his light touch and the instructions he'd given the others. They shouldn't make any noise, knowing as they did the terrain they were treading, and besides, the enemy—the two women—were too out of the way to be much of a worry. Nonetheless, at the slightest scare, his colleagues could swoop on them like sparrow hawks, smother their heads in black cloth, and tie them to their beds while he finished the job.

It was a moonlit night, and enough light was coming through the window for them to circulate easily.

As he crossed the dining room to get to the junk room, Nonat glimpsed Nas-Ratat clearing out the sideboard and the Valencian flitting like a will-o'-the-wisp from hallway to window and from window to dining room.

Nonat entered the junk room. Used to the dark, his eyes saw like a cat's . . . In any case, a silver thread of moonlight lit up the dining room balcony from top to bottom.

He noticed the old armoire Senyor Grisau had described. He walked over to it. His fingers caressed the keyhole and carefully slotted his screwdriver in. It was a flimsy lock that offered no resistance. *So that's how they protect their wealth!* thought Nonat, his lips moving with instinctive contempt. The two doors opened without a creak, as if the armoire was gifting its entrails to the bold intruder. Flat, extended like spatulas, his hands penetrated between folded clothes, twisted into corners, patted shelves, fluttered nervously from top to bottom, searching impatiently, flapping in a flurry like the wings of an insect being hunted.

The tradesman blanched in the gloom. He couldn't find any money. He became more agitated, started pulling clothes out onto on the floor. Nothing! He rummaged farther down. Thanks be to God! A chest! That must be the hiding place. And if he didn't find what he was after, he'd open the balcony and examine the other pieces of furniture.

He extracted the chest; the badly fitted wooden sides squealed in protest. Apparently in response, there was a small crack, a jarring sound like a dry tree branch being snapped, and the thief was inundated by a bright light from the ceiling. He was nonplussed and dazzled. As his sight returned, feeling crazier than he ever had, he saw, sitting on the bed in a corner of the room, a greenish ghost, a ready-made corpse spat out of the grave, eyes flashing like carbuncles, gaping horrendously at him.

Only three days ago, conscious of her unsightly appearance, Carmeta had decided to change rooms so she could cry when she felt like it, and also let her cousin get some sleep.

Nonat's steel springs self-activated and in an astonishing tiger-leap he hurtled toward the bed. But, before he landed, a horrendous howl shattered the night air, and the green ghost fainted and fell back on the pillow.

The burglar stayed still and numb by the couch. He didn't hear the sound of bare feet quickly approaching down the hall. He didn't come around until he saw Senyora Pepa standing in the doorway in a nightshirt, a white scarf around her head, holding a tiny oil lamp . . . She was frantic, like her upstairs neighbors, thinking Carmeta must be dying, but when she saw a man standing in the middle of the room, her blood froze and she too came to a halt. The Valencian stuck his knife into her ten or twelve times until her flesh was carved open. A gurgle, as from a simmering cauldron, was the only sound that escaped from her gullet.

The lamp burned in the oil spilled on the floor.

Nas-Ratat rushed in, holding a bundle.

"Why are you standing there like idiots? Are you waiting to get caught?" he exclaimed.

The men fled. The upstairs neighbors still hadn't left their apartment when the three of them reached the empty plot next door, quick as deer, and while the former rushed down and knocked on Senyora Pepa's door to no avail, that tragic trinity was off, quick as the wind, beyond the Bogatell beach . . .

They stopped in a deserted spot, out of breath and soaked in sweat.

A somber Nonat chewed his fists.

"Blasted night!" he bellowed hoarsely.

But the street porter wiped away the sweat and laughed quietly under the horrible remains of his nose.

"It could be worse, captain!"

Nonat glared at him, his gaze as penetrating as a snake's sting.

" . . ."

The other lifted his bundle.

"I've got the loot. It was hidden in the back of the drawers in the spare bedroom . . . But Nas-Ratat's nose has a keen sense of smell . . . Christ! We've hit the jackpot today!"

The next morning, street porter and bastard were sitting down in front of Paperines's tavern.

"I'll tell you again, captain: that *Xe* is a bad'un and one day he'll drop us in it. I don't like braggarts. Why did he need to kill that poor woman, who was as quiet as a mouse? It would have been enough to gag her and show her the knife . . . The difference being, if they catch us now, we'll be dangling in front of the public or thrown in the slammer for a good long spell."

But Nonat scowled and for a few hours one thought alone occupied his mind: will she or won't she sing . . . ? Because that light had been switched on, and he'd seen only too clearly that Carmeta's wild eyes had recognized . . . And Carmeta was still . . . was still in the land of the living! It boded ill!

Nevertheless, he clung to one secret hope . . .

He bought the evening papers, already reporting on the preliminary investigation and the dying woman's statement, and read every word frantically. He found no references to himself.

Nonat's forehead brightened; he smiled triumphantly.

She won't sing! he told himself, totally convinced that was true.

And, indeed, Carmeta did not "sing."

Sixth and
Final Part

Nas-Ratat had been spot-on with his prophecy: the dailies had been talking about Nonat for some time—naturally without naming him—reporting the deeds of that invisible "hero," who pounced all over the city in outrageous raids that shocked the peace-loving bourgeois, were admired enviously by professionals in the trade, and drove the outwitted police mad. But none would ever have claimed that such varied and isolated feats over such a long span of time had a common source, or, rather, were the work of a single, fertile, multifaceted mind . . . In fact, there was a vague fear that an international gang of criminals had invaded the city and was wreaking havoc by drawing on idiosyncratic skills and approaches. The burglary of an apartment followed the theft of a silversmith's stock, where holes had been drilled through doors and ceilings; the extraction of merchandise from goods wagons between one station and the next; the pickpocketing of a high-ranking bureaucrat's wallet; a horrible mugging in the middle of a crowded thoroughfare; the disappearance of a valuable chalice and candlestick holders from a convent chapel; the conning of a wealthy foreigner who'd handed over all his capital as an investment in a nonexistent business; the robbery of a gaming table in a suspect dive; a series of scares on unguarded stairs; a battle royal in a taxation office; the disappearance of fur coats from an aristocratic soirée; swooping in from nowhere to claim the contents of a clothes shop; the snaffling of lightning conductors from one entire district; the theft of items from clotheslines on terraces in another; a nighttime raid on a factory where the watchman was taken out with a hammer blow; the purloining of a priceless necklace from a lady alighting from a carriage; the relieving of pockets in crowds around the dentistry stalls in the port; the theft of a briefcase containing valuables; the unburdening of the savings of a famous physician from his home during his consultancy hours; the vaporizing of vintage wines from a grocery store. Why go on . . . ? It would be infinite. As it multiplied, as it burgeoned everywhere, El Senyoret's activity seemed boundless. He had injected his enterprise with the virtuoso skills and insights of a man with a vocation.

As if Barcelona were a chessboard and his hobby a fascinating gambit, drawing on his undeniable organizational talents, he deftly moved the pieces: quickly or slowly, but ever surprising, extraordinarily daring, and clever; with such a light touch you would have said it was effortless, although it was clearly the delectable flowering of a measured, upper-bracket temperament. Ideas came rapidly and matured in his mind, he foresaw the details and followed through in style . . . As in the workshop in Girona, as in Senyor Ramoneda's establishment, as in the Forge, he thought through every aspect: items, time, men, and context, and extracted the most from everyone. Thanks to his levelheadedness, it was maximum profit with minimum waste, the perfect equilibrium between every element in his business, simple at the core but complex and varied in its external expression. His agents—his eyes, his hands, his extra legs—were happy in their work, as previously his workmates had been at the factory, under his intelligent, competent leadership, efficacious and authoritative, all the more so because Nonat acted straightforwardly, generously, and calmly. He never argued or haggled: he took what he needed, whether a lot or a little, never giving explanations to anyone, and gave the remainder to his men with lordly, carefree disinterest; moreover, if his men ever argued about the division of spoils, he stopped them dead and imposed his imperious will that allowed no appeal. He always supplied those men with plentiful projects, plans in the process of development where everyone could chip in and shine, but he didn't like to mix with them, instead preferred to work in isolation and reserved for himself the riskiest, most sophisticated openings, those requiring skill rather than strength, brains rather than brawn. While he set up others with theatrical scenarios and ploys, he himself found exquisite joy in yielding to sudden inspiration, to impulses devoid of premeditated strategies. How exciting, say, to find in his fingers items he hadn't yet consciously registered! What salve for the soul to feel that almost magnetic power of every object of desire that, by virtue of that desire, seemed to make itself available to him, to come seek him out, to surrender and graciously offer itself up as if propelled by the most intimate, freest of wills! Conversely, violence and shabbiness were repellent to his instinctively subtle mind, to his artistic good taste; he accepted them in very few situations as unpleasant, inevitable requisites of the trade, but as far as he was directly involved he avoided them to the utmost, delegating them to his more uncouth colleagues, who had no clear sense of the dignity to be sought in all acts and who were oblivious to refinement.

Despite the material benefits that had accrued, he still harbored the memory of what happened at Senyora Pepa's with a sense of shame and bitter irritation, as if it had been a total failure and clumsy disaster; acts primitively conceived and grotesquely executed after rudimentary, amateur preparation—based on hearsay, like a nincompoop or beginner—with nasty surprises, foolish panicking, silly braggadocio and, above all, that laughable escape that could have been their ruin, leaving everything in a mess: clothes scattered around, doors open, the plank *in situ* making their route obvious, a woman still alive in her bed and able to betray the thieves, another on the floor, her nightshirt shamefully pulled up and her body stabbed to bits. If they were ever hunted down, there would be no hope of apologizing or finding clemency.

No, he hated things done brainlessly, that *brutish* way of working, as Nas-Ratat had dubbed it so aptly. That's why he felt only contempt for the Valencian's innate beastliness, which he deployed inopportunely, like the dish of the day, whenever they allowed him to operate instinctively, and for Senyor Grisau's unerring addiction to devious practices in every kind of job, as if they were all one and the same. At the end of the day Nonat got on much better with the street porter—a sensible, level-headed fellow who, without ever straying from his path, sidestepped as best he could dubious extremes, sagely declaring that his crimes needed no noise—or with Bielet—a lively, affable character—although Nonat couldn't be seen in public with Nas-Ratat because of his memorable face, or with Bielet because he always required cautious handling, his mischievous schoolboy wiles were dangerous and hovered between genius and blatant tomfoolery, and he often took excessive risks. That was why Nonat always said they should get on with it, each to his own interpretation of the bastard's orders, as long as they carried them out successfully, always preferring to spare himself the need to witness the idiotic or puerile behavior of others, allowing them the pleasure of peacefully doing their own thing on the jobs he assigned them.

His connection to Bielet had come about as the result of a comic scene at the time of Senyora Pepa's death. Nonat walked by chance past the doorway where he'd first met his future victim, and when he saw the down-at-heel shoe shine chairs in the shop, he suddenly had an idea. A well-organized shoe shine salon could be an excellent source of information and be exploited most profitably. He walked straight in. The hard-working lad pulled out his box of polishes and picked up a brush.

"No," said Nonat, "that's not why I am here. I expect you've heard what happened to your boss?"

Bielet's face immediately looked mournful.

"You bet I did! I know all about it!"

And he explained with picturesque expressions and serial exclamations how he had read about the evil deed in the newspapers, how he'd always been crazy about seeing and reading about every kind of crime at the movies and in the daily papers, how when he'd heard who had suffered that dastardly deed, he had run straight to the house in El Clot and seen for himself . . .

"It was a horrible mess, senyor, that made your hair stand on end!"

Nonat interrupted him curtly: "Well, in fact, I've . . . I've purchased all this from that lady."

And he looked around at the chairs, wooden steps, and even the shoeshine, who was taken aback.

"You have?"

Nonat nodded.

The young lad stared at him, scratched an ear, glanced back . . . and seemed at a loss.

"That's very odd," he finally mumbled.

Nonat stiffened.

"Why so?"

"Well . . . You know . . . Just so!" the shoeshine growled.

Nonat began to frown.

"So why so?"

Rather than answer, Bielet stared back, a mischievous glint in his cheeky schoolboy eyes.

"When do you think you purchased it from her?" he asked abruptly, as if genuinely not in the know.

A surprised Nonat hesitated for a second.

"When? Last week."

His voice was completely natural and he looked at the lad without so much as a blink. Although this time Bielet returned his stare; now the guile not only paraded in his eyes, but across his lips and whole face.

"I say odd because . . . By chance, the day before she died, Senyora Pepa dropped by and never mentioned this sale . . . On the contrary, she said: 'I want to buy new furniture, rent the ground floor next door, and set you up in a right and proper salon . . .'"

Nonat bit his lip, but now the dice were cast and he couldn't backtrack. He told Bielet he must have got it wrong, but the schoolboy laughed, shamelessly, sarcastically: "Believe me, senyor! That's the truth . . . true as the sun in the sky . . . Sure as can be, she even added these kind words: 'And as you're such a good boy, Bielet, I don't want anyone else to profit from the sweat of your brow, and right away I'll make you heir to all this when I die!'" He lowered his eyelids in comic grief: "Who'd have thought it, hey? Senyora Pepa loved me like a son, may she rest in heaven!"

Bielet lied so impishly Nonat couldn't think how to respond. It was the first time anyone had tried to trick him to his face, and he hadn't managed to gather his wits.

He looked quizzically at that youngster, without rancor or spite. The lad had talent and could wriggle out of a scrape. Might he have found flock and shepherd at a stroke? His expert lips smiled spontaneously, and his fingers tweaked the liar's ear in a benign reprimand.

"You're too clever by half, boy!"

And then he gave him a friendly pat on the back and added: "Fine, you shall have that 'right and proper salon' . . ."

And nobody ever referred again to who owned what or who was heir.

Nonat's life was pleasant, varied, and entertaining; he bivouacked from hotel to hotel—always a considerable source of income—in first- and second-rate establishments, and even the most modest, according to his professional needs; he attended all manner of spectacles, rode, dressed elegantly . . . At one point he spent time traveling. He visited Valencia, Majorca, went to Sevilla, Madrid, Zaragoza, Le Roussillon . . . And then, thinner, pricklier, and haughtier than ever, he returned to settle down in Barcelona. The income from his travels didn't match expectations. While he was in Catalan-speaking lands, everything went well, but as soon as he had to call on his backstreet Spanish, that undermined his gentlemanly airs, he felt so out of sorts and ridiculous he could have kicked himself. It was even worse with the French language, since he didn't know a word, and what's more, he lacked the retriever's scent that distinguishes the true vagabond and allows him to capture the intimate gesture, intonation, and mysterious resonance echoed by every living word, and grasp the hidden meaning of languages he doesn't know.

He was only too well aware that his terrible, irreparable ignorance would be the biggest obstacle to his advancement, perpetually disqualifying him and preventing him from flying through those infinite spaces he longed to visit. He understood that if he had put as much effort into cultivating his intellect as he had into cherishing his external appearance, there would be no limits to his power today, but he felt now, as before, a manifest aversion to books and a distaste for letters that were dead on the page. They would never come to his brain quickly enough, would never enhance or excite him with the magic of their powerful charm. He felt he was only stirred by his own anxieties, by his vital longing to dive in and swim in life itself, to breathe in and spit out its invigorating salt, to engage his energies in a war of movement—a colorful war full of ambushes and discoveries, where guile, insight, daring, sangfroid, ambition, naked passion, and strength of instinct could play out in their splendor, in complete freedom, without limits or controls . . . And, arrogant as he was, he thought only *visible* success was a worthy reward and acceptable culmination of that longing. Hence, he preferred not to confront his weaknesses and, so as not to confront them and feel his power diminished, he liked to avoid giving them an opportunity to surface by adopting the wisest of brave counsels: flee futile danger.

Consequently, he decided not to leave his land and was resigned to keeping to himself, without contacts in the higher echelons, without trying to force open the front door to that world he secretly envied, where, if he were ever to gain entry, he could never mount a defiant display of legitimate, public superiority. With the unconfessed spite of a defeated man, he told himself he would enjoy that comfortable hedonist world, with all the rights and none of the responsibilities, as a spectator enjoys a play from his private box, a bullfighting fan the *corrida* from his terrace seat, sheltered by pleasant shade. And one of these days—at the very worst, since it couldn't have been at the very best—he would stand unscrupulous and pitiless in that forbidden world, a sculpted figure held in place by a spider's web, by the incredible strength of his muscles of steel . . .

"I can't stand it any longer!" shouted Miquel, pacing up and down their bedroom like a madman escaped from the asylum, and he grabbed his pants and started to get dressed.

"What do you want to do now, you restless spirit?" asked his wife.

"Go to the Forge . . . I can least let off steam beating iron!"

"At this time of night?"

"What do I care about the time if it feels like a thousand witches are hexing me?"

And in a fury he pulled off his rice and wheat poultice, turned over the bowl where he spat out his plantain leaf water with milk, put on his jacket, said goodnight, and, ignoring his wife's tirade of complaints, strode out of the house like a man banished. By chance he'd seen the time on the alarm clock: 2.30 A.M.

It was raining: a fine drizzle that barely dampened his clothes. Miquel touched his cheek; the cold was making his jaw hurt even more, stinging so sharply his beard shivered.

The streets were empty and silent. As he walked up the slope, the houses brightened, and through the gaps he could see way off, down in the depths, the hazy, turbid glow of the city extending along the seashore like a phosphorescent mist. Now and then, a still, egg-yolk yellow revealed the nearby presence of lights under the drizzle's brittle veneer. A rooster called out in the air, as if invisibly suspended between earth and heaven . . . Three or four faint tunes from a barrel-organ waltz rose up from the bottom of a street . . . They were rhythms from a slags' ball that used to fire off in the early hours in the Gurugú tavern. One skinny cat after another scampered fearfully by. The Forge came into sight. He looked up instinctively, as he always did . . . His heart thudded violently. He thought he'd seen a gleam of light under the battered door, as in a nightmare, a hazy, reddish glow like the one from streetlamps. His heart stopped thudding, and he now felt it squeezed like a bird gripped by a fist. He thought there must be a fire, an idea soon swept away by another. They'd just stocked up on iron and coal, and what do you bet some scoundrel had gotten an idea and was after them? The anger of an honest man made Miquel's blood boil. The Forge was the apple of his eye and solace for his sorrow. He had toiled there for over thirty years, and he felt a lion's fury simmer in his chest as he prepared to defend his treasure.

All the heaviness in his paunch faded, evaporated, as if he had shed fat in order to skim over the ground rather than tread on it and approach the endangered works more stealthily. When he reached the door—apparently only pulled shut, not locked—he didn't dare give it a push and instead peered through the keyhole. A key was slotted on the other side. He snarled—could he have forgotten to lock up the previous day? He patted his pocket. His key was there, a big, ancient object heavy as the key to heaven . . . Bewildered, he paused for a moment . . . Suddenly, a piercing squeak from a file hit his eardrum. Miquel was so stunned he almost gave himself away . . . He took another look inside. The key had been turned; and what Miquel saw through the hole left him nonplussed. Two men were standing in one corner of the Forge under an oil lamp that had been moved from its usual place.

He recognized them immediately. It was the boss and . . . Salvi, his own son. What were they doing at that time of night? They were working; they were working intently, painstakingly, concentrating on the task at hand, which seemed delicate and demanding to judge by their attentive attitude; how they checked after every movement of the file. Every now and then they exchanged a quick, whispered word, pointed to their project, and got on with it: *sss-sss, sss-sss* . . .

Miquel was intrigued and brushed against the door, unawares. He would have sworn he hadn't made the slightest noise, but the alarmed nighttime toilers glanced up at the door and stuffed what they'd been holding under the big mechanical drill. For a minute they remained on alert . . . The moment they were over the scare, they resumed work. They were obviously afraid of being caught in the act. Miquel seemed rooted there. He wiped his brow and swallowed; a crusty crumb seemed stuck in his gullet . . . He moved cautiously away from the door and retraced his steps. He felt bitterly resentful. The boss and Salvi were doing something they evidently didn't want anyone else to find out about. Now, if it were anyone else, it wouldn't be *at all* peculiar, but how could they keep *him* out . . . ? That mistrust he felt he didn't deserve hurt deeply. Beavering in the Forge behind his back . . . the boss and his own lad, the ones who should hold him in high esteem. No, no, no; they didn't need to hide; for his part, he would give them all the leeway they needed . . . !

When he walked into his bedroom, disturbing his drowsy wife's slumber, in that nasal twang of hers she asked what he was doing.

"Nothing," replied Miquel, his voice shaking. "The fresh

air cured my toothache and I've come to get some shut-eye . . ."

True enough, he wasn't feeling a twinge of the toothache; it had disappeared some way or other, but as for shut-eye, that was another matter.

And at a quarter to five, he heard Salvi tiptoe in.

The next morning, when Miquel reached the Forge, he inspected everything, searching for the mysterious item they'd been fashioning a few hours earlier, but to no avail: he found no traces; the workshop tools and oil lamp were back in their rightful places . . . Miquel might even have thought he'd been the victim of a strange hallucination if he hadn't finally found, on the ground near the drilling machine, fresh iron filings that had been trampled or scattered on purpose by someone's foot.

Salvi didn't appear until almost midday; he had bags under his eyes and was sickly pale, tired and lethargic like an old man.

"So what did you get up to last night, you rascal?" his father rasped accusingly, heart thudding as he waited for the reply. It came slowly and faintly.

"I went to the theater."

"A performance that lasted till four in the morning?"

"It's a really long haul from there to here."

His father was livid. He was a straightforward, entirely upright soul who wouldn't have known how to lie even if he'd wanted to. He gritted his teeth to suppress the words rushing to his lips and merely growled again, bad-temperedly: "And what will the boss think of your gallivanting?"

Salvi shrugged and answered curtly: "Oh, don't you worry about the boss . . ."

Miquel gripped the pliers violently and once again that imaginary crusty crumb jammed his gullet. He swallowed repeatedly, trying to force it down, which made him miss the opportunity to state calmly that Salvi no longer seemed like his son and blast the boy with the curse he merited. He looked at him despairingly; Salvi didn't even notice. Miquel knew the boy was easily led, limp, fond of partying, but he wasn't a liar or a crook: that was all he needed, God Almighty! That boy was the nail he carried stuck deep in his heart, and this fresh hammer blow drove it deeper, wounding the most sensitive parts of Miquel's soul.

As if to finger his festering wound, Nonat had turned up at the Forge early that morning. He was wide awake and crisp as the fresh day that had followed the previous night's downpours. His vigorous body glowed euphorically. He jumped off his steed, and while Badoret tied it to a ring, the boss laughed and asked, as he dusted his boots with a crack of his whip: "How are we all, good folk? Long time no see, I've missed you!"

Miquel gawped, his hammer hanging midair . . . What, the boss was a liar as well? What was that all about? Spurred on by the wildest fantasies that piled into his brain like a barrowful of stones being unloaded, he did something he'd never done before: he spied on Nonat. He watched his boss on the sly, suspiciously, anxiously, like a traitor in a melodrama. But, in the scant half hour the boss spent at the Forge, giving orders, warnings, examining the fine detail of how things were going—as if, in effect, he hadn't been back for days—Miquel didn't glean the slightest clue to what had happened the previous night. Only in that last minute did he think he'd caught the boss giving a brief nod to Salvi's equally brief and quizzical glance.

Miquel felt his world was collapsing around him, he went cold, he went hot . . .

At lunch, his wife told him about the gossip at the market, that morning a bomb had exploded in the house of a Barcelona banker . . . Salvi glanced at his mother, seeking more detail . . . Then, a suspicion hacked its sinister way through his hapless father's vague doubts! Could that attack be connected to that mysterious nighttime toil? Could his son and boss be dangerous bombers? In a split second, doubt destroyed the very foundation of his ideals and battered the faith Miquel had in everything and everybody. And something he'd never considered struck him, shed light on a flurry of suspicious details. The boss was a tradesman like himself, yet he dressed like a gentleman and spent lavishly and showed off, and nobody had a clue where he got his money . . . Could he be someone in the grips of strange lunacy, like so many others in the city? Could he be—God forbid!—a criminal paid to hurt others? Anguished and grieving, Miquel swore to get to the bottom of all this . . . A man who never hid a thing, he became as taciturn and devious as his son, more so, even; he, who would have said Nonat and Salvi could do whatever they liked at the Forge, was transformed into the most perfidious policeman; a man who'd always lived by the light of the sun, he started on the quiet to lead a creepy, recondite second life, the reason for which he hid from everyone, including his wife.

When Miquel had jumped out of bed and been drenched in the downpour on the night of his big discovery, he'd caught a very nasty cold. He would have cured it if he had taken a couple of days off, but he was a stubborn, surly patient and had started doing what he'd never done before: going out each night, coming back late like his lad, getting up late, starting his day's work at noon . . . Surprised by his strange behavior, his wife wondered whether Miquel was losing his mind and told him in no uncertain terms that such disorders came with age and could only lead to bad ends.

And so they did: two were particularly damaging. The first was chronic bronchitis that brought on a sad, long-suffering state of untimely decrepitude, and the second was the discovery of the real nature of the mysterious tasks his boss and son were engaged in. Hiding near the works or looking through the keyhole, as if gazing into a kaleidoscope, on his long, vigilant nights, he saw the Valencian, Nas-Ratat, and even Senyor Grisau pay a visit . . .

The truth was that the Forge was providentially remote and isolated, out of sight of inopportune eyes, and had replaced Paperines's tavern as soon as the co-plotters realized their meetings there might attract unwanted attention.

Nonat had stopped in front of the Camps shop window in Plaça Reial. He had always been seduced by beautiful materials and styles. He heard someone say: "You just see: they wanted to charge me a hundred pessetes, and I thought: why not take the loot myself . . . I'll only have to spend a few hours away; I'll visit Mataró, where I've never been, clear my head and it will cost me fifteen or twenty pessetes at most."

He turned around: two gentlemen were walking along, their backs to him. He furtively followed them; he knew which one had to go to Mataró from his tone of voice; Nonat walked past them and registered that man's face and appearance. The following day, Nonat loitered around the station waiting for him, and sat down at a café terrace, watching the bustle that preceded and followed the arrival and departure of trains. That stingy, self-preoccupied gentleman never showed up . . . Those who did were a band of street hawkers selling cheap baubles. One was especially a pest. Engrossed in his observation of the scene, Nonat sent him packing several times with nods and gestures, as if swatting a fly, when the man stealthily showed him an obscene photograph. The bastard lost his calm and screamed: "Clear off, you dirty fool, or I'll call the police!"

The street seller ran off, though his very peculiar face left its imprint deep in Nonat's eyes: pock-marked, sallow-skinned, a forehead sloping backwards, a sharply bent nose that twisted down over his small upper lip and cast a shadow on two, domino-like teeth protruding over his lower lip, which in turn protruded over his beard, that retreated like his forehead and trailed down his neck.

"Where have I seen this *character* before?" the bastard wondered, intrigued, convinced he knew him, but unable to say from when or why. And he kept an anxious eye on the station. Then a clear, precise memory came to him: It was Parrot! The rag and bone man from Senyor Ramoneda's factory that he,

Nonat, had sacked because he'd presented fraudulent accounts!

Right then he saw Parrot again, walking into the station. Nonat paid for his drink, crossed the road, and entered the station. He patted Parrot on the shoulder; the other man turned around with a start.

"Recognize me?"

He stared and rolled his eyes: "Christ, it's Senyor Nonat!"

"Stick around, and we'll go for a drink . . ."

The miser from Plaça Reial had, quite unawares, played a bad trick on him. Nonat hadn't seen a whisker of him in two whole days of keeping watch. He must have postponed going to Mataró or given up on his hundred pessetes, because Nonat was certain he hadn't missed him. Even so, the bastard wasn't unhappy with how things had played out, because Parrot was a small fish who might be good bait, and one thing could lead to another . . .

Nonat had expressed his wish to see her, so the Valencian introduced her, and though he wasn't at all keen because he was wary of Nonat's handsome looks and status, he was unable to say no because he knew he'd pay the price, and, besides, the idea of a double income was too tempting. For many jobs, the boss would have preferred a woman to a man, though he employed none, but Nonat took a liking to La Pelada at first glance—and she was admitted into the brotherhood. No formalities or agreements preceded her admission. When someone seemed suited for what he wanted, the bastard simply gave orders. He didn't cloak himself or his business in any kind of mysterious rite, but neither did he enter into explanations, as if their pact was something agreed to a long time ago and the most natural, legitimate thing in the world. And he was so good at welding people together, and so smart in his choices, that all those he attracted combined naturally enough without a struggle and maintained a spontaneous, devoted faith and respect toward him, practically as if they were his children.

However, the Valencian's fears were entirely ill-founded, because La Pelada, grafted on like an implant of a very different ilk, brought to that crew of perverse degenerates even more disparate options. Apart from Nonat, who at all times displayed a perfectly dignified, aloof attitude toward his gang, and who held to that on this occasion as if La Pelada, despite her skirt, was merely another tool for him to manipulate; apart from Nas-Ratat, who felt an instinctive contempt for the woman, reckoning quite unconsciously that she was a wild-card who only existed to distract men from their goals and trip them up, everyone else would have thrown themselves at her feet if she'd so desired. As soon as she came into their sights, Senyor Grisau's big eyes glinted lecherously and he would bustle this way and that to help and woo her as if his slippers had Mercury's wings. Parrot, a mass of putrefying flesh, a body suppurating with sores and boils plugged with cotton wool, melted at the sight of the forty kilos that were La Pelada's hard, fibrous, as yet unblemished flesh. Even Bielet, by now the master of a salon *comme il fó* with a team of static and mobile assistants under his orders, winked mischievously the first time he saw her and noticed how easygoing she was and how eager to have her shoes polished, an operation always more demanding than a labor of Hercules, and a task that he always rounded off in more or less the same way; that is, by grasping her beloved foot, suddenly lifting it up with a comic twirl, and pressing it furiously against his heart while rolling his eyes.

Amàlia always found a sympathetic smile for Bielet, that crazy, garrulous, cunning lad full of fantasies—but was entirely disgusted by the other two, and in her calm, silent way she frankly let them know her feelings. However, the day would come when things would change, and that cold fish would experience the volcanic turmoil wrought by passion.

For several reasons, Nonat wasn't fond of writing when he had to give orders: a disaffection toward the pen, which wouldn't always faithfully translate his thoughts; his fear of the interpretation others—for the most part, hardly the literati—might give to his written words, and above all, a cautious wish not to leave compromising traces in his wake. He preferred to *say* it aloud, and tasked La Pelada with the job of delivering his verbal orders; she might not be right for many other jobs, but her very special way of being made her a first-rate messenger girl.

He once sent her to the Forge to tell Salvi something, naturally without his brother or father getting a whiff of the message. La Pelada delivered with her usual aplomb, and that was when she met the newest recruit to the crew, the young man she hadn't yet clapped her eyes on. The ex-electrician's handsome presence left the languid sinner thunderstruck; it was the spark that providentially ignites a pile of timber that burns to a cinder in seconds. She wasn't the only one caught by a sudden conflagration, the current of attraction was mutual; the blatant, ardent magnetism of true love enthralled them at a stroke, immediately sequestered and isolated them from the entire world, pitching them fatally, inevitably into each other's arms. And when his wet, eager lips soldered to her thin, red ones with the impulse and impetus of perpetual adherence, two bodies and two souls dissolved into one. They were instinctive lovers, classic lovers, without fear or hesitation, shame or regret; categorical lovers who only see, hear, and taste one another. Their connection was beyond words: a furtive glance, the slightest touch, a single hint of a thought without external manifestation placed one completely at the mercy of the other. La Pelada's listlessness vanished as if by magic, and her flesh and mind were aroused with the roar of a hungry beast and the might of a thunderous avalanche, and, as if in a fantastical garden created by demon spirits in the time a rooster takes to crow, flaming flowers of insatiable desire and a thousand thorny thistles erupted within in her simultaneously. A woman who had in her cold flesh unfeelingly suffered every possible outrage from the lowest of lusts, she now felt a rebellion hardening in her heart of hearts at the very idea that any man who wasn't *he, the only one,* might touch her.

The Valencian was eternally dismayed when he met energetic rejection, simpering revolt, looks that spat bile . . . And he noticed other kinds of changes in that woman, as radical as they were peculiar. Gone were the strips of rag or flimsy threads which hitherto she'd used to secure her stockings; gone were the blouses, stained or stiffened by dried sweat, falling apart on her body; her short hair was now splendidly thick and black as a crow's wing; her heavy-duty comb angrily lanced the last survivors of countless nomadic tribes . . . Even her skin, once brittle and wan, devoid of subtle softness like untreated leather, had become dewy, pliant, and warmly transparent; her skinny, tough torso that stank, almost defiantly, of a hermit's cave, assumed sweetly curvaceous shapes; her bosom expanded unnervingly; her hips sashayed in extraordinary rhythms; her lips moistened with divine flavors: her huge, night-black eyes filled with a deep inner glow from a remote, invisible sun . . . In brief, that amorphous instrument of solitary corruption gave way to a woman, a woman in love, ready for thrilling ecstasy and frenzied sweat . . . The Valencian was fully aware of this change in her, and felt an icy shudder shake every bone in his body as he wondered out loud: "Is this what we have come to?"

A shadowy veil hid his unhinged features; he concentrated his thoughts on a single image, his teeth chattering as if from an attack of marsh fever, and he delivered this harsh warning to the void: "If that be so, then beware . . ."

Nonat had told Parrot: "Pepe Martinez goes to Café del Liceu every afternoon; watch when he leaves, and follow him. You one day, Bielet the next—keep on him for a week, and then tell me every detail of what he does from one day to the next."

And he went to spend that week in Lleida. As on his trip to Girona, Nas-Ratat followed him at a distance like a remote satellite, and likewise, they came back quite dissatisfied with their trip. The haul from the fiestas had been adequate. Senyor Grisau would have work on his hands for days.

There were several passengers in the compartment when the train left Lleida, but one by one they got off and finally only Nonat and one other passenger remained. He seemed an upstanding gentleman whom the bastard, with a single professional glance, had immediately decided was someone without distinction. He was decently dressed, in good quality clothes, but had no kind of cachet. An ordinary suitcase, worn and battered at the corners, was tucked by his side on the seat with the quiet, innocuous air of a dozing cat. For a moment, that suitcase had drawn Nonat's attention rather than its owner. Sometimes, a canny miscreant keeps his wealth more securely in a cheap, shabby case than in any strongbox. But this time, instinct and experience told Nonat it contained nothing of value. Suitcase and owner melted away from his eyes as if they no longer existed, and our man became absorbed in his thoughts, which was his way to shorten hours of boredom on the rails. Even so, he began to feel uneasy, an uneasiness that only increased until he had this strange delusion: he'd been placed on one plate of an invisible scale that was rocking up and down at the mercy of the counterweight on the other plate. Panic suddenly roused him from his daydream . . . The fellow opposite was staring at him through the thick lenses of his spectacles. When he noticed that Nonat had noticed, he looked away, out the window. Nonat made an effort to concentrate again, but failed miserably. As soon as he felt that his will was about to triumph, immersing him, taking him out of himself, a greater force—the other passenger's gaze—sucked him into its orbit again, making him return time and again to the surface, to an awareness of that unwanted company. That gaze, that semi-intermittent stare—distancing itself when he sought it out, coming nearer when he avoided it—finally made him lose his patience. That traveler seemed to look at him not only with his eyes, but with his every feature, his shirt collar, his hat, his whole person; you might have said all of him was a gaze, a kind of emanation that was pinning Nonat down. So much so that, for a second, the bastard had the absurd sensation that the suitcase was staring at him too. That inanimate object, curled up like a tame pet at its master's side, appeared to enjoy a mysterious life of its own, bound to the latter by a magnetic pull that transmitted the commands from a superior will, forcing it to support him, to stare at their traveling companion too, with an entirely conscious insistence . . . The bastard felt a tremendous tightness in his chest and frantically inhaled air through his open mouth like a fish out of water. He got up, went for a walk down the car, checked the luggage in the rack, went to look out through the other door . . . Finally he sat down in the corner opposite to where the other passenger was seated and, pretending to look at the scenery, half-turned his back. All to no avail. Without looking, he could tell the other man had twisted around in his seat and was observing him from afar, just as he'd been observing him from close up. After making an effort not to budge, Nonat, almost feverish by now, got up and returned to his previous seat; he preferred to confront that gaze openly rather than feel it glued to his back, an intolerable intrusion, like some kind of hidden threat, as if he were about to be ambushed by a wild beast. Why was the man so rude? If he intended to stare at the bastard, the bastard would stare back, and they'd see who would tire first. And Nonat made himself comfortable, crossed his legs, crossed his arms, and looked straight ahead, cheekily challenging his neighbor . . . The latter didn't seem to notice, then, all of a sudden, everything went blank behind his lenses, like being behind a lampshade when the light is switched off, and that gentleman now seemed just like any other gentleman traveling by train.

Nonat felt highly embarrassed and blushed like an adolescent caught indulging some base desire. The other passenger's tact had betrayed his own poor manners and lack of discretion, evidenced by his cautious impatience at the least disruption, all so unlike the tolerance and courteous restraint that marks gentlemanly intercourse. Humiliated, in turn Nonat lowered his eyes, but the moment he sensed that hostile stare reviving and penetrating him again, a violation beyond words, he realized he couldn't stand it to the end of his journey and, to avoid creating a stir, he decided to switch cars. However, at the next station, something happened that was to deter Nonat from carrying out his resolve. The moment the train stopped in the station, a hue and cry went up on the platform, doors opened and slammed shut, and panicking passengers began to alight from cars and run. A crowd immediately formed at the end of the train, where the blue shirts and badged caps of station staff mingled with passengers.

Nonat and his neighbor peered out of their respective windows.

"What's the matter?" the latter asked a local walking back, who smiled and shrugged his shoulders.

"What do you think? A gentleman fell asleep and his watch and wallet were stolen . . . Now he's bawling and carrying on, but it won't do any good . . . In fact, serves him right, that might teach him and his kind to keep an eye out . . . It's only common sense not to nod off in the train . . ." and after giving voice to such charitable thoughts, he continued calmly along the platform.

Nonat had blanched and his heartbeats made his gullet tremble. That was too risky, Nas-Ratat, carrying, as he did, his gift from God! Because Nonat didn't doubt for a moment that the street porter was behind all the hullaballoo. And an extremely worried Nonat peered out of the window again to see what was happening; if they'd caught the thief, if there was any sign of Nas-Ratat . . .

He had entirely forgotten his neighbor, though the latter had kept *his* eye on Nonat the entire time, and when he saw that handsome young fellow looking perturbed, his stare became sharp as the blades of a sword.

Nonat's memory, once so wonderfully quick, had been slowing down as if it was getting lazy, and only after hours of journeying did it tell him that the stare of the man in his compartment was that of the judge who had been on duty on the occasion of foreman Rovira's suicide, the stare of a functionary who left in everyone else's eyes nothing of his own self or face beyond his stare, as if he were *only* that stare . . .

On the other hand, though Nonat hadn't immediately recognized the judge—currently a magistrate in Lleida—the judge had identified him straightaway. And the bastard would have felt even more alarmed if he'd known that the judge had been visiting Barcelona and the chief of police's office when news arrived of the fracas at Senyora Pepa's house, and had accompanied the police and carried out a brief inspection of the scene of the crime—not out of any professional obligation, but because of his fondness for criminological study, amateur sleuth that he was—and his sharp eye had discovered, by ferreting here and there, a photo of the bastard among Carmeta's clothes. He was about to call the attention of the police to that photo when the sight of the dying woman immediately reminded him that she was the sister of the man who'd been crushed by a tram, and that the man in the photo had lodged in the house of both brother and sister. Convinced he would only make himself look a fool if he revealed that intuitive but unproven suspicion, he decided to say nothing, just like wretched Carmeta . . .

Similarly, Miquel Vedià, the toiler in the Forge, also decided to say nothing after long, exhausting, inner struggles. His first impulse, as an honest soul, had been to inform on the thieves and cause them to be rounded up by the police, but paternal feelings immediately tied him hand and foot and sparked a cruel conflict in his anguished mind that, alongside the bronchitis he'd caught on that fatal night when he'd spotted Nonat and Salvi in the Forge, would ruin his peace of mind, health, and life.

"What can I do in good conscience?" he wondered constantly, every hour, pulled with increasing turmoil by two opposing currents; but rather than advancing one way or the other, he sank imperceptibly by the day into horrendous, complicit silence. He would have preferred to save the situation with expedient palliatives; complying with the law and sparing his son any slight, but he didn't know how. From the time he'd found out about the existence of that bunch of hoodlums, he'd felt it was his ineludible duty as an honest man to reveal to other honest folk the evil deeds they might be plotting—but he also sensed that no law, human or divine, could exist that obliged him, in the name of honesty, to throw his very own son into prison. All he was duty-bound to do was struggle to rescue Salvi from that lethal slide downhill . . . or punish him mercilessly, kill him if need be. That's right! Better dead than dishonest; better finished off by his father as a criminal, than lacerated and insulted by other men . . . And in a delirious frenzy, Miquel saw himself taking up the fight, challenging his wayward son, berating him for the unholy pit he'd fallen into, rescuing him from the dishonor he was pouring on his own family, hitherto free of any blemish; the dangers he was courting, the punishment he deserved from public opinion and the law, the awful future that awaited him when thrown into jail, deprived of sun and freedom, deprived even of a chunk of iron and a hammer to lighten the long, dark hours of remorse and solitude; or else, clad in that uniform, dragging a chain around his ankle—horror of horrors—or, even more terrify-ing, climbing in a black hood to a gallows and, with a post behind his back and a rope around his neck, executed as an example to evildoers . . . At that point, Salvi would turn pale and start to shake . . . Then squeezing everything he could out of his limited, rudimentary imagination, he would paint that scene in the most lurid colors possible, evoking the death of a criminal named the Comber, whom Miquel had seen garroted many years ago. That macabre scene would so startle Salvi that he could resist no more, and, driven by the warm, honest blood coursing through his veins to his conscience and flush-ing out the filthy sediments, he would throw himself at his father's feet, and, sobbing fit to break Miquel's heart, ask for forgiveness, beg to be saved and dragged from the abyss into which he was plunging . . . By now ecstatic, Miquel would press him against his chest, and, raising his eyes to heaven, give thanks to God for the miracle he had wrought with his words, a miracle that would restore the peace and happiness they had lost . . . But things didn't always go so smoothly, and the poor father, in his tormented imaginings, also anticipated his delinquent son's resistance, his stubbornness, his inability to heal his soul damaged by the worst kind of plague, and, unable to bear the infamy, Miquel would fire a bullet at him in a moment of madness . . . No, not a bullet! He had never handled a weapon and could never pick one up for the first time to fire at his own son, however disgraced Salvi might be . . . Though he would find the courage to hit the young man on the head with his hammer, just as he was now flattening the head of that screw on the anvil . . . And when he pictured his stunned son lying at his feet, gripped by the tragic despondency of a fated hero, the father felt the painful serenity of those who do their duty, however terrible that may be . . .

But ay, the gushing eloquence and energy the hapless father spilled into such romantic surges failed him in the dilemmas of real life. The moment he faced his son, the weak, beautiful creature he had fathered, his strength was erased by pathetic cowardice and fear, more suited to a baby rabbit than a man. He despaired, felt unable to raise his voice or reach a decision, and he cried like Mary Magdalen and pulled his hair out like a madman. It's the blood, the damned blood that binds me to him . . . If he were a stranger, it wouldn't be like this! And suddenly, when he came to the end of that mental cul-de-sac, a glimmer of light appeared . . . Miquel had an inspiration. Why not tackle the outsider in their midst? Why not ask his boss to help? Why not make him see reason? Why not make Nonat undo the wrong he'd done and return to him the son he'd taken? If he approached the boss, the root of all that evil, he was sure he could find the right tone to appeal to his feelings, to move mountains, to turn the most arrant sinner into a saint . . . And, naively in thrall to all that absurd nonsense he was inventing, he rehearsed his fantasy exactly, merely changing the character . . . He imagined Nonat striving to resist, to escape the force hurtling from his paternal sorrow, palpitating with faith and self-righteousness, but finally annihilated by it . . . or else, in parallel to Salvi's reactions, he too would stubbornly declare that he wanted, that *they* wanted, to continue along their evil path . . . Then, in his fantasy, Miquel would do his best to appeal to Nonat's better side, reasoning, imploring, warning . . . even—the shame of it!—compromising and offering to make a deal . . . He wouldn't say a word, he'd let Nonat pursue his criminal trade, he'd let him recruit and deprave as many youngsters as he wanted, but the bastard must return his son, return him . . . It wouldn't be the end of the world if he did so, now would it? And Miquel would keep quiet . . . He'd be forever crucified by remorse, but he'd keep quiet all the same . . . What more could Nonat ask of him? What more, for God's sake? But not even that would work! In Miquel's fearful imagination, Nonat wouldn't agree to a deal, and, to boot, would even dare suggest that Miquel should help him. And that would be the final straw, because when he heard that, Miquel would be beside himself, would forget all restraint, would pour out insults and threaten to blow all their cover. But what would that achieve? Since the other man, rather than taking fright, would surely start laughing, that soft titter he was so fond of, and retort matter-of-factly: "Well, get on with it, Miquel . . . Clear off, wherever I go, I won't ever want for company!" And, cast down from heights of expectation, power, and energy, Miquel would descend into the abyss, understanding that there was no cure, that whichever way he turned, he would stumble, always stumble across the horror he'd glimpsed: the inevitable, definitive loss of his beloved son, the dishonor and ruination of them all . . . !

Those inner quandaries ravaged the poor journeyman, and despite everything, both in front of his boss and in front of Salvi, he lowered his eyelids in embarrassment and avoided their stares as if he, and not the others, was the miscreant.

Day after day he wrestled with that inner turmoil in a state of shock, only managing to suggest to his heir that he should leave the Forge and start his own smithy, but Salvi had looked at him askance with that scornful, evasive look of his, reacting as if his father was an old man losing his mind: "Ugh! The things you come out with! Clear off, you fool!"

Consumed by that secret anguish, lashed by a roiling sea that battered his straightforward character and sapped his energies, terror inhabiting his soul, his physical strength gone, though still preserving his honest scruples, which flickered over the remnants of defeat like flames licking the logs of a tree trunk, the day came when Miquel could stand it no more. He plucked up his courage and told El Senyoret he was no longer in a fit state to manage the Forge and was going retire to his house, where he would install bellows and a smithy to do bits and pieces to keep the wolf from the door . . . That prospect, representing total impoverishment for the hapless worker, must have struck his boss with some force. Indeed, Nonat looked at his poor journeyman in surprise, as in the latter's dream, and his subtle intuition read in Miquel's eyes that all was not well. He thought for a moment, his fingers nervously tapping whatever they could find, and then declared, as affable and serious as ever: "I'm sorry, Miquel, principally for you, but for myself too, because you're an experienced tradesman and the Forge has functioned well under you, and I've never had to worry. But if you can't, you can't, one's health must come first. Salvi can take your place and you'll receive your pay as you always have . . ."

The setting sun that streaked the tatters of poor Miquel's life a blood red warmed his enfeebled spirit, perhaps for the last time, with a ray of courage. When he heard the thief's last words, he reared up, as if lanced by an invisible needle, and blurted out: "No, senyor! I only want to be paid with money that's been earned honestly!"

And Nonat glanced at him sternly, frowned, shrugged his shoulders, and retorted: "That's your business."

And he strode off, never looking back.

Miquel, heartbroken, left the Forge, the apple of his eye, forevermore, taking with him Badoret, his sane son, fortunately still after his own heart, but abandoning the other, a festering piece of his own flesh and soul, in the clutches of that devil from hell, whom *he*, Miquel, had loved and worshiped as a god.

Just as Nonat had set Bielet up with a brand new salon and a swarm of lads under his command who were scattered throughout Barcelona collecting valuable information—seedcorn for future operations—he'd also provided the Valencian with a carriage that, although for hire, wasn't shabby and battered, rather, quite to the contrary, it was adorned with luxury touches and cared for like the best private carriage. The coachman was always well-dressed, with a gleaming cap and a frock coat that wasn't mended, darned, or stained, and at every moment, whenever he stood to attention, took his cap off, and opened the door, he remembered how as a young boy he had served gentlemen of standing, though he performed even more deferentially now, and, wherever he was, his comportment made him stand out from the others and he immediately caught the attention of passersby, who made him their favorite.

Nonat liked to make the most of the attitudes or natural abilities of his men, to ensure they were always busy and that their faculties were never corroded by the rust of sloth, and to bolster, if not supply, a modest, regular income with bonus payments they earned from work of another kind.

When Parrot and Bielet had delivered their detailed reports on Pepe Martínez, his putative father, Nonat instructed the Valencian to always be near both his house and the exits from places where he usually dropped him off.

"Take note. He'll often use you, but won't always pay. Don't let that worry you; take him anyway and build up trust. When he can't pay you or he's been drinking champagne, he'll give you lots of lip and promise good tips. Accept the latter and listen to the former with good grace and never lose your calm. Let me know when you've become friends."

Friendship came quickly and the Valencian informed Nonat at once.

"Does he hail you on the street or does he give you a time?"

"Both . . . Last night, for example, he told me I should pick him up at four to go for a ride."

"That's good. Be there, and when I give you the nod, ride off, as if absentmindedly or ignoring his orders if he gives you contrary ones."

They met up a few hours later on Passeig de Gràcia. The carriage was trotting smartly up on the right. Nonat nodded to the Valencian, who used a passing removals van as an excuse to halt.

The bastard smiled, opened the door, and, taking his hat off, climbed in as if it were empty. The carriage immediately continued at a sprightly pace up Passeig de Gràcia. Leaning back, more to get a better view rather than out of surprise, the occupant eyed in astonishment the intruder who'd just got in so unexpectedly and sat beside him.

"My apologies, Senyor Martínez, but I needed a word . . ."

"Who are you, *caballero*, and what are you after?" the irritated old man inquired in Spanish after a moment's fearful silence.

"There'd be little point in saying; you don't know me . . ."

Nonat spoke in Catalan, either almost unthinkingly or quite deliberately as in effect he wanted to maintain his dignity in the eyes of that fellow from Madrid. The latter grimaced in disgust, and he made a move to the door as if intending to stop the carriage. But Nonat's hand came down heavily on his arm.

"Wait a minute. There's nothing to be afraid of. I just want a few words, and they're better said here than in your house. I need a service you can provide and that won't belittle you, and you will be well rewarded."

The former senator looked up in astonishment. This stranger was addressing him as if he were a trader or lackey.

"*Caballero!*" he exclaimed haughtily.

But the bastard smiled slyly.

"Bah! Don't worry, Senyor Martínez! As polite formulas can often hinder mutual understanding and I want to reach an agreement, I shall come straight to the point."

Nonat himself thought he was being rather vulgar, not acting in the refined manner he favored and which he so liked to cultivate. He could see he was having that impact, given the cold way the old man—though civil and courteous, it must be said—had received his familiar tone, but he was struggling to contain himself and not reveal, in a coarse outburst, the rancorous contempt he'd been harboring for so long.

The former political private secretary reared up in magnificent seigneurial style: "I think you are mistaken, *caballero*, I cannot see how you and I could *ever* agree with one another . . ."

The bastard's cheeks flushed and his eyes flashed with devilish cruelty; poor Martínez immediately realized he was in a bad place and, profoundly alarmed, again went to open the door, but the bastard spat words into his face like whiplashes that riveted him to his seat.

"You are the one who is mistaken, *senyor meu*, since any-one can reach the agreement he wants with Bianca Giannelli's murderer."

After a long minute of stupor, Pepe Martínez slowly raised his eyelids, and looked at the intruder in surprise and horror. Who was that fellow? What did he want from him? Why had he conjured up Bianca Giannelli, the beautiful diva from years ago, now lost in the mists of his distant memories?

Certain he would get a hearing, Nonat told his putative father of the wretched death of the abandoned singer, the possibility of a deserved, long-delayed revenge, the help Nonat sought from him, her seducer, in exchange for forgiveness, and how that simple help would be duly paid . . .

Finally, Nonat stuck his head out of the door and shouted: "Coachman! Stop in Avinguda del Tibidabo!"

Five minutes later, Nonat was alighting from the carriage and frostily wishing its remaining occupant a good afternoon, and the tinny-faced, stiff-backed driver did so without an ounce of surprise. It was the old rake who couldn't get over the shock. His manic eyes watched El Senyoret's silhouette walk gracefully off, and his fine gait, height, and proudly poised head brought back memories of his dead mistress. When she vanished from his world, she could have been only a little younger than that mysterious intruder, and, as if many years hadn't gone by since, his feeble, senile brain drew a curious conclusion: that fellow must be the singer's brother.

In the time they lived in close contact, Bianca had often spoken to him of a brother who lived in Italy, one she loved desperately and, for his part, Nonat had only alluded to her being cruelly abandoned and dying in a hospital without mentioning the specific illness or referring to any son. Italians bear rancor and incubate their hatred for years, and Pepe Martínez might have already felt the grip of that iron vice.

As an outlandish youth, Pepe Martínez had been a man of passionate moments, but years had watered down the wine and the veiled threat the stranger had just thrown his way had brought him out in a sweat. He went to wipe his forehead, then saw something in his hand. Two hundred-pesseta bills! What was that all about? Ah, no doubt it was his pay for services he was about to render . . . Who did that man think he was? And to restore his wounded dignity, Pepe Martínez went to tear those bills up . . . Then he recalled his previous night's disaster, when his pension had been vaporized at a green beige table . . . He stopped himself, acted as if he were thinking, though he thought nothing and, suddenly, with an expression of disgust, took out his wallet and slotted in the money.

As the Valencian drove the carriage, Salvi was soon to chauffer an automobile. One day Nonat had seen one go by transporting the consul's wife, as white and plump as ever, next to a swarthy Latin American gentleman with a shock of snowy hair, and soon after their son in another saloon. The sight of the two automobiles remained imprinted on Nonat's brain like on a photographic slide. After the gang's next successful round of *business*, its captain purchased the coveted vehicle and Salvi learned to drive it. When Nonat didn't need it, it could be for public use and, like the carriage, would provide two sources of income: the legal one, to cover costs, and the possibility of others.

Two basic journeymen were employed in the Forge, almost for appearance's sake, to keep it open, and they stuck to their jobs without any danger that they might waste their time prying or exercising their minds like Miquel.

The first time La Pelada saw Salvi dressed as a chauffeur, she stared at him long and hard in spellbound bliss. The electrician was so handsome in the becoming uniform, which lent an aristocratic air to his face and stance (which weren't commonplace anyway), and she became even more madly infatuated, experiencing new expectations and pleasures in her love. It seemed that only two things existed in this world for her: the orders from Nonat that she carried out rigorously but almost instinctively, as if all her old languid ways had adapted to them, and that other powerful new sentiment where everything alive and sensuous in her existence simmered. She and her lover were driven by blind, insatiable attraction, and constantly sought each other out, spending their time arranging dates and negotiating solitary trysts. From the moment the Valencian stepped into the coach box, La Pelada was free for most of the day, though Salvi wasn't; he had to find ploys and look for excuses, but the difficulties he encountered only served to intensify his desire.

"Come to the Gurugú," the electrician had begged at the beginning, "we can dance there . . . and be together without anyone bothering us."

And La Pelada had docilely gone to the Gurugú. When

he took her in his arms and they swayed from side to side for all to see, Salvi trembled with excitement and La Pelada clung tight, as if in a dream, swooning with happiness. Later, after they had danced they sat down in a corner to have a drink and, enrapt in each other, holding hands, her eyes locked in his, they spent hours oblivious to the world. They worshiped that strange tavern of ill repute and escaped there whenever they could.

When Salvi had the car, she loitered around the taxi ranks, and the couple made the most of his free time to chat and kiss, more or less out of sight. Sometimes he took her with him—Salvi knew his boss wasn't mean, provided they met their commitments properly—and he'd drive her at a break-neck pace to the outskirts, where they parked on a remote lane, and there inside the vehicle they entangled in an end-less, frenzied embrace, as if starved of passion, as if they had been waiting feverishly for that very moment for years and years . . .

The first to notice their folly, after the Valencian, was Nas-Ratat; the former merely suspected, but the latter had zero doubts because by chance he had twice caught the couple at it.

He shook his head in displeasure. He had never been in favor of bringing women into the company.

"Captain, a bit of skirt creates havoc, believe me. When skirt's around, the best of men loses his compass and throws everything away . . ."

But the captain had ignored him and now they had an *item* and an *issue* on their hands . . . Nas-Ratat deemed it was his duty to relate what was happening.

"They're on fire. They didn't notice me, even when I

brushed past them. We'll see how the Valencian takes it when he finds out . . . With the foul temper he's got! I told you, women are a plague . . ."

Nonat reacted sternly; he didn't like Salvi two-timing him; even so, he didn't want to get involved, at least not immediately. They'd decide on a course of action if all that looked as if it might damage the company.

Nonat wasn't renowned for being expansive with his men, but one night they were all in Senyor Grisau's little apartment, discussing with the alchemist, Nas-Ratat, and the Valencian a daring heist that had provoked a huge argument. All agreed it was a heist they wanted to pull off, but they couldn't agree on how to proceed. The focus was a Greek woman, a high-flying *poule de luxe* dripping in jewels. The threat of a court case had led her to flee Paris, and she was waiting in a semi-quiet state for the dust from the scandal to settle before she returned to the City of Light. Senyor Grisau, the only one familiar with her place of residence, suggested that La Pelada should enter the household as a serving wench and then act as spy and guide in that complex labyrinth, where there was never time to rest. But the Valencian leapt to his feet to refute the idea: "How could she go as a maid if she doesn't even know how to boil water? Forget it . . ."

Nas-Ratat said they should enter through the garden; the chauffeur, whom Salvi could befriend, slept in the garage there . . .

Nonat interjected: "No outsiders . . . That's always

dangerous; they are double-edged tools, you never know if they'll ring true, while we can do without, we will. After this lively exchange of opinion, I think we ought to take the shortest route, namely, the simplest. There's a vacant room in that building; we'll rent it, and from there we can comfortably climb down via the galleries . . ."

"No," Senyor Grisau interrupted, "there's a dressmaker's on the third floor with seamstresses at the back, and they work till very late."

"We'll wait until they're done."

"That's when there are the most people downstairs; they're gambling and making a din and there's always one customer who lingers on, and when downstairs thins out, the dress-maker goes back to work, that's obvious enough..."

Nonat wasn't at all fond of people contradicting him or erecting barriers.

"Look, we'll go down when it suits us, whether the dress-maker is around or not . . ."

He saw his two colleagues didn't approve of such a risky approach, but even so, they needed this heist because business had been slow for days.

"Anyone else would think this was your first time . . ." Nonat quipped a tad impatiently.

"No, captain," enjoined Nas-Ratat, "you know I won't put the kibosh on it, but if we can plan every move, you know . . ."

Then the Valencian spoke without looking at him: "And senyor, will you be joining us?"

Nonat immediately grasped why. Nonat very rarely went on jobs with them, but it wasn't a good idea if they thought of him as a rearguard general.

"Yes, I'll be there," he answered and, turning to Nas-Ratat and putting his hand on his shoulder, he added encouragingly: "And don't be scared, for Christ's sake, we'll do what we do, and we'll be fine."

The others looked at him, astonished by his confidence. And that was when Nonat took out his wallet with a flourish and showed them the doubloon from his Girona boss.

"This is something I carry that brings luck . . . As long as it's on me, we have nothing to fear." And with that he slipped the wallet back in his pocket.

The heist went wonderfully, and from then on the Valencian saw the bastard in a different light, and followed submissively in his footsteps whenever he could.

"Have you ever seen anyone fawn as much as Xe? All the kiss-your-ass stuff is because of that doubloon nonsense . . . He's always looking for something to protect his back . . . I mean, what kind of man behaves like that!? I tell you . . ."

But El Senyoret was pleased; he'd found a way to tame the Valencian. For his part, the Valencian now knew he had nothing to fear from El Senyoret.

Parrot had whispered in his ear the name of the individual stealing La Pelada from him, and when the Valencian, with a face like pigweed, asked for proof, the informant had no option but to take him to where Salvi's automobile happened to be parked at the time.

Whatever had become of Pepe Martínez, that wheeler-dealer? His degeneration had been as rapid as it had been sorry. All his fancy habits as an old rake and *bon viveur* collapsed like a castle of cards, just as his political future had. His dark, transparent, elemental eyes dimmed to ashen gray; his mustache curled upward in his nighttime binges, and the marrow in his bones inevitably shriveled, like new shoots withered by the frost; he dragged his feet, talked to himself, had bad dizzy spells the youngsters in the Circle laughingly put down to fondness for glasses of *Pipermint*, and his solemnly indifferent doctors to the advance of arteriosclerosis . . . The ex-dancer, bored by him—though of late he hadn't been so hard on her purse—had just shown him the door . . . Whatever had become of that happy-go-lucky old *roué* from Madrid? He'd been sledgehammered by the only thing that could have stopped his jollies: something serious . . . At first he had barely noticed. One can give introductions to anyone, and at the end of the day, that young fellow had only asked for an introduction for a certain jewel dealer to visit Senyora So-and-So today, and Senyora What-Do-You-Call-Her tomorrow, and Senyora Thingammyjig the day after. And in exchange for those introductions, whenever Martínez was short of funds, whenever his hands had frittered too much away at the card table, as if he had a real nose or quick intuition, as if he were providence itself, that young man generously rescued him from financial scrapes and, what's more, Batista the coachman was never a skinflint, and, as if the old rake were a nabob, always waited without protesting to be paid when he was in a position to do so. Pepe Martínez had thus reached what he felt was a soothing conclusion: everything in this world degenerates, and that if classical Italian revenge were now like that, he could be well-pleased with the way things had gone downhill.

However, his smug self-satisfaction was short-lived.

Like the good, feckless, sociable gadfly he was, Pepe Martínez was very given to visiting dames of his acquaintance. These ladies, young and old, were convinced that Martínez, that pleasing element of mundane diversion, would never desert their salons and soirées. It happened that one day he found one of his said lady friends down in the dumps. No doors had been broken, there was no mess in the apartment, but "all her jewels had been *lifted*" . . .

"Only one escaped, because I was wearing it around my neck . . . It was the one I bought last week from that jewel dealer you sent around."

Another day, he read in the papers about the scare another lady friend had experienced when she heard thieves in her bedroom in the middle of the night. Frightened off by screams and ringing bells, those thieves had fled without taking a thing, but left an iron bar as their visiting card; one morning, a third dame found her servants chloroformed and locked in their respective bedrooms, and every piece of furniture had had its locks broken and been cleared of its valuables, and the morning after, his friend H (a collector of weapons, antiquities, and precious bibelots), found that his collections had been ransacked by a fine connoisseur, who had gone about it with a fine-tooth comb . . . The coincidences stood out like dark spots on the sun, searing the consciousness of Pepe Martínez: each of those acts had followed, more or less exactly, an introduction he had provided that opened the doors wide to Senyor Grisau . . . First he was shocked, then scared, and finally he came to a clear-sighted conclusion. The hapless old fellow was struck down by a wave of profound indignation. Dear reader, was this the *straightforward* help that had been sought from him? Was he, a true gentleman, the paid *insider* of a gang of thieves? Beside himself, he decided to confront the young intruder and give him a slap with his glove . . . But then he realized he didn't know where to find him, or even what his name was . . . All their exchanges, like the first, had taken place in the carriage. When the stranger needed him, he organized the rendezvous, turned up with a welcoming smile, asked the coachman to stop, and jumped in like a colleague, like a close friend, and when he'd gotten the old man to write with his own pen the card he needed, he bid a cheerful farewell, alighted, and disappeared. Now our fine gentleman saw it all . . . He *was* the insider, or rather a plaything in the hands of someone or other who was, in any case, a criminal. He must escape from that trap, must unmask his tormenter, but how? Pepe Martínez remained flummoxed until he had an idea: Today or tomorrow the man would come back for a fresh card, and then . . . His flesh shook. It was no laughing matter. This *Italian* revenge was more horrendous than he could ever have imagined . . . he was dealing with a hardened criminal! His heart took a turn for the worse. The water diluting the wine wanted its way, but his mind was made up and, despite his frivolous nature, he kept to the righteous path and boldly won out. As he had, perforce, to wait for the hoodlum to reappear in order to respond to the outrage, Pepe Martínez reluctantly resigned himself to do so. But he didn't have to wait for long.

The new season was opening that night with a famous company from Madrid, his territory. Pepe Martínez couldn't miss out. He dressed elegantly, as usual, and was driven to the

Teatro Novedades.

"Hey, *chico*," he addressed the Valencian, "wait for me by the exit . . ."

The theater was a splendid sight, and Pepe Martínez fluttered around all night, which almost distracted him from his unpleasant situation when, at the end of the second act, he thought he glimpsed his loquacious stranger leaving the aisle on the right. He caught his breath, as if he had swallowed a mouthful of cold air, but a second later he was striding toward the stranger. And it definitely was *him*; alone, in evening dress, handsome, serious, elegant, impeccable . . .

Whether it was the dinner jacket or an association of ideas, Pepe Martínez then recognized his intruder as *the* stranger in the Liceu. As he thought the stranger had looked at him but not seen him, he indicated he was coming over, but the young man kept on walking, minding his own business. They met behind a large potted palm that hid them from the eyes of the crowd milling in the lobby. Martínez was about to say something . . . when the other lifted a finger to his nose.

"Not a word," he growled between gritted teeth, "we don't know each other . . . See you later in the carriage . . ."

"*The fact is* . . ." Pepe Martínez began violently, but an instant, terrifying glare silenced him. Pepe Martínez was afraid and instinctively patted his pocket, though he had never carried a weapon . . . When he came around, he was alone behind the palm tree like a fool. He didn't see that fellow during the rest of the performance, nor did he see him when he left the theater, but when they turned into Consell de Cent, they stopped for a moment because of two other carriages in front;

the door opened and *he* climbed into the old man's carriage.

Nonat had come prepared, as he'd analyzed the face and attitude of his victim during the performance. And as soon as Pepe Martínez began to bawl, he gave him the starkest message in the softest of tones: "Yes, that may be, but now's not the time to create a ruckus. The cards from you have opened the doors to all those houses and you should be aware that it's best for everyone that the police don't find out . . . So watch what you say! Goodnight!"

Three days later, Pepe Martínez's ex-dancer lady friend was found strangled in her junk room.

The previous night, her ex-lover had waited in vain for his favorite coachman to turn up.

From that moment on, Pepe Martínez began to fade, until he wasn't even a shadow of his former self. Driven by his instinctive frivolity, he had done lots of bad things in the course of his life, blindly, unconsciously. But his genuine gentlemanly feelings and habits never allowed him to do them voluntarily, or fully aware. However, that was small consolation, because the bastard now held him captive in tangled nets of steel, and the old rake, whether he liked it or not, couldn't refuse to do his bidding.

"How will Xe take it when he finds out?" Nas-Ratat had asked, afraid of the Valencian's devious instincts. On that occasion, though, the Valencian didn't react brutally. For a few days, his dirty, tin-yellow face wore a gallows grimace; his sunken eyes pursued La Pelada whenever she carelessly turned her back on him and his stubborn stare that didn't augur well. When she longingly fled their house to be near Salvi, the Valencian strove might and main to trail her, shaking from head to toe, blanching as he closed in on the lovers, but in the end, he said nothing, not a word. Nonetheless, he did seek revenge for the affront and pain they were inflicting, and even if it was bloodless, and went unnoticed, it was always subtle and cruel. He was a man of few friends, but he now sought Salvi's friendship with due resolve, and when the occasion arose, invited him for a drink, conversed with him, and coaxed him into worse behavior—often forcing the pace, albeit gently, overcoming as best he could the poor, impressionable youngster's reluctance—and then with brotherly candor he ribbed and joked about their adventures in front of La Pelada, who burnt like kindling. On the other hand, the Valencian was much more affectionate and forthcoming with his strumpet than ever before. He ignored her contempt and rebuttals, and always fondled her in front of the traitor; he mocked her embarrassment—as if it were the caprice of a spoiled child who found it hard to withstand the torture inflicted on her beloved; he choked her with constant gross acts and obscene references to their domestic life; he made her follow him whether she liked it or not, prevented her from seeing her lover, or always kept his eye on her in Salvi's company so they could never whisper a secret word, exchange loving glances, or unite those lips that burned with the desire to kiss . . . The lovers suffered so much that one day, when he learned from El Senyoret that the Valencian was out working, Salvi frantically looked for La Pelada and declared: "I can't live like this anymore! Move in with me once and for all . . . You're mine and I want . . . I want you to be mine alone, as if I were your husband. I'll rent the house next to the Forge, the one that's always shut up, and we can live there like man and wife."

She looked at him, panic-stricken, and suddenly felt the marrow in her bones freeze . . . What else did she crave in life but to live alone with him, forever and ever to the end of her life? But that couldn't be. It was impossible! It was impossible to dream of such happiness; it was impossible to defy the Valencian's rage. Only she knew how rabidly the Valencian loved her and what he would be capable of doing if he found out! How could she sentence her beloved's beautiful eyes to be shut eternally and his lips, red and sweet like strawberries, to turn to cold marble when touched by Xe or his wan, bewitched Infanta of Austria face be reduced to the chilling immobility of a lump of lard . . . The very thought sunk La Pelada into deep gloom, and she rejected Salvi's tempting offer with the same painful impulse with which she scratched and bit him—to make him more hers—in their moments of bliss . . . No, it couldn't be, better to live, to go on living and waiting, even if it was sad and exasperating . . . The Valencian was sick, his insides worm-eaten, and they, *they* were young . . . These shadows and anguish would give way to sun, peace and calm would follow . . .

And, keeping her innermost thoughts to herself, she chattered on—she who was usually so quiet—arguing, rebuffing his ideas, introducing more whimsical ones—brilliant verbal displays with no real value—to deter him from his intent, to distract him, to deflect him so things could stay as they were. Salvi tried to put up a struggle, tried to convince her, but after one futile, violent outburst, he softened and buckled before a will that was firmer than his and, as if faint from all his efforts, he put his head on her breast, letting her hold and fondle him as if he were a small child.

A big charity jamboree had been organized at the Park Güell by a committee of aristocratic ladies. The crème de la crème of Barcelona high society had come and the fiesta was magnificent in every respect.

Nonat was driven there in his automobile; he was never one to miss such an opportunity. The road was crawling with vehicles . . . Suddenly, a klaxon hooted behind them, a blast of air fanned his face, and another automobile overtook them at a lunatic pace, almost scraping them in a risky maneuver. It was the consul's wife's car. Traveling with her were two elegantly attired young ladies and the swarthy gentleman. The English brat was at the steering wheel, the chauffeur sitting beside him.

Nonat clenched his fists in fury. As the automobile had flashed by so near, he had started nervously, and the two young ladies, like the two maids years ago on Carrer Balmes, had guffawed.

His rage simmered and all afternoon he could only think of that incident.

Unfortunately, he kept bumping into those same individuals in the gardens, alone or in a huddle. Once the consul's wife's son was walking just ahead of him with one of the young ladies from the automobile; she looked at Nonat and no doubt recognized him, because she moistened her lips to stop herself from laughing and a moment later Nonat thought he overheard her utter that word "outsider." That ridiculous, instinctive reaction of his must have made them think he didn't belong to any select coterie, that he was "from the provinces," and that only rekindled his obsession, making him feel even more mortified.

He went on with his business, but tried not to lose sight of them, and the second he spotted them heading toward the exit at dusk, he followed them. People had only just begun to leave, so the street wasn't packed.

He instructed Salvi: "Follow them, and when they're least expecting it, drive as if you're gunning for them and give them the fright of their lives. They're the ones who overtook us, I want to teach them a lesson for laughing at us . . ."

Salvi was a youngster and the idea fired him up. He followed their automobile, waiting for the right moment to execute the maneuver. It came when the car in front slowed down because the English boy was talking and pointing out something on the road to the young lady.

At that point, they were alone, one in front, one behind, and the passengers in the consul's automobile weren't at all concentrating.

"Now!" the bastard shouted. "Show them what we're made of!"

Without warning, Salvi sped furiously at them like a ship about to ram another, sliding past in the craziest of swerves and leading the two chassis to brush against each other, then he stopped dead by the streetlamps for a moment . . . The women suddenly screamed, "Idiot!" and two hostile fists shook at them from the consul's car. Nonat swung around and grinned diabolically. Glances were exchanged . . . In a flash, the men's faces, contorted by anger, and the women's, by panic, became etched on his retina . . . Smiling as ever, Nonat doffed his hat and hailed them sarcastically while his automobile shot off like a bullet. More shaking fists and harsh, defiant words were directed his way as his car disappeared into the distance in a cloud of dust.

When they recovered from their shock, those assailed noticed that the fat, pale consul's wife was totally still, staring strangely into space like a sleepwalker. You would have said that fright had frozen her.

Nonat hadn't been a tenant of Senyora Maria's for some time. She was now his highly paid butler and housekeeper; he had refurbished the apartment to his taste with the necessary comforts, with a touch of nouveau riche excess that craves the latest craze. It had sumptuous carpets, huge armchairs, a telephone, bathroom, strongbox . . . To account for his growing prosperity, his vast wardrobe, his frequent absences, and the kind of people who sometimes visited, he had variously spoken of his scrap iron business, his agenting for foreign companies, his playing the Stock Exchange, his firms dealing with this or that, his partnerships here and there. As mentioned previously, Senyora Maria was no genius and Nonat needed her to be well prepared so she wasn't surprised by anything and could provide him with an alibi in a moment of danger, since the apartment was his main base and his official abode in the eyes of his other associates. In turn, Senyora Maria had only words of praise for "Senyor Nonat." He told her blithely about his plans, and when a windfall came he gave her a generous handout. They usually conversed over breakfast.

"Take a seat, Senyora Maria, I've got good news . . ."

"You do?" she laughed as she hastened to sit opposite him, a dust cloth dangling from her belt, a broom in her right hand, and a feather duster in her left, adding self-interestedly, "Tell me everything, Senyor Nonat."

"Do you remember the scrap metal from that factory that burned down?"

"Only too well! Its manager (Senyor Grisau) brought it to your attention, and that cost you five thousand *duros* . . ." answered Maria, proud of her good memory.

"That's right! The very same . . . Well, guess how much I made in the end?"

"How on earth should I know!"

"Ten thousand five hundred . . ."

Senyora Maria's mouth gaped open wide.

"Divine Providence! You mean, you made five thousand five hundred in twenty-four hours . . . !"

"Not quite that much, Senyora Maria! It took six months to conclude the deal; the money was locked and wasn't earning anything; then I had to pay out a lot in wages to repair the damaged goods. Even so, it's a fine net sum. So we must celebrate. I'll have supper with you tonight and we'll crack open a bottle of champagne . . ."

Senyora Maria clapped her hands.

"And so you too can profit from the good outcome, here you are." And Nonat threw a twenty-*duro* note on the table.

Nonat supped that night with Senyora Maria, and celebrated a piece of "good luck" as he did whenever he had a big job he was directly involved in on the same night.

On one such night, and while Nonat was waiting before dinner to get the latest on what was happening, he decided to take a bath in his en suite to ease his nerves. He was in the bath when Senyora Maria told him Senyor Pasqual's coachman had arrived. "Senyor Pasqual's coachman" was none other than the Valencian, the imaginary valet of Nonat's imaginary partner, in the same way that Nas-Ratat was "the warehouseman," the honorary security guard of an honorary scrap iron warehouse.

Nonat told her to usher the Valencian into his bedroom and tell him to wait by the bathroom door.

"Batista?"

"Senyor . . ."

"I can't come out right now, but tell me what's what. I can hear you."

"The people at 325 left at six. I didn't leave the station until the train left the platform; Parrot is downstairs to take him to the corner, if you don't have any other orders."

"I don't. Go. And don't budge until you see me. Then you and the carriage . . ."

"Right. Anything else?"

"No, that's all. And don't delay. Goodbye."

Before getting into the bath, Nonat had carefully laid out his jacket and waistcoat on the bed. The Valencian had given it a sly, feline once-over when he had come into the room. As he moved away from the bathroom door, he tiptoed toward the bed like a shadow . . . quickly rummaged in the jacket inside pocket . . . Nothing was there. He did the same with the waistcoat . . . When the Valencian's fingers extracted the wallet, the excitement turned him yellower than ever . . . He opened it, swiftly slipped out the doubloon and a couple of bills, put the wallet back in place, and ran out the bedroom like a naughty child, his footsteps ringing down the passage. All in all, his maneuver had lasted a second.

After his bath, Nonat slipped on his blue cotton trousers, combed his hair, smartened up, put on his waistcoat—instinctively patting it to check his wallet was in the inside pocket—and the jacket matching the trousers.

Senyora Maria laughed when she saw him: "What, dressed for the opera once again, Senyor Nonat?"

"Too true! One must adopt the disguise that best suits. The message from Senyor Pasqual was that we're meeting the scrap iron merchants, and we must make them believe we're hard workers if we want to get a good deal . . ."

El Senyoret had learned his lesson after what happened in Senyora Pepa's place, and never left anything to chance.

Salvi himself had communicated the orders to the Valencian, so he knew the man would be out the whole night.

"We've got five or six hours to ourselves. Why don't we go to the Gurugú, darling?" he asked La Pelada.

She didn't wait to be asked twice. He took her to the tavern; they ate, drank, then went to an outlying movie house, ever cheek to cheek, arms around each other, fingers interlaced, and though they were in seats, they sat with legs curled together, happy to clasp so tightly . . . When that was no longer enough, they drove to the Gurugú. They loved like never before, their flow of passion sustained and enhanced by the restrictions imposed by her cohabitation with another man. Every night of freedom was a honeymoon, full of blissful surprises, of tingling, supernatural delights. But that night, which their desire had told them would be endless, was violently truncated, for it must have been around 2 A.M. when the innkeeper informed Salvi that a man was asking after him. Salvi was shocked. They hadn't told anyone where they were going, so how could someone be asking after him? La Pelada asked what the man looked like. Immediately, they realized it was Parrot. They relaxed. Salvi knew Parrot must be on duty with the boss, who knew all about his subordinate's trips to the Gurugú. Parrot must be bringing orders from Nonat. With his pants rolled up, shirt collar open, and jacket unbuttoned, Salvi went out. It was indeed Parrot who was waiting; as usual, he wore a patch over one eye, and the hollow in his cheek, plugged by cotton, seemed deeper, suppurating more than ever.

"Well?" asked Salvi.

"Let's go outside," answered Parrot, looking around meaningfully.

La Pelada had stuck her head outside and was buttoning her blouse. Salvi did up his shirt as best he could and headed out. Parrot was already striding up the street. La Pelada followed behind as if it was something that didn't have to be kept secret from her, and besides, there was always a piece of twine pulling her wherever her beloved was heading. Parrot had walked into a wasteland half fenced-off in the middle of a field that, though only half-demolished, acted as a dump (and worse) for the whole neighborhood. Dogs had more than once pulled out bits of fetus or newborn babes from the stunted grass and piles of garbage; as a result, locals with a macabre sense of humor had christened that dump "The Morgue."

So they entered the Morgue, one after another. The two men had just stopped in the middle of the plot when La Pelada, who had just passed through the fence, unleashed a bloodcurdling scream strangled by fear, and staggered back as if drunk. A frenzied Batista was laughing opposite her, holding a knife that was dripping with blood. He had ruthlessly stabbed his strumpet.

The second he realized what had happened, Salvi went to throw himself at the assassin, howling in despair, but he knew he had been betrayed; his arms were held back like a pigeon with its wings pinioned, and although he struggled frantically, he couldn't break free from Parrot's grip.

Powerless, eyes bloodshot, mouth foaming, Salvi had to witness how the Valencian threw himself back on La Pelada, who had collapsed to the ground, and, as if the blood on the knife egged him on, he cursed horribly and began to hack away at her neck, and then, holding her decapitated head, walked over . . .

Holding La Pelada's head by the hair, brandishing it like a basket and bawling obscenities, he struck Salvi in the face, the chest, and the belly with that horrendous remnant of his disembodied love . . . But Salvi was no longer registering that monstrous act—he had lost his mind. A searing pain violently rent his body, and the force of that convulsion threw him from the arms that were subjecting him . . . The desolate, tearful howls that had filled the night suddenly stopped.

"Quick or they'll catch us . . ." muttered Parrot, shaking like a leaf.

"Don't be scared . . ." the Valencian answered, clutching to his chest, as confidently as Nonat, the lucky doubloon from Girona.

At the break of dawn, a gypsy woman discovered the crime, and when the crowds came, they found in the Morgue—amid the junk, piles of garbage, and bracken—the body of a disemboweled woman, a decapitated head with one eye still open in a grotesque wink, and the handsome chauffeur, drenched in a lake of his own blood, still gurgling a monstrous death rattle, and victim of the most barbaric mutilation . . .

"They still ain't got the murderers," people chorused months after, as they related the horrific acts in lurid tales of the year gone by. To catch them, the law would have had to go to South America. And the only people in Barcelona who might shed some light took great care not to open their mouths.

A lace-edged shawl around her shoulders, alone in the bay window of the sitting room, the pale and languid consul's wife was looking down at the garden as if spell-bound. Nothing seemed to be happening there to warrant her enchantment. After a leisurely midweek lunch, life seemed to plunge into such lethargy that even the leaves on the trees appeared to doze off. A single one, at the end of a new branch of an olive tree sticking out from a mass of green, shook now and then like a gliding bird darkly silhouetted against the limpid sky. From the right and from far across the garden came the sound of crockery being carried, and, from the left and much nearer, the sharp, hard click of billiard balls, echoing as they collided again. The consul's wife's attention seemed to be fixed between the three points of an imaginary triangle.

Indeed, between those three points, like in the frame of a stage set, the sandy paths and the green mass of tranquil garden were filled with bustle and movement, figures coming and going, and various scenes that assumed the character of an idyll, drama, or tragedy . . . evoking an entire life: her life.

As if prompted by a sudden cataclysm, by an inner volcanic eruption, that life surged in her memory in fragments, shredded and entangled, arbitrarily fractured and reset with no order or correlation between its component parts, as her memory expelled them—a cascading, incandescent magma pouring forth, burning crater walls, destroying and submerging everything in a violent, unstoppable flow.

Let's follow that lady in her thoughts, and try to connect the various facts with a chronological thread.

Time and again, as a matter of preference, she saw the magistrate, her lover's father, with his big, blue-green, glassy eyes, his angular, emaciated face, and his motionless thick, gray eyebrows, with three or four long, black bristles in the center of each that lent him a cunning, combative air so imposing in bygone days; his beard and mustache were trimmed military style and his usual old frock coat was buttoned from top to bottom . . . She saw him sitting at the table after drinking coffee, his fingers tapping on napkins, and, at the slightest sound, turning quickly to look as he always did, his head erect on his thin neck despite his age, a neck where a prominent Adam's apple bulged above an ironed collar; then pacing up and down his office, nervously scraping and boring between his long, yellow teeth with a toothpick; with his arms crossed and one leg over another, listening to some interlocutor with a constantly impatient air even though he wasn't, and persistently shifting his long, thin feet, always in baggy shoes . . . She also saw Doña Isidorina, his petite wife with her chickpea face, use the middle finger of her flattened right hand like a spatula, always feeling the cold, scurrying around the apartment like a mouse in her moth-eaten, black cashmere cape (now green with age) and a black, lace flounce that had turned red . . . And the five young misses, tall, thin, and untidy, with damaged hair like their mama, and the lean, angular cheeks and stained teeth of their father . . . And Master Isidoro, the older boy, short and round like a butterball, big, fatuous eyes on his round face and the little, intent mouth of a baby on the tit, so unlike Master Raimundo, his little brother, always laughing, lively, daring, and loving, who won over everyone's heart and ensured he was given whatever he wanted . . .

And she also saw herself weaving and walking between those people, graceful and straight-backed, being kicked by the little misses, lectured by the older ones, scolded by the mistress of the house, and curtly ordered around by the master . . . Working non-stop at all hours, and crying herself to sleep most nights from hunger . . . How hungry they all were in that place, from first to last, and how hard it was to hide how anemic they were, how bitter it made them, how they could stand it during the day, though it was unbearable at night . . . nights that were a torture stopping them from shutting their eyes! Luckily they were soon to be sweetened by furtive kisses, loving caresses, a gift of deep tenderness that made everything tolerable . . . After being fired by the magistrate, for no apparent reason at all, she remembered the horrors of her nostalgia when surrounded by new faces, bonding with her new mistress, that poor sick woman who loved her so much, the night she watched over her mistress in her death bed alongside the widower, who stared at her now and then, as if bewitched, as if completely absent . . . and his repeated emotional thanks, his faltering voice . . . and soon after, his surprising declaration, his proposal of marriage, and their first night together, on her side full of sadness and anguish, and then the long voyage between earth and sky, shut up in a cabin, soured by his repeated caresses, and arriving in unknown lands, and once again her nostalgia, that irrational nostalgia from when she'd left Donya Isidorina's household . . . A nostalgia she had been unable to pacify even when their baby girl was born, a nostalgia that only finally faded when Master Raimundo made a fresh appearance. His appearance was so amazing, so dazzling! Now it still seemed unreal, she still thought it must be a tale told by a kind fairy to deceive her and distract her from her terrible anxiety. That tale had been the only beautiful thing in her life, but also the source and cause of the greatest of her misfortunes; the casting away of her adorable little baby boy, and the loss of her other beloved, snatched from her loving arms by a cruel order banishing him from the fatherland that sent him to fight on that rebellious island, preparing the way for an obscure, inglorious death in a nighttime ambush when his regiment left La Trocha . . . Oh, what a stiletto thrust to her heart when she read that in the dispatches from the Cuban war! She turned cold and faint in the solitude of her bedroom, as she had almost done just the previous evening on the cushions in the automobile . . . When she came around, she felt such boundless grief at not dying there and then, at not losing once and for all that sad, sad life she now loathed so much. At that point she had felt there was no greater unhappiness in this world, but there was; her unhappiness had been deepened further by the death of her daughter, that horrible death that had her fighting frantically against the glands swollen by diphtheria . . . and then, yet more . . . with the miracle of a resurrection that gave her the final hope she might one day recover her son . . . Before retiring definitively to Europe, her sick husband had decided to consult a German specialist who, by recommending a simple diet, had cured his ailing stomach that had hitherto resisted all medicines . . . He was back by her side everywhere, the energy and love for his wife replenished, his wealth considerably increased, with crosses from two or three orders for services rendered to the fatherland by his steamships during the war and a couple of consulates of small South American republics. All her future had been shut down. The era of gloom, that long twilight, began with only a single burst of light from the birth of a third child, yet it wasn't accompanied by the comforting, total darkness where all is forgotten . . . Her sorrowing heart had slumbered for years and years in that vague gloom, muffled by three layers of fat, until yesterday when suddenly . . . that strange encounter and the defiant, hostile glint in the eyes of that young man in the other automobile had startled her, like a new, unpleasant resurrection, the resurrection of that man who, with a few, abrupt words, way back in her distant youth, had dashed her first, purest hopes . . . Yes, those eyes had pierced her yesterday with the same frosty rancor as the magistrate's glassy green eyes when he told her to get her clothes and leave his house . . .

The consul's wife swayed her shoulders, which trembled in waves of fear and tightened the lace flounce around her neck. Her small mouth and her lips, innocent like a child's, sagged limply, as they had over the last few years, sagged pitifully, as they had back when she had gone hungry.

Now and then the maid's monotonous singing drowned out the clink of crockery; the clatter of the billiard balls slowed as if they were exhausted, the leaf fluttering atop the branch finally stilled, as if it were asleep. Inside that imaginary triangle, the consul's wife's memory, the only wakeful item in that drowsy siesta, kept unreeling visions by the hour, and the weight of the past, always uneasy within her body oppressed by so much fat when disturbed by new impressions, rose hazily, cloud after cloud, misting a comatose present half-lit by so many painful filters . . .

Nonat was upset and furious when he realized the Valencian had disobeyed his orders, and wasn't with the carriage at the time and place he'd indicated. Nonat didn't like hanging around outside in those circumstances, and hated his staff interfering with his plans. It was too late to take any measures, but in the morning he wouldn't fail to punish his lack of discipline. That hoodlum was a wild animal: he only obeyed the stick, and woe betide Nonat if the Valencian ever lost his fear of him . . .

When Nonat woke, a bit later than usual, he phoned to order his horse be saddled up, and went to cast an eye over the Forge.

The two new workers were huddled in the entrance with three strangers, deep in animated conversation. They were talking about the crime in the Morgue. Nonat wondered what it was all about and listened with polite indifference to the three different versions he was given—and then alarm bells rang in his head. He stared blankly; cold sweat began to stream down his forehead and the sides of his nose. No doubt about it: that crime was too close to home. He had a clear sense of what had happened. The Valencian must have learned of La Pelada's treachery when he was on duty, and dropped everything else to hunt her down. That explained why he hadn't come to their rendezvous. Nonat forgave the Valencian for what he'd done, but as he put his fury behind him, he reproached himself for not intervening to avoid such excesses . . .

Nonat walked toward his horse, about to mount it and go and see what had happened for himself, when one of the strangers said: "When I was there, the chauffeur's father came: a miserable old man who seemed more dead than the dead man; he was pulling his hair out and was breathless after every word he said, he was so upset . . . Believe me, it was a sorry sight . . ."

Scowling, Nonat spurred on his horse, and rather than heading for the Morgue, shot down the street like an arrow, not stopping till he reached Bielet's salon. There, without

dismounting, he ordered the ex-altar boy to find Nas-Ratat
and tell him to come to Senyora Maria's house immediately.

He explained everything as soon as he saw the street porter.

"Captain, I told you that Xe would create problems for us.
He was only ever a piece of brawn, and would never do anything decently."

"You go, Nas-Ratat; hearsay won't do. Find out what went
on and where that fool is. I'll be waiting here!"

Nonat spent two long hours on tenterhooks during Nas-
Ratat's absence, and the moment he saw his long face, as sallow as if he were sick, the bastard knew the news was worse
than he'd been expecting.

"There are two swine, captain: him and stinking Parrot. If
you saw the butcher's job they did . . . ! Christ!" And the street
porter shook with repulsion and launched a gob of spit at the
balcony facing stone. "Don't expect to see them ever again.
When they finished, they went to the Valencian's place to
change clothes and then bought tickets to go to France. You've
lost the carriage too. Last night they sold it to the Chinaman
on the pretense it was a for-hire job and they were going to
work outside Barcelona."

Nonat went pale and wet his lips.

"Don't get too worked up, captain. They were garbage and
they've cleaned themselves away. We'll work better without
them, believe me. Better alone than in bad company. You see
how that doubloon was no use . . ."

But he broke off, and shot to his feet, because at the word
"doubloon" Nonat's pallor had turned a livid white and he'd
put both hands brusquely on his heart.

"What's wrong, for Christ's sake?"

Nonat gestured to him to sit and slowly extracted his wallet from his pocket. Before even looking, he knew the doubloon wasn't there. A flash of memory had just replayed the scene in his bedroom the day before and the real reason why Valencia was always prowling around him. The hoodlum had been waiting for the opportunity to grab the doubloon in order to punish the lovers and make his escape . . .

Nonat looked long and sad at his empty wallet, couldn't hold back any longer, and turned into a sobbing, convulsing mass. It was the first time he had cried as an adult.

Nas-Ratat's eyes went wide.

"Come now, lad! Don't tell me you really believe in all that gibberish?" He put a fatherly hand on Nonat's shoulder. "Don't be such a baby . . . Luck comes from the genius God gave you, not from that scrap of gold, that's like any other . . ."

The bastard was ashamed he had shown a moment of weakness and, reacting with a violent effort of will, replied with the flat tone that follows an emotional outburst: "No, but it was given to me by a man who loved me greatly . . ."

The street-porter's big, broad hand fell on his shoulder again, now in a protective gesture.

"If that's how it is, you shall have your doubloon. I, too, love you and I'll give you one . . . one doubloon's as good as another."

Nonat looked up, surprised. A spark of emotion shone in Nas-Ratat's eyes. Nonat squeezed his hand, as he had his master's in Girona. But, in his heart of hearts, something told him there are things without spiritual parallel and forces that cannot be transferred. The street porter's doubloon could never in a month of Sundays have the power of the one that had been stolen. And he felt, without knowing why, that along with that doubloon he had lost a dream, a hope, an expectation that was amorphous but intensely alive, like a fetus aborting in the innards of a woman; the dream, the hope, the expectation of that distant day when he would own that house that was the color of time, where the bright light of day fell like ash sieved through fine silk: that ancient seigneurial mansion where his seigneurial tastes could relax and be sweetly cradled, where he could create a mysterious harmony from a life with no foundations, a life like a mushroom, its roots reaching into a past of truly noble pedigree.

Nonat had seen him from a distance four or five times and experienced a repeated sense of loathing and a simultaneous impulse to exact revenge: a desire to do him down in some way. One day that need seemed particularly obsessive.

Nonat had retired for the day, as had Nas-Ratat, and they had agreed to meet the following morning at the port to watch people disembarking from a transatlantic liner that would dock that night.

He had woken up bleary-eyed and bad-tempered, and sat at his dressing table where the mirror suddenly revealed something as unpleasant as it was unexpected: he was ageing; his features had lost their freshness and elegance. In a state of shock, he gazed hard at himself. Every day he looked in the mirror, and though that new development had been hidden by the way his mind adapted to a face it knew, it was now cruelly there for his weary eyes to see. His eyelids were puffy, three wrinkles snaked out from each corner and spread to his temples; another thin, flat wrinkle was starting down his cheek; a hollow marked out a dip at once smooth temples, revealing the structure beneath; his hairline, always so flush, was now receding; his skin tightening over the bone . . . He spotted a metallic iciness in his pupils, a tendon's sinew visible on his neck . . . He knitted his eyebrows; his stare became harsher, more piercing; he blinked, moved away from the mirror, and plunged into a restorative bath.

When he emerged, he returned to the mirror; all traces of deterioration had disappeared; his skin was taut and silky; his calmed eyelids were clean and smooth; his forehead, a milky white, seemed hewn from Pentelic marble; his hair, tousled by the towel, airily crowned his head with a kind of black . . . halo. Nevertheless, Nonat had seen himself in that other guise and the worm inside still turned.

He quickly dressed and left. He caught a tram on Carrer Major. Now he had neither carriage nor automobile. To avoid any snags, he had made the Valencian owner of the first and Salvi the owner of the second, and the Valencian had sold his before taking flight, and after his chauffeur's horrific death, Nonat had taken care not to make any claims on the car; for a moment he had been tempted to get Senyor Grisau to repurchase it, but decided against because any contact with the law, direct or not, could at the slightest mishap lead much further than he desired. He would wait, and at a propitious time buy a new automobile and let Bielet handle it.

So he was going downtown by tram. The city was smiling and tranquil under a blazing sun, like his first days in Barcelona. Maids and shop assistants were bustling behind bay and shop windows in the sumptuous buildings on Passeig de Gràcia; on the desert that was Plaça de Catalunya the burlap palm trees seemed nostalgic for their opulent origins; a few women crowded around the fountain; the resonant chimes of the bells of Betlem and Santa Anna stirred the air; carts of vegetables were lined up side by side along La Rambla de Sant Josep, and in the port a liner whistled stridently . . . That Barcelona, half overwhelmed by a long, dark struggle, was reinvigorated, fresh, and carefree, reasserting its eternal youth, seemingly laughing at every attempt to oppress it, yet Nonat, the dominator, had risen weary and aged . . .

He reached the port . . . The transatlantic liner's passengers had begun to disembark. A string of individuals in their social disguises began to leave the huge mobile palace in heterogeneous attires that spoke of remote departure points, extended periods of danger, longing for the stability of dry land, disjointed faces, high color, skin exposed to sun and wind . . . Down on the quay, anxious faces thronged, pallid from the wait or unaccustomed to early rising, arms ready to clasp the welcome traveler; carriages private and for hire . . .

The bastard spotted Nas-Ratat in the throng, gold and red badge on his chest, ropes over his biceps . . . That wily retriever never missed a disembarking, his fine nose never missed a mark . . .

The last Argonauts left the ship . . . And suddenly Nonat felt a kind of electric charge. His likeness, the English brat had just popped up on the ship's gangway. As if to mock Nonat, he seemed more handsome, more refined, healthier than ever . . . A stretcher carried by two hospital porters followed behind him, and behind the stretcher came the swarthy-faced gentleman from the automobile, another shortish gentleman with a plump, freshly shaven, bespectacled face, and yet another, tall, thin, and wearing a monocle, followed by streams of people . . .

El Senyoret felt a twinge of intuition and slipped through the crowd toward Nas-Ratat.

"Follow that group, and at noon bring me all the information you can get. It's of great interest to me."

"But . . ." responded Nas-Ratat, his eyes indicating he had more than enough to do there.

"Forget it . . . This is the priority . . ."

"*Bueno*, captain. We've got all the information now . . . The white-haired gent with the face like a walnut is the consul for some place . . . in lands in the other world . . . South America, that is, you see? The other smooth-faced character is a notary, and the youngster . . ."

"Yes, I know who he . . . But what about the one on the stretcher?"

"I can tell you that too. He was a millionaire from those distant climes, and was very, very sick. Last night he took such a turn for the worse that he summoned the consul; he went to the liner, then left, and an hour later returned with his son, the doctor, and the notary . . . They took the millionaire to the hospital; he drew up a will before leaving the ship . . . I reckon the consul's got that paper gold in his place . . ."

Nonat smiled: "No, my friend, that's not how it is done.

If they're bonds, they'll deposit them in a bank, and if they are . . ."

Nas-Ratat interjected: "I know what I know! I think the consul's got most, if not all, of it in his mansion . . . His son was carrying a suitcase that was big and weighed a ton!"

"Are you sure?"

"For Christ's sake, I saw it as clearly as I'm seeing you now!"

Nonat's eyes flashed like a blade.

"Where's the consulate?"

"It's not at the consulate, but at the consul's private residence."

"I need to know how to get in and out of there."

"I'd expected you would. But I could do nothing more this morning because I needed to bring you the news, you'll have all you need tonight . . ."

"Don't leave it till tomorrow. And the more *data*, the better."

"Don't you worry."

Nas-Ratat's report had been accurate; all the evening papers carried the news of the wealthy South American's arrival and subsequent demise at the hospital. And they all added he had entrusted a considerable fortune in cash to the consul; it was destined to establish a large refuge for poor immigrants in Barcelona, plus a large amount of jewels that were to be sold, the proceeds of which would be used to support the school in the colony.

It was a cold night, blasted by gusts that seemed to chase the thick, black clouds swirling across the sky like smoke billowing from a conflagration, and down below all manner of creaking and noise awoke . . .

Jumpy as a cat because of the change in the weather and his suppressed longings, El Senyoret felt his nerves stretch tighter than the strings of a violin. Frenzied anticipation was making his heartbeat accelerate. Finally he had the opportunity to destroy that loathsome prig, that nasty brat, whose exquisite, lordly composure, innate, congenital distinction, and visibly lofty social status had quite involuntarily aroused profound envy in Nonat's déclassé soul . . .

He threw himself frantically into that adventure, trusting his instincts and good luck, for neither Nas-Ratat nor Senyor Grisau had managed to penetrate the house and allow him, by dint of precise information regarding household routines, to draw up a premeditated plan of attack.

"We know the little birdies are still in the nest because the young lad hasn't let the house out of his sight since that suitcase arrived; so wait two or three days (no need to rush, for Christ's sake!), and I'll find a way to get a good recon . . ." Nas-Ratat had advised, but impatience didn't let the bastard follow his sensible advice. He was afraid the suitcase or its contents might flee and deprive him of the chance to sink that smug blighter. He was eager to see the deed done as he'd imagined it: that fellow losing his stiff, British upper lip at the threat of a scandal, and the suspicion that would fall on his name after the robbery. The will, deposit, and its value were a matter in the public domain, and after the event, however much they tried, there would be no way to brush it under the carpet: everyone would seek an explanation, and they would find no explanation . . . Nonat had decided that, whatever it cost, he would leave no trace except for the fact that the valuables had disappeared with a few other trifles from the house, as if the latter was only to put the police off the track. Nobody would hear the slightest sound, nobody would be able to say they had seen anything to alarm them; consequently, it was inevitable that the household would fall under suspicion, and then, even if they paid up, even if they poured all their own wealth into the hole created, they could never remove the stain besmirching their reputation. The English brat would find his name was blemished, he would bear the stigma and have to wear that leprous placard in the midst of a high society that today applauded him . . . !

While he was sprucing up, that diabolical smile came and went from El Senyoret's lips, following the movement of his thoughts, with a joy so intense it hurt—like a bridegroom putting on a new suit before going to church to be blessed. After having a wash he put the blue silk thread around his neck, the only lucky charm he had left.

The mansion and its annexes sprawled over the area of a whole block, looking out over four streets. It was surrounded by a large garden the size of a small park, with shade provided by old trees, mostly the remnants of an ancient wood. There was a small green gate on the northern side that Nonat had closely inspected the previous day to ensure it wasn't barred or bolted in any way.

He told Nas-Ratat: "Position yourself on the corner of the street behind, and go in and out of the garden now and then so I can give you the nod and you can collect the suitcase or whatever from me. Once you've got it, beat it quick. I'll make sure the gate is properly shut. It's not likely that people will be around, especially on such a balmy night; besides, you saw how it's all gardens, except for the two cottages belonging to ordinary folk who don't go out at night. All the same, act as if you're tipsy, and don't carry any hardware on you, just in case the filth turn up. I'll have the necessary items. Then take a shortcut to the Forge: we'll see what's what when we get there. Don't go to the corner until I'm inside. I'll go along the street, you take the lane."

They went their separate ways. Raindrops fat as five-cent coins were falling; gusts of wind lashed and evaporated them before they reached the ground. Nonat used twine to secure his English peaked cap, which came nearly down to his eyes. Telephone wires shook wildly, and blared snatches of music accompanied Nonat a good part of his way. Those aerial tunes calmed his nerves and boosted his confidence, as he was so profoundly pleased by the trick he was about to play on the posh English brat.

He reached the green gate and effortlessly opened it. He looked up and down: a desert couldn't have been more solitary. He cautiously walked to the corner and eyed the lane: further down, a single figure was slowly walking despite the storm; his drunken zigzag from one pavement to the other indicating why he was so carefree. All of a sudden, the character started to whistle *Ven-y-ven* . . . Nonat quickly retraced his steps, pushed the gate, and strode into the garden, pulling it shut behind him. The gravel crunched under his white esparto sandals; a long-branched weeping willow battered by the gales twisted as if wanting to kiss the ground, cracking as if the wood was enjoying it . . .

Nonat tied a black kerchief around his face and walked warily on, silent and sure, like a shadow detaching itself from the somber expanse of trees.

The day before, he had climbed up the telephone post on the corner like an engineer doing repairs, and had seen at the back of the house a roomy glass gallery linking two sides of the mansion. It would have been extremely easy to gain entry there by breaking a pane if he hadn't been worried about leaving traces, but, as mentioned earlier, he didn't want to do that, preferring to act more cannily and open doors so nothing could be identified later.

Nas-Ratat had managed to find out at the consulate that the consul had a kind of office in his mansion where he conducted business related to his position whenever the weather or ravages of old age prevented him from going down to his official base. The black suitcase—or its contents—must be in that office. Nonat only had to find out where it was . . . Absorbed in such conjectures, he stopped for a second after following a U-shaped route around the house, the gallery, and the spacious rotundas. The wind furiously tore at the trees, and the odd window pane rattled. To the south was a balcony with a marble balustrade above the wrought-iron grilles of the basement. Nonat climbed nimbly up like a cat. He examined the two openings that looked over the balcony: they were shut with security bars; that wasn't the way. He climbed back down and went around the building. The light in the lobby was visible through the flowery wrought-iron skylight over the porch, which was lit all night, as they had noted on the previous two evenings . . . Finally, at the northern end, Nonat found a small servants' stairway tucked into the corner of the rotunda. A derisory little oak door studded with tin acorns led inside. Here was the ideal entrance Nonat had dreamed of! He cheerfully got to work. It wasn't as easy as he had thought. The padlock was unusual and tested his skills, and the pitch dark on that grim night didn't help. Nevertheless, the door finally yielded. He was in the house! It was equally dark inside, but he was helped by glimmers of light from the gloom outside. He oriented himself thanks to them and his own instincts. He was in a passage with two big doors on the right and a glass partition at the end. The first door was lined with green cloth. (Green like the garden gate, a good omen!) Nonat felt his heart thudding again. That must be the door to the office. Whether it was a study or at-home consular office, luck was with him. As Nonat focused all his hopes on the green-lined door, he reflected for a moment. The secret stairway opening he now spotted opposite that office was independent of the rest of the house and proved that people were received there who weren't part of the household, people who the consul perhaps wanted to keep separated from his domestic life. That, then, was his at-home office rather than a private study. Feverishly, with a heartbeat he found unnerving, Nonat opened the green-lined door at the moment a clock chimed a quarter to one. The distinct, silvery, if rather faint, ring of the three notes told Nonat that the clock was elsewhere in the house, in spaces used every day by the family. Only that sound and the wind had reached his alert ear. He concluded that that night and that house seemed expressly made for him. Even so, he closed the door behind him, just in case.

Once again he was plunged into total darkness. If he had known the layout, if he had visited it only once before, it wouldn't have been such a challenge because his groping fingers and beady eyes would have come to the rescue, but now, reluctantly, he had to rely on his torch. He shone its golden beam from ceiling to floor. It was all locked cupboards; in one corner, by the foot of a small ministerial desk, a wrought iron window with white glass panes seemed to receive light from a skylight or another room; a second, bigger door was opposite the entrance. Nonat opened it easily and found himself in the real office, to which the cupboard space was only the anteroom. He saw bookshelves, a sumptuous Louis XV table, and two small, matching cabinets with wooden doors . . . Where could the suitcase be? He worked at random, breaking first into the nearest cupboard. When the door opened, he was taken aback; it contained a strongbox. In case it was a trap, he opened the other cupboard . . . And felt his skull prickle, as if the roots of his hair were restless . . . He could see three shelves: there were stacks of papers on the top and bottom ones; on the center shelf was . . . a black suitcase! He gripped the cupboard door because his head had gone into a spin . . . He, who never lost his cool, had blanched an ivory white. After that first paralyzing wave of emotion, he put the torch on the floor, stuck both hands into the open space, and, thinking it must be quite heavy, took the suitcase at both ends and carefully tried to lift it—but it was *very* heavy and not easily budged. Then he twisted it around gradually, very gradually, to ease it out on its side. The effort made his kerchief slip from his face. He had moved the suitcase half-way out when *bang!* . . . A shot rang out and Nonat and the suitcase fell to the ground. The scene was instantly lit up as if it was broad daylight. A man stood calm and erect in the doorway from the anteroom; he was holding a revolver. It was the consul's wife's son.

The bullet had hit Nonat from behind and penetrated under his ear, shattering the bastard's jaw: half his face had been destroyed. Even so, he found the strength to rear up, like a viper that's been trodden on. Recognizing his enemy, he moved as if to reach for his knife. A second shot felled him to the floor again. The noise of the shots led to an uproar throughout the house. The first to appear was the nighttime valet, who had been dozing in the hallway waiting for his master to return; then came the consul in his dressing gown, holding a newspaper; next came his wife in her nightwear, her bare feet in purple silk slippers; finally, the other servants, in a state, struggling to tidy the clothes they had donned in haste . . . Everyone was terrified.

Husband and wife had spent the evening in tranquil conversation, and when they withdrew, while the wife undressed, the husband, who had been busy all day, had picked up the newspaper to read the latest news.

"*Hijo mío . . . ! Hijo mío . . . ! Hijo mío . . .*" the consul's wife bellowed, beside herself, unable to utter another word.

"Don't be scared! I'm fine!" her son replied with a smile, and without taking a stern eye off the man on the floor in the middle of the rotunda, he lovingly put his arm around his mother's neck.

"But what on earth . . . ?" the consul asked, totally bewildered.

"Well, you can imagine . . . Dinner at Mercedes's house finished and we hadn't had a chance to talk . . . I thought I'd write to her and, not wanting to make a noise inside, thinking you'd be asleep, I came in here . . . When I put the key in the lock, I noticed the door was slightly ajar . . . Naturally I concluded it must have been an oversight on Juan's part, but just in case, I had my revolver at the ready . . . And, lo and behold, the thief didn't hear me, I expect because everything else is creaking and crashing tonight and also because he was concentrating on the suitcase with the documents . . . I had to shoot to let him know I was here . . ."

Everyone in the house had crammed into the office.

The consul asked: *"Está muerto?"*

"No sé, vamos a verlo . . ."

And the son gently stepped away from his mother and went over to the bastard.

The consul's wife followed him breathlessly, her face drawn, holding out her arms as if wanting to protect him.

"Hijo mío . . . ! Hijo mío . . . !"

"Por Dios, mamá! No tengas miedo!"

Her son had put one knee on the floor and the revolver on the rug. He touched his victim's shoulder; the bastard didn't stir. Then, with the help of an old servant, he half-turned the inert body. Everyone cried out, horrified. Nonat had been horribly wounded; his shattered jaw was bubbling up blood and slivers of live flesh revealed splintered bones. The second bullet had hit him in the chest, in the right nipple. Those present gathered around, gaping. The consul's wife, as if stunned by fear and out of her mind, stood rooted next to her son.

Nonat gave no signs of life. His killer began to search his victim. Beneath the blue cotton jacket, he found the finest of shirts, and beneath that a monogrammed silk undershirt . . . Those present exchanged bemused glances. Beneath the undershirt, on the side opposite the wound, a clean, marble-white chest . . . The English brat pulled back the clothing and placed his bloodstained hand on the bastard's heart. At that moment Nonat opened his eyes . . . After a moment of unconsciousness, he remembered . . . Green-blue like the color of deep water, Nonat's piercing eyes bore into his assassin's . . . More focused on his search, the latter didn't notice, but attracted and instantly repelled by that cruel, searching gaze that echoed ominously across time, his mother was about to unleash a fearful scream when, as her son withdrew his hand, he lay bare the Montserrat medallion and the delicate lines of the cross tattooed on the wounded man's silken skin . . .

It was an extraordinary moment. Panic brought to Donya Tulita's snow-white face an expression of monstrous, frenzied happiness; her hands fluttered in exasperation; her body swayed backward and forward like a sawn tree trunk; her silent mouth distended horribly as she took the deepest of breaths . . .

When he saw that, the fratricide leapt to his feet and held out his arms to support her; his bloodied hands smearing his mother's face with the blood of the child she had abandoned . . .

Overwhelmed by the scene indoors, nobody realized what had simultaneously happened outside. The crack of the second bullet had been met with an immediate response in the street: a sharp, piercing sound and alarming gargles from a regulation whistle; staccato blasts that couldn't be mistaken for the aphonic gusts of the gale . . .

Here is the reason for those whistles.

As Nas-Ratat, on his wary watch on the street corner, noticed nothing untoward along the two streets he could see, he decided to go into the garden so he would be ready when the call came—which would be soon, according to his calculations. Listening intently, he crunched over the gravel toward the gallery, and once there, flattened himself like a communion wafer against the wall, making himself invisible in the corner formed by the smooth wall and the curve of the rotunda. He listened again with the alert, knowing look of a hare out hunting . . . Five minutes passed. Suddenly the sand on the path crunched . . . It must be his friend approaching. He emerged from his lair and slipped silently around the rotunda toward the nearing footsteps. When he entered the darkest area of the house's sheltered zone, the steps melted away . . . Nas-Ratat stopped abruptly and listened again. The first thing he heard after a short silence, close to where he was standing, was a bullet's frightening crackle. The street porter gave a start in the dark, and, shocked and numbed, was nonplussed. Should he flee, or go help Nonat? But before he could answer his own question, a second shot rang out like a rude interjection. It was all over! And he felt his feet sprout wings; he headed for the gate and flew down the street like a madman . . . A penetrating whistle pursued him as he fled; another whistle answered and two voices chorused: *"Alto!"* One from behind and one from in front. He was trapped between two of the neighborhood's private security guards: he couldn't escape or defend himself because he wasn't carrying any weapons . . . He shrugged his shoulders philosophically as he came to a halt, and let them arrest him. While they were tying his hands behind his back, a doubt crossed his suspicious, skeptical, commonsense mind. For Christ's sake, perhaps the luck brought by that doubloon wasn't such crazy nonsense after all?

Epilogue

Epilogue

THE LONG, EVENTFUL, SHOCKING TRIAL of Nas-Ratat and El Senyoret captured the imagination of the whole of Barcelona.

The consul's wife knew nothing of the ins and outs. After her terrible fit, she gradually faded in a slow death agony, a protracted torture, and her loving family, wanting to avoid any strong emotions that might upset her equilibrium, imprisoned her behind an impenetrable wall of silence she didn't dare defy with a single question. A sense of horror prevented her. She was sure one of her sons had killed the other and kept seeing those bloodied hands cradle her, hearing the ominous word come from lips that kissed her tenderly, covering the memory of her dead son in infamy . . .

The bastard's resurrection was slow and extremely painstaking, a true miracle of science. By dint of cutting and grafting, time and patience, his ruptured jaw was reset, the torn tissue mended, and they gradually healed and assumed a new normality, though he was branded forever by a horrendous scar that completely disfigured him.

When he was in a fit state to receive the judge, the latter came to take a statement, but the sick man refused to say a word and continued to do so whenever the judge repeated his attempt, first from his bed of pain and, later, during the trial proceedings.

Seated, back straight, arms crossed over his chest—to hide the deep hollow left by the bone-resetting operation—head erect and eyes cold, hard, impenetrable like when he was *at war*, svelte and lordly in profile and behavior despite everything, the bastard, like his mother, had enclosed himself in total silence. However much he was questioned, his lips never opened to answer.

In his courtroom seat, the prosecutor in the case—the former duty magistrate, the former judge from Lleida, so proud, in his heart of hearts, of his professional eye that had allowed him to divine the ignorant pretensions of that captain of industry—attributed Nonat's silence to a ruse and reflected, as he stared at the bastard: *It's bred in him, for heaven's sake! It's bred in him!*

And in turn, Nas-Ratat preened proudly at his own insights from the bench of the accused, full of the greatest admiration for his colleague in disgrace, for the bastard's hermetic, sphinx-like stubbornness, also muttering into his own hat, though with quite a different emphasis than the prosecutor's: *You show'em, captain. That's what you call pedigree!*

But both were quite mistaken in their deductions; the accused wasn't speechless for any reason of guile; it was because his cheek's nerves and muscles, violently compacted by stitches, didn't allow him to articulate words clearly. Before uttering anything, as if his mouth were stuffed with pebbles, from that chasm deformed by lead and a surgeon's knife, his voice emitted only one strange sound, like the *too-wit-too-woo* of an owl, and presumptuous in defeat, he didn't want to make the spectacle he presented seem even more ridiculous . . .

A year hadn't yet passed since the thieves had been caught . . .

There was a poor man who suffered from photophobia in the Sant Boi de Llobregat lunatic asylum. The man, who had loved freedom, light, and the weightless movement of a butterfly's eternally unconscious flight, was slowly disintegrating, crouched miserably in the darkest corner of his cell. He ate with his eyes shut and, even in the middle of the night, covered and anxiously pressed his skeletal fingers against them . . .

In his mangey yellow jacket, its ends stretching to his knees, his torn woolen slippers, and an extinguished cigar butt on the ominous abscess beginning to turn his lip purple; his hazy eyes set between puffy, inflamed eyelids, and a long white beard eating his cheeks, which looked scrambled like an egg yolk, Senyor Grisau, in the entrance to Santa Maria, holds out a greasy cloth cap to passersby. As he is a *decorative* pauper, an *ancien régime* painter occasionally uses him as a model. Apart from the meager earnings this brings him, Grisau's only other source of income are the alms he receives from compassionate souls . . . But even now the women who walk by, be they young or old, flee from his side, saying he tries to pinch them.

The one doing well for himself is Bielet. His salon is the bee's knees; he always sports caramel, patent leather shoes, smokes big cigars, invites a different woman for a drink every night, has a steady "relationship" with the boss of a pawnshop, is reckoned a card at the Faraón and Panchita clubs, and his posse of assistants still works to his orders, but now to profit himself . . .

When they were sentenced to *so many years* in the slammer, Nas-Ratat tittered, thinking that if he lived to do them, it wouldn't be his fault. The bastard thought the same.

His accuser's peroration had been a magnificent tirade that had caught the attention of the world of justice and would surely go down in history, but the charges raining down on him with the obvious approval of public opinion—which was an additional punitive blow—left him feeling indifferent; he was a cold fish, not a seeker of fame, as if such things didn't concern him.

In the final period of his convalescence, during the sessions of the hearing, night and day he had only one cruel, relentless thought on his mind: the destruction of his face. Though he hadn't seen it himself, from the comments of doctors and the endless, tireless way his own hand kept returning to touch it, from the reactions of people seeing him for the first time, he knew the damage was horrible and beyond repair, that his once handsome, fetching features were now repulsive and scarred where his gaze had always been calm and collected, and the bastard silently raged and despaired, felt his spirit rebel against such an affront, the fruit of happenstance. At times he felt the urge to commit suicide, but his instinct to live was so powerful and still sang with a strong voice, repeatedly defeating the muted voices of failure in the bitter, quiet isolation of prison, the prison that was his alone, that was his only pasture . . . But as soon as they took him from there and put him before the public, the rage in his soul turned blind and frenzied: the rage of a bull in the arena goaded by the stinging jabs of the picadors . . . If he had only listened to the dictates of rage, he would have insulted the onlookers, the court, everyone; he would have kicked them like dogs; would have spat in their faces . . . Nonetheless, the sense of good form that came so naturally to him kept him upright and dignified in his castle, like all the great seigneurs of history.

The sentence was read out . . . Nonat caught only one word: *prison* . . . Suddenly, his burning obsession with his face faded, erased for the first time, and gave way to a vision, a re-visitation, a memory sleeping in his gray matter that word had just conjured up. It was something he had seen at the movies, on an illustrated page, God knows where . . . A backdrop of rocks, a mine, a quarry, etc.; a gang of men with spades and pickaxes scurrying like ants against that arid landscape . . . They wore what looked like disguises, like clowns with the poorest of taste: baggy pants and loose Pierrot jackets criss-crossed with stripes . . . The nearest of those so disguised turns his head and looks wanly at Nonat . . . He's wearing a eunuch's cap on his shaven eunuch's head, with flaccid features swollen by female-style fat . . . The vision is repellent, grotesque, hateful, and Nonat quickly shuts his eyes to rebuff it. Immediately in the charged atmosphere of that room full of people, he felt a cool breeze, as if an invisible door had been opened next to him. That cool draught gently caressed his cheeks, entering his body through every pore of his skin, suffusing him with a sense of well-being . . .

The hearing is over and the crowds empty out of the court-room. After the rituals are rehearsed, those tried are returned to prison. Nonat feels at peace, with a youthful insouciance that makes him trip lightly along like a snowflake; letting himself be led here and there . . .

As he looks back at his trial, he retains the vague memory of a fresh, smiling mouth, the lively tip of a tongue slipping in and out, wetting its lips; a tawdry lady's hat with an over-curled feather and a cheap broach; a walnut-colored man, rubbery cuffs flapping on his jacket buttons whenever he moves his arm; a splendidly blue patch of sky, a cloudlet white and fluffy as a cotton boll . . . And his nose catches a whiff of gasoline . . . rubber . . . acacia . . . chocolate . . . sweat . . . dust . . .

The journey to Tarragona is pleasant, not to say jolly. Those sentenced are like a bevy of students on their way to new lodgings. As they alight from the train in a line, they laugh, exchange views, banter quietly . . . Suddenly, the line breaks abruptly, like a chain losing a link . . . A man runs down the platform like lightning through the throng of passengers . . . Astonishment all around . . . Confusion . . . Shouting, people running up and down, a flurry of *Altos!*, bangs from a round of gunfire, from Mausers aimed from the cheek . . .

The escapee, in full flight, jumps three feet in the air like a leaping deer and somersaults to the ground.

Everyone rushes over, crowds around him . . .

Nonat never wore that striped disguise again, and it was the last time the scar on his face was seen. With his neck laid open and his back peppered with lead, he sent the world, as an eternal farewell, the vision of his shiny, white teeth gleaming in the sun . . .

The End

Víctor Català was the pseudonym of the novelist and short story writer Caterina Albert (1869-1966). She was born into a family of small landowners, and lived in L'Escala, a fishing port on the Costa Brava. Her early works—especially *Solitude*—were representative of the Modernist movement in Spain and reflected her interest in tensions in rural life. She also owned a flat in Barcelona and experienced very different social conflicts and cultural change in the city, like the strike waves and anarcho-syndicalism and popularity of the new art of cinema in 1916-1917. She incorporated elements of cinematic narrative and factory strife into her writing, most notably in *A Film (3000 Meters)*, first published in Catalan in serial form in the literary magazine *Catalana* 1918-1921.

Peter Bush is an award-winning translator who lives in Oxford, UK. His translations include Juan Goytisolo's *The Marx Family Saga*, Teresa Solana's *The First Prehistoric Serial Killer and Other Stories*, Josep Pla's *Salt Water*, Rosa Maria Arquimbau's *Forty Lost Years*, and several collections by Quim Monzó, among many others.

OPEN LETTER

WWW.OPENLETTERBOOKS.ORG

**OPEN
LETTER**

WWW.OPENLETTERBOOKS.ORG

**OPEN
LETTER**